Praise for Barbara Wood

"Wood crafts vivid sketches of women who triumph over destiny."

—*Publishers Weekly*

"Entertainment fiction at its best."

—*Booklist*

"Absolutely splendid."

—Cynthia Freeman, *New York Times* bestselling author

"Wood creates genuine, engaging characters whose stories are fascinating."

—*Library Journal*

"A master storyteller."

—*Tulsa World*

"[Wood] never fails to leave the reader enthralled."

—Elizabeth Forsythe Hailey, author of *A Woman of Independent Means*

THE DIVINING

SCATINAVIA
NORTH SEA
ATLANTIC OCEAN
BALTIC SEA
York
BRITAIN
Londinium (London)
Elbe
GOTH
GERMANIA
Rhine
BELGICA
Seine
Lutetia (Paris)
LUGDUNENSIS
RHINELAND
NORICUM
HELVETII
GAUL
ALPS
Burdigala (Bordeaux)
Lugdunum
Po
AQUITAINE
PYRENEES
Ebro
Arelate
Massilia
Narbo
ILLYRIA
ADRIATIC SEA
Salonae
Caesarea Augusta
CORSICA
ITALY
Rome
HISPANIA
BALEARIC IS.
Tarentum
Brun
SARDINIA
Corduba
Carthago Nova
SICILY
Syracuse
Carthage
NUMIDIA
MAURETANIA
MARE IN
AFRICA
0 100 200 300 400 500 Miles
DES
Jean Paul Tremblay

H U N S
Volga
SARMATIA
CASPIAN SEA
CAUCASUS
BLACK SEA
Sinope
Trapezus
ARMENIA
THRACE
Byzantium
BITHYNIA & PONTUS
PERSIA
PARTHIAN EMPIRE
MESOPOTAMIA
GALATIA
Pergamum
CILICIA
Tarsus
Antioch
ASIA
AEGEAN SEA
Ephesus
Athens
Magna
Tigris
Euphrates
Ctesiphon
Seleucia
SYRIA
CYPRUS
RHODES
Palmyra
Babylon
Persepolis
Knossos
Damascus
CRETE
Jordan
Jerusalem
Dead Sea
ARABIA
Persian Gulf
Alexandria
Memphis
RENAICA
EGYPT
RED SEA
Nile
Thebes
DESERT

Other Books By
BARBARA WOOD

Virgins of Paradise
The Dreaming
Green City in the Sun
This Golden Land
Soul Flame
Vital Signs
Domina
The Watch Gods
Childsong
Night Trains
Yesterday's Child
Curse This House
Hounds and Jackals

Books By
KATHRYN HARVEY
Butterfly
Stars
Private Entrance

THE DIVINING

A NOVEL

BARBARA WOOD

TURNER

Turner Publishing Company

200 4th Avenue North • Suite 950
Nashville, Tennessee 37219

445 Park Avenue • 9th Floor
New York, NY 10022

www.turnerpublishing.com

Cover design by Gina Binkley
Interior design by Mike Penticost
Cover image: *St. Catherine of Alexandria,* 1507-8 (oil on panel)
by Raphael (Raffaello Sanzio of Urbino) (1483-1520)
National Gallery, London, UK/ The Bridgeman Art Library

Library of Congress Cataloging-in-Publication Data
Wood, Barbara, 1947-
The divining / Barbara Wood.
p. cm.
ISBN 978-1-59652-858-1 (hardcover)
1. Young women--Fiction. 2. Rome--History--Nero, 54-68--Fiction. I. Title.
PS3573.O5877D58 2012
813'.54--dc23

2011039853

Printed in the United States of America
12 13 14 15 16 17 18—0 9 8 7 6 5 4 3 2 1

To my husband Walt, with love.

BOOK ONE

ROME, 54 C.E.

1

SHE CAME SEEKING ANSWERS.

Nineteen-year-old Ulrika had awoken that morning with the feeling that something was wrong. The feeling had grown while she had bathed and dressed, and her slaves had bound up her hair and tied sandals to her feet, and brought her a breakfast of wheat porridge and goat's milk. When the inexplicable uneasiness did not go away, she decided to visit the Street of Fortune-Tellers, where seers and mystics, astrologers and soothsayers promised solutions to life's mysteries.

Now, as she was carried through the noisy streets of Rome in a curtained chair, she wondered what had caused her uneasiness. Yesterday, everything had been fine. She had visited friends, browsed in bookshops, spent time at her loom—the typical day of a young woman of her class and breeding. But then she had had a strange dream . . .

Just past the midnight hour, Ulrika had dreamed that she gotten out of bed, crossed to her window, climbed out, and landed barefoot in snow. In the dream, tall pines grew all around her, instead of the fruit trees behind her villa, a forest instead of an orchard, and clouds whispered across the face of a winter moon. She saw tracks—big paw prints in the snow, leading into the woods. Ulrika followed them, feeling moonlight brush her bare shoulders. She came upon a large, shaggy wolf with golden eyes. She sat down in the snow and he came to lie beside her, putting his head in her lap. The night was pure, as pure as the wolf's eyes gazing up at her, and she could feel the steady beat of his mighty heart beneath his ribs. The golden eyes blinked and seemed to say: Here is trust, here is love, here is home.

Ulrika had awoken disoriented. And then she had wondered: Why did I dream of a wolf? Wulf was my father's name. He died long ago in faraway Persia.

Is the dream a sign? But a sign of what?

Her slaves brought the chair to a halt, and Ulrika stepped down, a tall girl wearing a long gown of pale pink silk, with a matching stole that draped over her head and shoulders in proper maidenly modesty, hiding tawny hair and a graceful neck. She carried herself with a poise and confidence that concealed a growing anxiety.

The Street of Fortune-Tellers was a narrow alley obscured by the shadow of crowded tenement buildings. The tents and stalls of the psychics, augers, seers, and soothsayers looked promising, painted in bright colors, festooned with glittering objects, each one brighter than the next. Business was booming for purveyors of good-luck charms, magic relics, and amulets.

As Ulrika entered the lane, desperate to know the meaning of the wolf dream, hawkers called to her from tents and booths, claiming to be "genuine Chaldeans," to have direct channels to the future, to possess the Third Eye. She went first to the bird-reader, who kept crates of pigeons whose entrails he read for a few pennies. His hands caked with blood, he assured Ulrika that she would find a husband before the year was out. She went next to the stall of the smoke-reader, who declared that the incense predicted five healthy children for Ulrika.

She continued on until, three quarters along the crowded lane, she came upon a person of humble appearance, sitting only on a frayed mat, with no shade or booth or tent. The seer sat cross-legged in a long white robe that had known better days, long bony hands resting on bony knees. The head was bowed, showing a crown of hair that was blacker than jet, parted in the middle and streaming over the shoulders and back. Ulrika did not know why she would choose so impoverished a soothsayer—perhaps on some level she felt this one might be more interested in truth than in money—but she came to a halt before the curious person, and waited.

After a moment, the fortune-teller lifted her head, and Ulrika was startled by the unusual aspect of the face, which was long and narrow, all bone and yellow skin, framed by the streaming black hair. Mournful black eyes beneath highly arched brows looked up at Ulrika. The woman almost did not look human, and she was ageless. Was she twenty or eighty? A brown and black spotted cat lay curled asleep next to the fortune-teller. Ulrika recognized the breed as an Egyptian Mau, said to be the most ancient of cat breeds, possibly even the progenitor from which all cats had sprung.

Ulrika brought her attention back to the fortune-teller's swimming black eyes filled with sadness and wisdom.

"You have a question," the fortune-teller said in perfect Latin, eyes peering steadily from deep sockets.

The sounds of the alley faded. Ulrika was captured by the black Egyptian eyes, while the brown cat snoozed obliviously.

"You want to ask me about a wolf," the Egyptian said in a voice that sounded older than the Nile.

"It was in a dream, Wise One. Was it a sign?"

"A sign of what? Tell me your question."

"I do not know where I belong, Wise One. My mother is Roman, my father German. I was born in Persia and have spent most of my life roaming with my mother, for she followed a quest. Everywhere we went, I felt like an outsider. I am worried, Wise One, that if I do not know where I belong, I will never know who I am. Was the wolf dream a sign that I belong in the Rhineland with my father's people? Is it time for me to leave Rome?"

"There are signs all about you, daughter. The gods guide us everywhere, every moment."

"You speak in riddles, Wise One. Can you at least tell me my future?"

"There will be a man," the fortune-teller said, "who will offer you a key. Take it."

"A key? To what?"

"You will know when the time comes . . ."

2

As Ulrika entered the garden behind the high wall on the Esquiline Hill, she pressed her hand to her bosom and felt, beneath the silken fabric of her dress, the Cross of Odin, a protective amulet she had worn since she was a child. She felt its comforting shape and reassuring hardness against her breast, and tried to tell herself that everything was going to be all right. But the ill-ease she had awoken with that morning had stayed with her all day so that now, as a red-orange sun began to set behind Rome's marble monuments, Ulrika could hardly breathe. She wanted everything to be normal again. Even things that, just one day ago, had annoyed her, she would welcome on this late afternoon. The issue, for example, of everyone's expectation that she marry Drusus Fidelius.

Ulrika did not want to be disobedient. Rome raised its daughters to be wives and mothers. All of her friends were either married or betrothed (except for poor deformed Cassia, whose cleft lip guaranteed a lifetime of spinsterhood). No other aspirations were considered. A young woman on her own, without the protection of a man, was a rarity. Even widows were taken in by male relatives. Ulrika had confided in her best friend her wish *not* to marry, Drusus Fidelius or any man, and her friend had declared, "But no girl *chooses* to remain unmarried! Ulrika, what would you *do*?" Ulrika had no answer other than to say that she had always had the vague feeling that she was supposed to do something else. But what that was, she could not say. Her mother had trained her in basic healing arts, the manufacture and use of medicines, knowledge of human anatomy and how to diagnose illness, but Ulrika did not want to follow in her mother's profession, she did not wish to be a healer-woman.

As she stood in the garden and watched the guests arriving for the dinner party, she thought: Roman men greet their womenfolk with a kiss on the cheek, not out of affection but to see if they detect alcohol on their sisters or daughters—so controlling the men are. But Ulrika had heard that women in Germania were treated with greater respect and equality by their men.

Ulrika had flowered into womanhood among Rome's villas and streets and temples. She had known crowded and noisy cities, and a life of luxury in a fine house on the Esquiline Hill. But what of alpine forests shrouded in mist and mystery? Ulrika had devoured every book there was on her father's people, the Germans—had absorbed their culture and customs, their beliefs and history. She had even learned to speak their language.

To what end? she asked herself now as she watched the guests arriving in the courtyard of Aunt Paulina's house. She recognized them all, ladies in flowing gowns, gentlemen in long tunics and handsome togas. Had it all been in preparation to travel to the land where she truly belonged? It would not be an easy journey. Her father, Wulf, had died long ago, before she was born. And if he left behind kinfolk, Ulrika would have no way of knowing who they were, how to find them. She knew only that he had been a prince and hero of his forest people, and that he had bequeathed to her a bloodline of Rhineland chieftains and mystic seeresses.

A breeze wafted through the garden, stirring branches and leaves and the finely woven linen of Ulrika's long dress. She wore the latest fashion, which called for layers, an effect created by wearing a knee-length overdress as well as multiple shawls, all in varying lengths and shades of blue ranging from deep azure to the hue of the morning sky. Her long hair was braided and knotted at the back of her head, and concealed beneath a flowing saffron yellow veil, called a *palla,* that covered her arms and fell below her waist. Gold earrings and bracelets completed her wardrobe.

She shivered. If I am destined to leave, when and how would I go?

"There you are, my dear."

Ulrika turned to see her mother enter the garden. Selene, at forty, was poised and graceful, her slim figure draped in layers of fine linen in reds and oranges. Her dark brown hair was swept modestly to a knot at the back of her head and hidden beneath a scarlet veil.

"Paulina said I would find you out here," Selene said as she approached her daughter with hands outstretched.

Lady Paulina was a widowed noblewoman, and this was her house. Ulrika called her Aunt Paulina, as she was her mother's best friend, a woman who moved in Rome's highest circles. Paulina only invited the most elite citizens to her table, and Ulrika's mother, Selene, being a doctor *and* a close friend of Emperor Claudius, was one of them.

Ulrika linked her arm with her mother's, and as they neared the house, they came upon three men of stiff, military bearing debating a point of battle strategy. They wore long white tunics, their bodies draped in purple-edged togas. Seeing the two women, the men paused to greet them and introduce themselves, and when one, an archly handsome man with white teeth set in a tanned face, identified himself as Gaius Vatinius, Ulrika felt her mother stiffen. "*Commander* Vatinius?" Selene said. "Have I heard of you, sir?"

One of the other men laughed. "If you have not, dear lady, then you have ruined his day! Vatinius would be shattered to know that there was one beautiful woman in Rome who did not know who he was."

Hearing the strain in her mother's voice, Ulrika looked more closely at the man Selene had addressed as "Commander." He was tall, in his early forties, with deep-set eyes and a large, straight nose. His handsomeness was severe, as if he had been chiseled from marble, his manner arrogant as the hint of a smug smile played around his lips.

"Are you, by any chance," Ulrika heard her mother ask in a breathless voice, "the Gaius Vatinius who fought some years ago on the Rhine?"

His smile deepened. "You *have* heard of me, then."

Gaius Vatinius then looked at Ulrika. His eyes moved up and down her body, lingeringly, making her feel uncomfortable. In the next moment, a slave announced the serving of dinner, and the three men excused themselves and headed toward the house.

Ulrika turned to her mother and saw that she had gone pale. "Gaius Vatinius upset you, mother. Who is he?"

Selene avoided her daughter's eyes as she said, "He once commanded the legions on the Rhine. It was years ago, before you were born. Let us go in."

Four banquet tables were set, each bordered on three sides by couches. The placement of guests followed strict protocol, with the honored ones reclining on the left edge of each couch. The fourth side of the table was open, to allow slaves to come and go with food and drink. Roasted pheasant, dressed in their feathers, dominated the tables, surrounded by a variety of dishes from which the guests were to help themselves. The conversation of thirty-six people filled the dining room as they took their places, nearly drowning out the solo performance of a musician playing panpipes.

As Ulrika was about to take her place on a couch next to a lawyer named Maximus, she glanced across at Gaius Vatinius and stopped when she saw a peculiar sight.

Sitting on the floor at the Commander's side was a large dog.

Ulrika frowned. Why would a dinner guest bring his dog to the party? She looked around at the other guests, who were laughing and helping themselves to wine and delicacies. Did no one else think it odd?

Ulrika brought her gaze back to the dog. Her lips parted. The breath stopped in her chest. No, not a dog. A wolf! Large and gray and shaggy, with keen eyes and sharp ears, like the one in her dream. And it was looking straight at her while Gaius Vatinius engaged in conversation with his fellow diners.

Ulrika could not take her eyes off the handsome creature.

But as she stood and watched, the wolf slowly vanished until he was completely gone. Ulrika blinked. He had not risen from his seated posture. He had not left the dining room. He had simply faded away, right before her eyes.

Ulrika felt the floor drop from under her. She reached for the couch and slumped down. Her throat tightened in fear. Now she understood why the ill-ease had plagued her all day.

The sickness had returned.

3

ULRIKA HAD THOUGHT THE secret sickness that had clouded her childhood, and which she had told no one about, not even her mother, had ended when she was twelve.

She could not recall the first time she had seen something that other children did not, or had dreamed of an event before it happened, or had brushed someone's hand and had felt that person's emotional pain. *When she was eight years old, in a butcher shop with her mother, the butcher searching for a cleaver while customers waited impatiently, Ulrika speaking up, "It fell under a table in the back," the butcher disappearing into a room in the rear of the shop to return with the cleaver and a strange look on his face.* Ulrika had seen enough of those strange looks to know that the things she saw or sensed, in dreams or in visions, were not normal. As she already felt like an outsider in every city she and her mother briefly lived in, Ulrika had learned to hold her tongue and let people hunt for missing cleavers.

And then finally, on a summer day seven years ago, Ulrika and her mother had enjoyed a picnic in the countryside, and in the heat of that day, amid the drone of bees and the heady perfume of flowers, Ulrika had seen a young woman suddenly come running from the trees, her long hair flying behind her, mouth wide in a silent scream, arms stained with blood.

"Mother, what is that woman running from?" Ulrika had said, thinking they should go to her aid. "Her hands are covered in blood."

"What woman?" Selene had asked, looking around.

When the woman faded before her eyes, Ulrika realized in shock that it had been one of her secret visions, but more vivid and lifelike than any she had seen before. "No one, mother, she is gone now."

That was seven years ago, and no more hallucinations had visited Ulrika after that, no strange dreams of precognition or fantastical places, no sensing other people's emotions, no knowing where lost objects could be found. Ulrika had entered puberty and become at last like all other girls, normal and healthy. But now, at Aunt Paulina's dinner party, a vision like those of years ago had just visited her.

Ulrika was brought out of her thoughts by the voice of Gaius Vatinius.

"The Germans need to be taken in hand," he was saying to his table companions. "We signed peace treaties with the Barbarians during the reign of Tiberius, and now they are breaking them. I shall quell the unrest once and for all."

The guests in Lady Paulina's dining room reclined on couches, supporting themselves with their left arms while helping themselves to food with their right hands. The place of honor at Ulrika's table went to Commander Vatinius. Her mother, acting as hostess, lay on the couch to his left. Ulrika was opposite. In between were a couple named Maximus and Juno, a retired accountant named Horatius, and an elderly widow named Lady Aurelia. They reached for mushrooms fried in garlic and onions, crispy anchovies, plump sparrows stuffed with pine nuts.

When he saw how Ulrika stared at him, Commander Gaius Vatinius, a lifelong bachelor, fell silent and stared in turn. He could not fail to appreciate her unusual beauty—the ivory skin and hair the color of dark honey. Blue eyes were a rarity, too, among Rome's ladies. A glance at her left hand told him she was unmarried, which surprised him, as he guessed she was past the age.

He smiled charmingly and said, "I am boring you with military talk."

"Not at all, Commander," Ulrika said. "I have always been interested in the Rhineland."

Lady Aurelia said fretfully, "Why can't they settle down and be civilized? Look what we have done for the rest of the world. Our aqueducts, our roads."

Vatinius turned to the older woman. "What has the Barbarians so upset is that, four years ago, Emperor Claudius elevated a settlement on the Rhine from the status of garrison to colony, naming it Colonia Agrippinensis in honor of his wife, Agrippina, who was born there. That was when the new raids truly began. Apparently the Romanization of an old Germanic territory has stirred up feelings of some outmoded tribal patriotism and racial pride." Vatinius waved a long-fingered hand laden with rings. "Claudius has given me the honored duty of seeing to it that Colonia is defended at all costs."

Ulrika reached for her wine, but could not drink. The wolf . . . and now talk of renewed fighting in Germania.

"The Barbarians have been peaceful for such a long time," said Maximus, the rich and fat lawyer. He held up his hand and his personal slave stepped forward to wipe his greasy fingers. "I hear the tribes are being incited by one particular rebel leader. Do you know who he is?"

A dark look rippled across Vatinius's handsome face. "We do not know who he is, or even his name. We've never seen him. According to intelligence, he came from nowhere, all of a sudden, and is now leading Germanic tribes in fresh uprisings. They strike when we least expect it, and then vanish into the forest."

Vatinius sipped his wine, paused while a slave wiped his lips for him, then added with confidence, "But I shall find that rebel leader, and when I do I shall make an example of him by public execution as a warning to others who might have rebellious thoughts."

Ulrika said, "What makes you so certain, Commander, that you will be successful? I have read that the Germans are cunning, Commander Vatinius. What could you possibly have in mind that would assure you of such a certain victory?"

"A plan that cannot fail," he said with a confident smile. "Because it hinges upon the element of surprise."

Ulrika's heart raced. She reached for an olive with a trembling hand and said, "I would think by now that the Germans are wise to every form of strategy the legions use, even those intended for surprise."

"This plan will be different."

"How so?"

He shook his handsome head. "You wouldn't understand."

But she persisted. "Military talk does not bore me, Commander. I have read the memoirs of Julius Caesar. For instance, do you intend to use military engines in your campaign?"

He regarded her for a moment, appreciating the honey-brown hair, the delicately oval face, her frank expression—the girl was neither coy nor shy! —and then, flattered by her interest in his plan, and impressed with her ability to comprehend it, Vatinius could not resist saying, "That is precisely what the Barbarians will be expecting. And so I have a different plan in mind. This time I shall fight fire with fire."

She gave him a quizzical look.

"Emperor Claudius has granted me complete freedom in this campaign. I have the authority to call up as many legionaries as I require, as much siege machinery as I will need. And this is what the Barbarians will see. Catapults and movable towers, mounted troops and infantry units. All very organized and very Roman. What they will not see," he paused to taste his wine and to hold the delightful young lady captive a moment longer, "are the guerrilla units, trained and led by Barbarians themselves, deployed throughout the forests *behind* them."

Ulrika stared at Gaius Vatinius and she felt a cold fist squeeze her heart. He was going to use the Germans' own form of warfare against them.

She looked down at her hands, where she felt her pulse throbbing in her fingertips. And she thought: *It will be a slaughter.*

4

ULRIKA COULD NOT SLEEP.

She pulled her woolen cloak over her nightdress and left the bedroom. The house was dark and silent, but she knew her mother would not be asleep. This quiet time was when Selene wrote in her journal, studied medical texts, concocted medicines. And when Ulrika knocked on her mother's door, she saw that her mother was not surprised by the visit. "I thought you might come," Selene said, closing the door behind her daughter. Coals burned in a brazier, and two chairs with footstools were positioned close to it.

Ulrika had left Aunt Paulina's dinner party anxious and troubled, but she was somewhat comforted in this small room where her mother mixed healing potions, elixirs, powders, and ointments. It was a room filled with scrolls and books, ancient texts, papyrus sheets—all containing spells and prayers and incantations and words of magic for healing the sick. For that was what Ulrika's mother did—she healed people.

And now, for the first time, Ulrika wanted to tell her mother about the visions and dreams and premonitions of her childhood, tell her about the wolf vision at dinner this evening, and ask her what it meant, what cure was there for *her* sickness.

Instead, as she took a seat, she said, "Mother, at dinner tonight, you barely ate. You were pale and didn't speak. The way you stared at Commander Vatinius—why does he upset you so?"

Selene took the seat opposite and, picking up a long black poker, stirred the coals in the brazier. "It was Gaius Vatinius who burned your father's village to the ground many years ago, and took your father away in chains. In the years that Wulf and I were together, he spoke of returning to Germania and taking revenge upon Gaius Vatinius."

Selene released a weary sigh. She had known this day was coming, had dreaded it. And now that the moment had arrived, she felt courage abandon her. She recalled the day when Ulrika was nine and had run into the house crying because a neighborhood bully had called her a bastard. "He said bastards don't have fathers, and I don't have a father." Selene had consoled her by saying, "Do not listen to others. They speak out of ignorance. You *do* have a father, but he died and now he is with the Goddess."

Ulrika had started asking questions then, and Selene had taught her what she knew of Wulf's people, had told her about the World Tree, and the Land of the Frost Giants, and Middle Earth where Odin dwelt. She told Ulrika that she had been named for her German grandmother, the seeress of the tribe, whose name, Wulf had said, was Ulrika, which meant "wolf power." Selene had also told Ulrika that her father was a prince of his tribe, a son of the hero Arminius. (But Selene had not told her that Wulf had been a love-child, that he was a *secret* son of Arminius, for what good would come of that?)

Ulrika had created an imaginary father after that, playing games with wooden spoons that stood in for pine trees and a trench in the garden that, filled with water, made a perfect Rhine River. Ulrika had told herself stories of Prince Wulf and how, after many adventures and battles and romances, he always saved the day. "Tell me again, Mama," Ulrika would say, "what my father looked like," and Selene would describe the warrior Wulf with the long blond hair and beautiful muscled body. When Ulrika turned twelve and had outgrown dolls and games of the imagination, she had turned to books, devouring every tome and text on Germania to learn the truth and facts of her father's people and their land.

Ulrika now studied her mother's face in the amber glow of the coals. "There is something else, isn't there, Mother? There is something you are not telling me."

Selene faced her daughter with a direct gaze, and looked for a long moment at this child who had been surrounded by magic and mystery from the moment of her conception in faraway Persia. Selene thought again of the gift she suspected Ulrika might have inherited from her German bloodline—a form of clairvoyance that Selene had observed in her daughter as a child. Little Ulrika had known where lost objects could be found, would brace herself for surprising events as if she had known they were coming, would speak of another person's sadness when not even Selene herself sensed that sadness. Selene knew that Ulrika believed she had kept it a secret, and Selene had respected that, expecting her daughter to come to her one day to ask for an explanation, to talk about the special perceptions that visited her. Selene had thought that dialogue had finally arrived seven years ago on a day when they were having a picnic in the countryside and Ulrika had said she saw a frightened woman running through the trees. But there was no woman. Selene had known it was another of Ulrika's psychic visions. And then, curiously, the gift seemed to have gone away after that, as if the onset of womanhood had overwhelmed the tender, sensitive perceptive ability and covered it completely.

Releasing another sigh, Selene said, "It is something I should have told you long ago. I meant to. I didn't think I could explain it to you when you were little, so I kept telling myself: when Ulrika is older. But the right moment never came. Ulrika, I told you that your father was killed in a hunting accident before you were born, during the time he and I were living in Persia. That was a lie. He left Persia. Wulf went back to Germania."

Ulrika stared at her mother while distant sounds floated on the night—wheels creaking by in the deserted lane beyond the villa's high wall, the clip-clop of horse's hooves on the cobblestones, the lonely call of a nocturnal bird.

"He left at my insistence," Selene continued softly. "We had been in Persia only a short while when we heard that Gaius Vatinius had been there before us. We were told that he was on his way to the Rhineland. I urged your father to go, to hurry after him while I stayed behind in Persia."

"And he went? Knowing you were pregnant?"

"He did not know I was with child. I did not tell him. I knew he would have stayed with me then, because your father was a man of honor. And after the baby was born, I knew he would never leave us. I had no right to interfere with his life, Ulrika."

"No right! You were his wife!"

Selene shook her head. "I was not. We were never married."

Ulrika stared at her mother.

"Wulf already had a wife," Selene said quietly, not meeting her daughter's eyes. "He had a wife and son back in Germania. Oh Ulrika, your father and I were never meant to spend the rest of our lives together. He had his destiny in the Rhineland, and you know that I was on my own personal quest. We had to go our separate ways."

"He left Persia," Ulrika said slowly, "not knowing you were pregnant. He didn't know about me."

"No."

Ulrika was suddenly filled with wonder. "And he doesn't know about me now! My father doesn't know I exist!"

"He is not alive, Ulrika."

"How can you say that?"

"Because if he had reached Germania, your father would have found Gaius Vatinius and carried out his revenge."

Horror filled Ulrika's eyes. She said softly, "And Gaius Vatinius is alive. Which can only mean that my father is dead."

Selene reached for her daughter's hand, but Ulrika pulled away. "You had no right to keep it from me," she cried. "All these years have been a lie!"

"It was for your own sake, Ulrika. As a child, you wouldn't have been able to understand. You wouldn't have understood why I let your father leave."

"I haven't been a child for a long time, Mother," Ulrika said in a tight voice. "You could have told me before this, instead of letting me find out this way." Ulrika stood up. "You robbed me of my father. And tonight, Mother, you sat there while I shared bread with that monster."

"Ulrika—"

But she was out the door and gone.

5

Ulrika stared up at the ceiling as she listened to the distant rumble of night traffic in the city streets. Her head throbbed. She had cried for a short time, and then she had started to think. Now, as she lay on her back, her eyes peering into the darkness, she tried to sort out her emotions. She was filled with remorse over the terrible way she had treated her mother, walking out the way she had, disrespecting her.

I will apologize first thing in the morning. And perhaps we can talk about Father, perhaps it will help mend this rift that should not have happened between us.

Father . . .

How could her mother be so certain that he was in fact dead? How was Gaius Vatinius proof of it? Just because the general was still alive did not mean Wulf had not made it back to the Rhineland.

Ulrika rose from the bed and walked to the window, where she inhaled the springtime perfume on the night air. The ground was white, stretching away up the hill like a blanket of snow—petals from flowering fruit trees, pink and orange blossoms, dropped like snowflakes, looking white in the moonlight.

She thought of the snow-blanketed Rhineland, pictured her warrior father as her mother had described him so many times—tall, muscular, with a fierce, proud brow. If he had left Persia twenty years ago, as her mother said, then he would have arrived in Germania after the peace treaties had been signed and the region was stable and no longer at war with Rome. Wulf would have had to settle down, as so many of his compatriots did, to occupations and farming. It was only because of Claudius's recent decree that Colonia be elevated in status, and that the forests surrounding the colony be cleared for settlement, that old wounds were opened, old hatreds flared anew, and fighting began again.

Was it possible? Could her father be among those fighters? *Was he perhaps the new hero leading his people in rebellion?*

Now she understood the meaning of her wolf dream. It had indeed been a sign that she was to go to the Rhineland.

When Ulrika was younger and learning everything she could about her father's people, her mother had gone to one of Rome's many bookshops and purchased the latest map of Germania. Together, mother and daughter had analyzed the topographical features and, based upon how Wulf had described his home to Selene, down to the very curve of the tributary that fed the Rhine, they had been able to locate the place where his clan lived. There, Wulf had said, his mother was the clan caretaker of an ancient sacred site.

Selene had marked the spot in ink: the sacred grove of the Goddess of the Red-Gold Tears, explaining to her daughter, "It is said that Freya so loved her husband that whenever he went on long journeys, she wept tears of red-gold."

Hurrying to the mahogany storage chest that stood at the foot of her bed, Ulrika dropped to her knees and lifted the heavy lid to search through the linens and childhood clothes and precious mementoes from a life of wandering. She found the map and unrolled it with trembling hands. There was the place, still marked, indicating where Wulf's clan lived.

She pressed the map to her bosom, feeling courage suddenly flood her veins, and a new sense of purpose. And urgency as well. Gaius Vatinius was mustering his legions at that very moment. They were to begin their northward march tomorrow.

She reached for her robe. I must tell Mother. I must apologize for the selfish way I acted, ask forgiveness for my disrespect, and then ask her to help me plan my new journey.

But Ulrika found her mother's apartment dark and silent, and she did not wish to waken her. Selene worked long days, tirelessly helping others.

She would return in the morning.

6

Ulrika was wakened by her slaves as they brought breakfast and hot water for bathing. But she was anxious to make amends with her mother, and share the wonderful news.

I will need money, Ulrika decided as she approached the closed door. I will take only a few slaves with me so that I can travel quickly. Mother will know which route is best to take, the quickest. Gaius Vatinius is leaving today with a legion of sixty centuries—six thousand men. I must reach Germania before they do. I must find my father's secret camp, warn them—

"I am sorry, mistress," Erasmus, the old major domo, said as he opened Selene's bedroom door. "Your mother is not here. She was called away before dawn on an urgent errand. A difficult birth . . . she might be gone for two days."

Two days! Ulrika wrung her hands. She dared not linger even one day. "Do you know where she went, to whose house?"

But the old man did not know where in the city his mistress had gone.

Ulrika tried to think. Rome was vast, its population huge. Her mother could be anywhere in the endless warren of streets and alleys.

Hurrying back to her rooms, Ulrika altered her plans, thinking: I can do this on my own. Mother will understand. How many times did we leave a town or a village suddenly and under the cover of night? How often did we stay on the move because of Mother's personal quest?

Retrieving a clean sheet of papyrus from her writing desk, moistening a cake of ink, softening it with the tip of a reed pen, Ulrika thought for a moment, and then wrote: "Mother, I am leaving Rome. I believe my father is still alive, and I must warn him of Gaius Vatinius's plan to ambush his warriors. I want to help in the fight. And then I want to learn about his people, *my* people."

Ulrika paused to listen to the house come to life as slaves addressed their chores, voices called out, the creaky old voice of Erasmus barked orders. She saw the draperies over her windows stir with spring breezes, and she shivered with excitement and pride and newly found purpose. She thought of the people she was going to meet in those magical forests of which she had so often dreamed. And she realized, in surprise, that there was more to her quest, there were more reasons for her hurrying now to her father's homeland—it had to do with her secret sickness, the visions and dreams and knowing things that had frightened her in her childhood and which seemed to have returned. Perhaps that was the reason for the wolf vision the night before, perhaps the answer to her sickness—and the cure—would be found among her father's warrior people, in the misty forests of the far north.

She resumed writing. "I have been without a father for nineteen years. I want to make up for that lost time. And I want to give something back to the man who gave me life. I love you, Mother. You protected me when I was featherless and my nest was fragile. You said that I was a gift from the Goddess, the miracle child that came to you in your lonely exile, and as such you somehow knew that I was never completely yours, that the Goddess would call me someday to a special task. I believe that call is at hand. I believe I am soon to find out where I belong, and in belonging there, will understand who I am.

"Dearest Mother, I will love you and honor you always, and I pray that we are together again someday. And wherever my path takes me, Mother, whatever destiny awaits me, I will keep you in my heart."

She sprinkled dust over the ink, to dry it and set it, and as she rolled the papyrus and sealed the scroll with red wax, a tear fell from her eye onto the paper. She looked at the small water stain as it spread and then stopped, forming a curious little shape that resembled a star.

In the atrium, she found Erasmus overseeing the cleaning of marble birdbaths. Ulrika trusted no one but him to see that her mother got the letter. "Yes yes, mistress," Erasmus said, bobbing his bald head as he tucked the scroll into one of the many secret pockets of his colorful robe. "As soon as the Lady returns, I will give it to her."

As Ulrika carefully put together a traveling pack, her thoughts went round and round. How was she going to get to the far north? Colonia was almost at the top of the world. Should she take slaves or go alone? She briefly considered seeking Aunt Paulina's advice, or that of her best friend. And then she dismissed the notion, knowing that they would try to persuade her from this mission.

Her sturdiest clothes went into the pack, with toilet articles, money, a spare cloak. Then she took things from her mother's medical stores: jars of medicines, bags of herbs, bread mold, bandages, a scalpel, and sutures.

She left the villa without saying good-bye, and walked resolutely to the Forum, where she bought food and a skin of water from the marketplace.

Turning toward the main road that led through the city walls and northward into the countryside, Ulrika walked quickly, praying that the Goddess was with her, praying for the All-Mother to give her the strength to turn her back on the only family she had ever known, the only world—and to face an unknown destiny with courage and conviction.

7

SEBASTIANUS GALLUS PACED ANXIOUSLY as he awaited word from his personal star-reader. They *had* to leave Rome today.

The prosperous caravan leader, a broad-shouldered young man with bronze-colored hair and closely cropped beard, paused in front of his tent to observe his old friend.

The fat Greek was seated at a low table in the morning sunshine, bent over charts and star-maps, tools of his astrological trade in his chubby hands. Timonides had served the Gallus family all his life, for as long as Sebastianus could remember, and the wealthy trader never made a move without first consulting with the astrologer. This morning, however, something was wrong and Sebastianus was worried.

Timonides was a man of girth and gusto, having always been robust with never a day of illness. But he had been stricken recently by an affliction that was adversely affecting his ability to cast accurate horoscopes. Sebastianus had taken old Timonides to the best doctors in Rome, but all had shaken their heads and said there was nothing to be done, Timonides was doomed to live in pain for the rest of his life.

As he waited for poor Timonides, gray-faced with agony, to cast the day's horoscope, Sebastianus twisted the large gold bracelet on his right arm and squinted through the haze of a hundred morning campfires. The north-south caravan staging area lay beyond the city walls on the Via Flaminia.

This northern terminus, where Sebastianus Gallus was temporarily headquartered in a small compound of tents, merchandise, and workers, was alive with the hustle and bustle of caravans gathering from all corners of the earth, arriving with new goods or preparing to depart for far-off destinations. In the case of young Gallus, his own caravan, consisting of carriages, wagons, horses, mules, and slaves, was overdue for departure to Germania Inferior at the northern reaches of the Rhine River, where settlements were awaiting fresh shipments of Spanish wine, Egyptian cereal, Italian textiles, and assorted luxuries Sebastianus had picked up from traders who came from Egypt, Africa, and India.

They were to have departed two days ago, but Sebastianus dared not move from his private camp until Timonides said the stars had given permission. Sebastianus devoutly believed that the gods revealed their messages through the heavens and that a man needed only observe the celestial writing in stars, planets, moon, and comets to know which path he must take. But he had not anticipated his star-reader to be crippled by a mysterious ailment, leaving Gallus to watch helplessly as other merchants and traders called to their men to pull up stakes and strike off for the north, east, or west.

"Over here, miss! That man will cheat you whereas I am an honest man! I will take you anywhere you wish to go!"

Sebastianus turned in the direction of the barked words, recognizing the trumpet voice of Hashim al Adnan, a dark-skinned Arab who made a small fortune carrying Egyptian papyrus to book manufacturers in the north. He stood beneath the striped awning of his own tent, and appeared to be trying to steal a customer from a fellow caravan leader, a barrel-chested Syrian named Kaptah the Ninth (as he was the ninth of fifteen children). Kaptah was surrounded by amphorae filled with olive oil, ready to go north into alpine settlements, and he made a rude gesture at Hashim. Then he turned to the potential customer and said, "That man is a pig, dear lady. He will rob you blind and leave you in the mountains for the ravens to peck your eyes out. I am the most honest man around, ask anyone."

Trade caravans accepted independent travelers as long as they paid well and could take care of themselves. The protection of large caravans was the safest way to travel, whether on business or to visit relatives or just casual tourism. Sebastianus himself had that morning accepted a group of brothers heading to Masilia to attend a wedding. They had their own carriage and were paying handsomely for the safe escort.

Sebastianus studied the object of the competition between Arab and Syrian—a woman. Young, he deduced, from her slender body and bearing. And judging by the rich fabric of her dress, and the *palla* draped over her head, wealthy. Yet there seemed to be no personal slaves accompanying her, no bodyguards. More curious still, she carried bundles on her shoulders, as well as a waterskin and food bag. A young woman traveling alone? Surely she was not going far, to the next village perhaps.

As the two greedy traders fought over her like dogs over a bone, Sebastianus returned to his troubled thoughts and the reason for his urgency to depart. It had nothing to do with his regular commerce along the Rhine. Sebastianus Gallus was in a race to reach the farthest ends of the earth, where it was rumored that ships sailed over the edge and horses galloped into frothy mists, never to be seen again.

Sebastianus was in a race to win the coveted imperial *diploma* to escort a caravan to distant China. And what made him anxious on this spring morning filled with noise and smoke and sunshine was that he was competing against four other traders, men personally known to him as good, solid citizens who traded fairly and deserved the China route as much as he did. But Emperor Claudius was going to award the *diploma* to only one man.

Each trader was to complete his regular trade route while at the same time distinguishing himself in some endeavor. Sebastianus knew that his four competitors were going to succeed in making themselves stand out in Claudius's eyes. Badru the Egyptian had struck south for Africa, taking cheap clothes and trinkets to exchange for tortoise shell and ivory, and Sebastianus knew that Badru had the opportunity to bring back a rare beast for the arena. Sahir the Hindu was on his way to the southeast to pick up perfume and incense and was likely to find priceless books for the emperor. Adon the Phoenician was heading to Spain with pepper and cloves and would no doubt pick up vintage wine that Claudius had a specific taste for. And Gaspar the Persian, whose trade route carried him into the Zagros Mountains, would surely find a fabled rare flower with powerful aphrodisiac properties (everyone knew how desperate Claudius was to please his young wife, Agrippina). But Sebastianus Gallus the Spaniard was following his usual northward route to trade for amber and pewter, salt and fur. What could *he* find in the Rhineland that would catch Emperor Claudius's eye and persuade him to award Gallus the coveted *diploma?*

What troubled him further was the rumor that Roman legions, under the command of Gaius Vatinius, were marching north to engage renegade Barbarians in a major battle. Although war could be good for business, in this case it could hurt Sebastianus's chances to win the *diploma.*

He glanced impatiently at Timonides, who was trying to apply a copper protractor to a zodiacal chart, but with little success. Sebastianus wondered if he should seek the services of another astrologer. Time was slipping through his fingers!

Gallus was eager to make a name for himself. His father and grandfather and uncles had all carved new trade routes, distinguishing themselves, adding prestige to the already noted and respected Gallus family. Now Sebastianus wanted to prove himself by securing the China route for Emperor Claudius. It was the last unknown frontier, the last chance to carve a new route while at the same time earning the singular distinction of being the first man from the west to reach the imperial palace in China.

"I will take you all the way to Colonia! This man does not go beyond Lugdunum, he will abandon you there! I have a nice carriage, only three other passengers inside!"

At the sound of Hashim's barking voice, Sebastianus turned in surprise. The young lady was going all the way to Colonia?

He watched as Kaptah busily worked his abacus, a portable calculating device made of copper and beads, used by merchants, engineers, bankers, and tax collectors. The stocky Syrian was tallying the girl's fare by mile and food, throwing in extra fees here and there for water, the use of a donkey, even a place by the nightly campfire.

"Robbery!" shouted Hashim, his swarthy face turning purple. "Dear lady, with me you will not ride on a donkey but in a cart, and for that I will charge you only a slightly higher fee."

The young woman looked from one to the other in confusion, and when they saw her turn to the right, to glance down the row of tents and compounds that were all collected under a dusty sign that said GERMANIA INFERIOR, they both started talking at once, declaring that all other traders heading north would gouge her for every cent she had and then sell her to the Barbarians as a slave.

Seeing that the girl was at the mercy of these two vultures, both of whom Gallus knew very well—unscrupulous to the marrow, each of them—he spoke up. "My brothers!" he said congenially, striding up. "I have always noticed that the louder you both get, the bigger your lies."

He turned to the young lady and, before he could say another word, received a shock. As she turned to him, he glimpsed beneath the modest veil light-colored hair and blue eyes. She was holding a corner of her veil up to her chin, as Roman girls were taught, never to fully cover the face, but giving the effect of being ready to cover should the situation call for it. Sebastianus stared at the oval face drawing down to a delicately pointed chin, arched brows, small nose. But what arrested him most were her eyes.

He was momentarily speechless as he was remembering the time he had visited the famed Blue Grotto of Capri. Her eyes were the color of that lagoon.

"These men are not to be trusted," he said with a smile, casting the two men a warning glance when they started to protest. "They are rogues—lovable—but rogues all the same. If you wish, I can help you find an honest trader who will see to your safe passage to where you are going. What is your destination?" he asked, thinking that surely he had heard wrong.

But she replied, "Colonia," and he heard a confident tone, a strong voice, and then he looked around again for her companions. Perhaps they had yet to arrive, most likely because they had so much baggage to bring along for the wealthy young lady.

"How many are in your party?" he asked.

Ulrika looked up into the face of the stranger who had come to her aid. He stood a head taller than herself, the morning sun catching bronze highlights in his hair. He had a strong jaw, a straight and narrow nose, with a beard that was so closely cropped it was barely more than a shadow on his chin. Ulrika suspected he was not Roman because his Latin was lightly accented, as if it were not his mother tongue. Then she saw, lying upon his broad chest, suspended on a leather thong and resting against the white linen of his knee-length tunic, a scallop shell the size of her hand. She recognized it as a mollusk known to proliferate along the northwestern shore of Spain, and she had heard that Galicians wore these shells to remind them of home, and to show pride in their race and heritage.

She wondered briefly about this Spaniard. His brow seemed permanently furrowed, as if a problem had entered his head long ago and had yet to be solved. Not a man at peace with himself, she thought, or with the world. Impressions rushed at her: although his smile was easy, he was angry, but at whom or what she could not guess; his gaze was open, but he gave the impression of being guarded; and despite his relaxed stance, he seemed to be holding himself tightly, as if afraid of losing control. Had something—or someone—hurt him long ago?

"It is just myself," she replied, taking a small step back to put space between herself and this man, turning to look down the rows of camps. When she had left home that morning with such determination to reach the Rhineland, she had not anticipated difficulty in finding a party with whom to travel. Who could she trust?

"You travel to Colonia on your own?" the Galician asked in surprise. "But it is such a hostile place for a lone girl to visit."

She brought her eyes back to his—wondering where she had seen irises so green. "I have family there."

His frown deepened. "Still," he said. "A girl traveling on her own."

"Travel is not new to me. I was born in Persia, and from the age of three, when I left that distant city, I have traveled the world. I have seen Jerusalem and Alexandria. I have even crossed the Great Green on a ship."

"That may well be," he said, "but the world will only see a vulnerable female without protection. You will need to find a family that is going north and willing to have you join them, or a group of females. Unfortunately, my own caravan consists only of men, and I cannot be responsible for your safety at all times." He smiled. "My name is Sebastianus Gallus and I will help you find an honest guide to take you to Colonia. I am acquainted with nearly every man in the caravan trade, the honest ones as well as the cheats."

"I am Ulrika," she said, "and I welcome your kind assistance."

When Hashim and Kaptah, who had watched the exchange in curiosity, began to protest Sebastianus's stealing their customer, he shot them a look that silenced them. As he started to escort the young woman away, with the two traders accusing each other of causing the loss of a profitable fare, Sebastianus glanced back at his compound where Timonides the star-reader was still cradling his head and moaning.

Following his line of sight, Ulrika saw the fat, bloated man with a ring of white hair around his bald head. "What is wrong with him?" she asked.

"We do not know. He is my astrologer and he is unable to cast a horoscope."

Ulrika hesitated. She was in a hurry to start her journey northward, but the man was clearly in distress. "Perhaps I can help."

As THE STAR-CHARTS SWAM before his blurry eyes, Timonides thought he was going to burst into tears. Never had he known such despair, such bleakness. The stars were his life, his soul, and the messages contained within them were more precious to him than his own blood. He had dedicated his entire life to the heavens and interpreting the secrets written therein, but now look at him! Unable to distinguish Cassiopeia from Leo!

Lifting his head, hoping to dislodge the pain but feeling it only worsen, he saw his master walking toward him and he seemed to be accompanying a young lady.

Timonides momentarily forgot his pain as he watched Sebastianus take the girl's travel packs and water and food bags and shoulder them himself, leaving her free to hold her veil modestly in place—a skill known to Roman women that never ceased to amaze Timonides.

Strange girl, he thought as they drew near. By the drape and color of her dress and *palla,* she was patrician, yet she had been carrying her own packs. No doubt she was off to visit family, maybe attend a birth, for that was what motivated most women to travel. To his surprise, she stepped away from Sebastianus and approached.

"Is it a toothache, sir?"

He stared up into sky-blue eyes framed by hair the color of a young deer. Great Zeus, where had his master found this one? "Of the teeth remaining to me, mistress," Timonides said, "none give me grief, thank the gods. What ails me, miss, is my jaw."

"I am Ulrika," she said gently, "may I take a look?" To his surprise, she took the seat opposite him and, reaching out, gently palpated his jaw and neck with soft fingertips. "Is the pain worse when you eat?"

"That it is," he said in dismay. Timonides was fat for a reason. While astrology was the focus of his spiritual and religious life, food was the center of his mortal life. Timonides lived to eat. From his morning breakfast of wheat cakes and honey, to his late-night supper of pork fried in oil with mushrooms, his day consisted of chewing and swallowing and filling his belly in a continual feast of taste and texture sensations. When not eating, he was reminiscing on his last meal and anticipating his next. Timonides would give up women before he would give up food. And now, to be unable to eat! Was life even worth living?

"I believe I can help you," the young woman said in a voice soft yet confident.

"I doubt that!" he cried in misery. "My master took me to a doctor in the city who wrapped my neck and jaw in a hot mustard poultice that resulted in a burning rash. The second doctor prescribed poppy wine that sent me into deep sleeps. The third extracted my back teeth. No more doctors!"

He was wary as she continued to gently probe, but he had to admit that her touch was gentle and light, not like the ham-fisted doctors who had pried his mouth open so wide he thought his jaw would snap off.

When her finger touched a sensitive spot below his jaw, and he cried out, she nodded solemnly and asked Sebastianus to bring something sweet or sour for Timonides to eat. Sebastianus stepped inside a tent and returned with a small, yellow fruit, handing it to Ulrika, who recognized it as a costly fruit imported from India. Instead of peeling it, she slipped the entire lemon into the old Greek's mouth and said, "Bite down."

He did so with much protesting—didn't this girl know that lemons were a medicine, not food?—and while he struggled not to spit the sour thing out, Ulrika's fingers were immediately at the spot below his jaw, massaging and pushing mercilessly.

Sebastianus watched in fascination as saliva and spittle flowed from his astrologer's mouth, while those fingertips manipulated and probed until, after an agonizing moment, the girl said, "You may spit the lemon out."

Timonides did not need further encouragement. He spat saliva and lemon pulp into the girl's hand.

"Here was the cause of your distress," she said, showing him the speck in her palm. "A tiny calculus had formed in your salivary gland, and it needed the flow of saliva to flush it out."

"Great Zeus," Timonides murmured as he rubbed his jaw.

"You will have a little tenderness for a while," Ulrika said as she gracefully rose from the chair, "but it will go away and you will have no more distress." She delicately wiped her hand on the hem of her dress.

"What form of payment do you desire?" Sebastianus asked, amazed at what he had just witnessed. How had she known to do that?

"No payment," she said. "Just introduce me to an honest trader who will take me to Colonia as quickly as possible."

Sebastianus picked up her packs and bundles and said, "I know just the man." He paused to say to Timonides, "I assume you are now able to cast an accurate reading?"

"That I am, master, just as soon as I get some sustenance into my stomach!"

Sebastianus nodded curtly and led the way through the noisy throng, with Timonides watching his master and the strange girl vanish into the crowd.

An iron stewpot bubbled over a fire between two tents in the Gallus compound. Next to it, an oven made of portable stones gave off the aroma of baking bread. Upon the hot stones, fresh eggs sizzled in olive oil.

A large man in a gray, stained tunic stirred the pot with a wooden spoon. He had a round, flat face with slanting eyes and a baby's smile. When he saw Timonides approach, his smile brightened.

"Great news, my boy!" Timonides boomed. "I am cured! By the gods, I can eat again. Dish me up that stew, boy, I am ravenous."

Nestor was the chief cook for the Gallus caravan, preparing food for Sebastianus and his inner circle, which included a bookkeeper, a personal valet, a secretary, two assistants to help run the caravan, and Timonides the astrologer. Nestor had never learned to read, being simple-minded, and so he had never read a recipe. But he had a natural talent for concocting meals by instinct, knowing just which spice to add and how much. "Yes, Papa," he said with a giggle. Nestor was thirty years old and Timonides's only child.

As the old Greek sat down to the savory meal, looking forward with relish to every bite, he rubbed his jaw where there was no longer any pain, and he thought of the girl with the clever fingers, how quickly and easily she had rescued him from the worst hell imaginable. A hell that he prayed he would never visit again—

He froze. With bread in hand, ready to scoop up the pork and mushroom stew, Timonides squinted through the crowd of traders and workers, merchants and travelers, and a terrible thought sprang into his mind.

Timonides the astrologer held his office very seriously. Before casting a horoscope, he always bathed, meditated, changed into clean robes, purified himself physically and spiritually. He believed most deeply that the casting of horoscopes was as sacred and solemn as any temple ritual, that astrologers were as holy and reverent as any temple priest. The gods used the stars to send messages to mortals, and the interpretation of those messages was a serious and lofty affair.

Unlike with many seers and augurs, it never entered his mind to use his talents to his own benefit. Timonides was given food and lodging, and a secure place in the Gallus household, and he was content with that, knowing he was going about holy business. The world was full of soothsayers who used their art to make a profit, and some lived very well by telling lies. But those charlatans, he was certain, were going to burn in the fires of Hell for eternity. Not Timonides the astrologer, who held a close and secret wish in his heart.

And herein lay the tragic irony of Timonides the star-reader. Destined forever to read the stars for other people, the astrologer himself would never have his own horoscope cast. Timonides did not know the date of his birth, or where he was born, or who his parents were. He had been found on one of Rome's many trash heaps where unwanted infants were left exposed to die. Sometimes they were claimed for slavery, or by a barren woman desperate for a child. Mostly they perished, as people assumed such unwanted babies were defective or cursed. But a widow in Rome's Greek quarter had found the mewling infant lying among rotting meat and horse dung and, out of compassion, brought it home.

And so the astrologer grew up not knowing his own sign, his own planets and houses, where his moon and sun were supposed to be. Therefore it was his lifelong wish and most cherished prayer that someday, somehow, the gods would reveal to their humble servant the stars of his birth. To this end Timonides had kept his astrological practice pure. He had never cast an inaccurate horoscope, had never twisted the meaning in the stars to suit a more favorable reading.

Until now.

Because, the terrible thought that had suddenly entered his mind was: What if the stone comes back?

And he felt a blow to his chest as if a mule had kicked him. Was it possible his salivary gland would produce another calculus? Was the pain going to return?

Am I going to be kept from my precious food again?

And then he thought: I must keep the girl with me.

Timonides the honest and pure astrologer was instantly filled with terror.

Great Zeus, he thought, his mind racing along a track laid with blasphemy and sacrilege. He had to make sure the girl traveled with them. But he knew there would be no persuading his master to bring a lone female along on a caravan consisting of men and no other women. There was only one solution: Timonides the sacred astrologer must falsify Sebastianus's horoscope.

As it was never a good idea to make decisions on an empty stomach, he scooped some chunks of pork and gravy onto his bread, hefted it into his mouth, and munched with heavenly delight. As more and more of the stew went through his lips and down his throat, his every taste bud waking up to garlic and onion, reminding him of what it had been like to be unable to eat, filling him with dread that such deprivation would visit him again, Timonides the astrologer thought: But it would be just a small untruth. Not really a lie, more like a fiction. And I won't exactly say it is what the stars said, I will merely hint and let my master draw the vital conclusions.

Timonides washed the stew down with beer that had been kept cool in wet straw, and as he smacked his lips and signaled to Nestor for a second bowl, he told himself that what he was about to do was a small favor to ask of the gods. In all his years of serving the heavens and the stars, he had never asked for anything in return, had never once used astrology to his own gain. Surely they would not mind one tiny self-serving transgression from an old man who had been staunchly faithful.

As more greasy pork and piquant onions awoke his palate, reminding him of culinary pleasures to come, Timonides the astrologer started to feel good about what he had to do.

Sebastianus and Ulrika returned to the camp, having found a trustworthy guide to take her to Colonia, one who had families in his caravan. But a refreshed and considerably cheered Timonides greeted them and, with star-charts in his hands, declared, "Master, the message is astonishing but clear. This girl Ulrika is meant to travel with us."

Timonides spoke hurriedly lest his voice betray the lie. Showing Sebastianus his calculations, he said, "Master, you know that your sun sign is Libra with Capricorn your Moon sign." He went on to fill the air with words such as house and aspect, elliptic and ascendant, conjunctions and crescent, explaining the placement of the five planets in relation to the sun and moon and how they affected not only Sebastianus Gallus, but the caravan, the girl named Ulrika, and the outcome of the race for the imperial *diploma.*

Sebastianus frowned over the papyrus sheet covered in numbers but he had no reason to doubt the outcome of the calculations. Timonides used a small calibrated instrument to determine the intersecting angle between the horizon planes and the ecliptic, and his most prized possession was a zodiacal casting wheel made of finely hammered gold, with symbols and degrees imprinted in the metal. It was said to have belonged to the great Alexander himself. These left little room for error in the casting of horoscopes.

Still, this reading came as a surprise. "What does this young lady have to do with us?"

Timonides did not meet Sebastianus in the eyes, looking instead at Ulrika. "It makes logical sense, master. I was unable to make good readings because of my pain and hunger. The gods sent the girl to us to take away my pain and to fill my belly again. Now I am able to serve them once more. She is here for a reason, master, and that is only for the gods to know."

Sebastianus could not argue with this logic. He also could not deny that the girl had been able to affect a cure that Rome's physicians could not, so perhaps she would be an asset on the caravan. But how would she travel? Where would she sleep? How could he keep a watchful eye on all his men?

"But I am in a hurry," Ulrika said. "I must travel with speed and your caravan is too large, it will take too long."

"As it so happens," Timonides said quickly, "my master is also in a hurry and must reach Germania Inferior as fast as he can, and so we will be traveling at a healthy pace."

Timonides saw how his master hesitated and so he said, "Master, you know that in the next towns, a family will join us, or a group of women. They always do. It will only be for a short time that the young lady is unchaperoned."

Sebastianus considered this and then, as he had never questioned the stars, he finally said, "Very well," as Timonides had known he would.

It was done! The girl was coming along and Timonides was guaranteed of freedom from salivary pain. He struggled to conceal his joy.

They entered into an agreement. With the corner of her veil covering her fingers, Ulrika shook hands with Sebastianus and in that instant a startling vision filled her head: an explosion of small bright lights streaking across the black sky and coming to rest, like a shower of golden sprinkles, on a vast, grassy valley. The image was so strong, so vivid that it held her briefly transfixed.

In the next moment, her mind was filled with the vision of a breathtaking landscape of rolling green hills, a rocky coastline, winds blowing in from the sea. She knew it was a land called Galicia, although she had never been there. She knew it was this man's beloved home, verdant with thick forests, ending in a wild and rugged coastline, a place that his people called Land of the Thousand Rivers—and yet thoughts of Galicia caused him great pain. He is homesick, she thought, yet he can never go back. Sebastianus Gallus was a man without a country.

As Gallus picked up her travel packs and she followed him to a line of covered carriages, as her heart raced in anticipation of meeting her father at last, Ulrika shivered with a chilling thought. If her illness was indeed back, what other frightening visions and sensations awaited her on this journey into the unknown?

BOOK TWO
GERMANIA

8

"Stand aside in the name of Imperial Rome!"

Ulrika did not recognize the stranger demanding to be let in. "Who are you?"

"Agents of Claudius Caesar. You are hiding someone in there."

"I am hiding no one. We are a simple trade caravan, taking grain to the northern outposts. You must speak with Sebastianus Gallus, he is the leader of this caravan. You cannot mistake him. He is tall, with hair the color of bronze, and a deep commanding voice, and a way about him that makes one notice. He is unmarried, although I do not understand why, for he is very attractive, quite handsome, in fact—"

Ulrika opened her eyes to darkness and found herself in bed. Where was she? To whom had she been speaking?

It was another dream . . .

She held her breath and listened, and heard, beyond the cloth walls of her small tent, horses galloping through the encampment. Men shouting. Women crying out.

Ulrika frowned. It was barely dawn. The camp wasn't due to break up for another two hours.

Clutching her shawl at her throat, her long hair streaming over her shoulders, she stepped out and peered through the atmosphere thick with mist and smoke. Eerie figures were marching through the camp, brandishing swords and barking orders. Roman legionaries, rousing people from sleep, disrupting breakfasts, interrupting prayers.

As Ulrika watched the commotion in the pale morning light, Timonides appeared from around the side of the tent. "What's going on?" the astrologer asked with his mouth full. He held a greasy lamb chop with a bite taken out; his tunic was stained down the front where honey had dripped from wheat cakes. It was the first of several meals of the day for the corpulent Greek who had discovered the joy of eating again.

"I do not know," Ulrika murmured.

Timonides wrinkled his nose as he watched the red-caped legionaries stride through the crowded encampment, entering tents and covered wagons, kicking over hay bales, jabbing swords into barrels and bundles of merchandise. "They appear to be searching for something," he observed as he sank his teeth into the spicy chop.

Or some*one,* Ulrika thought.

"Where is your master?" she asked as she watched the legionaries brusquely pull people from tents, bringing torches close to their faces, to examine them and then push them away.

"Sebastianus will come soon. Mistress, go back inside. With your fair hair and that symbol you wear about your neck . . ."

Ulrika's hand went to her breast, where she wore the Germanic Cross of Odin. She turned and looked out over the Rhine—a wide, flat, silver river that, in the early morning mist, looked unreal. Roman naval vessels patrolled the waters, great ships moving under the power of sail or rhythmic oars, a constant reminder of Rome's imperial and mighty presence in this northern land. On the other side of the river, dark green forests holding ancient secrets stretched to the horizon.

Ulrika brought herself back to the camp and the intruders. The caravan of Sebastianus Gallus had stopped, along with several smaller caravans and groups of traders and travelers, at a garrison called Fort Bonna, one day's journey south of Colonia, birthplace of Empress Agrippina and the cause of the new outbreak of war in the region. Since leaving Lugdunum in Gaul and following the eastward road that skirted alpine foothills, the mood of the caravan had become one of nervousness and anxiety. Lugdunum was a major trading hub in Europe, a cosmopolitan city of marble towers and fortress walls and roads that stretched away like the spokes of a wagon wheel. And along those roads, men traveled, bringing with them word of fighting in the east, rumors and unconfirmed reports but no one saying for certain what was happening—or was going to happen, or had already happened—in Germania Inferior.

Now, after days of rising apprehension, they had come to a halt fifteen miles from Ulrika's destination. Her heart raced. Where was Gaius Vatinius and his legions? Everyone said that he was leading his troops directly across the Alps, a more hazardous route than the one caravans took, but a more direct one—thousands of men pushing northward like a deadly tide, bringing horses and weapons and war machines into the pristine forests of Ulrika's people. How far behind were the legions? How much time was left to her to find her father and warn him?

As she kept her eye on the soldiers, their armor clanking as they pushed their way into people's privacy, stamping the ground with their thick, hobnailed sandals, Ulrika wondered where Sebastianus was. She glanced at his tent. It was dark and deserted as usual. Once again, he had not slept in his own bed.

Where does he go every night?

As they had followed the busy trade route from Rome to Masilia, from Lugdunum to the Rhine, Ulrika had seen Sebastianus Gallus interact with merchants, traders, and travelers, inviting them to share his fire and a meal. Trade and commerce were conducted at each stopping point, with the abacus coming out, coins being counted, baskets and bundles of merchandise changing hands, and Gallus overseeing it all. When business was concluded, he would bathe in his tent, change into a fresh tunic and cloak, and leave the camp, usually bearing gifts, to head into the village or town, and return the next morning.

While Ulrika wondered what he did away from camp—while she wondered about many things concerning the master of her caravan—she did know one thing: his passion for the stars.

Ulrika had learned that Sebastianus Gallus was not a religious man in the traditional sense. He did not erect a small altar each time they camped, nor did he make a sacrifice of food and wine to the gods. Instead, he consulted the stars, making use of Timonides and his star-charts.

Ulrika thought about the gold bracelet on Sebastianus's wrist. It was a beautiful piece, finely molded with intricate designs. The surprising feature was a rather homely chunk of rock in the center, neither pleasing to the eye nor seeming to be of any value—a prosaic stone easily found in any street. She wondered at its significance.

As she watched the legionaries move through the camp, coming her way while a nervous Timonides stood at her side, Ulrika thought about the local people the caravan had encountered along the route, Germans who were not slaves, as Ulrika was used to seeing, but free men and women working their own farms, engaged in cultural arts and crafts and who came to the caravan to trade. She would stare at them, marveling at seeing this race in their own environment of forests and rolling hills and green, misty valleys. Women in long skirts and blouses, their hair worn in braids; men in leggings and tunics, hair worn long and nearly all of them bearded, reminding Ulrika that the term "barbarian" literally meant "bearded one," but that in recent years had come to mean any uncivilized person.

She trembled to think that she was near her father's territory. It filled her with pride to know that, not far from here, forty-five years ago, three legions commanded by Quinctilius Varus had been defeated by the German hero Arminius, Ulrika's grandfather! But sadness also filled her—leaving her mother without a proper good-bye. Fear was in her heart as well, that the childhood sickness that frightened her might never be cured, that she was going to be plagued forever with dreams that were too real and vivid to be mere dreams.

As two legionaries strode up to her tent, she braced herself.

Ulrika was familiar with the political climate of this region. Under the empire's *pax romana,* several important Germanic tribes worked peacefully with Rome, and seemed to have no problem with the presence of imperial forts and garrisons in their ancestral territory. So peaceful was this region, in fact, that Claudius had needed to pull idle troops from the Rhine and give them something to do: invade Britain. But now there was a new problem: an unnamed German warrior was firing up the tribes and uniting them against Rome for the first time in forty years.

And Ulrika was certain it was her father.

As the two legionaries approached, she tightened the shawl about her shoulders and drew herself up tall, ready to stand up to them. She would not let them search her tent. She had nothing to hide, but it was the principle.

On the far side of the camp, at the edge of the clearing where the western forest began, a leather-faced centurion scratched his testicles as he watched the proceedings with a jaded eye. A twenty-five-year veteran of foreign campaigns, the middle-aged soldier was looking forward to retiring with his fat wife to a vineyard in southern Italia, where he hoped to live out his days idling in the sunlight and telling war stories to his grandchildren. This search for insurgent Barbarians—in a trade caravan!—was useless. The whole military thrust north of the Alps was futile, in his seasoned mind. Germania was too big and its people too proud to ever be conquered. But the centurion never questioned orders. He did as told and drew his monthly pay.

He stiffened. His trained eye told him that trouble had just arrived.

"What is going on here?" boomed Sebastianus Gallus, riding through the trees at a gallop. Jumping down from his mare, he strode up to the centurion. "What are these soldiers doing here?"

"We're searching for rebels, sir," the officer said, recognizing the bronze-haired young man, in a fine white tunic and handsome blue cloak, as someone of rank and importance.

Sebastianus scowled as he surveyed the chaotic scene. It would be an hour before he could restore order and another hour to break camp and get the caravan underway. He had to reach Colonia before dark. "Upon whose orders?" he snapped. "And why wasn't I informed?"

"General Vatinius, sir," the centurion said wearily, reminding himself of the vineyard and warm Italian days. "He ordered a surprise search, the better to find the fugitives. No forewarning, no chance to get away."

"We are hiding no one here," Sebastianus growled and marched off.

Sebastianus's ill humor was due only in part to this unexpected upheaval of his camp. He had spent the night at a nearby farm, the guest of a Roman farmer he had known for years, but he had not slept well. It was because of the girl, Ulrika. The day before, she had announced her intention to leave the company of the caravan the moment they arrived in Colonia, to go off on her own in search of her father's people. Sebastianus had not expected that. He had thought he would help her put together a party that consisted of local Germanic guides, bodyguards, slaves. As safe an escort as he could muster.

But to go *alone*? Was she out of her mind? Was she so ignorant of the dangers she risked?

He wished he had never agreed to take her as a passenger. But Timonides had insisted that the stars showed her path aligning with his. And with each daily horoscope, there she was, still intertwined with Sebastianus's destiny. "When do our paths diverge?" he had asked in their camp outside of Lugdunum. Timonides had only shrugged and said, "The gods will let us know."

Although he had worried that a girl on her own in a caravan might be a problem, Ulrika had turned out to be no trouble at all. She had kept to herself, quiet, reading, going for walks—always modestly draped in the *palla* that covered her coiled hair and bare arms. She had traveled without complaint in an enclosed box-wagon drawn by two horses, a rocky carriage ride that always elicited grumbles from passengers when they stepped out at the end of the day. But Ulrika never spoke as she sought a place at the campfire while Sebastianus's slaves erected a tent for her privacy.

In a small way, she had even been an asset. Sebastianus had watched her heal people. A mere girl with a calming, quiet presence and a curious box filled with medicinal magic. She would listen to someone's problem and she would either say, "This is beyond my skill," or, "I can help."

She had said that she had learned healing arts from her mother, but

Sebastianus suspected her talent went beyond a mere apprenticeship, for those she had helped declared that she had somehow known exactly what ailed them, had known even without them being able to adequately describe their ills.

As he walked through his disordered camp, calming people down, assuring them that the soldiers would soon be gone, he squinted through the smoke and mist and saw her on the other side, standing outside her own small tent, talking to Timonides. Sebastianus was startled to see long hair flowing over her shoulders and down her back. She normally wore her tawny hair bound up in a Grecian knot and hidden beneath her veil.

He was further startled to feel a stab of sexual desire.

Pushing the girl from his thoughts—they were parting company tomorrow, after all—he strode through the camp bringing reassurances to his slaves and workers, and to those traveling under his protection, stopping to set hay bales aright, to soothe frazzled nerves, to restore order as he went. But his mind raced. It normally took him sixty days to reach Fort Bonna, yet he had arrived in a record forty-five. He had pushed to cover the miles, and had not conducted his usual extensive commerce in the towns and cities they had visited. By his calculations, if he could execute a swift turnaround in Colonia, he could have the caravan back in Rome in perhaps another forty-two days, with an excellent chance of beating the other four traders to the finish, which was the Imperial Palace and an audience with Emperor Claudius.

Unfortunately, simply getting there first was not enough. Sebastianus still had to find a way to distinguish himself before the emperor. What could he take back to Rome as a gift that would set him apart from Badru, Sahir, Adon, and Gaspar, who would surely present splendid trophies to Claudius?

As Sebastianus surveyed the camp, assessing damage and nerves, he saw two legionaries approach Ulrika's tent, where she stood her ground, tall and proud. He quickly made his way across, and as he neared, he heard her say, "There is no one in this tent."

"Sorry, miss, but we have to see for ourselves."

Ulrika did not budge. "I harbor no criminals."

"Just step aside."

She tipped her chin. "On what authority do you act?"

"Is General Vatinius good enough for you? Now just—"

Her clasped hands fell away. "*Who* did you say? General Vatinius? But he is miles from here, to the south—"

"The commander is at Colonia, with his legions."

Ulrika gasped. "Vatinius is *here?* Already?"

Sebastianus saw the color drain from her face. Before he could speak, Ulrika surprised him by suddenly standing aside and saying to the soldiers, "Search. You will find nothing."

As the legionaries conducted a quick sweep of the tent's interior, Ulrika wrung her hands. Sebastianus had never seen her so agitated. "You're worried about your father's family," he said, wishing he could offer something more. Sebastianus knew few details of the legions newly garrisoned at Colonia. He had heard conflicting reports, information being based more upon imagination and wishful thinking than fact.

Ulrika's eyes met his, and he saw fear there. "I must warn them," she whispered.

"Warn them—?"

The legionaries emerged from the tent, and Ulrika, without another word, quickly went inside. Sebastianus stood there for a moment, puzzled, then he turned on his heel and called out for Timonides.

As soon as he had seen his master enter the camp to stop and talk with the centurion, Timonides had tossed aside his unfinished lamb chop and rushed to the tent he shared with his son, Nestor, to prepare himself for the morning's astral reading. It was the first thing his master saw to when he returned to camp, before breakfasting even. When Sebastianus called for him, Timonides would be ready with the horoscope.

As he pored over his charts, using his instruments by lamplight, scribbling equations on a scrap of papyrus, Timonides felt a pang of guilt over the falsehoods he had uttered in the past few weeks. But he had wanted to keep the girl with them, in case his jaw acted up again, or another ailment befell him. He tried to assuage his conscience by reminding himself that in all his years of serving the gods and the stars, he had never asked for anything in return. Surely they would not mind this one small reward for faithful service, but the feelings of guilt—

He froze. Something was wrong.

He read his notes again, reset his protractor, made certain of degrees and houses and ascendants. And felt his blood run to ice. Great Zeus. There was no doubt. Yesterday, his master's horoscope had been as clear and uneventful as a summer's day. But now, unexpectedly . . .

A catastrophe lay ahead. Something great and fearsome that had not been there in prior days. Timonides licked his lips. Why now? What had changed? Had it something to do with the soldiers searching the camp?

Or is it my punishment for falsifying readings?

Timonides broke out in a sweat. He knew that when he reported this new reading, Sebastianus would demand an explanation as to why his horoscope had suddenly changed. If Timonides told him the truth, that he had lied back in Rome about bringing the girl along, what would Sebastianus do to punish him? Timonides did not mind for himself—he was an old man and had lived a good life and would accept any punishment within reason. It was Nestor he worried about. For his son's sake he must stay in his master's good graces. Pudgy and pie-faced, with the sweet temper of angels and the innocence of doves, Nestor would be helpless on his own.

Timonides wrestled with his conscience and indecision.

The day the newborn had been placed in his arms, the look of disgust on the midwife's face, the sisters and cousins all declaring it would be best for the child to leave him exposed on a garbage heap . . . Timonides had almost agreed, until he had felt that tender flesh, the tiny bones, the utter helplessness of the creature. His heart had turned upside down in that moment and Timonides had known he could not do to this infant what had been done to him. And so he had kept the son who had come late in life to the Greek and his wife, a surprise really, as Damaris had thought herself beyond childbearing age. And when Damaris had died when Nestor was only ten, Timonides had pledged himself anew to care for the boy at any cost.

Now, twenty years later, Timonides was being put to the test. And there was no question. He could not tell his master the truth—that a great catastrophe now lay before them because his faithful astrologer had committed sacrilege by falsifying horoscopes. For Nestor's sake, Timonides must save himself with yet another lie.

Rubbing his belly and wishing he hadn't dipped his lamb chops in so much garlic sauce, Timonides went out into the smoky morning to deliver the reading.

He found Sebastianus sitting at a table in front of the tent where the wealthy trader never slept, a scroll containing financial records opened before him, the ever-present abacus in his hand. The young Galician smelled of soap. He had changed into a clean white tunic, the close-cropped beard was freshly trimmed, his hands and feet were scrubbed clean. Timonides knew that, with his blue cloak fastened at his throat, Sebastianus was ready to break camp and make the last leg of the journey.

"The stars have a new message this morning, master. Something big is about to happen to you."

Bronze eyebrows arched. "Big? What does that mean? Nothing was said of this last night, in the evening reading."

"Things have changed," Timonides said, averting his eyes.

"Changed?" Sebastianus thought about this. "The soldiers," he said. Then he turned in the direction of Ulrika's tent, where he could see her silhouette moving about inside, and a strange new thought fluttered at the edge of his mind.

The soldiers . . .

Something about the soldiers and the girl named Ulrika. "I must warn my people," she had said.

What had she meant by that? Warn them of what? He had thought she was simply going home. That was all she had told him.

But . . . in the past few weeks, a word here, a comment there. "My people's land surrounds a sacred, hidden valley embraced by two small rivers that form half-moons. In the heart of this valley lies a sacred grove of oak trees, where it is said the goddess Freya wept red-gold tears." And another time, proudly, "My tribe are warriors."

Now, recalling her reaction to news of Commander Vatinius being in

Colonia, Sebastianus wondered: was it *her* people who were behind the new uprising? Were *they* the rebels Vatinius had been sent to vanquish once and for all?

And were those insurgents at that moment camped in the hidden valley Ulrika had spoken of?

Sebastianus rose to his feet, carefully considering his next words as new thoughts formed in his mind. "Old friend," he said to Timonides, "this great thing you speak of that lies in my path—could it be that I am about to meet someone very important?"

Timonides hesitated. What in the name of Great Zeus was his master talking about? The old Greek had no idea, but there was suddenly a look of hope, even excitement in his master's eyes, and so Timonides said, "Yes, yes, that is it," eagerly bobbing his head, hating himself for the lie, the sacrilege. But he had no choice. And if the gods struck him dead in that moment, he would not blame them. "You are about to meet someone very important who will change your life."

Sebastianus felt his blood suddenly run hot with excitement. It could only be Gaius Vatinius, commander of six legions! For who was more important in this region than he? And I have precious information to give him. I know where the Barbarian insurgents are headquartered!

With such information, Sebastianus knew, General Vatinius would be assured a victory. And Emperor Claudius would grant a handsome reward to the man who had brought it about. The imperial *diploma* to China.

I will ride north immediately and inform the General of a hidden valley embraced within two half-moon rivers . . .

ULRIKA HASTILY BOUND HER HAIR up in ribbons and reached for her travel packs. She decided she was not going to wait for Colonia. She must leave now. Vatinius was already here, and she alone knew of the secret trap he planned to set for her people.

Slipping out of her nightdress, she chose a practical traveling gown of plain white cotton with a matching *palla,* and as she dressed she thought of the myriad small vessels she had observed on the Rhine, local merchants plying their trade up and down the river under the eye of the Roman galleys. Ulrika spoke the dialect and had enough coins, she knew, to bribe one of them to carry her to the other side.

As she wrapped bread and cheese in cloths, she thought of Sebastianus Gallus. She should let him know that she was leaving the caravan this morning. But then she realized he might not allow her to leave, might even assign a guard to her to see that she stayed safely in his charge until he delivered her to Colonia—as per their agreement.

Saying a mental farewell to him, doubting she would see him again, Ulrika stepped out of her tent and headed for the Rhine.

9

SHE WAS LOST.

Ulrika had been walking for days, following the map, trying to recall the details her mother had told her long ago—so many small rivers shaped like half-moons!—and now she was deep in the forest eastward of the Rhine, and she had no idea where she was.

When Ulrika had made her way down to the Rhine, she had been able to bribe a boatman to take her across to the other side. And during the crossing, she had asked him if there was news of Vatinius and his legions, but the boatman had spoken quickly, his accent unfamiliar to Ulrika, so that she had garnered only bits and pieces.

One thing she did know: a major battle was about to take place.

But where?

She scanned the sunlit forest, where firs and oaks cast dark shadows, and birds called from overhead branches, and the silence was broken by the occasional snap of a twig, reminding Ulrika that creatures were watching her. Hungry creatures . . .

Where was she? As she had headed eastward from the river, leaving civilization behind, she had encountered fewer and fewer people until now she was alone in the deep woods, armed only with a dagger and inner fortitude. She knew she was moving in a northeasterly direction, but to where precisely, she no longer knew. Unlike in the city of Rome, there were no signposts in this wilderness.

She was dreading spending another night in this hostile terrain. Although the summer solstice lay just two weeks away and the days were warming up, the nights were cold. Ulrika had slept in hollows stuffed with leaves, against logs, and in the protection of boulders, wrapped in her *palla* and praying that tomorrow she would find her father. Her food was gone. Her dress was torn, her sandals falling apart. And now she trekked wearily through a forest that looked the same as the forest the day before, and the day before that.

With each gnarled root that caused her to trip, each thorny bush that snagged her skirt, each owl that screeched and each shadow that menaced, Ulrika felt herself drawing closer to tears. She had thought that the land of her ancestors would feel like home. After years of not knowing where she belonged, of feeling like an outsider, even in the house she shared with her mother in Rome, Ulrika had been so certain that Germania would feel safe and familiar and comfortable. Instead, this wild, unpredictable forest frightened her.

She was appalled at her naïveté. How could she have thought it would be so simple to find her father, when all the experienced spies and agents that made up Caesar's intelligence network could not?

She paused to lean against a tree and catch her breath. The sun was directly overhead. How many hours of daylight were left before she had to find a safe place to spend the night? Should I turn back? Do I even know the way back?

The map, purchased from a cartographer in Lugdunum who had hawked his wares from a booth in the marketplace, guaranteeing "the latest precise geographic details," had proven useless. Rivers and streams indicated on the map did not exist, while those Ulrika had drunk from were not drawn at all. As for the valley between two half-moon rivers—she could have already passed through it without knowing it.

She wished belatedly that she had not snuck out of the caravan camp, that she had at least told Timonides where she was going. Instead, when she had packed her bags and was ready to travel, she had made sure no one saw her as she made her way down to the riverbank. Were Sebastianus Gallus and the Greek astrologer worried about her at this moment? Or did Gallus assume she had gone in search of her family? Was Sebastianus Gallus at that moment in Colonia, resting up for the return trip to Rome?

Is he even thinking about me?

Ulrika was not surprised that the Galician should appear in her thoughts, in this place and at this time, because she had dreamed about him every night since leaving the camp.

Reminding herself of her mission, and that time was growing dangerously short, she paused to listen to the forest and imagined the thousands of troops wheeling war machines into place, officers riding to and fro shouting commands, foot soldiers and cavalry being positioned into columns and lines. She knew that the battle would begin with the release of missile weapons—javelins, crossbows, and spears.

She resumed her trek. A chilly wind blew through the forest. A sandal strap broke and suddenly Ulrika was barefoot. Pain shot through the sole of her right foot, causing her to cry out. Her travel packs grew heavy on her shoulders, and her legs became sluggish. She had never known such hunger. A voice from the past, Aunt Paulina's, whispered, "A young lady never cleans her plate. It is always ladylike to leave food."

Aunt Paulina was like a second mother to Ulrika because her own mother, Selene, was so busy with her healing practice and her many patients. "A well brought up Roman girl," Paulina would say, "never exposes her hair in public. She never fidgets. She never speaks out of turn. She works quietly at her loom every afternoon. She is always nice and polite and looks forward to the day she will marry and have children."

As Ulrika stumbled over the uneven forest floor, sharp twigs and rocks cutting into her foot, she thought: Is this my punishment for breaking the rules?

The wind shifted, rustling overhead leaves and branches, but this time bringing into the forest the smell of smoke. Ulrika stopped and lifted her face. Yes! There were campfires nearby! Perhaps a hearth with food in a pot, meat turning on a spit. But most of all—people . . .

As she stumbled through the trees, she heard voices. She came through the pines and into a vast, green meadow. Ulrika scanned for huts, signs of life, and saw a man lying in the tall grass. She approached him with caution. The man was sprawled in a strange position.

She slowly reached down and touched him. He was stiff and cold.

Ulrika snatched her hand back. She looked around the meadow.

And then she saw—

Another body.

And then another . . .

Ulrika lifted her eyes to the edge of the meadow, where she saw the beginning of blackened earth—a shocking landscape of misshapen trees, many still giving off wisps of smoke. The earth had been set afire, a trademark of victorious Romans, whose policy was slash and burn after a battle.

Numbness creeping through her body, she continued into the meadow, where she found more corpses, until soon she came into a valley that was strewn with hundreds of dead, perhaps thousands.

She continued through the stench, the flies, the mutilations and bloated bodies, disembodied heads among decapitated corpses, a grotesque scattering of limbs and internal organs. She saw bulging eyes and tongues gaping up at her as if angry that she should see them in this condition. Ravens were pecking at faces, flying up, startled, with swollen tongues in their talons. Squawking and fighting over exposed testicles, ripping and devouring the tender flesh. Wolves chewing on bones.

Nausea swept over her as she staggered among the dead. She sobbed to find men impaled on trees, their arms hacked off, blood that had run in rivers now congealed black. She heard groaning. Some were still alive!

She followed the soft groans and came upon a German warrior lying in an unnatural position. His legs were twisted in an impossible way, as if his torso had snapped. The upper half of his body lay supine while his legs were almost prone. His eyes were open. Ulrika couldn't move. She stood over the dying warrior, frozen, not breathing, her eyes wide with shock and horror.

His lips parted. Bearded chin moved. He whispered something. He wanted her to kill him, to end his misery.

Unsheathing her dagger and clasping it tightly in both hands, Ulrika raised the weapon above her head and, with a strangled cry, drove the blade into his breast. His eyes remained open, but she saw the light fade and he stopped breathing.

Sobbing, blinded by tears, Ulrika fell back and looked around the battlefield. At the *thousands* of dead. Was her father among them?

She desperately searched for the hero named Wulf. But she saw only decomposing bodies nailed to trees. The remains of women who had been raped—women who had joined their husbands and sons in battle and suffered terrible fates.

Ulrika stood frozen to the spot. She had misunderstood the boatman who had carried her across the Rhine. He had not warned of a battle about to be fought, but one that had already been fought. Vatinius had not just arrived in Colonia with his legions! He had already marched into battle—and won.

I could have saved them! I came too late!

She sobbed, tears rolling down her cheeks as she staggered among the butchered dead. "I am sorry," she whispered to the slain warriors. "I am so sorry. Please forgive me."

The sun dipped behind the tall pines, casting the battlefield in gloomy shadow. Ulrika was suddenly engulfed in an eerie silence. She turned in a slow circle, her eyes sweeping over the corpses, and felt a strange chill invade her bones. It was death, she thought, coming to steal her soul.

The silence was suddenly broken by a loud snap. Ulrika spun around. Her eyes widened as she saw movement in the forest. She could not move as shapes shifted among the pines. Cold sweat sprouted between her shoulder blades. The ghosts of the dead!

Finally, white apparitions came voicelessly through the trees—tall figures with long, flowing hair. Ulrika felt her heart rise to her throat. Terror gripped her. When the figures emerged from the trees and into the clearing, Ulrika's eyes widened. Not ghosts—women. Stepping silently among the corpses, bending, retrieving, gesturing to the sky. What were they doing?

Ulrika watched as two stunningly beautiful women paused in their queer posturing, looked at Ulrika, and then, straightening, walked toward her—tall women, long-limbed and robust in full skirts and colorful blouses, thick blond tresses draped over generous bosoms. Ulrika knew who they were: "victory women," or "shield maidens." In the local dialect, they were Valkyries, handmaidens of Odin who singled out those heroes slain in battle to take them to sit in the great Val Hall and drink mead for eternity.

As the two approached, stepping over severed limbs, bending to touch cold foreheads, murmuring, chanting softly, moving among the fallen dead to whisper—what?—their images shifted and changed until Ulrika realized they were not young and robust at all, but old women, their heads crowned with white braids, their aged bodies draped in belted tunics and long skirts, coarse shawls around bony shoulders. Despite advanced years, however, they walked with erect spines, straight shoulders. Years had aged them, she thought, but pride had kept them strong.

When the first came near, Ulrika saw that around the crown of her head lay a handsome circlet of twisted silver, twined and curled with silver leaves and stems, coming together on the old woman's forehead to support a tiny silver owl resting on two silver oak leaves, a pale moonstone between the leaves, like an egg, as if the owl were waiting to hatch it.

The two women paused to give her close scrutiny. When the second of the two saw the Cross of Odin on Ulrika's breast, she pointed and murmured, while the other pursed her wrinkled lips. Milky blue eyes peered at Ulrika from beneath white brows. "Are you lost, daughter?"

It was a dialect Ulrika understood. "I am looking for—" Ulrika could barely breathe.

"You should not be here," the woman said gently, "among the dead."

"I need to find—"

The old woman had sharply chiseled cheekbones and jaw, a thin aquiline nose, making Ulrika think that in her youth she must have been a very striking woman. But now the young flesh was gone, leaving her with bone and sinew, but an air of strength all the same. She reached out and laid a hand on Ulrika's arm. "You are weary. Come, daughter. Away from all this death."

"I am looking for my father. He is Wulf, the son of Arminius."

The old woman shook her head in sadness. "Wulf is dead. His family all perished. Come now, you must eat and rest."

"Dead! No, you are mistaken. I am searching for him. He cannot be dead."

But the women turned to lead the way, lifting their skirts as they stepped over corpses, allowing Ulrika a glimpse of leather boots lined with fur. She fell wordlessly into step behind them, carrying her travel packs, her burdens, her pain as she walked with one sandaled foot and one bare foot over ground that was soaked with blood.

At the edge of the meadow they approached an area of blackened earth where the Romans had set fire as they had retreated with captives and weapons looted from the dead. Nearby, Ulrika knew, the legionaries would have given their own slain a decent burial, in mass graves with prayers and offerings to the gods.

As she followed the two old women over scorched ground where not a blade of grass had survived, she realized that they had entered what was left of a village. All that remained after the Roman fires were the charred foundations of what had once been sturdy log halls. Ulrika's eyes stung with smoke as she passed places where embers still glowed, and straw and wood smoldered. Trees that had once been magnificent pines and oaks were now stunted and black, twisted and grotesque. The stench was overwhelming.

The old woman with the silver circlet around her head stopped in front of what appeared to be a pile of grass and twigs but which turned out to be a crude shelter. "Inside is food and drink."

Ulrika bent to enter the hut, finding darkness inside. But when her eyes adjusted, she saw a bare, earthen floor with fur pelts, waterskins, woven baskets holding vegetables and fruit.

She gratefully accepted what she suspected was the last of their food, and so although she was ravenous, she ate sparingly, and then drank from the proffered waterskin.

"Who are you?" she asked of the two women who sat watching her.

"We are the caretakers of a sacred grove. We have been so for countless generations, ever since the Goddess Freya wept her red-gold tears among the ancient oaks. You must sleep now," the old woman said, "while we return to the task of burying our sons and husbands."

"Yes," Ulrika said wearily, laying back on a blanket made of thick bear skin. "I am so very tired . . ."

She did not know how long she slept, but when she awoke it was dark and the two caretakers of the sacred grove were lighting torches and stirring something in a hot cooking pot. As Ulrika struggled to sit up—every bone and muscle ached—the one with the owl and moonstone circlet came to her side. "Here," she said with a smile. "Mushroom broth. It will give you strength."

Ulrika rubbed her eyes as, once again, the two elderly women seemed to grow young. In the flickering torchlight, their wrinkled skin became smooth, their milky eyes turned luminous, their white hair was miraculously black.

"Why did you come here?" the one with the moonstone asked. So far, her companion had yet to speak.

Ulrika blinked. They were old again. "I came to warn my father's people of the coming invasion. But I was too late."

Ancient eyes filled with wisdom settled on Ulrika's face and stayed there for a long moment while outside, night birds called and the wind whistled. Finally, the caretaker of the grove said, "That is not why you came here. That was not your purpose. You were brought here for a different destiny, daughter." She pointed to the wooden cross that hung about Ulrika's neck. "You wear the sacred symbol of Odin. You are the servant of the gods, you are doing their bidding."

"Why would they choose me to be their servant?"

"Because, daughter, you have inherited a special gift." She paused. "You do have a special gift, do you not?"

The old woman waited, while her companion sat in watchful silence.

The bowl of broth stopped at Ulrika's lips. She lowered it to her lap and said, "What special gift?"

A long bony arm reached out, and for an instant Ulrika glimpsed smooth skin and strong muscles. The old woman touched Ulrika's forehead and whispered, "It is called the Divining."

The smoke from the sputtering torch seemed to grow stronger. Ulrika's head swam for a moment, and then she said, "Do you mean my visions? But it is an illness."

The woman shook her head, casting platinum highlights off her white hair. "It is a gift, daughter. You are afraid of the visions. You must not be.

You must embrace them because they came from the gods and are therefore sacred."

"How do you know this?"

"You say you are the daughter of Wulf. The Divining is in his bloodline."

"But my visions make no sense. Nor can I command them. They are like random dreams that come and go and are beyond interpretation. What sort of gift is that?"

"You will learn to control them and read them."

"To what purpose? I have no wish to know the future."

"That is not the purpose of your visions."

"Then what?" Ulrika set the bowl aside. "What good do such nonsensical visions do for me?"

"They are not for you, daughter. You must use your gift to help others, not yourself."

Ulrika massaged her temples. "I still do not understand."

"Your gift has been handed down to you from a long line of women who possessed it. But your gift is young and undisciplined, which is why your visions make no sense. You must learn to tame your gift, control it. Learn to use it to help others."

"But what is the Divining?"

"That you will learn when you learn discipline."

"Who will teach me this discipline?"

"It must come from within yourself. But there will be teachers. You will not know them. Only when you have left them behind will you know who they were. That is why you must open your mind and heart to all whom you encounter in your life's path. Sleep again, child. Rest. Tomorrow you must return to where you belong. Tomorrow you begin a new and special journey."

Beneath the soft comfort of wolf pelts, in the coziness of the forest hut, Ulrika closed her eyes and slipped away into deep, welcome sleep.

When she awoke to find sunlight streaming through the overhead twigs and branches, her memory of the night before came back. As she bathed in a nearby stream and refreshed herself on a humble breakfast of mushrooms and acorns, Ulrika pondered the mysterious words the old woman had spoken.

When she was ready to leave, the senior caretaker of the grove supplied

Ulrika with nuts and berries, a waterskin, and fresh boots for her feet. "Do not go back by way of the battleground," she cautioned. "Directly south of here, you will come to another stream. Follow its current and it will take you to the river your people call the Rhine. You will be safe along the way, daughter, for the spirits of the stream will protect you."

As an added precaution, the caretaker of the grove reached into a leather pouch on her belt and withdrew a handful of curious stones, flat and variously shaped, each with a symbol drawn on it. She cast these stones onto the ground and studied the symbols for a long moment while birdsong filled the air. She frowned, white brows coming together, then she straightened and said, "The runes say that you have strayed from your destined path. You must go back to the beginning of your path and set out upon it again. This time you will stay true to your destiny."

Ulrika looked down at the flat stones. "Where is the beginning?"

"At the place where you were conceived, for that is when your life began."

"But that is in Persia, which is a vast land! How will I find such a place?"

"It is where you must go. There, you will find your destiny."

Her mind filled with puzzled thoughts, Ulrika thanked the two women, and struck off southward.

As they watched her go, the other old woman, who had not spoken, rested her gnarled hand on the first one's arm and said, "Sister, how can you be so calm about this?"

"I am not calm, Hilde. I wanted to embrace her, but I had to hold myself back, for her sake."

"Did Wulf know she was coming?"

"Wulf does not even know she exists."

As they watched Ulrika disappear through charred trees, the second of the old women said, "But why did you lie to her? Why not tell her the truth?"

She could not, for the truth was a great secret: after the deaths of Arminius's wife Thusnelda and their only son, the German hero never married again. But when Arminius was grieving bitterly for his loss, he found comfort in the sacred grove dedicated to the Goddess of the Red-Gold Tears, where the beautiful young priestess took him into her arms. Wulf was the result of that secret union.

"Could you not at least tell her that her father is alive?" Hilde asked gently.

Milky blue eyes filled with tears. "A great and strange destiny awaits my granddaughter, and if she knew her father was still alive, she would stay here and go in search of him and never fulfill that destiny. Believing him to be dead, she will follow the correct path."

"Will she come back to us?"

"Perhaps someday, the gods willing," said the elder seeress of the Cherusci tribe, herself called Ulrika and after whom her granddaughter had been named.

10

THE DAY DIED, THE FOREST GREW MENACING.

Ulrika had been following the stream as the old woman had instructed, but it seemed to be leading nowhere. How far was the river? Her packs grew heavy as the stream seemed to meander aimlessly through dense pines and oaks, down a narrow valley pocked with ancient caves. Ulrika felt the eyes of woodland creatures measure her progress as she stumbled, her right foot bare, over prickly ground.

Snap!

She stopped, held her breath to listen.

Snap!

Footfall. Too heavy for an animal.

Rustling in the underbrush. Something—or someone—was following her.

She scanned the forest, her eyes wide in the dying daylight. Shadows took on forbidding shapes, seemed to move. The gurgle of the stream faded while other sounds grew loud—the screech of a hawk, the wind high in treetops, another snap of underbrush.

Wondering if she could outrun whatever was following her, Ulrika turned in the direction of the sounds, saw silhouettes moving, and realized they were men. When the first emerged into the small clearing beside the stream, and Ulrika saw that he was tall and bearded, wearing a belted tunic and leather leggings, when she saw the tribal tattoos and long twisted hair, she frantically searched for a place to hide.

Four more emerged from the oaks and pines, swords in hand, angry looks on their faces. One had dried blood caked on his arm, another limped on an injured leg. As they drew near, brandishing swords smeared with blood, Ulrika saw the crazed look in their eyes. She thought of her own dagger, tucked out of reach in one of her packs.

She fell back a step. The strangers exchanged words which she did not understand. But she understood their intent. Killing lust burned in the eyes of these survivors of a humiliating defeat.

She fell back another step and felt the slope of the ground as it began the descent to the bank of the stream. The sun had left the forest; gloom surrounded Ulrika and the five warriors. They crept closer. She smelled their sweat. She saw scars, old and new. The long blond beards, unruly hair. The faces smeared with blood and dirt.

Then she saw the man at the rear, a barrel-chested giant with red hair, separate himself from the others and inch around to come up from behind. He leered at Ulrika with a gap-toothed grin. Reaching for the strap of one of her travel packs, she drew it from her shoulder and swung it with all her might. The warrior laughed as he grabbed the pack and tossed it away.

Ulrika tried another, swinging it at her assailants, but it too was wrenched from her grasp and thrown out of reach. She tried to step to the side, but a third man blocked her way. They encircled her. Ulrika could not watch all of them.

The leader raised his sword, grinning like his comrades, the look in his eyes no longer one of killing lust but lust of another kind. The man behind grabbed Ulrika's hair, as half had come uncoiled during her forest trek. She cried out. He dragged her to him. She felt strong arms go around her waist. She kicked, tried to bite. The leader seized her ankles. Ulrika cursed her weakness. Afternoons sitting at her loom, browsing in bookstores—

They dragged her to the ground and pinned her down. The leader bent over her, grinning as he tugged at her dress. He lowered himself, and then suddenly looked at her in surprise. Ulrika stared up into his scarred face and their eyes met for an instant before he collapsed onto her, suffocating her with his weight. The others were suddenly on their feet, shouting. Pushing the unconscious man away, Ulrika sat up and saw Sebastianus Gallus, in a white tunic and blue cloak, come flying out of the forest, swinging a sword. She watched in amazement as the four warriors descended upon him, their swords meeting his.

Ulrika shot to her feet and searched for something to use as a weapon. She saw the dagger in the dead man's back, which Gallus had thrown on the run. She yanked it out and looked for a target, but the men were moving too quickly.

As metal clanged with metal, the Galician reached for the fastening at his throat, drew his cloak from his shoulders and threw it over the heads of Ulrika's assailants. One of them became tangled in the cloth and fell backwards. The other three continued to fight, attacking from all sides, with the Spaniard deftly meeting each plunge of a Barbarian's sword.

Gripping Gallus's dagger, Ulrika gave a cry and flew at the man with red hair, sinking the weapon into the meat of his shoulder. He bellowed and swung about. Ulrika managed to pull the dagger out and jump aside, to jab at another warrior.

With the clang of metal ringing in her ears as she thrust and hit and screamed, driven by fury and grief and self-recrimination, her eyes blinded by tears, Ulrika caught flashes of Sebastianus Gallus as he fought the Barbarians. She saw thickly muscled arms, broad shoulders, and a strong back as he swung his massive sword again and again, sending his foes reeling, staggering beneath his blows.

Gallus kept up with them, even though outnumbered, thrusting, slicing, spinning this way and that, meeting each blow that came his way until one attacker fell, and then another. With one man left standing, and Gallus advancing with his sword, relentlessly driving the Barbarian backwards, the others scrambled to their feet and ran off, shouting oaths over their shoulders as they plunged into the woods and disappeared.

Heaving for breath, Sebastianus watched them go, then he wiped his brow and looked at Ulrika. "Are you all right?"

She stared at him. "Yes—" she began. Was he truly here, or was he a vision? *Why* was he here? How had he found her? Gallus gulped for air, his chest expanding, muscles straining the fabric of his tunic. His closely cropped bronze hair and beard glistened with the sweat of combat. Ulrika was speechless at the sight of him. Sebastianus's sword was massive, yet he had swung it with ease.

"They will come back," he said as he retrieved his cloak from the ground and then picked up Ulrika's packs. He looked around the forest gloom. The sun had gone, night was nearly upon them. "I got separated from my party. I'll never find them in the dark. Those caves look safe for now."

Ulrika fell wordlessly into step at his side. She was numb with shock. Judging by their tribal tattoos, her attackers had been Cherusci, her father's countrymen. And yet her rescuer was really a stranger to her, with whom she had no connection, materializing out of nowhere, startling her with his strength and power—a man who sat with his abacus, counting sacks of grain.

"Here," Sebastianus said when they reached a cave surrounded by stunted trees and trailing blackberries. The fissure was small, barely visible, with just enough room for them to slip inside. "They won't find us in here."

But Ulrika held back. "No, not this one," she said.

"Why not? It's defensible. And we can camouflage the opening." Sebastianus glanced back toward the forest. They needed to find a hiding place quickly. As he stepped toward the cave entrance, Ulrika said, "No, they will find us in there."

She turned and surveyed the dark woods, listened to the stream trickling nearby. In the darkening twilight she saw ahead, on the other side of a stand of oak trees, a larger cave, with a wide opening, and no brush surrounding it. "There," she said, pointing. "We will be safe in there."

Sebastianus looked at her in surprise. "They will find us for certain in there!"

But she sprinted ahead, turning ghostly white in the purple dusk. Sebastianus ran after her. Ulrika disappeared through the entrance and Sebastianus had no choice but to follow.

Inside, he saw that the cave was deep and wide, with no openings branching off, no large rock formations behind which to hide. They might as well be sitting in the middle of a meadow! Before he could voice his objection, they heard voices—deep, angry, shouting. The Barbarians had returned and, from the sound of it, had brought friends.

Sebastianus dropped the travel packs and gripped his sword, ready to fight. But Ulrika seemed unconcerned as she slowly looked around the deep, black cave, turning in a circle, looking up at the rocky ceiling, until she was facing the entrance and Sebastianus. "We will be safe here," she said again.

Whispering a curse, Sebastianus took Ulrika by the wrist and drew her away from the opening, to press her against the cold wall while he peered around to watch the Barbarians.

But Ulrika did not mark the progress of the Germans as they tramped through the forest, drawing nearer to the cave. Instead, she found herself staring at Sebastianus's muscular arms and broad shoulders. His tunic was sweat-soaked from the fight, the fabric clinging to his back, defining hard muscles. The breath caught in her throat.

But then she saw the tear in the cloth, the red stain spreading over his upper arm. He was wounded! Ulrika placed her hand over the injury and pressed gently. Sebastianus flinched, then said, "Shhh."

They watched the Barbarians go inside nearby caves, search behind boulders, run their swords into dense brush, cursing oaths, wondering where the Romans had gone. To Sebastianus's surprise, they did not even glance toward the cave where he and Ulrika were hiding, did not come near, even though surely they must have seen it. He waited with held breath as the German warriors continued deeper into the woods, stamping over twigs and leaves until their footfall and voices could no longer be heard.

He turned to Ulrika, his face inches from hers. "How did you know they would do that?" he asked softly.

But she stepped away and opened one of her travel packs. Sebastianus watched as she sorted through the contents, bringing out a small, stoppered jar and a roll of cotton. Her dress was torn and soiled, her *palla* beyond repair, and her long, lion-colored hair streamed over one shoulder while still touchingly coiled on one side of her head. She looked tragic, yet proud, he thought. The bend of her slender body, the graceful movements of her hands—everything about her was fluid, elegant.

Sebastianus looked away and concentrated on watching the forest.

Even though the German warriors had moved on and could no longer be heard, Sebastianus remained watchful by the cave's entrance, his sword ready. Ulrika came up to him and, lifting the torn sleeve of his tunic, gently dabbed ointment on his wound. Sebastianus thought it a minor injury and would have let it dry and scab on its own, but she was cleaning it, and then applying more salve and finally wrapping his upper arm with strips of cotton fabric. Expertly done, he noticed, recalling what she had told him about her mother being a healer.

When she was finished, she lifted her eyes to his and for a moment both stood breathless in the darkness of the cave. Sebastianus felt the shadows move and shift about them, as if cosmic changes were taking place, and he remembered that he was cut off from his group, separated from his astrologer. Tonight, for the first time since he could remember, Sebastianus would sleep without his evening horoscope.

The thought unsettled him. As did the girl's proximity. She stood too close. He could feel her soft breath on his neck. He stared at her lower lip, full and moist and sensuous.

He stepped back, drew down his bloody sleeve, murmured a thank-you, and wanted to ask again how she knew the Barbarians would not search for them in this cave. But he was held by her blue eyes. He saw the smudges of dirt on her cheeks. Recalled how she had fought her attackers. "Night is upon us," he said. "We will need a fire."

Ulrika sat wearily on the cold dirt floor and watched Sebastianus strike the flint and coax a flame out of a pile of dried leaves. He had collected stones and placed them in a circle for a campfire, and now he added twigs and pieces of wood. "Thank you," Ulrika said.

"For what?" He concentrated on laying the sticks. The girl was filling his thoughts in a way that made him uneasy. He knew it was not just her proximity. Sebastianus suspected that if they were a thousand miles apart, he still would not be able to rid his mind of her. Aside from Ulrika's beauty, her grace and femininity, there was a curious strength about her—the way she had flown at the Barbarians with a dagger, and then had held her emotions together as they searched for a safe hiding place. Now, quietly watching him with those compelling blue eyes.

"For saving my life," she said.

"As long as you travel with my caravan, you are under my protection. It is my duty to see that you reach your destination safely. When you turned up missing from our camp, I put a party together to go looking for you." He didn't look at her as he added, "I was furious when I realized you had left. I had to send the caravan on ahead while I put together a search party."

When Ulrika trembled and wrapped her arms around herself, Sebastianus unclasped his blue cloak and draped it around her shoulders, drawing it snugly tight. In the flickering firelight, Ulrika saw the pewter pin that held the cloak at the throat. It was a beautiful Gallic design.

Sebastianus saw how it caught her interest. "That was given to me by a widow in Lugdunum. A man in the neighborhood was making unwelcome advances and she had no male relatives to protect her. So I paid the man a visit. He will not bother her again."

His words reminded Ulrika of something Timonides had said outside the city of Masilia, when Sebastianus had gone into town that night, bearing gifts. "My master has friends all over the empire. He takes care of people who have no protection. He need only make it known that this man or that woman is under the care of Sebastianus Gallus the merchant trader, and that person is safe."

Ulrika had asked what these people gave Sebastianus in return and Timonides had said, "Their friendship."

As Ulrika touched the fashioned metal, she received a brief vision of the widow who had given him this gift—a pretty woman left alone by a husband who drank too much—and Ulrika knew that the Greek astrologer had spoken the truth when he had said that all Sebastianus asked in return was friendship, for she sensed that there had been nothing more between Gallus and the widow.

"How did you find me?" she asked.

Sebastianus poked the flames with a green stick. "I became separated from my group and met an old woman who told me a Roman girl had come through here recently, a girl on her own. The old woman directed me to the stream. Why did you leave the caravan? Why not wait until we reached Colonia?"

"I wanted to warn my father's people."

Sebastianus finally looked up, firelight reflected in his green eyes. "Warn them of what?"

"Gaius Vatinius had a plan that would ensure his victory." She explained about the dinner at Paulina's villa, the secret strategy Vatinius had bragged about. "But I came too late."

Sebastianus absorbed her remarkable tale while silently building a warm, bright fire. He looked across the flames and saw how pale she was in the hot glow, how she trembled, not from cold but from shock. She had seen a battlefield strewn with corpses. She had traveled a great distance to be reunited with a father she never knew, only to be told he was dead.

"You are very courageous," he said.

"I am very reckless. I could have gotten myself killed. I could have gotten you killed. I'm sorry."

"At least you brought us to the safety of this cave. You knew those men would not come in here. How did you know?"

She mutely shook her head and looked at her hands.

"I have food," he said, reaching for his travel pack. "You must be hungry."

When she did not respond, he turned to her, to find Ulrika with her back to him and to the fire, her eyes delving the darkness at the rear of the cave. "What is it?" he asked.

"I thought," she began, but then turned around, shaking her head.

Sebastianus brought out coarse bread and sharp cheese, cutting off chunks with his knife and handing them to Ulrika. As she nibbled delicately, staring into the flames, Sebastianus noticed that her eyes flickered toward the cave entrance, beyond which lay a dark and forbidding forest. He knew she was not worried about their stalkers coming back. The look in her wide, blue eyes was haunted, as if she were seeing images not there.

She is back on the battlefield, he thought, searching for her father . . .

"What will you do now?" he asked. "Stay here and perhaps search for survivors of your father's family?"

"I do not know what I will do now. I was so certain when I left Rome that

I would find answers here. Yet I am more confused than ever." She thought for a moment, holding him in her gaze with damp eyes. *You must return to the place of your beginning.* "I do not know if there is anything, or anyone, here in the Rhineland for me. But if I return to Rome, I will be expected to marry." She bit into the bread and chewed. "Are you married, Sebastianus Gallus?"

He shook his head. "I am never in one place long enough to be a good husband and father. I have a villa in Rome, but I am rarely there. Sometimes my journeys keep me away for years. What woman would want that kind of husband?"

He fell silent then, and found himself held captive by a pair of frank, blue eyes. He gazed at Ulrika across the golden flames of the campfire, and felt unaccustomed yearnings stir deep within him.

Breaking away from the spell of her eyes, Sebastianus cleared his throat, looked at his hands, and then surveyed their saturnine surroundings. "This cave evokes a memory from my boyhood in Galicia, when I was thirteen years old. There was a man, Malachi, who owned the largest vineyard in the area. He was fat and rich and my brother Lucius and I had heard our father say that Malachi was cruel to his slaves and animals. We did not like that. So Lucius and I would sneak among Malachi's vines and eat his grapes until he chased us off with a whip. One night we crept into his vineyard and stole bunches of ripe grapes, taking them into town and selling them. When Malachi complained to our father, he gave us the thrashing of our lives. This meant revenge. Our plan involved a cave very much like this one."

Ulrika kept her eyes on Sebastianus as he spoke.

"Lucius and I dug a pit just inside the cave's entrance and filled it with pig manure. And then we ran past Malachi's house, making sure he heard us, exclaiming about treasure we had found in the cave. Because he was greedy, or so we thought, we knew he could not resist following us. We paraded in and out of that cave carrying bags, knowing Malachi was watching. And then Lucius and I loudly agreed that we had enough treasure and should go home."

Sebastianus laughed softly. "We thought we were so clever. We did not know, of course, that Malachi was onto us. As we watched the entrance, he came up behind us. He shouted, 'BAH!' We jumped up and yelped and dashed straight into the cave and the manure pit. My mother scrubbed us with soap for a week to get the smell out. And Father gave us yet another thrashing. Lucius and I didn't laugh at the time, but in later years we did."

Sebastianus shook his head. "I was always looking for trouble and Lucius, being younger, followed. Neighbors called us 'those Gallus devils.' My father was forever apologizing for our pranks. But he secretly admired us. He had a way of smiling when he thought we weren't looking."

"Tell me about your family," Ulrika said, finding comfort in the sound of his voice.

"We have been traders for generations. It is in our blood. My ancestors journeyed the length and breadth of Iberia, taking goods to the many tribes that have lived there for millennia. When the Romans crossed the Pyrenees into our land, two centuries ago, my family did not fight them, as others of my race did. Instead, they saw it as an opportunity to expand commerce. My forefathers entered into contracts with the invading Romans, and began carving out routes to distant lands, following the new roads being laid down by Roman legionaries. When Julius Caesar made the conquest of Iberia complete, my family adopted Roman names and Roman ways, we learned to speak Latin and cultivate Roman friendships, and when we were offered Roman citizenship, we embraced it. My ancestral home, Galicia, is the northwesternmost tip of Hispania. I own land there, and a villa.

"My three sisters live there with their husbands and children. I have not seen them in five years, but I write to them regularly, and send money home, even though they are prosperous. I miss my home and my family very much."

"My mother is the only family I have ever known," Ulrika said, picturing a Galician villa filled with children. "We never had a home, we were always on the move because of her personal quest. We came to Rome seven years ago, but it has never felt like home to me. I have never really known where I belong. I had thought perhaps here . . ." She sighed. "It must be nice to have an ancestral home, to know that blood relations are still there, that you can always go back someday."

"Someday . . ." Sebastianus said as he stared into the fire. That was the problem. Sebastianus Gallus was a man who wanted to walk two streets at the same time: he wanted to remain unmarried and free to explore the world, open new trade routes. But he also yearned to go home, settle down, marry, and have a family. He could not do both, and so he traveled his exotic trade routes with a divided heart.

"My next journey, the gods willing," he said, "will be to China. If Emperor Claudius will grant me the imperial *diploma*." And if, he added silently, I can find a way to distinguish myself over Badru, Gaspar, Adon, and Sahir.

Sebastianus had been on his way to meet with Gaius Vatinius, to inform the general of the location of the hidden rebel camp, when he had been stopped by a stab of conscience. Although the information he carried to the Roman commander was priceless beyond measure, and would surely guarantee the granting of the *diploma* to him by Claudius, Sebastianus had suddenly thought: the insurgents might be this girl's family. And he could not betray her. She trusted him, had placed herself in his care, and Sebastianus always prided himself on being an honorable man. So he had turned back, deciding that he must earn the *diploma* by other means.

"Can you not go to China without one?" she asked. "Do merchants not travel that route already?"

"No merchants from Rome have ever gone as far as China. The route is long and fraught with danger. Caravans are constantly being attacked by brigands and mountain tribes. A *diploma* from the imperial court at Rome guarantees some degree of safety, but only as far as Persia. Beyond that, little is known about that fabled far-off land."

Hoot! Hoot!

Ulrika turned to the entrance, her eyes widening.

Sebastianus stirred the fire. "It is but an owl," he said quietly. Or, he thought, it is a secret signal. And he imagined the Barbarians using the cover of night to plan their assault on the cave. He kept his sword close.

Ulrika turned then to peer into the darkness at the back of the cave. "What is it?" he asked.

"I thought I heard . . ."

"There is nothing there," he said, looking into the black abyss beyond the fire's glow and feeling the dark forest at his back with its myriad sounds and whisperings.

Ulrika slowly rose, her body stiff as she leaned toward the darkness.

Sebastianus reached out, touched her arm, to reassure her. She gave a cry and whipped about. "It's only me," he said.

Ulrika's eyes went to the scallop shell that lay on his chest, a cream-colored mollusk with fluted ribs and a wavy outer edge. "What does it mean?" she asked as she sat down.

Sebastianus looked down at the shell suspended on a leather cord and said, "There is an ancient altar near my town. No one knows who built it or when, or to which god it was originally dedicated. Since the arrival of the Romans, someone has carved the word 'Jupiter' into the stone, but I believe the altar was originally dedicated to a goddess because it is decorated with hundreds of scallop shells which, as everyone knows, is the symbol sacred to the goddesses Ishtar and Mari. For many years pilgrims came from all over, each adding a scallop shell. In this way the altar became large and beautiful."

Sebastianus was proud that he was a descendant of the distant ancestress who had built the altar. In fact, he had taken his scallop shell directly from the altar instead of collecting it at the shore as others did. The shell around his neck was very old and might possibly be one of the originals placed there by his ancestress herself, and so it carried great power.

"Unfortunately," he added wistfully, "the highways to the remote altar became rife with brigands who set upon the unarmed pilgrims. Visits are sparse now. I fear the altar might someday be forgotten."

"It means a lot to you?" Ulrika asked.

He gave this some thought, weighing his answer. "I was praying there one night, ten years ago, and . . . " He hesitated.

Lucius, she thought, holding him with her eyes.

The flames crackled and snapped. The darkness of the forest hovered at the cave's entrance, a constant reminder of the dangers beyond. Behind her, Ulrika felt the darkness of the cave's belly, empty and hungry. She saw how the fire brought out the bronze highlights in Sebastianus's hair.

"Ten years ago," he said quietly, his green eyes reflecting the light as he relived a memory, "I was to accompany a shipment of wine to Cypress with a fleet of our merchant ships. My brother Lucius was to take a local caravan in Hispania. But he knew of my desire to go to China, that I had recently come into possession of new maps to the East, that I needed to study them, plan my route, meet with traders who had recently come from kingdoms that lie on the road to China. And so Lucius offered to change places with me. Our father would not have approved, but he was in Rome at the time, and would not have known of the switch. So Lucius accompanied the ships to Cypress. He perished during a storm at sea."

He touched the gold bracelet on his wrist. "I was at the scallop-shell altar," he said, "the night a shower of stars fell from the sky. A river of debris covered the countryside, mostly bits of ice and rock no bigger than a grain of sand, but that night, as the star-shower streaked the sky, I saw a star fall to earth, and I ran out into the hills to find it." He touched the small, gray stone on his gold bracelet. "The crust was hot at first, but it cooled, and I kept it as a trophy, an actual fragment of a star."

His face darkened, his gaze going inward as he said, "And then the letter came, informing me of Lucius's death, and when the author of the letter specified the exact date—the tenth day of that month named for Julius Caesar—and I realized it was the same day on which I had found the star-stone, I knew it was a sign from my brother. But I also realized that I had sent my brother to a death that should have been my own, and so I made a vow that day, on the sacred scallop shell, never to remove this bracelet, in memory of my brother."

"I'm sorry," Ulrika said. "That is a sad story." She suddenly sat up. "Did you hear that?"

"Hear what?"

Ulrika listened. Beyond the cave's entrance, the forest stood in complete darkness, with not even moon glow to relieve the night. She turned and looked toward the back of the cave, also plunged in darkness. "We are not alone," she whispered. "Someone is in here."

Sebastianus shook his head. "It is impossible. There is no other entrance."

"There is someone at the back of the cave. I'm sure of it."

Wrapping a dried vine around the end of a stick to form a torch, Sebastianus rose and walked toward the back of the cave, Ulrika following. But the light illuminated only cold, stone walls and an earthen floor, with a ceiling so low they had to lower their heads. When they reached the end, they found no exit, no way for an intruder to get inside.

"You see?" Sebastianus said. "There is no one here."

"Look!" Ulrika whispered, pointing.

He turned and, lifting the torch, saw the rock wall suddenly spring to life. It was covered in vivid paintings, and as Sebastianus examined the figures rendered in bright reds and yellows and browns, he was able to identify bison, deer, wolves. There were also small figures of men carrying spears, chasing the animals, hunting them. All executed in a lifelike manner. Sebastianus had never seen anything like it.

"Someone is buried here," Ulrika murmured. "He was a holy man . . . a long time ago."

Sebastianus turned to her and saw Ulrika's face cast in strange shadows. Her eyes were wide as they swept the darkness, as if searching for that ancient holy man, as if expecting to find him there, welcoming the two intruders.

"This is why we are safe in here," she added quietly. "This is why those men outside will not come in here. It is a holy place, and taboo for them to walk on this ground."

"How did you know?"

"I think—" she began. "Do you remember the old woman who told you in which direction I had gone? She took me into her hut for a while and she told me that I have a gift."

"What sort of gift?"

"I am visited by visions, dreams. I thought it was a sickness, but the old woman said it is a power given to me by the gods and that I am to use it to help others."

Sebastianus nodded. "My mother believed in such powers. She called it the Invisible Eye." He took in the loose tawny hair, trailing over one shoulder but still coiled on the other side, the smudges on her cheeks and chin, the tattered dress that spoke of disappointment and grief. And suddenly he was gripped with the impulse to take her into his arms and hold her, keep her safe, make love to her. "It is late. You need to sleep."

As he led the way back to the reassuring fire, they both tried to ignore the forest beyond the cave's entrance, an uncanny realm of ghosts and owls and Barbarian rebels awaiting the unsuspecting trespasser. Ulrika gave Sebastianus's cloak back to him, saying her own would be sufficient now that the fire had warmed the cave, and then she took a place by the amber flames, to lie down and curl up in her cloak.

Soon, troubling images filled her slumbering mind. The valley strewn with the victims of Roman treachery. Her father, cut down by an imperial sword. Did he fight to the very end? Did it take ten soldiers to finally bring the great Wulf to his knees? In her dream, Ulrika wept until she thought her heart would break.

And then she realized she was not sleeping by the fire anymore but had somehow made her way to the back of the cave, where she was alone beneath the stony vault ceiling.

In the next moment, sandaled feet stood before her. Ulrika pushed herself up and saw an old man looming over her, robed in a bear skin and carrying a spear. His hair and beard where white and long. He spoke. "I am the shaman of our tribe. We are Wolf Clan. I created these paintings eons ago. They tell the story of our people. *Your* people. You have forgotten who you are, your ancient names, your purpose and destiny. It is not for you, Ulrika of the Cherusci, to sit at a loom, recline on silken couches, and have slaves attend you. Ancient blood swims in your veins. Feel it. You know in your bones, you know in your sinew, who you are. You know, too, that the gods have singled you out for a special purpose. You have been given a great gift, which you must use for the good of humankind. But first you must return to the place of your beginning."

"My beginning," Ulrika whispered. "I do not know where that is."

"Your mother told you the story long ago. You have not forgotten. The name of the place sleeps in the deepest part of your soul. Think, Ulrika!"

She struggled with her thoughts. Yes, her mother had told her of her journey through Persia with Wulf. But there had been many place names—

"Go deep into that place you rarely venture, Ulrika, to that part of your soul which slumbers, a repository of precious memories. Your mother and father stopped to rest at a place called . . ."

"I remember," Ulrika said in wonder. "They stayed beside the Crystal Pools of Shalamandar."

"And that is where you must go . . ."

The old man was bent and wizened, skin and bone, but as he stood before Ulrika against the backdrop of vividly painted bison and deer, the flesh began to grow on his limbs, muscles filled out beneath the shriveled skin, he grew tall. His hair turned from white to bronze, the fragile jaw filled in and grew a stubbled beard.

Sebastianus!

He wore only a loincloth. She saw the wound on his upper arm, which she had cleaned and bandaged, an injury to muscles that had wielded the heavy sword when he came to her rescue. He glistened with sweat.

What had *he* to do with this cave, with the shaman who slept here?

Sebastianus filled the stone chamber with his masculine power. Ulrika had never known a man so strong, so *male*. She became warm, feverish. She rose to her feet to stand before him, to face this powerful man.

He spoke in the voice of the ancient shaman: "You must not turn your back on the call from the gods. You are courageous, Ulrika. You will not deny your destiny."

"But I do not know how to find the Crystal Pools of Shalamandar. And it is such a long and hazardous journey."

"Great destinies do not come easily."

Sebastianus reached up and drew down the other side of her hair, undoing the Grecian knot entirely. At his touch, her skin caught on fire. She had never known such sexual hunger. But she felt something else, too, a power she had never sensed before, as if it were waking up, stirring from a deep, ancient slumber.

He swept her into his arms then and, pulling her to him, pressed his lips to hers. Ulrika's arms went around his neck. She clung to him, kissing him back, relishing the hardness of his body, his masculine power and strength.

And then he began to fade, leaving her arms empty and cold.

Don't leave me . . .

ACROSS THE FIRE, SEBASTIANUS watched Ulrika as she slept. It was a fitful sleep, her eyelids fluttering and small sounds coming from her throat. Of what did she dream, he wondered? She was enchanted somehow, touched by a special magic. The admission of her special gift did not surprise him. But where in all the world did such a special creature belong?

When she started to shiver violently, he took his cloak and laid down beside her, covering her with the thick blue fabric and drawing her into his arms. Her hand went up to his neck, and Sebastianus struggled against desire. Ulrika was asleep, vulnerable, and he was her protector. He would never betray that trust.

He stroked her hair and whispered words of comfort, and after a moment she grew quiet and the shivering stopped. As he watched her closed eyelids, the long lashes resting on white skin, he thought of the wondrous gift she had given him and did not know it—a priceless commodity that was going to be presented to Claudius Caesar upon Sebastianus's return to Rome and that was going to guarantee the awarding of the China *diploma* to him.

With such exciting thoughts in his head, Sebastianus fell asleep, holding the enchanted girl, protecting her with his strength and his warmth. And presently he sighed deeply, his broad chest expanding, and as he exhaled, a low groan came from this throat.

Ulrika opened her eyes and felt the scratch of beard stubble on her forehead. When she felt the strong arms encircling her, inhaled the masculine smell, and realized that she lay in a man's embrace, she gasped.

Ulrika had grown up in the company of women. She had no brothers, uncles, or male cousins. Wherever she and her mother had lived, it was always at a residence of females. She had never experienced the touch of a man, had never lain with a man, had never felt his heat and strength. She held her breath now, overwhelmed by the power of this man as he cradled her in his muscular arms, as she pressed her hands to his shoulders and felt the hardness beneath. She rested her face on his chest, relishing the steady thumping of his heart.

She recalled the dream she had just had. What did it mean? What had this Galician to do with a thousand-year-old medicine man? Filled with questions, Ulrika felt her doubts begin to subside. She started to see that she had not come to the Rhineland on her own, but rather had been brought here.

I was summoned here to learn the true nature of what I had thought an illness. I cannot turn my back on my calling. Mother will tell me where to find the Crystal Pools of Shalamandar, and from there I will start my true path.

Ulrika laid fingertips on Sebastianus's upper arm and drew comfort from the hardness beneath the fabric of his tunic. Sebastianus Gallus made her feel safe and secure in a way she had never felt before. It overwhelmed her. And then it soothed her until, after a while, Ulrika drifted back to peaceful slumber.

Voices woke her, and sharp rays of bright sunlight that streamed into the cave. She found herself alone by a cold campfire.

Rising, adjusting her dress, her *palla* and her hair, she went to the cave's entrance and saw Sebastianus standing among green trees and grass, shining like gold in the morning sun, talking quietly with Timonides, Nestor, and a company of slaves and soldiers.

When he turned to look at her, Ulrika smiled. She knew now what she must do. She would not turn her back on the gift from the gods, she would not call it an illness anymore. She was filled with fresh resolve and determination to search for the meaning and purpose of her visions, and in so doing find her own meaning and purpose, and finally, where she belonged.

BOOK THREE
ITALIA

11

As Nestor followed the girl with the sunlight hair through the busy marketplace, his keen nose picked up, among the many scents in the air, the spicy aroma of mutton roasting over a fire.

He swiveled his big head this way and that, and when he saw the great shank, peppered and darkly crisp, being turned on a spit, he loped over to the stall where it was being cooked and knew at once that the meat would be perfectly pink in the middle, the fat slightly yellow and ready to melt on the tongue, the skin crunchy and easy to peel.

He would take it home to Father.

The man who was cooking the meat, a chubby Armenian with a big nose and ringlet curls cascading over his shoulders, gave Nestor a suspicious look. "What do you want?" he snapped.

Nestor smiled and reached out to lift the mutton leg from the fire.

"Hey!" the Armenian shouted, drawing the attention of his wife and sons, who were busy at the wooden counter with other customers, exchanging meat and beer for coins.

Before the man could strike Nestor with a stick, a gentle voice said, "No, Nestor, you must not take that." And he felt a hand on his arm, coaxing him away from the stall.

It was the girl with the sunlight-hair. Her name was Reeka and she was kind to him. Other people called him names and told him he should never have been born. Some people even hit him with sticks and caused him pain. But Reeka was always gentle, she always smiled at him.

And so he turned and followed her, the mutton roast forgotten.

Offering a word of apology to the Armenian, Ulrika guided Nestor back to the direction they had been heading, toward the temple of Minerva. She did not mind keeping an eye on Nestor while Timonides visited the public baths in town. Taking care of his son was a full-time job, and Ulrika knew that once in a while the astrologer appreciated a spell of time for himself.

Nestor needed watching because he had no grasp of the concept of purchasing or trading in the marketplace. He thought everything was there for the taking. He also needed to be watched because he had a tendency to frighten people. Ulrika knew that the simpleton wouldn't harm a flea, but he was large and lumbering and walked with a rolling gait that gave him an aggressive aspect. And although Timonides tried to keep his son clean, Nestor had a habit of spilling on himself, and wiping his hands on his tunic, which made him appear out of control—another reason for people to fear him.

But Ulrika knew the biggest reason people shied away from Nestor was his round face with tiny slanting eyes and perpetual smile. These features made people uneasy because they were reminders of the perversity of nature and that it was only through the grace of the gods that they and their own children were normal.

However, it was an easy and pleasant task, taking care of Nestor. He never argued or disobeyed. He was always agreeable, and seemed to know only two emotions: happiness and sadness, with the former much more prevalent than the latter.

And his astonishing gift never ceased to amaze Ulrika. One taste of a new sauce, one sip of an unfamiliar soup, and Nestor could return to camp and re-create the dish down to the last grain of salt.

"Here we are," she said to her companions—two female attendants and a male bodyguard. They had arrived at the temple of Minerva.

After leaving Fort Bonna, the Gallus caravan had continued on to Colonia, where Sebastianus had conducted trade and commerce with local merchants, exchanging goods brought from Egypt and Spain for German products currently in demand in Rome—mead, silver and amber jewelry, animal hides and fur. Travelers who had journeyed with the caravan said farewell to Sebastianus, while new travelers purchased places in the caravan for its return trip south.

He had cut their stay short, as both he and Ulrika were eager to get back to Rome. Now the caravan was camped outside Pisa, one hundred and sixty miles north of their destination. While Sebastianus stopped long enough to drop off goods and passengers, and take on new travelers and supplies, Ulrika seized the opportunity to visit a local temple, one famed for housing a powerful goddess.

Here, in Minerva's place of worship, Ulrika hoped to find guidance. The old woman in the Rhineland had told her she must teach herself discipline. But how could that be accomplished without help?

The prospect of discovering her true destiny, of learning at last where she belonged, filled Ulrika with excitement. Unfortunately, seeking her destiny meant that she and Sebastianus must part ways.

The closer they drew to Rome, the more he consulted maps of the distant, mysterious East. Where, exactly, *was* China? His anxiousness to get started grew with each passing hour. Ulrika knew that Sebastianus had received reports that two of his four competitors for the *diploma* were now ahead in the race! Adon the Phoenician was but a sea voyage away from Rome and was bringing a rare animal called a "gryphon" for the emperor, and Gaspar the Persian was on his way back from the Zagros Mountains with a pair of conjoined twins, sisters fused at the hip since birth, who were said to be able to pleasure several men at once. Tempting prizes for Claudius. Nonetheless, Sebastianus had assured Ulrika that he was confident his own offering would appeal to the emperor even more.

As she thought of Sebastianus, Ulrika felt her heart turning toward him as a flower turned to the sun. She knew she was falling in love with this handsome man who had come flying out of the forest like a hero from myth, wielding a massive sword as he cut down, one by one, her savage assailants. That image, imprinted on her brain, was as vivid as if he were at that moment fighting off enemies, his sword whistling through the air as he protected her with his strength and power.

But she knew that such a love was a luxury that could never be hers. Sebastianus was bound for the ends of the earth, while she herself was on her own personal path.

As she and Nestor and their companions mounted the temple steps, Ulrika thought of the many shrines and holy places she had visited since leaving Colonia, to light incense, offer sacrifice, and ask each god to illuminate her. If her gift came from the gods, she reasoned, then it was they who must instruct her in what to do next.

She purchased a small white bird from the dove vendor on the temple steps, giving him a copper coin and receiving the assurance that the bird was perfect and free of blemish. As she took the small cage from the vendor, Ulrika saw a young man standing next to him—a youth who had not been there a moment before. Ulrika waited, listened, and then the vision faded.

It frustrated her. She had experienced several such visual and auditory spells during the return trip to Rome, and they were all random and without meaning. Perhaps, she thought with hope as they reached the main entrance at the top of the marble stairs—perhaps compassionate Minerva will show the way.

They entered the dim interior and saw a large sanctuary stretch before them—a circular hall fringed with white columns, a shining marble floor, with lamps hanging from the ceiling, and at the opposite end, the goddess herself, larger than life, seated on a throne. Priests were lighting incense and chanting while citizens handed over their offerings of doves and lambs.

Ulrika paused inside the entrance, to calm her mind, to open her heart to whatever message the goddess might send, and her companions halted also, looking around at the magnificent marble walls and domed ceiling and thinking that the goddess of poetry and music, healing and sewing—but most of all, the goddess of wisdom—must be very influential indeed.

A portly priest in a white robe and smelling of oils and incense, approached. "How may the Goddess help you, dear visitors?"

His voice was softly feminine, his eyes kind and smiling. "I have come seeking guidance on a personal problem," Ulrika said, and she handed him the caged dove.

"You have come to the right place, dear lady, for Minerva is the Goddess of Nearness, and she is near you now, to hear your prayer. Come this way."

As he turned, a ring of keys jingled at his belt, and Ulrika wondered if the prophecy of the Egyptian seer were about to come true.

But the priest neither offered her a key nor unlocked a door as he took her and her companions to a quiet alcove where Minerva was depicted in mosaic tiles above an altar. To Ulrika's astonishment, the priest opened the cage and allowed the dove to fly free. She had expected him to slaughter it, as most gods demanded. Instead, they watched it flutter and circle and then fly out of the temple and toward the sunlight.

The priest smiled. "That is a good sign. Doves are the messengers of the gods. Minerva has heard your prayer."

"How will I hear her answer?"

The priest stepped up to the altar, where Ulrika now saw a series of scrolls lined up, each with a different color ribbon. "Choose," he said.

She pointed to the one tied with a blue ribbon.

He opened it, and read out loud, softly, "Your lungs are in a hurry. It is as if they are in a chariot race." Then, to Ulrika's surprise, he rolled the parchment up and re-tied the ribbon, replacing the scroll on the altar.

"That's all?" she said.

"The Goddess heard your prayer and guided your hand. That is her answer."

"But what does it mean?"

"The gods speak to us in their own language. Sometimes interpretation is elusive and does not come to us right away." He bowed slightly, said, "Minerva's blessings," and left.

They descended the steps and entered the busy marketplace again, Ulrika's companions thinking of the approaching midday meal, Ulrika puzzling over the goddess's cryptic message, and Nestor eyeing a bowl containing round, shiny objects that he thought he would like to take with him.

Ulrika did not see the blind beggar squatting in the shadow of Minerva's temple, did not see Nestor suddenly reach down and grab a handful of coins that generous citizens had tossed into the beggar's bowl.

It happened quickly: the man shot to his feet, shouting, "You dare to steal from a cripple! And a blind one at that!" And before she could react, his blind man's staff, which kept him from bumping into buildings, went up in the air and came down with a resounding crack on Nestor's head.

Nestor fell. He started to cry. The pain was more than he could bear. Why had the man hit him? And then Reeka was there, grabbing the staff as it started to come down again, stopping it, protecting Nestor from his attacker, saying to the man, "He has the mind of a child, do not strike him again. And who are you to accuse of theft, when you yourself steal from good citizens by pretending to be blind?"

And then she was on her knees and speaking soothingly to Nestor, touching his head where it hurt, where blood now trickled. But the pain went away beneath Reeka's gentle touch. The fragrance of her hair and clothes entered his nose and filled his head in the way food aromas did. He felt better. His tears and fears subsided as he listened to her soft voice and felt her tender touch.

He wanted her to hold him in her arms and never let go. Nestor, who had only ever known two emotions in his life, now felt a third settle into his heart like a radiant sunflower.

Nestor had fallen in love.

SEBASTIANUS WAS AT THE CARAVAN CAMP, conducting trade with a wine merchant, when he saw Ulrika and her party return. Nestor's head was bandaged, and Ulrika herself was looking distraught.

Sebastianus went to meet them. "What happened?"

As Ulrika recounted the incident to him, he saw afternoon sunshine glow in her blue eyes. He noticed the way the long honey-colored hair seemed to peek teasingly from beneath her palla, and how the blue of her soft linen gown brought out the hues of her eyes. He was acutely aware of the rise and fall of her bosom as she spoke in one breath about false cripples and the honesty of the innocent, and Minerva's cryptic message in the next.

Sebastianus knew he could easily fall in love with her. He desired her. He wanted to make love to her. But he was not free to do so. In Rome they would say good-bye.

"Hoy there!" came voices from the crowd. They saw an anxious Timonides hurrying toward them. "Terrible news, master!" the astrologer shouted.

"What is it?"

"It is Emperor Claudius," Timonides said breathlessly as he drew near. "He is dead!"

"Dead!" Ulrika cried.

"Assassinated, according to rumor. But, master, they are saying that Lucius Domitius Ahenobarbus has been proclaimed his successor, and that he is systematically destroying all who were closely connected to Claudius. You cannot go back to Rome, master! You are now an enemy of the state!"

12

As they neared the city of Rome, after days of hearing reports of chaos and riots in the city, the members of Sebastianus's caravan were quiet and somber, not knowing what they were going to find.

They had passed through peaceful countryside that appeared to be unaffected by the political news, the farmers' cottages and villas of the rich, nestled in green hills among pastures and vineyards, as sleepy and serene as they had been for centuries. But Sebastianus had not gone into towns and villages at night as was his habit, he had not left the caravan for even a moment, nor had he entertained guests, but had stayed close to his passengers and workers, making his presence known, calming raw nerves and reassuring those who traveled with him that everything was under control. Noon and afternoon horoscopes were added to his usual morning and evening readings, keeping Timonides busy with his charts and instruments while Ulrika's worried thoughts were upon her mother and their friends—all allies of the assassinated Claudius.

And now they were nearing their destination, Sebastianus leading the way on his mare with Ulrika riding behind in a private covered wagon.

Although Rome was a dangerous place now for them, there had been no question of staying away. Ulrika needed to return as quickly as possible to her mother's house, to make sure Selene and her friends were safe. Sebastianus was worried about his villa in Rome and the staff who served him.

But foremost on his mind was the question of the *diploma* for China. Would the new emperor even be interested?

Sebastianus had been able to glean some information along the way about Claudius's successor, a sixteen-year-old youth with the birth name Domitius Ahenobarbus but who, it was rumored, had changed his name upon succession to the rather grandiose Nero Claudius Caesar Augustus Germanicus. People were saying that young Nero had declared a new era for Rome and that he had ambitions to expand diplomacy and trade. This offered a glimmer of hope for Sebastianus, if he could avoid being arrested for his very loose affiliation with Claudius (Sebastianus had met the deceased emperor only once, and briefly). What he knew he must do was somehow get close to the emperor, who surely was surrounded by an army of guards, tutors, protectors, not to forget his powerful mother, Agrippina, who was also Claudius's widow. Sebastianus needed to let the ambitious young man know of his plans to open a new trade route to China and establish diplomatic connections with foreign nations along the way, expanding the Roman empire beyond even Nero's vision.

But how to get close enough to Nero to explain all this?

Riding at Sebastianus's side on a trotting donkey, Timonides was likewise plagued with worry. He thought about the catastrophe that had appeared in his master's stars back in Fort Bonna and continued to shadow his master's daily star-readings. Did the nameless disaster lie just ahead, in the eerily quiet city of Rome? And had he, Timonides the erstwhile honest astrologer, brought it about with his falsified horoscopes? What if the new emperor had Sebastianus executed? What would become of Timonides and Nestor? They had no money, and Timonides was old, Nestor simple-minded. It made his blood run to ice to think of the pair of them in the streets, begging.

This is all my fault! he lamented in his heart, despising the crowds that they now joined, hating the city walls, angry at Emperor Claudius for getting killed, and furious with himself for having tricked Sebastianus into taking Ulrika with them. By the gods, the crusty old heart of Timonides the astrologer cried. I swear upon all that is holy, upon the very soul of my beloved Damaris, that I will never again falsify a sacred horoscope or blaspheme in the name of the stars! Please, just get me and my son through this dark hour, and I shall serve the gods and the heavens with the utmost honor and respect and will never tell another lie for as long as I live!

They arrived at the vast terminus and, making sure the caravan was safe and secure, Sebastianus and Ulrika, Timonides and Nestor, and a few slaves and guards, struck off on foot, to join the throng trying to get into the city. With his impressive credentials and merchant-trader's pass, Sebastianus was allowed through the smaller pedestrian gate, where the members of his party were scrutinized and questioned, their travel packs inspected. With an admonition to go straight to their residences and nowhere else, as curfew was strictly enforced during martial law, they were passed through.

To their surprise, the city was neither in chaos nor disrupted by civil rebellion but eerily quiet as the day died and evening curfew was marked by the blare of trumpets. They reached the Esquiline Hill as the stars were coming out, and as they climbed the cobblestoned lane, Ulrika saw subdued residences behind high walls, and more silence than was usual for a balmy evening. But, to her relief, up ahead and on the left, she saw Aunt Paulina's house illuminated with torches and lamps, and heard voices rising in laughter as music played up into the dusky sky. She saw, beyond Paulina's villa, the house she shared with her mother. It was dark and silent, but that was not unusual, as Selene frequently spent evenings with her best friend, often staying the night at Paulina's. During these hazardous times, until the new emperor calmed everyone's nerves and assured the populace that life was going on as before, it made sense to Ulrika that her mother would seek the safety of Paulina's house.

Ulrika thanked Sebastianus and assured him that she would be all right.

He insisted on going inside with her, but Ulrika reminded Sebastianus that he had his own house and people to see to, that he must not waste time.

You and I can go no further, she whispered to him in her heart, taking in his handsome countenance, the bronze-colored hair in the torchlight, his height and strength. They had been in each other's company for six months, had shared food and fire, and had slept together in a magical cave. But he was destined to go to far-off China, and Ulrika's path was fated to lead elsewhere.

Telling himself that he must simply say good-bye and walk away, Sebastianus reached for Ulrika, placing his hands on her arms, and then he stepped close, to look deeply into her eyes. He wanted to swim in that inviting blue, refresh himself in the grotto that was the iris of her eye.

He bent his head and brushed his lips on her cheek. Ulrika gasped. Her heart rose in her throat. She wanted to turn her head, bring her mouth to his. Instead, tears rose in her eyes and trickled down her face. These, too, Sebastianus kissed—fluttering kisses that felt like butterflies. They made her skin burn and her body cry out for his touch.

"May the gods be good to you, Ulrika," he murmured against her ear, reluctant to let her go, "and may the stars guide you to happiness. If you ever need me, you have but to send word."

After saying good-bye to Timonides and Nestor—who cried like a child at having to leave her—and watching them retreat down the steep lane, Ulrika turned to the gate set in the high wall. Finding it locked, she pulled the bell rope, and when a slave answered, she said, "Please tell Lady Paulina that Ulrika is here."

He wrinkled his nose. "Who's Paulina?"

Ulrika's eyes widened. "Your mistress, of course." And then, realizing she did not recognize this slave, looked past him and saw people in Paulina's atrium, laughing and drinking. There was not a familiar face among them. "Who's house is this?" she asked.

"It belongs to Senator Publius now." And he slammed the gate in her face.

Ulrika stood in shock. Aunt Paulina's villa had been confiscated? Where were Paulina and her household staff? Ulrika looked up the lane at her own dark and deserted house.

Where was her mother?

She ran to their villa and received a second shock: a sign on the gate warned that the property had been seized by the imperial government and that trespass was a criminal offense. Ulrika broke the seals and slipped inside.

The garden had a neglected look, weedy and dusty, with dry fountains and marble benches littered with dried leaves. Ulrika went through a deserted atrium and reception room, down empty corridors and into silent bedrooms. In the rear, kitchens, laundry, and slaves' quarters were all deserted and dark.

Making her way back to the atrium, Ulrika surveyed the dark house in rising dismay. Had her mother been taken away by imperial guards? Was she now in prison, or worse: had she already been executed?

Ulrika went in search of a lamp. Finding one, still full of oil, and a flint, she lit the lamp and brought it back to the atrium, where she tried to think. Should she stay here, in the hope that her mother would come back, or would soldiers return? She had broken the seal on the gate, which in itself was a crime. Now she was trespassing against imperial orders—

When she heard a scraping sound, she shot to her feet, and was startled to see Erasmus, the old major domo, passing along a colonnaded corridor with his travel packs. "Erasmus!" she called.

He jumped. "Huh? Is it a ghost? Ah, mistress!" he said when his eyes focused. "Praise the gods you are alive. But you can't stay here. I was ordered to get the house in order for new owners, and now I too must leave."

"Where is my mother?"

"Gone," he said sadly in a raspy voice. "She and everyone left Rome days ago. They went in a hurry. They knew the city was no longer safe for them."

"But *where* did they go?" Ulrika cried.

Bony shoulders lifted in a shrug. "The Lady left a letter for me to give you in case you came back." He dug into one of the many secret pockets of his colorful robe and withdrew a scroll tied with a red ribbon. As he started to hurry away, he paused and, thrusting his hand back inside his robe, pulled out a second scroll and said, "Here is another. Good-bye. Be careful, mistress, for these are dangerous times for the friends of Claudius, may he find peace in the afterlife."

Ulrika looked at the two scrolled letters, recognizing the wax seal on her mother's but puzzling over the second. Who else had left her a letter? Turning the scroll, searching for a seal, she saw a dried water stain on the paper. It looked as if someone had cried and a tear had dropped, leaving a star-shaped stain—

She froze. It was her own letter, written months ago! "Wait," she said, hurrying after the old man. "Why did you give me my letter back?" But he was gone. The lane was deserted.

Ulrika looked at her letter again and, seeing that it had never been opened, realized that the old man had removed it from the very same pocket he had slipped it into the day she left Rome.

My mother never received my letter.

Ulrika sat down and read by lamplight the letter from her mother.

"My dearest daughter, I write in haste because we are forced to flee. I do not know where I am going. All the family is with me. I do not know if my political enemies will turn on you. Rome is no longer safe for you. Perhaps by the grace of the Goddess, you and I will find each other one day. I pray also, dearest daughter who came to me in love and in my hour of need, that you find what you are looking for. I am sorry you felt you had to leave Rome without saying good-bye to me, without leaving word. But I understand. Please do not forget your Roman half, and do not despise your Roman blood, for I am part of you, as is your father, Wulf."

A night breeze gusted and moonlight illuminated dried leaves rustling over paving stones, and Ulrika thought: I went in search of my father and, by doing that, lost my mother.

And then she recalled the last time she had seen her mother, the row they had had, and how Ulrika had turned on her heel and left while her mother was still speaking. *That is my mother's last memory of me!* For Selene never read the words of apology and love.

A sob escaped Ulrika's throat and her eyes filled with tears that dropped onto her mother's letter, wetting black ink, smearing words that said, "Do not despise your Roman half."

As she watched dried leaves skim the paving stones of the atrium, brushed along by a cool night breeze, she tried to figure out what she should do next. Go in search of her mother? Try to seek her old friends? She thought of Sebastianus, wondered briefly if she could go to him for help, but then realized that, with her connections to Paulina and this house that had been seized by the government, she would be placing him in jeopardy.

One thing was certain: she could not stay here.

As she rose from the bench, she heard the sound of footfall. She spun about and saw a man silhouetted in the moonlight.

Sebastianus.

He came into the atrium. "I was not comfortable leaving you. I needed to make sure you were all right. When the slave at Paulina's gate said a strange woman had tried to enter the home of Senator Publius, I knew something was wrong."

"They're gone, Sebastianus," she whispered. "My mother, my family. All gone. I am alone."

He took her into his arms and held her tight, caressing her hair, feeling her warm breath on his neck.

"You are not alone, Ulrika," he said, drawing back. "You are coming home with me."

"We'll all be murdered in our beds!"

Primo seized the hysterical laundress by her arm and growled, "Hold your tongue, woman, or you'll make matters worse." He gave her a painful squeeze with his coarse ham-fist and sent her on her way.

Holy blood of Mithras, Primo cursed silently as he spat on the floor. Women could never be counted on to keep a level head in times of emergency.

And tonight's was the worst of all possible emergencies, with word coming down the street that soldiers of the new emperor were systematically assassinating anyone who had anything to do with Claudius Caesar, including a caravan trader named Sebastianus Gallus who had met Claudius only once fleetingly, but whose name was recorded on the roster of those to be admitted to the Imperial Palace.

Primo resumed his inspection of the house, lumbering through the rooms of the Gallus villa like a war machine, his head turning this way and that as he oversaw the industry that always marked his master's return.

Primo was a large, ugly man whose nose had been broken so many times it barely resembled a nose anymore, and he would have been condemned to a life of begging in the streets had it not been for Sebastianus Gallus, whose house he now ran with the discipline and precision of the dedicated soldier he had once been. Without his steadying presence, Primo knew, this house on the edge of the city would have fallen apart days ago. Even now, there was barely enough staff to keep the kitchen, gardens, laundry, and animal care going, so many slaves had run off in the night. A tense atmosphere hung over rooms glowing with lamplight as slaves prepared the house for their master's return—all under the watchful eye of big, ugly Primo, veteran of so many foreign campaigns and survivor of so much combat that little fazed him anymore.

But he did *not* like the piercing screams of a hysterical laundress!

As Primo strode from room to room, making his presence known, instilling obedience in the slaves from his mere appearance—he still wore the leather breastplate, short tunic, and military sandals from his army days—he could not have explained, had he been asked, where his hatred of women came from. He might have simply said, "They are silly, useless creatures."

Or perhaps he might admit that it stemmed from shame for his own mother, who had been a waterfront whore servicing sailors while her son lay curled in a corner pretending not to hear the animal sounds coming from her bed. She was beaten to death by a customer when Primo was twelve, and he managed to survive on his own in the streets of Rome until he reached the age of military enlistment.

Or possibly his contempt for womankind sprang from the fact that he had never forgiven his witless mother for naming her only child Fidus, which meant "faithful," not realizing in her perpetually drunken state that the name would subject her son to a life of mockery and ridicule, as the nickname for Fidus was Fido, a popular name for Rome's pet dogs. So humiliating was this name—his friends would bark whenever he was around—that when he enlisted as a legionary, he said his name was Primo, as it sounded important, and so Primo he had been ever since.

But the truth of it—should Primo ever truly examine his close-fisted heart—was that he neither hated his mother nor women. In fact, the self-proclaimed despiser of women actually loved them.

If only they loved him in return.

Although there had been one, long ago, who had not only shown him a kindness, she had saved his life . . .

"Primo! Primo!" a young slave called as he came running into the atrium where a dozen burning torches kept the night away. "The caravan has arrived! The master is in the city!"

Primo dashed through the atrium, through the front garden, out the entry gate, and onto the narrow lane embraced by the high walls of private residences. As he peered into the darkness—there were few street lamps in this sector of the city—he recalled the day, eight years ago, when he had walked along this same street, going from gate to gate, knocking, asking for work, as he was a soldier recently retired from military service and needed employment to supplement his meager pension.

He had served his emperor and the empire well, until he was mustered out after the requisite twenty-five years, finding himself alone and on the streets with little to live on. Primo refused to resort to what most old soldiers did—telling war tales in taverns in exchange for beer—and so he had sought honest employment.

But what had he to offer? Many legionaries were trained beyond the usual combat skills of the regular soldier—they were "specialist" soldiers with secondary roles such as engineer, artilleryman, drill and weapons instructor, carpenter, medic. Such men, when they mustered out of the military, had professions to fall upon.

Not Primo, who had been an ordinary infantryman. All he could offer were strength and brawn, which he possessed in great supply, as life in the army had built up his already large body. On the march in unfriendly terrain, a foot soldier was loaded down with a shield, helmet, two javelins, a short sword, a dagger, a pair of heavy sandals, a marching pack, fourteen days' worth of food, a waterskin, cooking equipment, stakes for the construction of palisades, and a shovel or wicker basket. And so there was nothing Primo the army veteran could not move or lift with ease.

However, as he sought honest employment, gates had been slammed in his face, until he had come to the house of merchant-trader Sebastianus Gallus and had found appalling disorder. The slave at the gate was sullen and rude, the house steward wore a stained tunic. Food droppings littered the floors, raucous laughter came from the kitchens and laundry, animals roamed freely in the main rooms. Learning the identity of the homeowner, who was away on a caravan, Primo had hired a horse and ridden out to meet the returning caravan, whereupon Sebastianus Gallus, hearing the shocking report of his household, left the caravan and rode back with Primo to catch his steward and staff by surprise, learning that they only got the house into shape when they knew their master was almost home. Primo averred that he would keep things in order while Sebastianus was gone, and he was hired on the spot. Primo had taken on the role of Chief Steward, but in the years since had also become bodyguard, chariot driver, and overseer of general maintenance of the household.

When he saw the party now coming up the lane, and heard Timonides loudly complaining about something, Primo scratched his backside and spat on the ground. He didn't like Timonides or his simpleton son. The Greek astrologer was self-righteous with his charts and instruments. Like most soldiers, Primo did not know how to read, nor could he do sums, and so he was scornful of men of higher learning. Timonides further irritated him with his spouting about there being order in the universe, that everything happened for a reason, and that a man could control his destiny through star-reading. Primo knew otherwise. Nothing happened for a reason, the universe was chaos, and there was no way to control one's destiny. All of life was random and accidental. And as for the life after death Timonides preached about, it had nothing to do with *this* life, so why would a man concern himself with it?

Primo frowned when he saw a woman with them.

He knew what women thought when they looked at him—this ugly brute with too many battle scars on his face to have any saving grace. Only if he paid generous coinage would a woman allow him access to her body. He sometimes wondered if sworn celibacy, especially in the name of a god, was easier on a man's vanity than repeated rejections by women—and certainly easier on his purse!

As Primo stepped away from the gate to greet his master, soldiers appeared suddenly at the other end of the street, armor clanking, booted feet stamping on the paving stones. Primo's eyes widened. He saw by the scorpion insignia on their metal breastplates that they were Praetorians, an elite military cohort operating directly under the emperor. Primo was further shocked by their blatant carrying of weapons, defying the ancient tradition that soldiers were forbidden to be armed within the city walls.

This was not a good sign.

The captain of the guard, a short, wiry man with a narrow face, and wearing the red-plumed helmet of an officer, strode up and said, "Are you Sebastianus Gallus?"

Sebastianus maintained his composure as he strode up and said, "I am he."

"You are to come with us by order of the emperor."

Sebastianus nodded and turned to Primo. But as he gave orders to his chief steward to see to the rest of his party, the Praetorians began rounding everyone up, no questions asked, using their spears as goads.

Sebastianus protested. "Let them go. They have done nothing."

But his words fell on deaf ears. And so they were all taken: Sebastianus and Ulrika, Timonides and Nestor, as well as Primo who, as a veteran of the legions, instinctively fell into step with the guards upon the words: "by order of the emperor."

They were taken by wagon to the Palatine Hill where, according to legend, a she-wolf had suckled the babies Romulus and Remus, founders of Rome, thus imbuing the spot with great mystical power. Here, overlooking the Forum and the Circus Maximus, the Imperial Palace loomed majestically, its white marble walls, terraces, columns, and fountains glowing against the night sky with lamps and torches beyond counting, as if the new emperor were trying to command even the night to retreat.

As the wagon rumbled beneath massive arches and past colossal statues, Timonides silently blamed himself for the terrible fate they were about to suffer. All those falsified horoscopes! Had he really thought he could get away with it?

Primo, standing in the swaying wagon as if riding out a storm at sea, thought grimly of the battles he had survived, only to end up suffering a coward's death.

Sebastianus held onto Ulrika, his arm tight about her waist as he tried to think of what he could say, whom he could bribe to obtain his friends' release, for if Nero wanted to punish the friends of Claudius, then only he, Sebastianus Gallus, should be held accountable. Surely this girl, an elderly astrologer and his simpleton son, and the chief steward of his household had nothing to do with it.

But Sebastianus had heard what emperors did to ensure themselves of complete loyalty among their subjects—they left not a single friend of their predecessors alive. Would Nero be any different from Tiberius and Caligula and Claudius before him?

Down a narrow lane lit by torches in sconces, the wagon was brought to a halt and the detainees ordered down. Surrounded by the elite cohort, Sebastianus and his companions were hurried through an unmarked, unguarded door, down a long dim corridor, up steep stairs, and along yet more narrow halls, the sound of their footsteps whispering off marble walls, their shadows stretching and shrinking in flickering light. Sebastianus saw fear on his companions' faces and tried to think of words of assurance.

As they were taken into a wider corridor where servants now slipped past bearing platters and pitchers, they heard a dull roar of voices, and when the captain of the guard drew aside a heavy tapestry to reveal an audience chamber ablaze with light, Sebastianus and his companions blinked in surprise.

The imperial reception hall was vast, with a forest of columns, towering statues adorned in gold and precious stones, a marble floor that shone like glass, and it was crammed with people milling about in Roman togas, military uniforms, foreign dress. Sebastianus and his companions stared in amazement at the visitors awaiting audience: statesmen and senators, officials and foreign dignitaries, ambassadors and princes. There were couriers bearing the winged staffs of messengers as they hurried to and fro, secretaries recording in shorthand on wax tablets and papyrus, sycophantic courtiers bowing and scraping, slaves and servants—all creating a din that rose to the high ceiling, where dazzling gold and silver mosaics proclaimed the wealth and majesty of the Caesars.

When he realized where they were, that this was where Claudius had received visitors and foreign dignitaries, that in fact this was the imperial throne room (although the throne and the new Caesar could not be seen through the crowd) Sebastianus said to the Praetorian captain, "Why have we been brought before the emperor?" From what he had heard, enemies of Claudius had simply been arrested and taken straight to prison or execution. None had been granted an audience by the new Caesar.

The captain did not reply but kept his small eyes fixed across the immense hall, as if awaiting a signal.

Standing with his master, and momentarily forgetting his fear, Timonides eyed the platters of food passing by, his mouth watering as he wondered who it was all for and why it appeared that untouched platters were being returned to the kitchens. At his side, Nestor smiled and giggled at the colorful people, at the amusing sounds of different languages and dialects, the comical way men gestured as they argued, told tales, expressed opinions.

Primo, a veteran of foreign wars, observed the scene with a jaded eye. He knew that ambassadors were here to create or break treaties, that envoys had come to make or break promises, that men had come to beseech, cajole, praise, or kiss the imperial buttocks, and that nothing any of these self-important men accomplished here today was going to be worth a jot in a hundred years.

At Sebastianus's side, Ulrika watched and waited in apprehension. She, too, was wondering why they had been brought before the emperor.

And then she saw, standing between two dignitaries in the distinctive robes and headdresses of the Parthian Empire, a familiar woman. Her mouth was open in a silent scream, and her arms and hands were stained with blood. In shock, Ulrika realized it was the apparition she had seen in the countryside when she was twelve. Why are you here? she silently asked the ghost. Why do you haunt *this* place?

Realizing that her heart raced and that she was breathing rapidly, Ulrika placed a hand on her breast and tried to force herself to calm down. Her visions were no longer something to be afraid of, but to control. And so first she must overcome her fear—

The breath stopped in her chest.

Your lungs are in a hurry . . .

Minerva's strange message! Did it have meaning after all? As her companions shifted on their feet, waiting to be called, Ulrika focused on her respirations and forced them to slow down, calming herself, suppressing her fear. As she did so, she heard faint whispering—a soft susurration that lay just below the din in the marble hall. She looked around—were there more apparitions? What were they trying to tell her? And then the whispering receded and the frightened woman slowly faded before her eyes.

But Ulrika was excited. She had gained some small control over her gift. That was what the Goddess had told her. Ulrika must be conscious of her respirations before she could control the Divining. Minerva had been the first of her teachers!

The Praetorian captain came to life at that moment and grunted an order to his guards, and the six newcomers were prodded forward.

No one cleared the way as they had to shoulder through knots of men, and a few women, who looked by turns bored, impatient, angry, or hopeful as everyone awaited his or her turn before the new emperor.

But even as they drew near, Sebastianus and his friends were afforded no clear glimpse of the young Nero, as he was surrounded by advisors, in purple-edged togas or military dress, all leaning toward the throne like mother hens, clucking advice into the imperial ear.

The personage whom everyone saw, and who stood tall and powerful at the side of the white marble throne, was Empress Agrippina, a handsome woman in her forties, widely known to be ruthless, ambitious, violent, and domineering. It was also said she had a double canine in her upper right mandible, a sign of good fortune.

Agrippina wore a purple gown under a saffron-yellow *palla* edged in gold, her head crowned with hundreds of tiny curls. She was known to take long soaking baths in goat's milk, and employed a daily regimen of applying egg whites and flour to her face to enhance her fashionable paleness. As she was a great-granddaughter of the emperor Augustus, a great-niece and adoptive granddaughter of the emperor Tiberius, as well as sister to the emperor Caligula, niece and fourth wife of the emperor Claudius, and finally mother of the newly seated Emperor Nero, Agrippina bestowed upon her son an illustrious bloodline.

That she had poisoned her husband Claudius so that Nero could claim the throne, no one doubted for a moment. But where was the proof? Imperial household staff told of the empress's heroic efforts at the dinner table to save her stricken husband, kneeling at his side, forcing his mouth open so that she could insert a quill feather to induce vomiting. And Claudius did indeed vomit, which should have expressed the ingested poison (from mushrooms, it was whispered) but then he died anyway. No one could fault the empress, as she did try to save his life, although rumor had it that the quill had been dipped in toxin obtained from a rare fish and that it was the *second* poisoning that had done the emperor in.

The empress leaned forward now, long pincer-like fingers gripping her son's shoulder, and murmured something, and the clot of advisors dissolved. As the men drew back, Sebastianus and his friends saw a youth on the white marble throne, wearing a white tunic under a white purple-edge toga, with a laurel wreath above his brow. The sixteen-year-old possessed regular features, a light downy beard on his jaw, and surprisingly blue eyes. His neck was unusually thick for one so young, giving him an athletic appearance that he otherwise did not have. "The reputation of the Gallus family is well known, Sebastianus," the young Caesar said without preamble. "You and your father and grandfather have served Rome and her people well. And now we are told you wish to open a diplomatic route to China?"

"That is true, sire," Sebastianus said, blinking in surprise. He had not been expecting *this*. "I wish for the men of China to know the might and grandeur of Rome. I wish also to expand Caesar's network of friends and allies."

"Other men wish to do the same. Why should I select you above the others?"

Sebastianus glanced at Ulrika. Thinking of the idea that had come to him from something Ulrika had said the night they spent in the cave, and knowing his idea would completely distinguish him from his competitors, he said, "Because, sire, I alone can guarantee that I shall make it to the distant Orient. Where others will certainly fail, I shall be successful. And I promise that not only will I return with new friends of Rome, and their treaties, I will return with treasure beyond imagining."

Nero bent his head back and looked down his nose at the supplicant, a mannerism that made Sebastianus wonder if the boy had practiced it in a mirror. "Tell me, Gallus, how can you make such a guarantee when no other trader can?"

"I have recently come from Germania Inferior, where I regularly conduct business in Colonia, and there I learned a special secret."

"And what might that be?" Nero asked, and Agrippina, the imperial advisors, and those nearest, listened with interest.

Sebastianus's heart raced. This was a moment he had dreamed of all his life. "It is being said, sire, that Commander Gaius Vatinius employed deceptive measures to give his soldiers a tactical advantage. He operated under the clever strategy that things are not always what they seem. When I heard this, I saw how such tactics could be employed along a trade route. For example, brigands who prey upon caravans are blinded by greed and tend to see only what they *expect* to see. They know that merchants and traders spend more time at the dinner table than at the gymnasium, and so the thieves who lie in wait for a caravan expect to descend upon soft, weak men. And that is how such missions fail. But in this case, using General Vatinius' strategy, my caravan will be different. The brigands will not know that our robes and turbans and beards disguise trained fighting men. What the brigands will not be expecting is the element of surprise."

Nero pursed his lips as one of his advisors, a man in military dress, leaned forward to murmur in his ear.

"Continue, Sebastianus Gallus," the young emperor said after a moment.

"In addition, sire, when the brigands attack my caravan, not only will they find themselves suddenly fighting soldiers, they will also find themselves being attacked from behind. Another tactic I learned from General Vatinius."

The military advisor again murmured something to Nero, who said, "Clever strategy, Sebastianus Gallus. But how will you be able to create such a fighting unit?"

"May I call my steward forward, sire? He is not a slave, but a freeman, and a veteran of Rome's elite legions."

When Primo stepped forward, a look of awe and bewilderment on his disfigured face, Sebastianus continued: "What my trusted steward has told me of warfare, and how to win, is three essential rules: attack before being attacked, wage the battle in the enemy's territory so that his losses are all the greater, and use the element of surprise, for that is the deadliest weapon. These guarantee victory, great Caesar, and Primo is a master at all three."

"You expect one man to do all that?" Nero said with a trace of scorn.

Sebastianus did not take offense. "Although Primo is retired from the army, he still has military connections, friends who serve the Empire at this moment, and so he has entry into all garrisons, forts, barracks. In addition, Primo knows many retired legionaries who would be more than eager to fight again for Rome. But there is more," Sebastianus added, warming to his topic. "As I travel the eastern route, I will send spies ahead, men dressed as local folk, to blend in and talk in taverns and at waysides, to learn what they can of planned attacks. And then I will send soldiers ahead to hide and come in behind any brigands who lie in wait."

"Tell me, Gallus," Nero said, peering down his nose. "How did you learn of General Vatinius's secret strategies? Commander Vatinius enjoyed a triumphal entry into Rome after his victory in Germania, and as a reward he was granted command of the legions in Britain, where he is currently employing his strategies again. But how did *you* learn his secrets?"

Sebastianus felt many eyes on him, including Ulrika's, which were wide and blue and full of question. "All of Colonia speaks of them, sire," Sebastianus said, "for that was how the battle was won. They are no longer secret."

Agrippina leaned forward and said something in her son's ear, upon which his advisors drew in close and a conference was held with much nodding and shaking of gray and white heads.

When Nero's advisors were done, the old men in togas drew back from the sixteen-year-old, whose voice still cracked when he spoke, and Caesar said, "Very well, Sebastianus Gallus, it is our wish that you carry our imperial *diploma* to China, there to establish an international mission with the ruler of that land. Along the way, you will make allies of monarchs and chieftains, offering them our protection in exchange for small favors. We will send you with gifts for these rulers, to show Roman generosity, and in return you will bring back examples of their resources. We will also send men trained in foreign diplomacy, who will establish political connections along the way. It is our wish that, someday, Roman eagles will protect the entire world."

Nero yawned then, and the captain of the Praetorians quickly stepped forward. Gesturing to his guards, he rounded up the five and escorted them away from the throne. But they were not escorted far. The captain and his guards soon withdrew, vanishing behind a tapestry that hid a door, to leave Sebastianus and his companions standing in the crowded reception hall in speechless silence.

Finally Sebastianus spoke, and there was disbelief in his tone as he said to his companions, "It appears that I have won the China route! Timonides, we will need the most accurate and precise star-charts drawn up. I want to know the most propitious day for departure."

"At once, master," he said. "But I can feel it in my old bones that the reading is going to be very favorable toward you. After tonight's victory, how can it be otherwise?" Timonides could barely contain his joy. The catastrophe that he had expected tonight had not only not occurred, but a wonderful gift had been given to his master instead!

China! Timonides had heard great stories of the food there, the delicacies, the rare treats! A specialty called rice, fluffy and subtle, to be mixed with meat or vegetables, fried or boiled and seasoned to one's own taste. And did not Babylon lie along the route? Timonides had heard of a special dish there that involved crunchy fish fins dipped in sesame oil and wrapped in bread. His paunchy stomach rumbled. He could hardly wait for the journey to begin.

As he took Nestor by the arm to hurry out, Timonides vowed that from now on, he was going to lead an exemplary life. No more falsifying horoscopes, no more lying about the stars for his own personal gain.

Sebastianus said to his chief steward, "Primo, you will need to get started at once recruiting men, as we sail as soon as possible for Antioch."

"Yes, master," the old veteran said with uncharacteristic animation. A military mission! One involving strategy and warfare. His face lit up until he was almost no longer ugly, and his soldier's mind awoke from slumber to begin racing ahead with names, plans, strategies, lists of supplies he would need. He turned on his heel and left.

Sebastianus finally faced Ulrika. "I owe you a tremendous debt," he said, looking at her for a long moment, oblivious of the crowd milling around them, aware only of her nearness. He wanted these people, this colossal hall, all of Rome to vanish and leave him alone with her. "How can I thank you?"

Ulrika could hardly catch her breath as she looked up at him. Sebastianus stood so close, his eyes holding hers, his voice drowning out the din so that the rich tones coming from his throat were all she heard. No one else existed, the world was silent and far away. She wanted to slip into his arms, press her body against his, feel his heat and warmth and reassuring strength.

"You need not thank me," she whispered, thinking: I do not want to be parted from this man. "But I will ask a favor. Just now, you told your steward that you would be departing for Antioch. My mother lived there as a girl, she grew up in the house of Mera the healer woman until she was sixteen years old. Perhaps that is where she and my family went when they fled Rome. I can think of no other place they would go. I need to know that she is safe. And she is the only one who can tell me where to find the Crystal Pools of Shalamandar."

Sebastianus was flooded with relief. He had feared these were his final moments with her, that they would be parting ways in this remarkable hall. "I will gladly take you to Antioch," he said.

As they fell silent then, looking into each other's eyes, thinking of the coming weeks and months together, for Antioch was far away—as Sebastianus thought excitedly about the new adventure he was to begin and the mythical realm that lay at the end of an unknown road, as Ulrika thought of Antioch, the third largest city in the world and home to many gods, many temples and sacred groves where answers were to be found—neither saw Empress Agrippina give covert orders to a slave, who then crossed through the crowd to detain Primo at the door and escort him back to the throne, where he was admitted through a doorway concealed behind a tapestry.

Inside a private chamber where flames flickered in golden lamps, Primo the loyal soldier listened to words that made him go gray-faced and wish he had never been born. For the first time in a life of dedication to duty and following orders without question, Primo the veteran considered running away and making sure he was never found.

"Do you understand your orders?" Empress Agrippina asked sharply.

"Yes, mistress," he said, sick at heart, knowing that his beloved master, Sebastianus Gallus, was at that moment celebrating an empty victory. What Primo the loyal friend had learned was that the new emperor was not a generous benefactor after all, but a very dangerous and deadly enemy.

BOOK FOUR

SYRIA

13

When Ulrika saw the apparition standing behind the innkeeper as he wiped down his stained counter, unaware of the numinous visitation, she set aside her cup of warm wine, settled back in the chair, turned a deaf ear to the soft voices in the tavern, and concentrated on slowing her respirations.

In the weeks since discovering, in Nero's audience chamber, that controlling her lungs brought her closer to controlling her visions, Ulrika had practiced what she thought of as "conscious breathing." It had taken her several tries—twice more in Rome, three times on the ship crossing the Great Green, and once prior to this evening in an Antioch street—to learn that not only must she breathe slowly, but in a measured cadence, drawing air through her nose, expelling it through her mouth.

And so now she inhaled the aromas of the tavern on this late, rainy night—the smells of stale beer, roasted lamb, smoke from the fireplace where flames roared and kept out the winter cold—and as she withdrew into herself and grew calm, she sent a silent voice across the smoky room, across the supernatural ethers, and said, "Who are you? What is it you wish me to do?"

Ulrika still did not know what the Divining was, the nature of her special gift. But because her visions consisted mostly of people—of all ages and walks of life—she assumed she was able to speak to the dead. She assumed also that they, sensing that this living human was a conduit to their world, were trying make contact with loved ones through her.

She watched the young man, who had long hair and wore a plain tunic, as he gazed at the innkeeper with soulful eyes. A son, perhaps? "Tell me your message," she said silently, but the youth did not acknowledge her and, like the previous visions, finally faded away.

Ulrika sighed in frustration. Although she was able to hold the visions longer, and in some way make them appear more solid and detailed, they still disappeared. She had also discovered, to her frustration, that while she had made progress with the visions when they came, she still could not bid visions to come to her, she still had no control over when or where one might materialize.

In the Rhineland, the keeper of the sacred groves had told her she would never know who her teachers would be until she looked back. Ulrika saw only Minerva. And the Egyptian seer had told her to accept a key when offered. Their rooms above this tavern had doors that locked, but the innkeeper offered them no keys. Who would her next teacher be? And when would she receive a key—to what?

While Timonides and Nestor, who shared her table, consumed their meal of oily fish and stewed leeks, oblivious to Ulrika's brief withdrawal from the moment, she turned her attention to the tavern's entrance, where the closed door kept out the cold and the rain.

Where was Sebastianus? He had gone out into the city earlier that day. Had he gotten lost?

The inn was located north of the Jewish Quarter in Antioch, on a narrow, hilly lane called Green Wizard Street for reasons no one knew, since no wizards lived there, nor were there any trees or shrubs or greenery of any kind. But it was in a maze where a man could easily lose his way. And as it was nearly midnight, the weather outside inclement, Ulrika was worried that he had gotten lost, or worse.

She tried not to worry, but the tavern was quiet and filled with shadows. No one had come through the front door in the past hour, and few patrons lingered in the smoky atmosphere. Two very drunk carpenters, complaining about lack of employment, leaned on the counter with beer mugs in their hands, and three tables accommodated patrons quietly snoozing in their cups. The innkeeper was a portly jolly man who was himself tipsy from sampling his own wares.

Ulrika felt her heart begin to gallop, and her respirations quicken. She had discovered that, in her conscious-breathing, not only did she have a stronger hold on her visions, a side benefit was a great inner calming for herself. And so she slowed her breathing now, reminding herself that Sebastianus left the inn every morning and always managed to find his way back through the warren of twisting, winding streets. The caravan to China was going to be the largest he had ever handled and so he had much to organize and see to.

And once again, Ulrika was impressed by Sebastianus's network of friends and connections. Even in a city so far from Rome, he seemed to know many men who owed him favors or who were simply happy to be of help.

However, the man he had gone out to meet with tonight had nothing to do with the caravan. He was helping Ulrika in her quest. She had not found her mother in Antioch. And so she decided to see if anyone in this port town had heard of the Crystal Pools of Shalamandar. Sebastianus had asked about and learned of a hermit living in the wilderness of Daphne outside Antioch, a foreigner named Bessas who had come to this Syrian city long ago, and who, it was said, possessed knowledge of rare and esoteric places. But Ulrika had been cautioned that no one had ever been able to get such information out of the old hermit. Nothing had worked, everyone said. Bribery, reasoning, pleading, even threats.

Sebastianus had said that *he* could get the information from the old man, and Ulrika half believed he would, for Sebastianus Gallus could be a very persuasive man. He was visiting the hermit at that moment, and Ulrika prayed that he would be successful.

The clock in the corner of the room—a stone urn marked with hours, and from which water dripped, lowering the level each hour—now indicated that it was past midnight.

Feeling a tug on her arm, Ulrika turned to see Nestor offering her a plump peach. Ulrika thanked him and bit into the juicy fruit. Ever since the episode with the false blind beggar in Pisa, Nestor had followed her about like a puppy, smiling adoringly and giving her gifts. She did not mind. His childlike innocence, in the body of so large a grown man, and his guileless nature, touched her.

Ulrika suspected that Nestor had a poor grasp of time and distance and that, most likely, the attack by the beggar seemed to him to have occurred only yesterday, and in this city. Because of this, unlike most people, his memory of it would never fade, nor would his gratitude to her for saving him.

She turned toward the tavern's entrance, where she hoped Sebastianus would soon appear, and felt her heart flutter. Sebastianus had taken residence there, she carried him day and night in her breast and in her thoughts. When she was in his presence, her body grew warm and she ached for his touch. She had never known such desire. Once, during the voyage from Rome, a storm had struck and Sebastianus had held her and comforted her as the ship was tossed mercilessly on high seas. Ulrika had thought they would kiss, that they would make love. But he never took that crucial step.

She had seen the way Sebastianus looked at her when he thought she was unaware, and knew that he welcomed her touch. They both found ways and excuses to be in each other's company. But neither had dared utter words that could not be called back. She knew it was because neither was free. Both were committed to separate destinies.

As she finished the peach, a rare fruit that had been brought, over many years and by many brave caravans, from China, she saw its presence in this particular tavern on this particular night as a sign that Sebastianus was on the right road.

Her eyes strayed again to the clock, and her worry grew.

"I pray that my master is successful," Timonides said as he, too, noted the hour and wondered where Sebastianus was. Had he been able to find the hermit Bessas? Was he successful in obtaining the location of the Crystal Pools? Timonides had no idea what ploy Sebastianus was going to use, or why his stubborn young master thought it would work where others had failed, but he hoped Sebastianus was successful.

"If not," Timonides muttered as he ran his bread around his greasy plate, catching fried onion and the last bits of fish, "my master should just pluck the bastard's head from his neck and *scoop* the information out!"

The fire cracked and sparks flew upward. Nestor smiled and giggled. His chin was greasy from dinner, his tunic spotted and stained, but Timonides would take care of those things later, as he always did. Nestor had earlier astonished the innkeeper by replicating one of the man's own specialty dishes—a delicacy made of chopped nuts and honey. Over the years, innkeepers and wealthy housewives had tried to buy Timonides's son—with his talent, one could steal the secret recipes of Rome's renowned chefs and serve them at one's own table. But Timonides would never sell Nestor, and it wasn't just because he himself enjoyed his son's unique skills. Nestor was the center of the old Greek's universe, and to Timonides Nestor wasn't simple minded, he was just a very sweet boy. It didn't matter that Nestor had no idea where they were at that moment or where they were going. Even the ocean voyage hadn't fazed him, as he had stood at the ship's railing, smiling at the sea. And soon, they would be seeing yet new and different sights to delight the child-man.

If only they would get going!

Timonides was tired of lingering in Antioch. And it had taken over a month for them to finally arrive here. After securing a transport vessel for Sebastianus's goods and slaves, they were first delayed by a bad dream that had visited the ship's captain the night before they were due to sail. The second delay, as they were about to depart, was caused by a crow being sighted on one of the masts—a very bad omen for sailing. But after a week of such delays, the *Poseidon* had finally set sail and, enjoying decent weather, arrived in Antioch ten days later.

But now a month had passed, they had just celebrated the winter solstice. Gray skies hung over the city, and rain had been coming down all day. Even so, it had not been a month spent in idleness. Primo, who had taken up temporary residence at the local Roman garrison, had spent the past thirty days recruiting and training men for his special military unit, drilling them, arming them, preparing them for the hazardous journey ahead, and especially schooling them in the secret strategies and military tactics they would be using. Sebastianus in the meantime had been busy putting together his massive caravan, buying camels and slaves, meeting with trade merchants, taking on merchandise, conferring with bankers—all the business of commerce. Timonides, of course, had passed each day in diligent study of the stars, their alignments, houses, ascents, and descents, paying particular attention to the moon and constellations and the planets. This mission to China must not fail. Rumor had it that Nero was prone to petulance and did not like disappointment.

As thunder cracked and shook the centuries-old inn, Timonides looked through the smoky gloom at Ulrika, who was watching the street door.

She was quite handy with her medical kit, he thought, recalling how on the voyage from Rome, he had been stricken with such seasickness that he had not been able to eat. Once again, Ulrika had come to his rescue, giving him a tonic made from a rare and expensive root called ginger. It had done the trick so that Timonides had been able to eat again, and now he was doubly indebted to her!

Back in Ostia, awaiting the order to set sail, Ulrika had surprised Timonides by suggesting that she might be of some help to Nestor. Not his mind, of course, for that could never be helped. But Nestor had never learned to speak properly beyond a few garbled syllables. Timonides understood what the boy was saying, but it was gibberish to everyone else. Ulrika had speculated that Nestor could have something called a "tied tongue." Her own mother, she said, had been born tongue-tied and had had her tongue freed when she was seven years old. She recommended that Timonides take his son to a doctor skilled with the knife. Timonides had been tempted, but then he had thought: Do I really want Nestor to be able to talk? Didn't people mock him enough as it was? And what if, in gaining speech, Nestor lost his gift for cooking? Such things were known to happen, unexpected consequences to good fortune, a trade-off as it were, the gods being the capricious pranksters they were known to be.

No, best to leave things as they were. Especially as he had more urgent matters requiring his attention, primarily the problem of the catastrophe that continued to lie in his master's future. The first time Timonides had noted the possibility of calamity ahead for Sebastianus, at Fort Bonna months ago, he had been alarmed. But as he had watched the stars and charted their courses, and as he had observed the dark omen continuing to lie in the future—as if, in fact, it moved in time as Sebastianus himself did—Timonides's panic turned to a more objective frame of mind.

There was no doubt—something terrible awaited his master, it hovered like a dark cloud on the horizon, staying always distant no matter how quickly one traveled toward it. But where or when the catastrophe was going to happen was any man's guess. Timonides had stopped blaming himself for it, and he had told not a single lie since leaving Rome—he had held himself to his usual noble standards, had held the gods and astrology in the highest esteem, had kept himself morally and physically clean and pure, and had arrived at this rainy night feeling spiritually immaculate and without blemish.

So whatever the catastrophe was, and whenever it was going to happen, no one could blame Timonides the astrologer for it.

As SEBASTIANUS MADE HIS way up the narrow street, leaning into the rain, looking forward to a hot fire and spiced wine, he thought of the remarkable series of events that had brought him to this even more remarkable moment.

Tomorrow they would depart for Babylon! And after Babylon . . .

He owed this good fortune to Ulrika.

Sebastianus would not be here tonight, about to embark upon the adventure of a lifetime, had Ulrika not told him the remarkable facts of Gaius Vatinius's secret battle strategy. While Adon's gryphon or Gaspar's conjoined twins would be far more appealing to a sixteen-year-old, Nero's seasoned advisors saw merit in a caravan trader who could guarantee the safe passage of imperial ambassadors and goods to the Far East, thus expanding the reach of the Empire.

And Sebastianus was certain he would be successful. Primo had been working with his hand-picked unit, drilling them relentlessly, a small fighting force of mercenaries, loyal veterans, retired gladiators, and marksmen with bows and arrows. A force to be feared.

He owed it all to Ulrika, and now he had a gift for her!

Sebastianus neared the tavern with its sign that swung in the wind. No one could read it, as the lamp had been doused by the rain. But the Inn of the Blue Peacock had stood in this spot for generations, a warm beacon in the winter, cool harbor in the summer, offering food and drink to the weary wayfarer, gathering place for those who lived on Green Wizard Street. And temporary home to Sebastianus and his three companions.

Ulrika slept in the room next to his, on the floor above the tavern, while Timonides and Nestor shared another. But sleep had been elusive for Sebastianus. He had found himself tossing and turning, waking at all hours to kick his blanket off despite the winter night. He dreamed about Ulrika, just as she filled his daytime thoughts. He had come close several times, when he had held her during a storm at sea, or in a rocky chariot, or as they passed through a crowded marketplace, to revealing his feelings for her. But she was still under his protection as a caravan leader, and that was a personal rule Sebastianus would never break.

And how did she feel about *him*? he wondered as he pushed on the heavy, rain-soaked door. There were moments when he caught her staring at him. At other times, she seemed to move close to him, or she would touch him more than was necessary. If only he could hold her just once, kiss her, caress her . . .

Sebastianus entered the tavern loudly announcing his great news: He had found Bessas and presented the old hermit with a proposition he could not refuse!

Timonides jumped to his feet, wheezing as he did so. The other patrons had already left, the innkeeper had vanished into his private quarters, and Nestor had gone upstairs to bed. Only the astrologer and Ulrika remained. "Did he tell you how to find Shalamandar?" Timonides asked.

Ulrika rose and went to Sebastianus, taking him by the arm to lead him to the fire, lifting his damp cloak away from his shoulders. A goblet of warm wine awaited him, and she pressed it between his cold hands.

Sebastianus fell silent for a moment, filling his eyes with the sight of this fair-haired maiden silhouetted in front of a dying fire. I wish, Sebastianus said silently, I could give you so much more. I wish I could find your mother for you, or explain your gift from the gods. I wish I could take you into my arms and never let go.

Instead, he sipped the wine and said, "Bessas does indeed know of Shalamandar and the crystal pools. Even better, he will show us the way."

"And you believe him?" Timonides cried. "He is not going to take your money and vanish?"

Sebastianus smiled as he looked into Ulrika's eyes. "Bessas is called a holy man, and people around Daphne revere him, they take him food and offerings, and bless his name. They say he has brought luck to them. And he asks for no money."

"But he did tell you how to reach Shalamandar?" Timonides said in irritation. He had seen this lovesickness blossom between Sebastianus and Ulrika over the weeks, and knowing that nothing could come of it, wished his master would find a cure for it!

"He said he will guide us to it," Sebastianus said as he turned to the astrologer. "I offered Bessas what no one else had thought to, what all travelers in foreign lands yearn for: passage home. We depart for Babylon in the morning!"

Timonides awoke with swimming bowels. Moaning softly, he crawled out of bed and padded across the wooden floor on bare feet, cursing himself for taking that third helping of leeks. The innkeeper's wife had stewed them in too much oil and now he was paying for it.

A floorboard creaked and he stopped, looking at the other bed, which was a sack filled with straw on the floor, covered by woolen blankets. He didn't want to wake Nestor, who sometimes had difficulty getting back to sleep.

Timonides blinked in the darkness. The rain had passed and the stars were out. Enough light seeped through the cracks of the window shutters to reveal a vacant bed. Where was Nestor?

Deciding that his son must have gone outside to answer nature's call,

Timonides resumed his journey across the small chamber, to rifle through his travel pack for a stomach powder he always traveled with. A few pinches in a cup of water, and his insides would calm down.

When he heard the door, he muttered, "Go back to sleep, son, I'm all right," knowing that Nestor would worry about his father.

But instead of mumbling his incomprehensible, "Yes, Papa, good-night," Nestor remained standing in the doorway.

Timonides turned to frown at him. Nestor was grinning, and in his right hand he clutched a sack.

"What's that then, eh?" Timonides said, eyeing the sack. "What do you have there?"

Nestor's child-grin widened as he lifted the sack. "Reeka," he said with delight.

Timonides waddled up to him, cursing leeks, innkeeper's wives, winter nights, and life in general. "A gift for Ulrika? At this hour?"

He held out his hand, wondering what the boy had gotten into now—Nestor had a penchant for bringing flowers for Ulrika, or colored pebbles—and took the sack, thinking it held a melon of some sort, by the weight and shape.

Praying the boy hadn't stolen it, and that Timonides wouldn't have to find the owner in the morning, and explain things, he opened the sack and peered in, wrinkling his nose, letting his eyes adjust to the dim light in the room. "What—" he began. Narrowed his eyes. Brought the sack closer. "I don't . . ."

And then—

Timonides cried out.

He dropped the sack and tripped backwards to land on his buttocks. "Nestor!" he cried. "Nestor! What have you done?"

For Nestor's gift was the head of Bessas, the holy man whom all of Antioch revered.

14

It was a long moment before a stunned Timonides could scramble to his feet. And then it was to rush to the small window, throw open the shutters, and thrust his head out in time to vomit down to the street below. He broke out in a cold sweat and let the night air revive him.

The head of Bessas . . .

What had possessed Nestor?

His mind reeling, Timonides closed his eyes and tried to think. As sweat poured from his face and dripped from his nose—as wave after wave of nausea hit him—he recalled words he had spoken earlier by the fire: "My master should just pluck the bastard's head from his neck and *scoop* the information out!"

And there sat Nestor with his knack for two things: taking words literally, and always wanting to please. Especially Ulrika.

"By the stars," Timonides whispered, feeling the leeks swim in his belly and come up again. He vomited twice more before he could bring his head inside, and then it was to worry that his scream might have been heard. But the mudbrick walls of the inn were thick. Had he disturbed the others, he would have known by now. But the night continued on in its objective silence, and Timonides was alone with a monstrous problem on his hands.

A problem that grew in size and proportion as several facts began to sink in: primarily, that Sebastianus had said Bessas was believed to have brought luck to people.

And people didn't take kindly to holy men getting their heads cut off.

As the immensity of Nestor's act began to sink in, Timonides felt his bones and muscles melt. He feared he was going to faint. But he had to maintain a stout heart and a clear head. What was he going to do?

They will be coming for my son . . .

For it was certain that Nestor, who continued to stand there smiling, oblivious of what he had done, would surely not have been careful to go about his grisly task unseen, nor would he have covered his traces. Knowing Nestor, he might have even shown his "gift" to a passerby! The hue and cry could be out at that moment, the guards of the night watch stamping down the street that very minute, to take Nestor away for certain execution.

Timonides's legs gave way and he slumped to the floor. They will crucify my son . . .

As HE WATCHED HIS FATHER take a seat on the floor, Nestor thought of the gift he had just brought, and was thoroughly delighted with himself. He hadn't done it for his father, it was for the lady with the sunlight hair.

Nestor loved Reeka and would do anything for her, she talked to him so soothingly, calming him, telling him that everything was going to be all right. He loved her voice. It caressed his inside mind. Like a mother's touch.

He giggled when he looked at the sack on the floor. In the simple mechanisms of his mind, Nestor had discerned that Papa and Uncle Sebastianus were looking for a pool. They hoped to take Reeka there, to make her happy. But Papa and Uncle Sebastianus had seemed to be having a hard time finding the pool, and there was a man who knew where it was, but he wasn't telling. Papa said it could be scooped from his brain. Uncle Sebastianus had said the man lived in a hut near the big statue of Daphne. Nestor remembered the statue because it looked so comical, a woman with tree branches growing out of her hair. Papa needed to scoop the pool from the man's brain, so here it was!

A gift for Reeka, the lady with the sunlight hair.

LIFTING HIS WEARY HEAD, Timonides looked up at his son, still standing in the doorway with a smile on his face, and Timonides felt his heart break into a million pieces.

He suddenly felt big and lumpy and stupid, this astrologer who could read the messages in the stars with such precision that he could advise a fellow on whether to choose beans or lentils for supper—a man who could lift his face to the dark bowl of night, pick out Venus, and tell you exactly where she would be in an hour, in a month—a man who could close his eyes and point directly at red, distant Mars while other men would be searching wide-eyed and saying, "Where is it?"

A man of precision and control, and yet whose life had just unraveled into the myriad fibers that had made up its fabric.

This is it, he thought in weary surrender. This is the catastrophe that was foretold. And it is all my fault. I brought this about. I used the stars and my sacred calling for my own personal gain. I wanted to keep the girl and her healing skills at my side, and in so doing brought calamity to myself and my master's house. I alone can fix it.

And there was only one way. Timonides the astrologer had to lie again.

My punishment, he thought, for having lied in the first place. And the punishment, ironically, was that he was doomed to continue to lie. He could never, for as long as he lived, tell Sebastianus the truth of what had happened tonight.

Hoisting his bulk from the floor, he searched the cold night for a plan. They must leave the city at once and be well away before the magistrate was able to determine the identity of the cold-blooded killer of Bessas the holy hermit. *It will be easy to convince Sebastianus to move at a quick pace. He always obeys the stars—*

Timonides groaned as he suddenly remembered Ulrika. He could not let her come along, for Nestor would continue to commit crimes to please her.

I will tell her that I have done her chart and found that her mother is living in Jerusalem.

Sebastianus will ask about Bessas. I will tell him that the hermit is not to be trusted.

Telling Nestor to go to bed, assuring him that his gift was good and that Papa was pleased, Timonides went to his travel pack to bring out his box of charts and instruments. The old astrologer felt the weight of the world on his back. He did not want to do this—he did not want to lie again, to blaspheme and commit sacrilege, to outrage the gods and bring their wrath upon his head. But he had no choice. He must save his son, even at the risk of his own immortal soul.

When he had cradled Nestor as a baby, Timonides had learned a primal truth: that it was not the parent who created the child, but the child who created the parent. And while others saw a simpleton, Timonides the believer in the transmigration of souls looked beyond the homely features and thought of the migrant soul that might lurk behind them. Perhaps Nestor possessed the reincarnated soul of the greatest philosopher who ever lived.

Either way, precious son or great philosopher, Timonides could not let him be executed.

Lighting a lamp, Timonides got down to the business of casting his master's horoscope, hoping to find some truth to mix in with the falsehood. He did not go through his usual ritual of bathing and praying and changing into clean robes, for the lie would only make him filthy again.

But as Timonides went through his calculations, wrote down figures and degrees and angles, noted sun signs and moon houses, as Antioch slept and the stars wheeled overhead unconcerned with the star-reader at the Inn of the Blue Peacock who perspired over his equations and numbers, he saw a new and unexpected indicator emerge.

He froze. Whispered an oath. Rubbed his sweating face. Picked up his pen and re-calculated.

Finally Timonides sat back in shock. There was no question: the aspects of the progressing and transiting planets to that of Sebastianus's birth planet definitely indicated a new direction for him! The gods, through their precise arrangement of heavenly bodies, were crisply clear in their new message: Sebastianus was to take a turn *southward* from Antioch—he and Ulrika were now both to take a southern journey together.

Timonides closed his eyes and swallowed with a dry throat. Calamity upon calamity! His doom was sealed, for not only was he going to falsify a horoscope, he was now going to disobey the unmistakable, divine message in the stars.

Sick at heart, but knowing he had no choice, and that they were running out of time, Timonides hurried across the hall to pound loudly on his master's door.

ULRIKA WAS NOT ASLEEP when the knock sounded at her door. She had been awakened earlier by a cry, and she had lain in the darkness trying to discern if it had been real or dreamed. And then she had heard muffled voices, a spell of silence, followed by footsteps across the hall, a banging on a door, and more muffled voices, but loud this time and sounding urgent.

She had been about to get out of bed to see what the trouble was, when a knock announced someone at her door, and she opened it now to find Sebastianus on the other side. Clearly roused from sleep, he had hastily thrown a cloak over his shoulders, and underneath he wore only a loincloth.

When he stared at her for a moment, Ulrika became aware of her own lack of clothing. She wore only a night dress—a thin shift that reached her knees—and her hair was undone and tumbled over her breasts. She felt naked.

Collecting himself, Sebastianus said, "Ulrika, Timonides says your mother is in Jerusalem."

"My mother! What—"

The astrologer pushed his way through, waving a sheet of papyrus. "Yes yes, there is no doubt of it. Your mother is there, living with friends."

She blinked, looked from Sebastianus to the astrologer. "But why are you doing a reading at this hour? And why my—"

Timonides spoke rapidly. "A dream woke me up, ordering me to look out my window, where I saw a star streak across the sky. I knew this was a message that I must cast my master's horoscope, and there it was! A new message from the gods. My master is to leave Antioch at once for Babylon and you are to go to Jerusalem."

"We did live for a while in Jerusalem," Ulrika said, "in the house of a woman named Elizabeth."

"Yes yes," Timonides said as he shambled out of the room, talking as he left, "you must go at once to Jerusalem, reach your mother before she leaves. The house of Elizabeth . . ."

Timonides's voice faded down the corridor, and Ulrika found herself alone with Sebastianus, their eyes meeting in the dim light, unspoken words on their lips.

"My mother can help me," Ulrika heard herself say, breathless at the sight of Sebastianus's bare chest, glimpsed between the folds of his disarrayed cloak, wondering why she wasn't more excited by the astrologer's news. "She will tell me where Shalamandar is, and the Crystal Pools."

"I will take you to Jerusalem—"

Ulrika placed her fingertips on his lips. "No, Sebastianus, you are to continue eastward. You must depart at dawn, as the stars command."

They fell silent, held by the night and by their mutual desire. Longing burned in their eyes, and each knew the other's yearning. But both were bound by duty and oaths spoken long before Sebastianus and Ulrika had ever met.

He found his voice. "I will send Syphax and a contingent of men with you so that you are well protected."

"Thank you," she said, thinking that once again this strong and powerful man had come to her rescue. Ulrika knew Syphax, a stony-faced Numidian from the northern coast of Africa who hired himself out as a bodyguard and mercenary. He had escorted and protected Sebastianus's caravans for six years, and she knew he could be trusted.

Sebastianus added, "He will see that you are safely delivered into your mother's care in Jerusalem." He looked at her for another long moment, and then on an impulse took her by the shoulders, drew her close, and said in a husky voice, "Ulrika, all going well and the gods willing, I will arrive in Babylon within six weeks. I plan not to depart for the Far East until the festival of the summer solstice, for the day after is the most propitious day in the year to begin a long journey. After you find your mother and learn the whereabouts of Shalamandar, join me in Babylon. I shall wait until the last possible moment before departing for China."

"Yes," she whispered. "I will join you in Babylon." She reached up to touch Sebastianus's jaw, and when her fingertips met the fine, bronze-colored stubble of his beard, she saw—

Sebastianus frowned. "What is it?"

Ulrika opened her mouth but couldn't speak.

He waited, wondering if she were receiving a vision. He had witnessed it before, had seen her delicate nostrils flare, her pupils dilate. The color left her face, and the skin at her temples grew taut.

Outside, over the sleeping city of Antioch, a cloud sailed across the moon and bright stars, plunging the rooms of the inn into darkness. Momentarily blinded, Sebastianus and Ulrika felt their other senses heighten. Sebastianus felt Ulrika's warm skin beneath his hands as he continued to hold her shoulders, making him think of the softness of swans and mist. Ulrika smelled the rain still on him, reminding her of verdant forests and meadows. He heard her gentle respirations. She felt his warmth.

And then the cloud sailed on, like a great trireme across the ocean of night, and starlight washed once more into the small room at the inn. Sebastianus saw a pale, feminine face. She saw eyes the color of a meadow.

"There is treachery in your party," she finally said. "One of your men, who is close to you, will betray you."

"Who? Which one?"

"I do not know. I cannot see his face."

The truth was, there was no face to see, for it was not a true vision that had just visited her, but a *feeling*. As her fingertips had touched Sebastianus's face, the most overwhelming sense of disappointment and disillusionment swept over her. Utter betrayal. Like a physical blow, and it was going to knock the spirit out of Sebastianus Gallus.

"Is it perhaps one of Primo's recruits?"

She shook her head. "He is a friend."

"I trust all who are close to me," he said, "but I also trust *you,* Ulrika, and your instincts. And so I will be careful and watchful. We will say farewell in the morning, when we depart at the caravanserai."

Ulrika watched him cross the hall and slip into his own room. Closing her door, she stayed with her back to it and whispered to the gods, "Please take care of this man. Watch over him. Bring him safely back to me."

Sebastianus didn't even have to knock. Ulrika already knew he had come back, that he stood now on the other side of her door. She opened it and there he was, the cloak gone, bare chest and arms exposed, a look of hunger and uncertainty on his face. He held out his hand and Ulrika saw the scallop shell from an ancient altar in Galicia. "Take this," he said. "It holds great power."

She took the shell, vowing to wear it always.

"I need to touch you," he whispered.

She looked up into his eyes and felt them embrace her, draw her inside, into his mind and heart. "And I, you," she said.

They reached for each other at the same time, arms gliding perfectly against each other, slipping into and around the right places, with Ulrika delivering herself into a refuge she had yearned for and Sebastianus drawing a sweetness to himself that he had hungered for. Their mouths met in heat and passion. Each tasted the other. Hands hurriedly explored, grasped, kneaded. Words came whispered breathlessly through clenched lips: "I want—" "I need—" "You are—" "We are—"

Ulrika pressed herself to Sebastianus and felt his hardness. She burst into flame, or so it felt, her skin so hot now and damp and wanting to be devoured by the Galician's mouth. And Sebastianus wanted to delve into her, to join his body and life force to hers, to become part of her, making her part of him.

But then they heard a crash, and heavy footfall, and the grumpy voice of Timonides in the next room as he was apparently packing his bags and complaining, and speaking very loudly of the urgency with which they must be going.

Reluctantly, Sebastianus drew back. "It seems we are not to know a moment alone together," he said, glancing toward the wall which almost vibrated with the energy of the astrologer's industry. "Timonides meant it when he said the stars have commanded us to hurry."

Why? she wanted to ask, hating the feel of his withdrawal, the cold air that rushed between them, the awful emptiness that now filled her arms. And the burning of her lips, the tingling on her tongue. She did not want to stop.

"Ulrika," Sebastianus said as he drew her close one last time, "I want to stay with you, be with you. But Timonides is right. I must go. To love you and to enjoy your love in return—such a privilege and luxury cannot be mine, not now that I am under Caesar's command."

He bent and kissed her forehead.

"Ulrika, Ulrika," he said, filling his mouth with her name. "It is said that Eros, the god of love and desire, is continually taking humans apart and putting them back together. And it is true! My former self has been utterly shattered and re-shaped. The man I once was, so guarded in his feelings, so in control of his heart, no longer exists. Why Eros singled me out for this particular joy, I do not know, but I still firmly hold that I am not deserving of it.

"I do not want to leave you! But I must do as the stars dictate, for it is the will of the gods. No man can defy his stars, for they map out his destiny. This I believe most passionately and with all my heart: there is an order to the universe. And if the gods deem we not join again in Babylon, then I pray that you find what you are looking for, and the answers to the mysteries within yourself. And when I come back from China, and surely I will for the stars have promised, I will search for you, and I *will* find you, my dearest Ulrika."

15

THE PUNGENT SMELL OF lamb's wool and goat hides mingled with the scent from the oil lamp as Ulrika struck a flint and lit the wick.

Flickering light illuminated the tent, which was still dark inside as the sun had yet to rise. Soon, sunlight would flood the tent and cooking aromas would invade the cloistered atmosphere of her private tent.

As Ulrika combed her long hair, she paused to lay her hand upon the scallop shell on her breast, its presence a reassuring promise of her reunion with Sebastianus. She and her escort had left Antioch weeks ago, but in the time since, she had been unsuccessful in finding her mother in Jerusalem. And so Ulrika had given orders to Syphax to take her to Babylon, where she would join Sebastianus's caravan.

Her heart raced at the thought of seeing him again. When they had said farewell in Antioch, to follow their separate roads, Ulrika had not been prepared for the terrible feeling of emptiness that had filled her in the days that followed. As she had ridden in the covered carriage, in the escort of Syphax and his men, following an ancient road southward, an unaccustomed sadness had enveloped her. She had needed to tap into all her will power to keep from giving orders to turn back and join Sebastianus.

She could not bear to be parted from him.

She and her escort had left Jerusalem the day before and stopped for the night at the base of the hills that looked out upon a bleak, arid region of unending rock and sand. Their next stop was Jericho, from which they would take an ancient trade route across the desert to Babylon. Ulrika trembled with excitement. She had spent every waking moment thinking about Sebastianus, their last night together in Antioch, their passionate kiss. She would close her eyes and feel him again, his body, his power. His touch. His taste. In Babylon, Ulrika and Sebastianus would be free to love at last.

And then Sebastianus will go to China while I search for Shalamandar and its crystal pools. My love and I will be reunited after that, of this I am sure.

Stepping out of the tent, Ulrika was surprised to find, in the crisp pale dawn, a deserted campsite. She looked around. Syphax and his men were nowhere to be seen. Had they gone hunting, perhaps? Or in search of fuel for the fire? As sunlight broke over the ragged cliffs, illuminating the campsite, Ulrika saw that the horses and pack mules and tents were gone.

Turning in a slow circle, she scanned the wilderness, the sharp wind in her face, and all she saw were barren cliffs and dun-colored hills. Golden rays of dawn were dissolving shadows in their path, leaving a tawny wilderness to stretch in all directions beneath a clear blue sky. There was little greenery, despite the spring equinox having just been celebrated. This barren land was populated with rocks and stones, boulders and sand, canyons and plateaus—but no people.

Ulrika knew why the men had snuck off into the night: she had told Syphax she was out of money and that he and his men would only be compensated when they re-joined his employer's caravan. Ulrika knew the sort of men Syphax and his comrades were: men who followed the nearest coin. They had grumbled about going to China and falling off the edge of the earth. This would have been their chance to cut ties with Sebastianus Gallus and find safer and more profitable employment elsewhere. No doubt they had heard of more lucrative employment while they were in Jerusalem.

At least, Ulrika saw with relief, they had not left her without provisions. At the doorway of the tent were a sack of lentils, a bag of bread, and a generous waterskin. And they had left one donkey, its tether tied to a rock while the beast munched on weeds.

As the sun crested the hilltops, Ulrika took her bearings. Jericho lay a few miles to the northeast. Directly ahead, although she could not see it, lay the Sea of Salt, the terminus of the Jordan River. I will go east, she decided, and turn northward when I reach the sea. At Jericho I can join a caravan to Babylon.

She decided she would leave the tent, as it was too cumbersome to dismantle, fold, and pack onto the donkey. The little creature would carry the food, water, and her possessions, and she would walk. But as Ulrika bent to pick up the sacks, she saw with dismay that they had been slit open, the contents scattered and covered in bird droppings. Ruined! The waterskin, too, had been cut. In alarm she saw animal prints in the sand, left by the paws of a giant cat—a lion or leopard. And the water had long since seeped into the earth.

Which meant she was alone in the Judean wilderness without food or water.

THE MORNING AIR WAS fresh and biting, the sky a deep blue with scattered white clouds. Ulrika led the donkey by its tether, her travel packs and medical box tied to its back. She picked her way around rocks and boulders, expecting the terrain to flatten soon and show more growth. Although it was spring, and rains had recently visited this region, the wilderness blossoms and grasses were already withering and drying up, leaving only dun-colored hills with deep ravines.

With the sun in her eyes, Ulrika trekked steadily eastward, looking for signs of habitation, even if just a lone shepherd's tent. But as the sun climbed in the sky and the day grew warm, she encountered no other souls. A wild donkey fled from their path, and birds circled overhead. Ulrika kept her eye out for leopards and lions, for surely at her slow pace, she must appear easy prey.

It was a desolate land, the barren, striated hills pocked with caves, like dovecotes, one of which had been the abode, long ago, of two women who lived in a cave with their father. Ulrika had heard the local legend of two sisters who were childless and without husbands, and who had conspired to get their father drunk, have sex with him, and thereby perpetuate the family line. The story went that they were successful in seducing their father, a man named Lot, and became pregnant with sons who went on to be patriarchs of new nations.

Noon came and went. The sun began its descent toward the west as Ulrika pressed on through a region of limestone and chalk, dried vegetation and stones, and no water.

Finally the brown, barren landscape flattened. Ulrika left the hills and ravines behind, and saw up ahead, in the near distance, the shimmer of pale blue water. The Sea of Salt.

Although hungry and weary, Ulrika pressed on. There would be people there—food and rest.

Shadows were growing long, the sun turning orange when she finally arrived at the shore. Ulrika stared at the strange shoreline that seemed layered with a fine, white ash. She had known this was not a freshwater lake, but a "dead" sea of salt, with no plants or fish. However, she had hoped to find drinkable water. But for as far as she could see, all along the salty shore thick with foul-smelling mineral deposits, there were no tents, no people, not even a lone camel. Which meant no fresh water.

On the other side of the flat, glassy sea, on the far eastern shore, mountains rose, with no signs of towns or cities. Northward, to her left, the River Jordan flowed near the populous and prosperous city of Jericho—but that was miles away, too far for her to reach tonight. Southward, to her right, lay unknown territory. And behind her, westward, the rocky hills seemed to support no life.

The shore of the sea was riddled with dangerous quicksand pits, hazardous tar pits and pools of asphalt that gave of an acrid stench. She dared not venture farther in such hostile terrain as night was falling.

Ulrika scanned the hills for refuge. A cave, perhaps. She would search for a well or an underground spring.

Suddenly, a chilling sound filled the desert silence. The wail of a jackal. A moment later, more wails rose to the darkening sky. Ulrika tried to determine their location. A pack of hungry jackals would not be shy about attacking a defenseless human.

As she reached for the donkey's tether, to lead him back to the safety of the hills, the jackals screamed again and the donkey bolted. "Wait!" Ulrika cried. He galloped off, taking her packs with him.

She looked up and saw the first pale stars wink into existence. She thought of Sebastianus looking up at the same stars.

Then she returned her focus to the western hills, which were now jagged black shapes against a lavender sky. The sun had set. Dusk was upon her. She knew it would be brief—quick twilight and then the desert would be plunged into darkness. And danger.

Tightening her *palla* about herself, she struck off westward, to the foothills, where deep shadows offered the promise of protection from the night.

As the moon had yet to rise, and the stars were not yet bright beacons in the sky, the terrain was cast in darkness. Ulrika had to step with care. Pebbles and rocks covered the ground, with snake and rodent holes pocking the earth.

The wind picked up, chilly, biting. It cut through her *palla,* and she thought of her heavy cloak, bundled up on the back of the donkey. He would not have trotted far, but there was no hope of finding him in this darkness.

The jackals wailed again, and they sounded closer. Ulrika picked up her pace. Suddenly, the ground gave way and she fell, sharp pain radiating up her leg. Pushing herself to her feet, she saw that she had stepped in a hole, twisting her ankle. She could barely walk on it. Now she limped, slowly and painfully, chastising herself for not having been more careful, for not having the good sense to ride the donkey in the first place.

With each step, her ankle screamed in pain. It soon became agony to walk. She thought of the supplies in her medical box, the painkillers that would enable her to walk. Even so, such medicines came either in powdered or pill form, both of which required drinking water. A willow-bark syrup would ease her pain, but it too required water for dilution.

As she neared the foothills, Ulrika scanned the narrow ravines. The gulleys and canyons were cloaked in darkness. She could not make out features. Was that one blocked by boulders? Did that one have green shrubs that might mean water? Could that dark spot indicate a cave or an animal's lair?

Which to choose?

As she looked this way and that, up and down the stretch of desolation that lay between the hills and the sea, she caught a dark movement at the corner of her eye. Turning, she saw an animal, watching her.

Ulrika froze at the sight of the hungry beast that eyed her with golden irises. A wolf.

But as Ulrika held her breath and watched the wolf—a brown, shaggy creature with upright ears and a tail that went straight out—she wondered if in fact the animal was real, or a vision. Wind whipped around them, whistling down through the small canyons with a mournful song. Sand flew up and blew over the ground like a strange mist.

Ulrika and the wolf locked eyes. She was afraid to move. If he was real, he would attack.

But the wolf finally turned and began to lope away, hugging the foothill, its head held high. After a short distance, it stopped and looked back and it occurred to Ulrika that the wolf wanted her to follow. But it did not seem to be headed into a ravine, toward shelter and protection; rather it was staying on the flat wasteland, out in the open, where she would be unprotected and vulnerable.

"You are wrong," she murmured to the vision, and turned toward one of the protected canyons where she saw a cave. She would be safe in there.

But the wolf continued in the opposite direction, out into the open. He stopped again and looked back, golden eyes commanding her to follow.

You would lead me into exposed space! she wanted to cry. But the wolf waited until Ulrika, no longer able to stand up to its power, gave in. She turned and followed it.

The animal came to a halt at last, stopping, turning, waiting for her to catch up. Then he sat on his haunches like a stone idol awaiting sacrifice. He watched Ulrika with his acute golden eyes, his ears pricked and alert.

When she neared him, Ulrika said, "What do you want of me?" and then he vanished before her eyes, fading like shadows at noon, fading as the wolf at General Vatinius's side had faded, until he was gone and Ulrika was left in the barren wilderness, her ankle throbbing, her mouth and throat parched with thirst, while jackals sent their unearthly yelps to the stars. Other predators, Ulrika knew, would soon be on the prowl.

She turned and took a step, but her ankle gave way. With a cry she fell. When she tried to stand, she realized in horror that she could not. She was unable to walk.

Exhaustion overwhelmed her. Every ounce of strength and energy seemed to have drained from her body. Tears stung her eyes as she massaged her leg and sensed the gathering of night creatures, circling her, watching, waiting.

Ulrika felt the impersonal stars looking down at her, witnessing her distress. She felt the black sky and the cold winds as nature went about its business, ignoring the woman in peril.

Help me, cried her frightened mind, sending her silent plea to the All Mother whom she had revered all her life.

As she lay there, trying to gather strength to crawl back to the hills, Ulrika placed her hand over Sebastianus's scallop shell. It brought comfort. She pictured the man she loved, tall and strong, she conjured up his voice, his scent, the feel of his warmth and power. She wished she had gone to Babylon with him.

Overcome with fatigue, Ulrika laid her head down and felt the desert sand beneath her cheek turn to cool grass, and when she opened her eyes, it was the middle of the day, with a pale blue sky above. And before her stood a woman, tall and beautiful, creating an altar of scallop shells, a wild, untamed countryside surrounding her, wind whipping her long hair, sculpting her long white gown into a marble masterpiece.

"Who are you?" Ulrika said.

The woman smiled in a secretive way, and whispered: You already know the answer.

And Ulrika did know. She was the ancestress Sebastianus had spoken of. A distant priestess named Gaia, from whom he had descended.

"Why do you appear to me?" Ulrika asked.

"To tell you that there is nothing to fear."

And then the altar and coastline vanished, and Ulrika was back in the mocking wasteland, stars winking overhead.

And then she saw—

Sebastianus!

Ulrika sobbed with joy. He was here! In the Judean wilderness, coming toward her over the arid, salt-crusted ground, his blue cloak billowing about him like the sail of a mighty ship. She reached for him. "Sebastianus, you came back!"

But it wasn't Sebastianus—a stranger stood before her. She could not get a good look at him, for light now emanated from his body—a blinding light glowing about his head like a brilliant nimbus, streaming out into the cosmos.

And then a voice—it was not something she heard but rather felt all around her—a man's voice commanding: "Call out for help, Ulrika."

"No, I must not, for then the animals will know where I am."

"They already know where you are. They are closing in."

Ulrika held her breath and listened. She heard soft footfall, rapid breathing, grunts.

Her blood ran to ice. The beasts of the night were drawing near.

"Call out for help," the glowing apparition said again. "Quickly! Now! Shout, Ulrika, fill the night with your voice."

She opened her mouth but no sound came out. Her throat was too dry.

"Again!" the shining spirit said. "At once! With all your strength!"

Ulrika reached deep within herself, gathered the last of her strength and life force and, stretching her mouth wide, screamed at the top of her lungs. "Help me! Someone, please! *Help!*"

And suddenly Ulrika was surrounded by a warm light. It engulfed her, embraced her like loving arms, lifting her up, buoying as if on a golden sea. She felt waves of compassion and security wash over her. She heard the voice, deep and mellow, say, "Do not be afraid. Everything is going to be all right."

Ulrika felt peaceful and serene. She had never known such calm, such quiescence. It was beautiful.

I am dying, she thought in detachment. The animals have found me.

They are devouring me. This is what it is like to die. But I do not mind.

"Hello? Is someone out there?"

She ignored the call. It was only her imagination. And she didn't want to leave the light. The warmth was soft and precious. She wanted to stay in it forever.

"Who is out there?"

She opened her eyes. She blinked up at frigid stars overhead, felt the night cold sweep into her flesh, swift and biting. Where did the warmth and light go?

Ulrika sucked air into her lungs, tried to gather strength into her limbs. What had just happened? Struggling to a sitting position, she looked around. The hills stood black and silent behind her. Ahead, the salt-sea lay silver in eerie starlight. Who had spoken just now?

And then she saw the lights, bright little sparks growing larger as they drew near. A voice called, "Is someone there? Call out so that we can find you."

"I am here!" Ulrika cried, struggling to sit up. She waved her arms. "Here, over here!"

The bright glows drew near, and Ulrika saw that they were torches carried by two women. "Are you all right?" one of them asked.

"Dear child," the older of them said, "are you out here all alone?"

"I hurt my leg," Ulrika said. The women spoke a dialect that was prevalent in this part of the Empire—a mixture of "common" Greek and Aramaic, with which Ulrika was familiar.

They reached for her and, each taking one of her arms, lifted Ulrika to her feet. The younger of the two, a woman in her forties with strength in her body, steadied Ulrika and helped her along over the ground.

Wordlessly, they made their way to an outcropping of rock, passing around it and up a narrow ravine, where Ulrika saw a group of black goatskin tents standing protected from the wind. The older of the two women went into the largest of the tents, while the second placed her torch in a sconce outside, and then she helped Ulrika into the tent.

Ulrika welcomed the blessed warmth and light within, and sank with relief onto a bed of blankets and sheepskins. As the younger of the two women handed Ulrika a cup of water, she said, "I am Rachel. This is Almah.

Welcome to our home, and peace be upon you."

Ulrika gratefully sipped the water and told them her name, adding, "I was certain I was going to perish out there. I do not know what I would have done had you not found me."

"We did not know you were out there," Rachel said. "And then we heard your call for help. It is a good thing you had the strength to cry out."

"I almost didn't," Ulrika said, trying to recollect the vision that had come to her—first, an ancient priestess named Gaia, and then a stranger who seemed to glow with an inner light. It was he who had commanded Ulrika to call for help.

Details of the dwelling's interior began to register on Ulrika's brain as the water refreshed her. Rachel's home was a typical desert tent with a center post holding up the ceiling, creating a spacious living area that was warmed by a charcoal brazier, brass and clay lamps glowing here and there. Rugs covered the floor, a small table held bowls, pitcher, utensils. A pair of sandals hung on a peg, along with a cloak, small and feminine. Ulrika assumed that the other tents she had glimpsed, smaller than this, were used for storage, or perhaps other people were sleeping there.

With a smile, the older woman, Almah, gray-haired and bent beneath black clothes and a black veil, handed Ulrika a plate of sweet fig cakes and a bowl of dates. "Thank you," Ulrika said as she accepted this most welcome offering.

While she ate, she wondered about her rescuers. Rachel was in her early forties, Ulrika would guess, slender, and dressed in a long gown that was gathered at the waist with a sash. The gown was made of soft wool dyed in brown and cream vertical stripes, and Rachel's thick black hair was concealed beneath a cowl-like veil of soft brown wool that pooled around her shoulders in gentle folds. She wore no jewelry, no cosmetics. But her face was arresting: square and tanned with large black eyes, wrinkled at the corners and framed by black lashes, thick black brows. Ulrika wondered why Rachel and her elderly companion seemed to live alone in this desolate place, or were there perhaps others whom she would meet in the morning?

"What happened?" Rachel asked, taking a seat on a large cushion and drawing her feet under her skirt. "Why were you out there alone?"

Ulrika told them about her search for her mother in Jerusalem, her intention to go to Jericho and from there to Babylon, and then about her abandonment that morning. "My donkey is out there with all my things."

"We shall find it in the morning," Rachel said. "When you have eaten your fill, I will treat your ankle. It is quite swollen."

"Thank you," Ulrika murmured and then addressed her food with singular attention. But after a moment she felt her hostess's eyes upon her, saw a question in them.

"The place where you fell," Rachel said after a moment. "Were you in that spot for a reason?"

"What do you mean?"

Rachel smiled and shook her head. "It is nothing. Here, let me bind your ankle. Almah has something for the pain."

Ulrika accepted the wooden cup containing a dark brew. She recognized the aroma. Her own mother, back in Rome, had made such a bracing tonic by setting twice-baked barley bread into water, leaving it to ferment in a large clay vat, and then, straining the liquid through a cloth, producing a strong, medicinal beer.

As Ulrika brought the cup to her lips, she thought again about her vision in the desert. It had been much more intense than any she had experienced. And this time, two people had spoken directly to her. Had it perhaps only been a trick of her mind? But what troubled her most was the peaceful, loving feeling that had engulfed her, a sweet state that, for one brief moment, she had not wished to leave.

And had she remembered to practice her new conscious breathing, to control the vision and make it last longer, would she have indeed stayed in there forever?

16

As Ulrika surveyed her new surroundings in the morning sunshine, she wondered about this curious group of tents in the middle of nowhere, inhabited by two women on their own, with no family or friends, not even the humblest servant, just the company of chickens and a pair of goats.

Rachel had told her that an oasis lay three miles away, northward along the foothills, where a natural spring came from the dun earth and gave life to date palms, fish, and birds. Several families lived there year-round, and travelers stopped there to rest. Rachel and Almah visited the oasis to fetch fresh water and other supplies, but they did not live there, preferring to return to this lonely spot in the embrace of a barren canyon.

Why?

Hearing footfall, she turned to see Rachel leading Ulrika's donkey up the ravine, her travel packs and medicine box still attached. "He didn't wander far," Rachel said with a smile. "How is your ankle?"

It was feeling better, although Ulrika couldn't put any weight on it.

Nonetheless, she was anxious to resume her journey to Babylon, and was determined to find a way, a passing caravan, a traveling family who would take her.

As Rachel tethered the beast and untied Ulrika's packs to take them into the tent, Ulrika wanted to ask her why she and Almah didn't live at the oasis. Why did they stay in this barren place where not even a thorn grew?

Rachel emerged from the tent and as she bent over the cooking pot that was suspended over a fire, to stir a simmering lentil soup, she glanced at Ulrika. "Please," she said, pointing to the stool beside the tent door. "Take the weight off your ankle."

Ulrika gratefully took a seat and turned her face to the refreshing morning breeze. From the vantage point of this small encampment, she could see all the way to the crusty white shore of the salty sea, could see the desolate wasteland that stretched from the acrid water to the base of these cliffs. And then she realized in shock that she could see the very spot where she had fallen and had experienced a vision that even now, in the comforting light of a bright sun, continued to trouble her.

Ulrika scanned the small camp, the tiny tents, deserted, the larger tent that was Almah's, and the largest, Rachel's, which looked upon a little compound of campfire, stools, a pen for chickens, two goats. Wet clothing, washed at the oasis and brought back by an uncomplaining Almah, was spread out on boulders to dry.

When Rachel saw how Ulrika looked around in curiosity, she said, "I am a widow, and my beloved husband died before he could bless me with children. So I am alone. Others lived here with me for a while, but they left, one by one, until there is only Almah."

Ulrika thought of the Vestal Virgins—a sect of nuns in Rome who took vows of chastity and who lived a cloistered life devoted to prayer. But Rachel was Jewish—Ulrika had recognized the menorah inside the tent—and she had never heard of Jewish nuns.

"What is in Babylon?" Rachel asked with a smile. "You are in such a hurry to go there."

"There is a caravan about to depart for lands in the Far East. A . . . friend is the caravaneer, a Spaniard named Sebastianus Gallus. We parted in Antioch when I had to come to Jerusalem where I thought I would find my mother. But I promised to join him in Babylon if I could."

"There is something special in Babylon?"

Ulrika paused to give Rachel a thoughtful look. The handsome Jewish woman possessed a unique voice. Deep for a woman, but smooth and soothing. It made Ulrika think of warm honey. A voice that one could not ignore. Ulrika wondered how much to tell Rachel, wondered if her hostess would think her mad—visions that were a gift from the gods, and a necessary quest to find a place called Shalamandar, the place of her conception. "I am searching for something," she said. "I was told it is in the back of the east wind, in mountains that have no name. Sebastianus is helping me to search for it."

Rachel stirred the soup, adding a pinch of salt. "Sebastianus is a good friend?"

"I have known him but a year, yet it seems I have known him forever." The words tumbled from her lips—meeting Sebastianus at the caravan staging area, the journey to Germania in Sebastianus's company, Sebastianus rescuing her from attackers in the forest, a night spent in hiding with Sebastianus, the journey back, getting to know more about him, an ocean voyage, a rainy night at an inn in Antioch. Ulrika blushed, suddenly realizing how she must sound. Every sentence began, "Sebastianus . . ."

Bringing two bowls of soup, Rachel sat next to Ulrika, giving her one, and said, "When I first fell in love with my Jacob, I could speak of nothing but him. Sometimes, I just spoke his name because it felt good in my mouth and I loved to hear it spoken. You speak the name of Sebastianus the same way."

A small table stood between the two stools, and upon it lay a plate of flat, round bread, a small bowl of salt, two cups of water. They ate in silence, scooping the thick lentils onto the bread, two women deep in thought, each curious about the other, both pondering the uniqueness of this moment as women from very different worlds shared a humble meal.

When they were done, Ulrika started to rise, but Rachel bent her head and said, "*Hav lan u-nevarekh . . .*"

Ulrika listened politely as Rachel recited a prayer. When she was finished, Rachel said, "We always give blessing to God after we eat."

Ulrika recalled that, the night before, when Rachel extinguished the last lamp before they went to sleep, she had recited a prayer in Hebrew. She had recited another that morning, upon rising.

Rachel said, "Prayer is ever-present in our lives. Prayer is witness to our covenant with God. It confirms and renews our faith on a daily basis."

As she took the empty dishes, Rachel said, "I will take you to the oasis so you can bathe. I go there myself once a month for the *mikvah*—a ritual cleansing bath following the menstrual cycle—in a secluded pool set aside for women. It is very private."

A day passed, and another, and Ulrika fell in with the rhythm of Rachel's and Almah's strange life. As her ankle healed, she went with them to the oasis to trade chicken eggs and goat's cheese for water and dates and fish. One day they brought back live locusts, which Rachel placed in a basket to be set it out in the sun until they died, and then she sat and painstakingly plucked off the locusts' wings, legs, and heads, placing them in her clay oven to dry-roast them for a special treat. Rachel cooked chicken eggs served with a sauce made of pine nuts and vinegar. Almonds and pistachios baked in honey were dessert. The three women drank watered date wine in the evenings, in moderation, as the sun went down and the valley of salt grew still and quiet.

Ulrika became interested in her hostess. There were no idols of gods in Rachel's tent, no relics of ancestors, no altars for sacrifice. She was not familiar with the religion of the Jews, except to understand that their god was invisible, and therefore they did not carve his likeness. Every dawn and every evening, Rachel went outside and prayed to her god, whom she called "Father." And Rachel's faith seemed to have many food rules, called *kosher*, so that Ulrika marveled that Rachel could remember them all.

They spent evenings talking over the campfire beneath the spring stars, and while Ulrika repaired her sandals and Almah worked at the loom, Rachel chopped vegetables and told stories about the heroes of the past.

"Jewish history is filled with many stories of brave heroes," Rachel said in her thick, honey-warm voice. "There was David who slew a giant, a peasant named Saul who became a king, Gideon who conquered the Midianites with a handful of men, Moses who brought the Israelites out of Egypt, and

Joseph who saved an entire nation from famine. We look upon these forefathers as heroes, but they were in fact weak men. David, when he slew Goliath, had been a mere boy. Saul came from the smallest and least important clan. Gideon was from the weakest clan, and he himself was the weakest in that clan. Moses was slow of speech and tongue and begged God to send someone else to bring the Israelites out of Egypt. And Joseph was a slave. None of these heroes came from impressive backgrounds, or were men of any particular distinction. The rabbis tell us that God purposely chose these men because He showed Himself strong through their weakness."

Rachel's compelling voice, her piercing eyes, the graceful gestures of her hands often captivated her audience, making them see and feel and hear the very story she was relating. She had a unique way of bringing the past to life, so that listeners held their breath, waiting for more. Ulrika told Rachel that she had a rare and special gift, and asked her if she ever told her fabulous tales to the people of the oasis.

"I had never thought to," Rachel replied, but Ulrika could see that Rachel liked the notion of sharing her sacred stories with others. "Perhaps," she said. "At the least, my stories entertain and keep away the fears of the night."

But Rachel did engage in one practice that Ulrika could not fathom, and which she was too polite to inquire about. Periodically, Rachel would leave the camp and take herself away from everything, to a secluded spot, and there she would sit, cover her face with her hands, and sway rhythmically while whispering softly.

At first, Ulrika had thought she was weeping—a widow who occasionally remembered her loss and went into seclusion to deal with her grief. But then she had noticed that Rachel always returned with a smile, her eyes dry and with no sign of having wept. Finally Ulrika asked, and Rachel replied, "It is my meditation. It is more powerful than prayer for it is focused. With such concentration, one can connect with God, the Divine."

The Divine . . .

Ulrika found herself desiring this woman's opinion and advice, and suspected she could confide in Rachel, so she set aside her broken sandal, the awl and leather laces, and said, "I have been told I have a spiritual gift called the Divining. Do you know of it?"

Rachel shook her head. "But in the history of my people there are many with spiritual gifts—prophets and visionaries."

After Ulrika explained about her personal quest, Rachel said, "Let me share with you my private meditation."

Ulrika listened with interest while Rachel described a technique of visualization, and also of repetition of a word or phrase. "It takes much practice, for the mind has a will of its own and is not easily commanded. This is why meditation is best conducted in a secluded setting. The rabbis tell us that when a person prays outdoors, the birds join in with the prayer and increase its effectiveness. So it must be also with meditation."

"Perhaps," she added after a moment of thought, "this meditation will help you understand your own connection to the Divine."

As Rachel seemed to have opened a personal door, Ulrika decided to ask another question that had stood at her lips ever since she first came here. "Rachel, what holds you to this place? Wouldn't you rather live in a town or a city? Come to Babylon with me."

"I still serve my husband."

"Even though he is dead?"

Rachel added with a smile, "He will come back someday."

"What do you mean?"

"Jacob and I will be reunited in the Resurrection." Seeing that Ulrika did not understand, Rachel said, "In the Book of Job it is written, 'Once more my skin shall clothe me, and in my flesh I will have sight of God.' Another prophet, named Daniel, said that those who lie sleeping in the dust of the earth shall wake, to enjoy life everlasting. And our Teacher, who was crucified by Rome, said that we shall rise again at the resurrection, when the Last Day comes."

Rachel added, "Because I trust you, Ulrika, and because of the circumstances of how we met, I am going to tell you what I have never told another soul. My husband is buried here and it is my task in life to protect his grave. This is why I stay."

Ulrika looked around, but saw no grave marker. "What do you mean, the circumstances of how we met?

"The place where Almah and I found you, on that spot where you hurt your ankle and called out for help, that is where my Jacob is buried."

Ulrika's eyes flew open. "I was lying upon a *grave*?"

"Eleven years ago, my husband's political enemies assassinated him and I knew that their persecution of him would not stop with his death, that they would not be satisfied until they had scattered his bones to the winds. And so I and a few loyal friends brought my Jacob's body down here and buried it in a secret place, with no marker, nothing to indicate that he rested there. My friends stayed with me, but over the years, one by one they left. This is why I do not live at the oasis, and why I cannot go to Babylon with you, for I must keep eternal vigil on Jacob's resting place, to protect it from his enemies."

Ulrika was stunned. *She* had not chosen the place but had been led there by the spirit of a wolf. And then she recalled the profound vision she had experienced on that place—the man with blinding light radiating from his head and hands.

17

Ulrika could not stop thinking about Rachel's focused meditation. If it connected a person to the Divine, then might it not also connect *her* to the Divining?

She chose a day when Rachel and Almah went to the oasis. With the aid of a walking staff, for her ankle was still tender, Ulrika walked down to the place where the two women had found her, injured and calling for help. She supposed she could have experimented with the meditation anywhere in this wilderness, but this was where she had experienced two intense visions. And a man was buried here. Perhaps this place possessed a special energy, and that was why the visions had been so startling.

Recalling the steps Rachel had outlined, Ulrika sat with her face into the wind as sunshine shimmered off the surface of the distant Sea of Salt. She crossed her legs, covered her face with her hands, and concentrated on slowing her respiration, controlling her lungs. When she was breathing deeply, in a measured rhythm , she chose an image upon which to center her thoughts. "Choose something that is personal," Rachel had advised. "Something simple and pure." And so Ulrika conjured up in her mind the inner flame which burns in every soul, and then she began a whispered chant. As the words came over and over, as her hands blocked out the world, Ulrika began to sway, for as Rachel said, "We put our entire bodies into prayer so that we pray even with our sinew and bones."

Ulrika watched the inner light, the glimmering soul flame, and sent her repeated prayer into the cosmos: "Compassionate All Mother, hear my plea. Compassionate All Mother, hear my plea." And gradually Ulrika began to feel a sweet peace steal over her, felt her worries and fears melt away. The image of the flame grew until she could feel its heat, and she trembled to think that the image of the radiant man, that had filled her with such joyous ecstasy, was about to materialize.

But instead, a wild countryside of rolling green hills and barren rocks coalesced in her mind's eye, trees twisted by constant winds filled her inner vision, and she saw the scallop-shell altar, the beautiful woman in flowing white robes.

It was Gaia, again, the distant ancestress of Sebastianus Gallus.

Ulrika formed a question in her mind and sent it forth. "Can you help me, Honored One?"

"You are arrogant, daughter," Gaia said. "You do not come to this sacred place with a humble heart, but rather seeking ecstasy and joy. And you are impatient and impulsive. Remember the recklessness in the Rhineland, when you left the caravan and endangered your companions."

"I am sorry for that," Ulrika said, surprised that she was being chastised, and then accepting that she deserved it. "But I wish to understand my gift. What is the Divining? What am I to do with it? And where is Shalamandar?"

"So many questions in your arrogance. You wish all things to come to you without any effort on your part. Overcome your flaws, daughter. Turn your weaknesses into strengths, and your spiritual power will grow."

"But how do I do that?"

"You must be taught, you must learn."

"But I have learned. I am doing everything right."

"You are not yet ready. You have not yet learned all you need to know."

"But from whom do I learn?" Ulrika cried silently. "It makes no sense, the student teaching herself!"

The Galician countryside shimmered and grew unfocused. Ulrika now saw palm trees and stars. Once again, she saw Sebastianus walking toward her. "Gaia!" she called out. "Please come back."

Now Ulrika found herself in the warm tavern in Antioch, and then it too grew distorted until she was back in the shaman's cave in the Rhineland.

I cannot control my visions . . .

She summoned the inner flame again, struggled with her respirations, attempted the repetitious chant once more, but the visions faded, the soul flame dimmed, and when Ulrika finally took her hands away from her face, she saw that the sun was near the western horizon, and that she was lying on her side in the sand.

She had fallen asleep!

Gaia was right, she thought in disappointment. I came here with an arrogant heart, thinking I had mastered my thoughts, thinking I had perfected Rachel's meditation. I still have no control. My gift is still in its infancy.

But as Ulrika lifted herself to her feet, steadying herself on the walking staff, she realized that although she had not made better progress in gaining answers, she was excited nonetheless about a new development: the vision of Gaia had not come to her unbidden. Ulrika had been the one to command a vision—*she* had chosen the time and the place.

It was the first step, she knew, toward controlling her gift. From now on, she was confident, her power would grow.

18

Ulrika's ankle healed over the course of the weeks she spent with the two women, and eventually the day came to say goodbye. A small wine caravan had rested at the oasis, and the owner was willing to take Ulrika as far as Petra in the south, which was located at a major trade crossroads and where she would find a caravan to take her eastward to Babylon.

Rachel and Almah accompanied her to the oasis, where Almah wept and embraced Ulrika as a daughter.

Then Ulrika turned to Rachel, her new friend whom she would never forget. "I have a gift for you," she said.

During one of her first nights in the camp, Ulrika had asked, "You have sacrificed so much. What do you miss the most?" And Rachel, after a moment, had replied, "Perfume."

Ulrika now opened her medicine kit and brought out a small glass vial stoppered with wax. An Egyptian hieroglyphic identified the precious contents. Pressing this into Rachel's hands, she said, "This is oil of lilies. It soothes the troubled heart."

In return, Rachel placed a talisman around Ulrika's neck, to join the scallop shell and Cross of Odin. It was small and carved from cedar, and hung at the end of a slender hemp thread. "It is called the *mogan david*," she said, "which means the Shield of David." Ulrika saw that the talisman was made of two triangles united around a central point, making it resemble a six-pointed star. "Between here and Babylon," Rachel said, "you will enter into Jewish communities, and when they see this star, they will take you in as one of their own."

"Tell your stories at the oasis, Rachel, as you told them to me."

"I will," Rachel said. And then she took Ulrika's hands into her own and said, "'For you shall go out with joy and be led out with peace; the mountains and the hills shall break forth into singing before you.'" She squeezed Ulrika's hand. "That is from the prophet Isaiah. Peace unto you, Ulrika. And God's blessings. I pray you find what you are searching for."

BOOK FIVE
BABYLON

19

THEY WERE SIX SISTERS in search of husbands, and they had come to Babylon to find them.

Ulrika was not sure the young women, ranging from thirteen years old to twenty-four, had been given accurate information, but they were hopeful and full of cheer, and had livened the journey from the oasis at Bir Abbas, where they had joined the flax caravan and told their remarkable tale. Their father, a widower, had had to sell his house, his sheep, and himself into slavery to cover gambling debts. And so he had been forced to send his daughters out into the world in the hope of finding a better life.

They rode on the back of a flat dray drawn by mules, seven young women, two grandmothers, and one elderly carpenter, swaying with the vehicle as they watched the towers and smoke fires of Babylon draw near. Ulrika had joined the caravan in the town of Petra, where a Babylonian flax trader had brought massive sacks of fibers, seed, and flowers to sell to makers of linens, medicines, and dyes. To fill his empty drays for the return trip, he took paying passengers who joined or left at various settlements and farms along the way. Now he was reaching the terminus of his biannual journey, and his passengers looked forward to food and lodgings and a steady ground beneath their feet.

Ulrika's excitement grew. After weeks of desert travel, camping at oases, walking, riding, constantly on the move, she felt the fresh breeze from the Euphrates River whisper against her face. The desert gradually gave over to lush green farms, dense groves of date palms, fields of wheat and barley. Marshes and ponds appeared now, from which lively waterfowl flew up in rainbows of color. Beyond, a ribbon of blue lazily wound its way between banks thick with poplars and tamarisks, to disappear under city walls—Babylon straddled the Euphrates—and emerge on the other side, bringing water to thirsty sheep and goats.

As Ulrika's small caravan neared the Adad Gate, a major entry in the western wall, through which heavy traffic was passing to and fro, she recited a silent prayer of thanks to the All Mother. She had come through the long trek unscathed, and now would soon be reunited with the man she loved—her love growing with every dawn as she held the handsome Sebastianus in her heart and mind, picturing his bronze-colored hair in the sunshine, hearing his deep authoritative voice, seeing his dimpled smile. Although many in Ulrika's group would leave the caravan here and enter the city on foot, Ulrika would stay on the road and follow it to the southern tip of the walled city, where she had been told the caravans to the East were launched. She knew she would find Sebastianus there.

Whenever the leaders of caravans met along the many trade routes of the Roman empire, they exchanged gossip as well as goods. And during their last camp, at an oasis called Bir Abbas, the flax merchant had shared his fire with a wine trader traveling west, and from him had heard of a great caravan being prepared for a diplomatic trip to China, a Spaniard traveling under the auspices of the Roman emperor himself.

Ulrika knew it was Sebastianus of whom they had spoken, and she knew he was still in Babylon because the summer solstice had yet to be marked, and he had said he would leave after that.

The flax caravan wound its way through congested settlements of people who had come to the city to find work. Ulrika had heard of the power and might of Marduk, called by his followers as the most powerful deity in the universe. I will consult with his priests, she thought now. Perhaps Marduk can tell me where to find Shalamandar.

The flax trader brought his line of animals and wagons to a slow crawl, and those with whom Ulrika shared the dray gathered their bundles and prepared to head into the city on foot. Ulrika said farewell to the six sisters, wishing them luck.

As the dray neared the road that led past the Adad Gate—a massive archway in the city walls with guards in towers and colorful pennants snapping in the wind—they heard the sudden garish blare of trumpets. In the next moment, riders on horseback came galloping through the gate, hooves thundering across the moat bridge. The riders were shouting, "Make way! Make way! Fall on your faces in honor of the Divine God Marduk!"

The flax trader brought his dray to a halt, as all other traffic and pedestrians came to a stop on the highway and surrounding lanes. The thunder of drums came next and Ulrika watched as, immediately behind the horses, drummers marched, banging their instruments in unison, creating a formidable sound.

"What is it?" she asked of the flax merchant.

"They are parading the Great God," he said. "They say that getting a glimpse of Marduk brings luck. Keep your eye open."

As she waited for the procession to pass, Ulrika turned her face to the east, toward the feathery palms and blue sky that embraced the caravan staging area.

Tonight, she thought with racing pulse, I will be with Sebastianus . . .

"MY FRIEND, IT HAS been a pleasure doing business with you. I promise you, my fine wines will open doors and gateways to you, they will make men want to give you their virgin daughters. I say in all modesty that my grapes are the envy of Marduk himself!"

Sebastianus smiled at the loquacious Babylonian as he conducted a final check of his animals and their packs. Recently added to his caravan was wine stored in silver jars, the way the Phoenicians had done for centuries, as the silver prevented spoilage. And mules were draped with bags of fresh milk strapped to their sides. Fermentation would take place in the bags, causing the milk to curdle. The constant motion of the animals would then break up the resulting cheese into curds while the remaining liquid, the whey, would provide a potable drink in case no water was found.

Sebastianus's caravan was nearly ready to depart. All he had to do was wait until after the solstice celebrations.

At which time, he prayed, Ulrika would appear and he could persuade her to join him for the journey eastward.

Was it a foolish prayer, he wondered? Surely Syphax had delivered her safely to her mother in Jerusalem, where Ulrika would have learned the location of Shalamandar. And now she would be on her way to join him. Perhaps she was nearby already, and the same wind that blew gently on Sebastianus's face caressed Ulrika's.

"I thank you for your help, Jerash," he said, seizing the Babylonian's wrist and giving it a manly squeeze. Jerash, garbed in a colorful fringed robe with a cone-shaped hat on his head, was the cousin of a man whom Sebastianus had befriended in Antioch, and now Jerash had given him the names of relatives who lived in settlements eastward along the trade route. "You have but to mention my name, noble Gallus," the Babylonian said as he reached into a deep, embroidered pocket and brought out clay tablets, "and give these letters of introduction to my uncles and cousins, and they will offer you all the help you need! Your mission to China will be like riding on a breeze, my friend! The gods will carry you on their shoulders and you will fly like a dove!"

Nearby, sitting at the campsite with his pie-faced son Nestor, who was stirring a stew of lamb and vegetables, Timonides watched the exchange between Sebastianus and the Babylonian with a jaundiced eye. He alone knew that Sebastianus's caravan to China was going to be no dove's flight because it lay upon a route plagued by pitfalls, traps, treachery, and setbacks. Not that any of this was apparent to ordinary men, or could be seen with the naked eye. Only Timonides knew of the great dangers that lay ahead, because only he had read his master's stars and had seen the calamities that awaited him.

And it was all the fault of Timonides the astrologer! He could not stop falsifying his horoscopes, but must keep lying, must keep Sebastianus moving eastward in order to save Nestor from certain execution. The hue and cry from Antioch had not yet reached Babylon, but the royal mail routes along the Euphrates River were swift and efficient. A word from one magistrate to another, and the guards of the city would be knocking upon every door, looking under every rug, overturning every man-sized jar in search of the assassin of the beloved Bessas the holy man.

It made Timonides almost too sick to eat.

The stars did not lie. Sebastianus was supposed to be, at that moment, somewhere south of Antioch, perhaps as far south as Petra. Anywhere but here! Yet Timonides, interpreter of the will of the gods, urged his master ever eastward, uttering blasphemy upon blasphemy, at the sacrifice of his own immortal soul. For surely he was going to Hell for his sacrilege. Worse, by bringing Nestor along on his caravan he made Sebastianus an unwitting participant in a capital crime. Sebastianus was giving aid to a fugitive, which meant certain execution for him as well, should they be caught.

If only they would leave! Timonides had gently suggested that they start for the East today, this minute, not waste a precious moment, but Sebastianus, he knew, was thinking of that girl! Ulrika. She was like an insidious disease, itching just below Sebastianus's skin. Timonides saw how his master looked westward every evening, pausing in his work to gaze wistfully over the miles and horizon, picturing the fair-haired girl who had bewitched him. Timonides had been tempted to falsify a horoscope and insist they leave, but it would just be one sin too many. Wherever he could be honest, he would be so. Besides, why put his master to the test? What if he told Sebastianus that the gods insist they leave at once, and Sebastianus, waiting for Ulrika, said no?

To make matters worse, Sebastianus was considering altering the first leg of their journey to accommodate that girl. He had asked around for information on the whereabouts of Shalamandar, but no one had heard of it. She had said the place was in Persia, and so Sebastianus had declared his intention of going north at first, to accompany her to her own destination before getting on to the business of China!

With a sigh, and thinking that the philosophers were right when they said it was impossible to love and be wise, Timonides returned to his charts and instruments for the noon horoscope, and as he re-calculated his master's stars, taking into account the comet that had appeared in Sebastianus's moon-house, and the unexpected falling star that had streaked past Mars—

Timonides froze, and his breakfast of eggplant and garlic rose to the back of his throat.

Not again . . .

He wanted to cry out against the injustice of life. Destined forever to read the stars for other people, Timonides the astrologer, who had been abandoned on a trash heap as an infant, had hoped that someday the gods would reveal to their humble servant the stars of his own birth. To this end Timonides had tried to keep his astrological practice pure.

But the gods were perverse. They toyed with him, tormented him. Gave him glimmers of hope only to dash them.

The girl was in Babylon.

There was no doubt about it. Sebastianus's horoscope had changed. The two lovers were about to cross paths again.

And so once more, despite oaths to the contrary, Timonides must falsify another reading. He could not allow Ulrika to join the caravan. Nestor had behaved himself during the journey from Antioch and during their stay in Babylon. But with Ulrika in his company once again, the boy would certainly commit another crime to please her.

Even if it meant sending his own immortal soul to Hell, Timonides had to protect his son.

"Master," he called, rising from his table. "I have found her at last. The stars have revealed Ulrika's location."

Sebastianus turned such a hopeful smile to him that Timonides feared the eggplant was going to come all the way up. Swallowing back his bile, he said, "She is in Jerusalem. She is with her mother and family."

The smile turned to a frown. "Are you sure?"

"The stars do not lie, master. Even if the girl were to leave Jerusalem today, she would not reach Babylon for weeks. But master, a journey does not lie in her future. She is *staying* in Jerusalem."

It pierced the old man's heart to see such disappointment on Sebastianus's face. He loved young Gallus almost as much as he loved Nestor. Cursing his life, cursing the parents who had abandoned him on a trash heap, cursing Babylon and the gods and even the stars, Timonides said, "There is something else. The comet last night, and the falling star against Mars, indicate that we must leave at once. We cannot stay another day in this city. It is crucial, master."

"But the Summer Solstice is days away!"

"Master, the worst calamity will befall this caravan if we delay. *Today* is the most propitious day for departure. The gods have made themselves clear."

With a scowl, Sebastianus weighed his decision.

He had spent his time in Babylon collecting as much information as he could about China. Precious little was to be had. Goods from that distant land never came directly to this part of the world, but passed through a series of middlemen. A bolt of Chinese silk might cross the hands of twenty traders before it reached the Babylonian market. It was the same with information. Place names, in particular, did not travel well, and so each man he spoke to, every map he consulted, had different names for cities and geographical features.

One, however, seemed more consistent. The city where China's emperor was throned. Sebastianus had a name at last, an identifiable goal to set before himself each dawn and sunset, keeping it in his mind like a fixed star.

"Very well," he said reluctantly. "Where is Primo? Timonides, send someone into the city to find him."

"Yes yes, master," Timonides said with relief. Later, in the next city or valley or mountain, when they were far enough away from the threat of Ulrika's presence, he would make sacrifice to as many gods as he could, offer penance and self-denial, dedicate himself to fasting and celibacy if he must—Timonides would do everything in his power to get himself back into the good graces of the Divine.

"Make certain Primo comes back at once," Sebastianus said, and then he turned and strode into his tent, his mind already composing the letter he was going to write to Ulrika and leave in the care of the Caravan Master.

Across the river in the Western City, in the shadow of the Temple of Shamash, Primo the retired legionary, Chief Steward of the Gallus villa in Rome but now second in command of his master's caravan to China, lay back as a whore massaged his thick penis. His thoughts were not upon the woman and her carnal ministrations but upon the long journey he and his specially trained men were about to take. And he mentally reviewed the things he was to see to that day: provisions, weapons, the duties roster.

The prostitute straddled him without a word. Those were always his instructions: "Don't speak." Primo could only enjoy a woman if she was nameless—and even then it wasn't really enjoyment, more of a need.

Letting the prostitute do all the work, the veteran of military campaigns and a hard life decided that his crack archer, a Bithynian named Zipoites, would be best for gathering intelligence along the journey—he was solidly built enough to look fat under merchant's robes, no one would suspect his strength or that he was a trained fighter. Yes, Zipoites would be the one to send ahead to settlements along the road, to visit taverns and talk with the local men. Zipoites could hold his wine where other men's tongues loosened. He was adept at getting information out of—

"Ungh." Primo gave a cry as he climaxed, and then he lay motionless for a few moments while the whore wordlessly removed herself from the bed and slipped into a robe to cover her nakedness. Outside, the city of Babylon bustled beneath its usual din as citizens hurried to and fro in the narrow streets, their minds concentrated upon their own immediate worries, fears, hopes, and yearnings. They were preparing for the coming week of summer solstice celebrations, which also meant they were preparing for a season of heat and dust. Many were unemployed, and so their thoughts were on food and the gods.

But Primo didn't care about this city or its people. His job was to see that his master, Sebastianus Gallus, reached China safely and that their diplomatic missions to the East were a success.

And there was the *secret* job, commanded by Nero Caesar himself . . .

As he slipped back into his clothes—the old soldier's costume of white tunic, leather breastplate, military sandals laced to the knee—Primo spat on the floor. He wished he had not been recruited into Nero's spy-ring. He would obey, of course. His loyalty might be to his employer and the man who had saved him from a life of begging in the streets, but a greater duty compelled him, as a soldier, to uphold his allegiance to Emperor and Empire. Even if it meant betraying the man he loved.

As he left, he reached into the leather pouch at his waist in which he carried money and his lucky talisman—a bronze arrowhead that had been dug out of his chest by a military surgeon who had declared Primo the luckiest man on earth, as the German arrow had missed his heart by a breath. Primo pulled out a coin and threw it down. It had a Caesar on it, so the whore knew it was good. Primo didn't look at her face. They never looked at his.

As Primo walked along the Street of Harlots, he realized that, more and more of late, he was coming away from his paid women with diminished feelings of satisfaction. Physically, they satisfied him. Primo had no difficulty getting erect or coming to orgasm. But, increasingly, he was leaving whorehouses with little gratification.

And he found himself thinking of a woman he had met long ago, the one woman in his life to whom he had given his heart.

Primo and his regiment had been passing through yet another small, nameless village when his Centurion had sent him ahead to find the local blacksmith. It was spring, Primo recalled, with a blue sky dotted with white puff clouds, the scent of blossoms in the air, the breezes fresh and full of promise. His boots had stamped over cobblestones as he had entered a narrow alley and found himself suddenly surrounded by a group of angry men. They carried clubs and daggers, and seemed intent upon using them.

Hatred of Roman soldiers was universal throughout the empire, especially in newly conquered regions, and so Primo knew the anger in these men was fresh and sharp. They would mindlessly attack and only ponder the foolishness of their actions later, as they were nailed to crosses. It had briefly entered his mind to try to warn them off—for surely they meant to kill him, and he was greatly outnumbered—when a young woman appeared. "Wait," she called, and the villagers stopped advancing upon the lone soldier.

She drew near, and Primo saw that she carried an infant close to her breast. Her head was veiled, but an exquisite face was exposed to the spring sunshine.

One man growled, "This is none of your concern, daughter of Zebediah. This is men's business."

"And is it men's business to make widows of their wives and orphans of their children? Shame on you."

"Rome is evil!" shouted another. And they began to press forward again.

But she placed herself in front of Primo, so that he caught a sweet fragrance from her veiled hair, and she said, "This soldier is not Rome. He is but a man. Return to your homes before it is too late for all of us."

They shifted on their feet. They fingered their clubs. They looked at one another and then at the infant sleeping in her arms until finally they turned and drifted away.

The young woman faced Primo and said, "The fault is not yours, Roman. You are only doing your job. Go in peace."

And Primo, the soldier whose heart was the size and hardness of a pebble, fell in love.

He watched her walk away, a slim figure draped in a long blue veil, as if she had descended from the sky, and he stood frozen in that moment of time, as if the world had come to a standstill and he and the young mother were all who inhabited it. She had not smiled at him, but she had not looked upon him with revulsion either, though he was indeed ugly. She had simply looked at him—he had seen lovely features, heard a gentle voice—

Even now, simply from the memory of it, Primo was rocked with intense emotion. She had intervened on his behalf. Although she had done it to spare her neighbors from Rome's wrath and the punishment of those who did not obey their new masters, she had looked at him with clear brown eyes and told him it was not his fault. And in that moment he had fallen in love, irrevocably and without condition. He had also known in that moment that he would love her for as long as he lived, and that he would never, for the rest of his life, love another woman as he loved that young mother.

A powerful stink suddenly washed over him, bringing him out of his nostalgic reverie. He wrinkled his nose and turned in the direction the stench was coming from. Rotting corpses hanging on the city walls. Most had their hands cut off, or their genitals, indicators of their crimes: thieves and rapists. Justice in Babylon was swift. A thief suffered having his hand cut off, and then he was strung up by his ankles and left to die. Sometimes it took days. To Primo, it seemed an extreme punishment. Most likely the thief had stolen from a rich man, because who cared if someone stole from a poor man?

Such was justice in the world in general. It was a rich man's world, no doubt of that.

And an emperor's.

"You are to watch Gallus's movements," young Nero had said that night in the room at the back of the imperial audience chamber. "You are to commit to memory his words, observe how he presents himself and Rome to foreign potentates. We cannot have an ambassador who puts his own interests first. You will report to me any actions or words that might be considered seditious or treasonous."

Thinking of it made Primo scowl on this smoke-filled morning, making his face appear even uglier than it normally was. He would do the job, but he wouldn't like it.

"Sir!" came a shout from the end of the lane. Primo recognized a slave from the caravan. The man was breathless from running. "I was sent to fetch you at once. The caravan departs today."

Primo looked at him in surprise. And then, thinking it was about time, broke into a sprint and headed toward the Enlil Gate.

❧

WHILE SEBASTIANUS WENT UP and down the line, checking camels and horses, giving last-minute instructions, patting men on the back and telling them a great adventure lay ahead of them, Timonides paid a secret, hasty visit to the Caravan Master, whom Sebastianus had visited moments earlier. Timonides knew Sebastianus had given the man a letter for Ulrika. Timonides could not help that. But he also knew that Sebastianus had given the Caravan Master a verbal message to give to a fair-haired girl should she come inquiring about the Gallus caravan. "Tell her we departed on the day before the Summer Solstice. Tell her we will wait at Basra until the next full moon. From there, we take the old northern route to Samarkand." He had given the man a silver coin for his trouble.

Now Timonides gave the man a new message, and slipped him a *gold* coin to help his memory. The astrologer returned to the caravan in time to mount his donkey and wave readiness to Sebastianus who sat high atop his horse.

And then Sebastianus, looking back toward the west one last time, to picture fair hair that framed blue eyes and to whisper a prayer for Ulrika's safekeeping, turned in his saddle and faced ahead, toward the east, where mountains and rivers and deserts awaited him.

And a fabled city called Luoyang.

THE MARDUK PROCESSION SEEMED to go on for miles, and Ulrika grew so impatient that she was tempted to abandon the dray and hurry to the caravan area on foot. But no one dared move while the supreme god of Babylon was making an appearance in public, and so she had to wait.

Finally, the last of the drummers and priests and mounted soldiers had passed by, and the flax merchant whipped his donkeys into forward progress. At the caravan staging area, which was vast and crowded with men and beasts, tents and enormous piles of merchandise, Ulrika went straight to the tent of the Caravan Master, who could point her in the right direction.

He wrinkled his bulbous nose. "Eh? The Gallus caravan? They left over a month ago. Long gone, by now." Gallus had given him a silver coin to tell the girl the truth. But the Greek had given him a gold coin to say they had departed a month ago. For this amount of money, the man would have happily made it a year! "And this is for you," he added, handing Ulrika a small scroll.

She quickly opened it and saw that it was a letter from Sebastianus, written in Latin. "My dearest Ulrika, the stars have decreed that we must depart early. It is with a heavy heart that I leave, for I had hoped to have you at my side on this journey into the fabulous unknown. But I go also with joy, knowing that I will soon fulfill my life's dream to visit distant China. I carry you in my heart, Ulrika. You will be in my thoughts and in my dreams. And when I stand before the throne of the emperor of China, you will be at my side. I pray, my dearest, that you receive this letter, and that you will wait for me in Babylon. I love you."

"Do you know which route the caravan took?" she asked, her eyes filling with tears.

The man frowned. Gallus had left explicit instructions, but surely the gold coin warranted a false rendering of that information as well. So he said, "They were to board ships at the Gulf. They'll be far away at sea by now."

Crushed with disappointment, Ulrika thanked the man and turned away, toward the towering gates of Babylon, turning her back on the eastern horizon where still could be seen, in the dying light of day, dust rising up from the hooves and wheels and feet of the great caravan that had just departed for China.

20

Ulrika had discovered that Babylon, being at the crossroads between east and west, was a cosmopolitan city, tolerant of all faiths. Here, any foreigner to the city would find the god or goddess of his choice. Greek visitors found shrines to Aphrodite, Zeus, and Diana. Romans, when not at war with Persia, were welcome in temples devoted to Jupiter and Venus. Phoenicians could offer sacrifice to Baal, Egyptians to Isis and Osiris, Persians to Mithras. And of course, Babylon's own gods, Marduk and Ishtar, resided here in the most magnificent temples.

Ulrika had visited them all, speaking with priests and oracles and wise-women, seeking to further her inner self-discipline. She engaged in focused meditation every evening, and while she had enjoyed some success in conjuring up visions at will, they did not last long. She grew sleepy, or her mind wandered, and she lost concentration. While the various temples and priests offered different forms of prayer, none could set her on the path toward deeper meditation.

She had also searched for clues as to where she could find the Crystal Pools of Shalamandar, with no success.

But the whole while she had been in this great city on the Euphrates, Ulrika's heart had been with Sebastianus, who she prayed was making steady progress toward China.

She read his letter every night, and had developed the ritual of speaking to him before falling asleep, picturing his handsome face, his smile, sensing his strength and power, recalling the feel of his hands on her arms that last night in Antioch as he had declared his love for her. Ulrika would lie on her pallet as the city of Babylon stirred in restless slumber and whisper to Sebastianus in the darkness, telling him of her day, what she had achieved, assuring him that he was in her thoughts and heart from morning until night, hoping that Mercury, messenger of the gods and patron god of merchants and traders, would carry her words to her beloved.

Ulrika turned toward Enlil Street, where she rented a small room from a widow named Nanna who supported herself and her five children by painting Ishtar-eggs. Nanna had great skill and a delicate touch, whether carving designs into clay eggs, or painting birds' eggs from which yolks and whites had been removed. Such eggs were popular as gifts to family and friends, and also a favorite temple offering in Babylon. In exchange for room and board, Ulrika helped Nanna take care of her five little ones. She also shared her healing knowledge with the neighbors in that quarter—prescribing elixirs and tonics, lancing boils, delivering babies—all the things her mother had taught her back in Rome.

But Ulrika always took time to visit the caravan terminus at the south of the city, to inquire among traders returning from the East for any news on Sebastianus. The last report on the imperial diplomatic caravan to China had been six months ago, when a merchant of Bactrian camels had told Ulrika that he had heard of the Gallus expedition making a safe and successful passage through the treacherous passes of Samarkand. Ulrika had heard no word of Sebastianus since.

She stood now in the sunlight of the marketplace as people bustled around her, ignoring the young woman in plain homespun with a veil covering her hair. The only feature to distinguish Ulrika from other young women in Babylon was a wooden box hanging from her shoulder on a leather strap, symbols in Egyptian hieroglyphs and Babylonian cuneiform identifying it as a medicine kit.

Thinking of the money she had just been paid for draining an abscess, and what she might purchase with it, Ulrika stopped suddenly and stared. In front of a vendor selling onions, leeks, and lentils, on the dusty ground before the display tables, a big brown hound sat on shaggy haunches.

Ulrika did not know why she had stopped, or why the creature had caught her interest. He was an unremarkable dog, and the market square was crowded with animals—pens of geese and chickens for sale, crates of ducks and doves, roosts where exotic parrots and hawks sat tethered. Pigs and goats oinked and bleated in straw-packed pens, cats and dogs—for food and temple sacrifice—paced in small cages. There were even snakes dancing as charmers played their flutes, and scorpions hanging from the faces of mystics, to the amazement of onlookers.

Yet Ulrika could not take her eyes off an ordinary dog.

And then she realized that it was, of course, not a dog but a wolf.

She had not experienced the wolf vision again since the night in the Judean wilderness when it had led her to a secret grave. She stared at it now in wonder and curiosity. And then something occurred to her. Keeping her eyes on the vision, she slowed her breathing, removed all thoughts from her mind except for the wolf, and focused on him with renewed intensity. "Lead me to where I must go," she whispered. "Show me the way."

The handsome creature turned and loped away, through a crowd that was unaware of a spirit-wolf passing in their midst. It led Ulrika under a stone archway, and she found herself in a small square bordered on all sides by residences with wooden doorways and shuttered windows. In the center of the square, a small knot of people watched a man in their midst. Such sights were common in Babylon, as street entertainers were common—magicians, storytellers, even seers and necromancers.

But the man in the midst of this quiet crowd was different from the usual street hawkers, who always wore colorful costumes to catch people's eye. This man's attire was subdued, modest. Ulrika recognized the long curls framing his face, the white, fringed shawl with blue stripes, and the leather straps around his arms and across his forehead as the trappings of a devout Jew. And the people gathered around him were unusually subdued. Instead of being rowdy and pushy, this gathering was small and quiet and consisted of, Ulrika saw, mostly women and slaves. A few men stood on the edge, arms folded, skeptical expressions on their faces.

When she saw that many in the audience suffered from injuries and disease, it occurred to her that this man worked healing miracles. Babylon was full of such healers.

She focused her attention on the Jewish wonder-worker, who stood with a woman and held up his hands as he softly chanted. To Ulrika's surprise, the woman was chanting as well. And then she realized: they were praying together.

As everyone watched in silence, listening to the soft murmur of two voices, Ulrika studied those around her, saw the looks of hope and anticipation on their faces, and wondered what they expected to see happen here today. "Pardon me," she whispered to a woman standing next to her. "Who is that man?" Ulrika asked.

"That is Rabbi Judah," the woman said. "He has come recently from Palmyra. They say he is a worker of wonders."

Ulrika returned her attention to the two standing in the center of the silent crowd, and saw that the praying woman had begun to sob. Covering her face with her hands, she bent her head and wept. The Jewish wonder-worker laid a hand on her shoulder and said, "Do you understand now, sister?"

The woman nodded, too overcome to speak.

The small crowd began to shift and murmur. It was someone else's turn. Yet there was no pushing and shoving, no calling out or holding up coins. Ulrika wondered if they had been told ahead of time to be respectful of Judah, or if it was something they instinctively sensed.

The woman left—trying to give Judah coins, which he refused—and now the small gathering grew tense as each hoped the Jewish wonder-worker would choose her or him next. To their disappointment, however, the middle-aged Jew cleared his throat and said in a sonorous voice, "Brothers and sisters, mercy unto you and peace, and charity fulfilled. Remember this: nothing is lost, nothing is hidden. Ask, and it will be given. Seek, and it will be found. There is redemption in forgiveness, as a man should be remembered for his good deeds and not for his sins. But know this above all: there is no death, there is only eternal life as long you keep yourselves in the love of God. And draw comfort, too, in the knowledge that God has a divine plan, the final goal of which is the highest good for humankind. We have only to obey his sacred Law and we will be redeemed."

The gathering broke up peacefully. Ulrika did not understand what had just taken place. There had been no dramatic demonstration of magic, no explosive powders, no transformation of water into wine, no spontaneous healing of blindness and paralysis, and certainly none of the attendant noise and cheering from the mob that one saw in other market squares with other wonder-workers.

She wondered why her wolf vision had led her here.

But in the next instant, the rabbi turned and looked right at her and Ulrika felt something fly across the small, sunlit square, brush against her eyes like invisible wings, and soar down through her body to the center of her soul. She gasped. She could not move.

Judah came toward her. He walked with a limp. He smelled of bread and onions, and Ulrika saw close-up, in the prodigious gray beard that fanned across his broad chest, a pistachio shell.

"Blessings, daughter," he said in Aramaic. "What is it you seek?"

Ulrika looked at the others drifting away from the small square, and wondered why he had singled her out. "Are you a mystic, honorable father?" she asked.

He smiled. "I am an unworthy servant of God, glory and majesty to Him."

She looked in the direction the weeping woman had gone, under a stone archway flanked by two Ishtar-egg vendors who were, at that moment, snoozing in the sun.

"That dear sister had lost something, and now she knows where to find it," Judah said, anticipating Ulrika's question. "But you seek something yourself, daughter. Can I help?"

Ulrika scanned the leathery face for signs of deceit. But Judah's eyes were open and honest, his middle-aged features clear of the slightest shadow of guile. And he had not asked for money, something all charlatans did before offering a service. It occurred to Ulrika that he might be a genuinely honest man—he made her think of Sebastianus—and so she said, "I am learning to meditate. But I cannot seem to concentrate. It is a form of prayer, I was told, and so I thought . . ."

He nodded. "Come, break bread with us."

Ulrika had expected to be in the company of a small family, a private affair, but the house of Rabbi Judah was open to all. The courtyard was crowded with people of all ages and social status. And the gathering was lively and full of joy, with singing and testimonials and spiritual revelations. Judah asked for silence and he preached to the excited company, a message centering upon the End of Days and a new age approaching, which he called "the kingdom."

The crowd burst into praise and singing while Judah moved among them, blessing them and thanking them for coming. When he reached Ulrika, he gave her a long, searching look and said, "Why do you wish to learn meditation?"

"Honorable Rabbi," she said, "I have been visited by visions all my life. They are inexplicable, they come randomly and seem to have no purpose. I seek a way to command them, and to learn how to put them to good use."

Judah said, "Many of our faithful are blessed with visions and spiritual phenomena. Some are even touched by the Spirit and then speak in tongues. Come, you will want to confer with Miriam."

Judah led her inside the house, which was quieter and with fewer people. A middle-aged woman dressed all in brown with a brown veil covering her hair sat upon a chair with several people seated on the floor at her feet. She was plump and reminded Ulrika of a rosy-faced partridge.

Judah said, "My wife Miriam is like Deborah of old, a judge who was also a prophetess. Like Deborah, Miriam is not one who foretells the future but who hears a message from God and passes it on to others."

When Judah introduced the young woman to his wife, Miriam reached for Ulrika's hands and said, "Do not be troubled, daughter, for you are blessed. God has given you a gift."

"But I do not know how to use it." Ulrika replied. "I have been practicing focused meditation, but I cannot concentrate long enough. I fall asleep, or my mind wanders. What else must I do?"

Taking Ulrika's hands, she looked deep into her eyes and said, "Do you fast before you meditate?"

"Fast? No."

Miriam said, "Fasting cleanses the body of the impurities that impede clarity of prayer. Fasting also keeps one awake. Hunger sharpens the senses, your mind will not wander. Do this, and you will be successful."

"Thank you, Honored Mother."

"I hear doubt in your voice. Let me tell you this, daughter: imagine your gift as a house filled with wonderful treasure. You do not know the way inside, but as you circle the house, you catch glimpses through windows, and you see fabulous things. Is this how it is with your spiritual gift?"

"Yes," Ulrika whispered.

"You need to find the door, daughter, and the key to its lock. Once you are inside, the treasure is yours."

"Key!" Ulrika said, recalling what the Egyptian seer had told her in the Street of Fortune Tellers. "Is meditation this key?

"I do not know," Miriam said. "But you are searching for a place, are you not, for the beginnings of your soul? You must find this place for it is essential to the spiritual path. I sense that you have strayed and must start again."

"That is what I have been told. Do you know where Shalamandar is?"

"I know nothing of Shalamandar, but there is one who does. He will take you there."

"Who is it?" Ulrika asked in rising excitement.

Miriam closed her eyes and, swaying in her chair, murmured words that Ulrika did not understand—it did not even sound like a human language but a kind of gibberish. When she stopped, the rabbi's wife opened her eyes and said, "You must go to Persia and save a prince and his people."

"A prince!" Ulrika frowned. "But how can I save a prince?"

"If you do not, his bloodline will end. His people will be no more."

"Is it this prince who will take me to Shalamandar? Will he give me a key? Can you tell me his name?"

"All answers lie in Persia. Go in peace, daughter."

BOOK SIX
PERSIA

21

HE STOOD BEHIND THE cover of trees as he watched the tavern, the patrons coming and going with lanterns glowing against the forest night.

He had followed her to this place, from the last village, tracking her along the mountain trail as cautiously as he would a deer. She had not known she was being followed—a young woman with fair hair and a confident stride. Her cloak covered her from head to foot, creating a tall, slim figure, with travel packs hung securely over her shoulders and on her back. She appeared to be strong, but as far as he could see, she carried no weapon. And she traveled alone, which was unusual, but which was going to make it easy for him to snatch her.

As soon as she emerged from the tavern, one swift move and she was his.

"I BELIEVE I CAN help you, sir," Ulrika said.

"No one can help me!" the man cried. "A thousand devils plague my head! They spin the world about me in a fiendish game. I cannot sleep. I am at my sanity's end. I wish only for death!"

"Good sir," Ulrika said calmly, in a soothing tone as the other patrons in the wooden shack, where travelers and local people gathered against the cold night, looked on in interest. "I have seen this disorder before, and I have skill in treating it. If you would but allow me to touch you."

The poor man had been complaining loudly when she had entered the small establishment and had taken a stool by the fire. A paunchy Persian with a stringy beard and shadows under his eyes, he had lamented to his companions about the affliction that kept him from working his small farm, that made it almost impossible for him to walk even, until Ulrika had risen from her stool and approached him, offering to help.

This was how she had journeyed for the past fourteen months—going from settlement to settlement, earning her keep with her healing skills, staying always on the move, never in one place for more than a day or a night, keeping to herself, not even telling people her name, her mind focused on but one goal—to find the prince who needed her help.

When Miriam the rabbi's wife had told her there was a stranger in Persia whom she was to rescue, Ulrika had believed her. After all, Miriam enjoyed a reputation for being a prophetess. But also, Ulrika had been born in Persia. This journey to aid a prince was meant to be.

But there was another reason Ulrika had decided to undertake the mission to find the prince. Long ago, when she and her mother had journeyed through this ancient land, when Ulrika was not more than three or four years old, they had encountered a very striking-looking man seated on a magnificent throne and dressed in splendid robes. A tall round hat crowned his head, beneath which thick curls cascaded to his shoulders. His beard was prodigious, covering his chest to his waist, and coiled in tight ringlets. He held a staff in one hand and, curiously, a flower in the other. In front of him, a golden censer burned incense.

Ulrika could not recall how long she and her mother had visited the nobleman, if they had dined with him, or slept in his house. She did not remember his name. But his appearance had struck her as so magnificent that she remembered him in detail. Was *he* the prince Miriam had spoken of? It seemed likely that this could be so. And perhaps he lived near the Crystal Pools of Shalamandar. Finding the man, Ulrika had decided, would surely be a simple task: all she needed to do was re-trace the route she and her mother had followed out of Persia eighteen years ago and she would cross his path.

But the task had turned out to be not so simple after all. She had been following that route for over a year now, she was nearing the end, in fact, and was no closer to knowing the identity of that magnificent man, or where he could be found.

Ulrika asked the farmer to lie down on a long table, while everyone gathered around and watched, men and women in woolen mountain garb, bearing the distinctive features of a race that had sprung from ancient Parthian blood mingled with that of invading Greeks. A handsome race, Ulrika thought.

She paused to look at a niche in the far wall, where a solitary lamp flickered. She had seen many such niches since entering this mountain territory called the Place of Silent Pines. They were shrines to local deities called *daevi,* which meant "celestial" or "bright"—holy and beneficent divinities who had been worshipped in this region for thousands of years. Ulrika thought of the statues of gods and goddesses around Rome, and the massive Marduk effigies dominating the streets of Babylon. She thought of the oak trees in Germania, carved in the likeness of Odin, and Rachel's god near the sea of salt, who had no likeness at all. And now here in this remote mountain region, gods who were represented by solitary flames kept burning eternally.

Deities, Ulrika realized, were as diverse and various as the people who worshipped them.

Positioning herself at the head of the table, she said to the farmer, "Please look up at the ceiling." She spoke Greek, a language of these people—another legacy of Alexander's conquering ways.

"It spins," the man moaned.

"Just a moment more, please. Say a prayer, it will help."

He did so, muttering his god's name three times in clusters of three, while he traced signs in the air three times each with one hand and clutched what appeared to be a rabbit's foot in the other. Ulrika had learned that although people's religions might vary around the world, and even be at odds, one human trait remained universal: superstition. Whether they were warriors in Germania, citizens in Rome, sailors in Antioch, tent dwellers in Judea, onion sellers in Babylon, or mountain folk in Persia, all believed in good luck and bad luck, and the many ways to invite the first and fend off the latter.

Everyone in the tavern watched in silence as Ulrika placed her hands on either side of the man's head and then, gently, rolled his head from side to side, bringing his face to look upward again. "Quickly now," she said. "Sit up!"

He sat bolt upright on the table with eyes wide, jaw slack. The onlookers held their breath in anticipation. And when he cried, "Breasts of Ishtar! The dizziness is gone!" they threw up their arms and cheered.

Ulrika was secretly relieved, as some forms of dizziness could not be cured by this treatment. But this was a simple therapy for an affliction that sometimes drove men to suicide, and she was glad she could help.

"Dear lady!" the Persian farmer cried, falling to his knees on the earthen floor. "I am forever in your debt! I had become so desperate I was going to search for the Magus and beg him to put me out of my misery."

Ulrika helped the man to his feet. "The Magus?"

The Persian blinked owlishly. "You do not know of the Magus? But everyone in this territory knows of him! He lives in the City of Ghosts, in a high tower, a man of royal blood who is the last of his kind. He is said to work healing miracles, if he can be found. Dear lady, how can I pay you for saving me from certain suicide?"

Before Ulrika could reply—*a man of royal blood, the last of his kind*—the Persian shouted, "Wait wait!" Reaching around his neck, he pulled a cord over his head and held the offering to Ulrika. "This is a claw from a sacred gryphon, an ancient beast whose spirit will protect you from harm."

Ulrika accepted the talisman—a leather thong at the end of which was suspended what looked like a raven's talon. She would place it in her medicine kit with other amulets and charms she had received from grateful patients. "You are very kind," she said. "But I need a place to stay tonight so if you could direct me—"

"Say no more! My house is the humblest in the village, as anyone will tell you, but it is *yours,* dear woman! I will run ahead now and tell my wife, may the gods bless her womb, that a most esteemed guest will be honoring us tonight! Anyone here will tell you where to find the house of Koozog. Just follow the path and when you come to the pen of spotted pigs, there you will find a welcome fit for a queen!"

Three more patrons approached Ulrika, requesting cures for: a boil, an abscessed tooth, hemorrhoids. The first two she lanced, and for the third she prescribed a concoction made from the *hamamelis* plant, found in abundance in this region. They paid her with: a copper coin, a hair from the head of the Prophet Zoroaster, and an earnest handshake.

Before others could run home and bring family members with various ailments, Ulrika declared that she was weary and must rest, but that she would return in the morning.

She was thinking about what the pig farmer had just said: a man whom they called Magus, and who lived in the City of Ghosts, which lay along the very route she and her mother had taken years ago! Ulrika planned to be there in a few days. Was it possible the prince of her memory—the man seated on a magnificent throne—was this Magus?

Encouraged by the new information, and feeling more hopeful than she had in weeks, Ulrika pulled her hood over her head and left.

Outside, she felt cold, biting night air. Flickering torches illuminated the small enclosure of tavern, stables, animal yard, and collection of tents where travelers snored through the night.

The Magus, Ulrika thought in rising excitement. Of royal blood and the last of his kind . . .

Was this what they called fate? Was this was why she had been diverted along her path earlier that day, when she had set out for a small town named Tirgiz and instead had had to take a steep mountain track due to a fallen tree across the road?

Over a year ago, Ulrika had left Babylon on a cargo ship laden with wool and grain. At the vast gulf where the Euphrates emptied, Ulrika had said good-bye to the kindly captain and had found passage with a caravan heading southeast, carrying dates and figs to be traded for mined metals and gems. The caravan had followed an ancient royal road built hundreds of years before by Cyrus, the first king of the Persians, with the flatland rising gradually from the coast into gently rolling hills, which in turn had lifted the travelers up into the steep slopes of the Zagros Mountains. At a crossroads near a place called Al Haza, Ulrika had left the caravan to wait for another group of travelers to pass by—in this case, monks headed for a monastery high in the snowy mountain peaks. They had taken her with them on the condition that she not speak to them or sit with them at meals. Ulrika had been glad to isolate herself from them, riding a donkey and sleeping under the stars. Village after village, farm after farm went by until she said good-bye to the monks and next joined a large boisterous family on its way to a wedding.

Ulrika had said farewell to them at their destination and had set off on the next leg of her journey, which would take her within miles of where she and her mother had lived eighteen years ago and where Ulrika had been born, only to find the road blocked by a fallen tree. There had been but one way around it, a steep mountain track, with the detour bringing her to this forest settlement, which she had not planned to visit, but where she had learned of a prince who was the last of his line!

This was no accident, she decided. The Magus had to be the prince of her long-ago memory.

Ulrika took it as a good sign—confirmation that she was on the right road and going where she was meant to go.

Because it was imperative she find the Crystal Pools of Shalamandar.

Although Miriam's suggestion that she fast before meditating had helped Ulrika to command visions at will, she still could not hold a vision long enough to interpret its meaning—the beautiful young woman who had haunted an unaware ship's captain, the shining light that accompanied the monks who did not see it, the woman with a baby, following the wedding party.

What was she supposed to do with such visions?

She looked up at the late-summer moon, full and effulgent, sailing against the black night. Was Sebastianus at that moment looking at the same moon? Had he reached China even? He had estimated it would take him three years to arrive at the capital city of the East. If so, would he, in a year's time, be starting back on his return trip to Rome?

I will be in Babylon to meet you, she thought in excitement.

Ulrika shivered as she peered into the darkness in the direction of Koozog's pig farm. Drawing her cloak more snugly about herself, she did not hear the sudden footfall approach from behind, did not see the large hand come up before her face to clamp down over her nose and mouth. A strong arm went around her waist, pinning her arms. Ulrika tried to cry out but could not. When her feet left the ground she kicked and struggled.

She could not breathe. Her lungs fought for air but the hand was clasped too tightly over her nose and mouth.

In horror Ulrika saw darkness roll toward her until it swallowed her up and dropped her into oblivion.

22

WHY WAS THE RIDE so rough? Could the driver not have found a smoother road? And when would they reach Babylon? The trip was becoming more and more uncomfortable. Her wrists hurt. Why would her wrists hurt?

Ulrika opened her eyes. She blinked. It was night and she didn't seem to be in a wagon at all but looking down at the ground. And it was passing beneath her.

When she realized that her hands were tied behind her back and that she was being carried on someone's shoulder, like a sack of grain, she tried to cry out, only to discover that a cloth had been tied over her mouth.

She struggled against her abductor's hold. His grip tightened. She tried to kick. He pinned her legs down. She writhed against her bonds. Another arm went over her thighs, holding her fast. But Ulrika fought, twisting this way and that, jerking her body so that her kidnapper lost his footing.

"Enough!" she heard a voice snap in Farsi. "Be still!" he then hissed in Greek.

It only made her struggle all the more until her kidnapper came to a halt and dumped her unceremoniously to the ground. Realizing that her feet were not bound, Ulrika scrambled backward over the leaf-strew forest floor, her eyes on a tall, forbidding mountain man garbed in furs. He seemed disinterested in her attempt to escape, but merely turned his back as he lowered travel packs, and Ulrika's medicine box, to the ground.

She did not get far. Her feet became entangled in her long cloak. And when her head and shoulders came against something hard, Ulrika looked up and saw in the moonlight a massive pine tree towering over her. She looked frantically to her left and right, but all was dense woodland.

As she wriggled against her bonds, she kept an eye on her abductor. He was using a long stick to dig a hole.

Her grave!

Fresh fear and determination empowered Ulrika so that she was able to push the gag from her mouth, the cloth slipping down to her chin. "Who are you?" she cried. "Why have you kidnapped me?"

In an instant he was at her side, knife unsheathed, the blade pressed to her throat. "I told you to be still," he growled. "Do you understand me?" he said in Greek.

She nodded mutely.

"Not another word," he said, "or I will silence you myself."

She watched in terror as he returned to his task, digging a hole that was wide and deep enough to hold a body, and then he sat down and proceeded to sharpen tree branches into lethal points.

Trembling beneath her cloak, Ulrika tried to twist her hands free of their bonds. She kept her eyes on the stranger, taking the measure of him in the moonlight that filtered through the canopy of leafy treetops. From his voice she judged he was young. His hair looked black. He was tall and slender, and deceptively strong. He wore a fur tunic and leather leggings. His arms were bare, despite the night coldness in the mountains, so that Ulrika saw sculpted muscles and pale skin smudged with dirt.

In as calm a tone as she could manage, she said, "What is your name?"

He didn't look up from his labor. "You do not want to know my name, and I do not want to know yours. For the last time, be silent."

She bit her lip and, watching him as he sharpened sticks, kept silent.

He sat cross-legged on the ground facing her, his head bent over his task, to look up every now and then to listen to the forest, which was alive with nocturnal sounds. He never looked at Ulrika, never spoke until finally he stood up and climbed into the freshly dug hole where, as far as Ulrika could discern in the light from the moon, he planted the sharp stakes into the ground. When he was finished and all stakes were in place, he climbed out and covered the pit with loose grass and shrubbery.

Ulrika realized he had set a trap.

As he came up to her and reached for her mouth gag, Ulrika shook her head. He studied her for a moment—in the moonlight Ulrika saw black eyes framed by black lashes and brows—then he murmured, "As long as you keep quiet."

He lifted her to her feet. He did not remove her wrist bonds but gestured that she was to walk with him. Then he picked up the travel packs and medicine box and, without another word, resumed his trek through the night.

WHEN DAWN BROKE THROUGH THE TREES, and Ulrika thought she would drop from exhaustion, the stranger came to a halt. Gesturing to her to sit, he vanished through the trees and returned with a goatskin filled with fresh, crisp water. Holding it to her lips, he let Ulrika drink her fill, then he slaked his own thirst.

"Please," Ulrika whispered. "My arms hurt . . ."

He paused, looked down at her. As sunlight crept across the forest floor, illuminating mossy trees and gnarled trunks, Ulrika got a better look at her captor.

He was slender and wiry, with lanky arms and legs—a young man in his twenties, she realized. His hair was ink-black and fell to his shoulders in curls. His eyes were dark, his nose long and thin, but his lips were voluptuous, almost feminine, and his jaw was smooth and beardless. He looked, in fact, surprisingly well groomed for a wild mountain man. Stranger still was his unusually pale skin. Ulrika would have thought that a man so otherwise dark would be olive-complexioned, but he seemed to be in fact whiter than Ulrika herself, and she wondered from what strange race he had sprung.

Unsheathing his dagger, he reached behind her and cut the bonds. As Ulrika felt sensation, and then pain, return to her hands, she watched him cross to their travel packs and open one of his own. He returned and held out a small cloth bag. Ulrika saw that it contained nuts and dried berries and she discovered that she was ravenous.

"I cannot build a fire," he murmured apologetically as he walked away, and Ulrika had the odd sense that he was not addressing her.

And then he did a curious thing. While Ulrika watched, and the woodland came alive with birdsong and the whisper of a morning breeze, the mountain man gathered twigs and leaves and created kindling for a good campfire. He even brought out a flint and held it over the small mound, but did not strike a spark. He chanted as he did so, a prayer in a dialect Ulrika could not identify. And when he was done, he reached for the corded belt at his waist and removed an object that hung there.

As he placed the object next to the unlit fire, Ulrika saw that it was cornet-shaped and the color of old ivory, perhaps half a cubit long, and straight. An animal horn of some kind, she thought, with a gold seal at the wider end, as if something were contained within.

"Please tell me where you are taking me."

He ignored her as he busied himself with a long rope, which he threw over a tree branch, anchoring one end to the trunk and laying the other on the ground in a knotted coil. Ulrika realized he was creating another trap, and while he worked, once again kept lifting his head to listen, his body tense and alert.

"You would travel much faster without me," Ulrika said, guessing that he was evading someone who was in pursuit.

He said nothing as he covered the coiled rope with leaves and grass, and slowly bent the tree branch, tying it down with a string, creating a trigger that, Ulrika guessed, when touched, would spring the rope into the air.

"Leave me here," Ulrika said. "I am no use to you—"

Snap!

He spun around.

Snap!

Ulrika shot to her feet.

They listened. Heard footfall. Someone was coming.

"We must go!" he said, sheathing his dagger and scooping up their travel packs. "Quickly!"

Ulrika gathered up the bag of nuts, and then she retrieved the water-skin. As she reached for her medicine box, which the stranger had dropped near the mound of kindling, Ulrika picked up the ivory horn he had laid there and—

Her mind exploded with a vision of such brilliance and passion that she staggered back. A massive bonfire. Sparks rising to the night sky. People dancing in a frenzy, shouting, beating drums. It filled her head. It made the earth spin beneath her. Fear, anger, hope, desire. Tears drenched her. Laughter lifted her up. She was swept up into the sky, and dropped to the earth.

Ulrika felt a tug on her hand. The vision vanished. She blinked. The stranger was glaring at her. "You do not touch this!" he growled. She saw that he had snatched the horn from her.

"I'm sorry. I meant no disrespect."

He hastily reattached the ivory horn to his belt. "This is sacred. Not for unbelievers. We must go now."

He sprinted ahead of her, and Ulrika kept up with him as they heard heavy footfall behind.

They had gone only a short distance into the forest when they heard a sudden cry. Ulrika and her abductor paused briefly to look back and to listen to angry shouts and sounds of frantic chopping.

The trap had worked.

"WAIT," ULRIKA GASPED AS she stumbled over the ground. "I cannot go any farther. I must rest."

The stranger turned and grabbed her wrist, to pull her along as she staggered and protested. The sun was high now, they had stayed on the move all morning. It had been hours since they had heard their pursuers.

"Please," Ulrika said, when suddenly he came to a halt and Ulrika ran into him, nearly causing them both to fall.

"We are here," he said, and dashed ahead.

Ulrika looked around and saw only oaks and pines forming a dense forest, and dappled sunlight. She watched in amazement as her abductor disappeared into a thicket, to reappear a moment later, gesturing impatiently for her to join him.

As she neared the brush that looked too tangled for anyone to cut through, Ulrika saw an opening. She entered and found herself inside a small hut, cleverly hidden and disguised in the middle of the woods. To Ulrika's surprise, the hut had a comfortable feel to it, despite being a temporary shelter, with rugs on the floor and brass lamps suspended from the grass ceiling, little golden flames flickering to create an intimate atmosphere.

In the center of the floor, lying on a bed of animal skins, a young girl lay feverish and sleeping.

All thoughts of fatigue and hunger left Ulrika as she ran to the girl's side, dropped to her knees and immediately felt the burning forehead.

"How is she?" the mountain man asked as he knelt at Ulrika's side. "I left her a day and a half ago. I had no choice."

Ulrika lifted eyelids to look at dilated pupils. She detected a rapid pulse. The girl's breathing was shallow. "She is very sick."

"I did not want to leave her," he said. Lifting the blanket made of soft deer skin, he exposed a nasty wound. "She fell and injured herself. I tried my best to fix it, but infection set in. I knew that the only way to save her was to find help." He looked at Ulrika. "I saw you in the village. I saw how you treated a man's injury. And I recognize these symbols." He pointed to her medicine box with the Egyptian hieroglyphics and Babylonian cuneiform painted on the sides.

"Do not let her die, do you understand? *You cannot let her die.*"

Ulrika was momentarily arrested by black eyes that seemed deeper than night, and filled with unspoken emotion. It struck her that her young kidnapper was desperate, on the run, frightened, and angry, and perhaps not as dangerous as she had initially thought.

He was also, she realized, quite handsome, and it crossed her mind that, should he ever smile, his sensuous lips would be most attractive.

Ulrika reached for her medicine kit. "I will administer Hecate's cure. It is made from willow bark, which is inhabited by a very powerful spirit."

"Are you a physician?"

"No. My mother is a healer. She taught me."

"You do not live here in Persia. This is not your home."

She kept her eyes on her own hands as she busily dispensed powder into a cup, and mixed water into it. Her abductor sat uncomfortably close. She could smell his sweat, and the wild scent of animal skins, pine, and loamy earth. "I have come to find someone," she said.

She did not look at him, but sensed his question.

"I am seeking answers to a personal question," Ulrika said as she stirred the powder until it dissolved. "And I believe there is a man, called the Magus, who can help me."

When he said nothing, Ulrika asked, "Is this girl your sister or perhaps your niece?" The girl's coloring was the same as his—an unusually white complexion framed by raven-black hair. But they were not father and daughter. The girl would be around thirteen and the young man appeared to be just a little older than Ulrika herself.

"She is from another tribe," he said, and Ulrika thought: But sharing the same Persian-Greek ancestry I would wager.

He suddenly turned toward the opening of the thicket-hut. "I will stand watch," he murmured. Removing the ivory horn from his belt, he laid it on the girl's chest and said, "The god of my people is Ahura Mazda, the Wise Lord of the sky, and this is sacred ash from his first Fire Temple. It is white and clean, and protects from evil." He stood, his midnight hair brushing the tangled weeds that made the ceiling. "Her name is Veeda," he said, and then he was gone.

❧

By the time the stranger returned, Ulrika had been able to encourage the girl to take a few sips of Hecate's Cure. The medicine was famous for reducing fever, taking away pain, and conquering the evil spirits of infection. Then she had tended the wound on the girl's leg, cleaning it, washing away the dead flesh to apply fresh salves and bandages. Ulrika did not fully understand how healing worked—the greatest Greek physicians in the world could not entirely explain how a cure worked—but Ulrika had used a method so ancient and proven that, once she was done, she felt confident the girl would soon begin to recover.

"How is she?" the stranger asked, coming to Veeda's side.

"You brought me to her in time."

He nodded. "I have been praying."

Ulrika had left the ivory horn in place on the girl's chest, wondering about the ash he had said it contained. She thought of the mound of kindling he had built but had not lit, and how he had apologized for not making a fire. "I cannot light a fire," he said softly now, and once again the words did not seem directed at Ulrika. She wondered who he was speaking to. "It would draw our pursuers to us. I have to keep moving. I must survive in order for this girl to survive." He kept his eyes on Veeda's face as he said this, and once again Ulrika wondered about their relationship.

Veeda was from another tribe, he had said. Was she his bride?

"I will find food," he said abruptly. "You must rest now. There," he added, pointing to folded rugs against the grassy wall. "You can make a bed. I will let you sleep. Do not fear. I have set traps, and I will be on the lookout."

As he once again left the hut, and Ulrika suddenly found the prospect of sleep very inviting, it occurred to her that her abductor had not himself slept in a long time.

He had sacrificed his own comfort and well-being to save this girl, she thought. He had risked getting caught by men who pursued him—*and for whom he set deadly traps*—in order to find medical help. Who was Veeda to him, and why was her survival so important?

23

ULRIKA DREAMED OF SEBASTIANUS.

He stood on a vast, windswept landscape with a boiling ocean on one side, violent crags and tors on the other. He appeared to be building an altar of shells and fire. He wore only a loincloth, his tight muscles gleaming in the sun. Ulrika tried to call to him, but as she drew near, Sebastianus began to climb the altar, which had become a golden tower rising in tiers shot with blinding sunlight. He was trying to reach the stars, she knew, for he was seeking answers that could be found only in the celestial bodies of the cosmos.

But Ulrika saw that the top of the tower was a raging bonfire—a dreadful conflagration that she knew would devour him once he reached it. She called out, frantic, desperate to stop him.

You cannot save him, a voice whispered all around her, on the wind, in the clouds. A woman's voice. Gaia . . .

Ulrika snapped her eyes open. Her heart galloped, and a fine sweat covered her body. In the dim light of the camouflaged hut, she saw that the girl continued to sleep beneath soft deerskin blankets. Ulrika tuned her ears to the forest outside and heard heavy footsteps going to and fro. Her kidnapper, pacing.

She thought of the dream she had just had. During her lonely days of journeying into Persia, Ulrika had continued her nightly ritual of speaking to Sebastianus. Every night before falling asleep, she would tenderly take the scallop shell between her hands, holding it safe and loved, and whisper words of hope and devotion to Sebastianus, closing her eyes to mentally send her message across the miles and days in the hope that they would reach him. She did so now, sending out a prayer that her beloved was alive and well and reaching his goal.

At dusk the stranger brought fish that, though it must be eaten raw, was a welcome feast to Ulrika, who could not remember ever being this hungry. But first she checked on her patient and found with relief that Veeda's fever had already begun to abate, her breathing becoming more regular.

As they quietly ate, with the stranger pausing now and again to listen to the deepening night, Ulrika asked him about the ivory horn that contained sacred ash. She had learned in her travels that encouraging someone to speak about their religious beliefs often broke down barriers.

"Fire temples are our places of worship," he said as he picked at the fish flesh with his fingers. He had delicate hands, Ulrika thought. Feminine hands, and she adjusted her impression of him once more, from brutish mountain man to someone more refined.

"We do not revere fire itself," he said in a low voice, glancing at the sleeping girl, "but rather the ritual purity that it symbolizes. Our faith was founded by the prophet Zoroaster in a fight against the image-cults brought to our land long ago by the Babylonians. We deplore imagery of any kind. We worship the open sky, ascending mounds to light our fires, so that Ahura Mazda, the Uncreated God, will see them. The prophet Zoroaster assured us that the Creator Ahura Mazda is all good, and no evil originates from Him. Good and evil are forever in conflict, and we humans must play a large part in that conflict, in making sure that evil never triumphs over good. We achieve this by living a life of good thoughts, good words, and good deeds. This keeps the chaos at bay."

His words echoed those of Sebastianus, when he had told Ulrika that only through reading the gods' messages in the stars could chaos be averted.

"Yours is an interesting faith," Ulrika commented as she lifted Veeda's wrist and counted the pulse, finding it normal.

"It is the only faith," he said. Then he fell silent, and Ulrika wondered if he was curious about her. There was a constant tension within him, and she suspected it was not completely due to the fact that he was being pursued.

She asked where he and Veeda were going, but instead of responding, he gathered up their fish bones and left the hut.

As she listened to night descend over the forest, with mountain chill stealing into the hut, Ulrika wondered if she should try to escape. Would she get far? There were the deadly traps, and the pursuers. And she was not certain which way it was to the tavern. Besides, she no longer felt threatened by the young man, and Veeda still needed her help.

The girl stirred and sighed beneath her blankets, and when Ulrika went to her side, Veeda opened her eyes and gazed at Ulrika with black irises framed by black lashes. "Who are you?" she asked.

Slipping an arm beneath the girl's shoulders, Ulrika lifted her up to drink from the water skin. "I am Ulrika. Do not worry, Veeda, I am here to help you. How do you feel?"

"I am all right, but my leg hurts."

"We will take care of that."

The girl looked around the hut. "Where is Iskander?"

"He's just outside, keeping watch. So that's his name? Iskander? Is he your uncle? A cousin?"

The girl shook her head. "He is from another tribe."

"Where is he taking you?"

"Away. To keep me safe."

Ulrika's brows arched. "Safe from what?"

"Evil men who wish to kill us. Please," a small hand reached for Ulrika's, "where is Iskander?"

Ulrika paused to feel Veeda's forehead—she was a very pretty girl, and the fever only enhanced her natural beauty—then she said, "I will be right back."

Ulrika found Iskander seated on a boulder, spear in hand. "She is awake."

He was instantly inside the hut and at Veeda's side, looking anxiously into her face. "Are you feeling better?"

"I woke up and you were gone. I was frightened."

He stroked her damp hair. "I had to go for help. I hoped you would sleep until I returned. I did not mean to frighten you."

Ulrika watched the scene in curiosity. Despite the tenderness between the two, there was a sense of formality also, as if they had not known each other for long.

"Did Ulrika save my life?" Veeda asked.

Iskander looked up and offered Ulrika a grateful smile that did indeed transform his face. "Yes," he said. "Ulrika saved your life."

That evening, Veeda was able to sit up and eat a little food, and she asked Ulrika many questions about the world beyond their mountain realm. They slept after that, but when Ulrika awoke during the night, she found Iskander gone, and once again heard him pacing outside.

The next day Iskander determined that they must resume their trek, although once again, despite her inquiries, he would not tell Ulrika where he and the girl were headed, or the identity of their pursuers. While Ulrika shouldered her own packs, Iskander took Veeda onto his back and carried her. She held onto him with her arms around his neck and they made a curious pair, for Veeda's dependence upon Iskander seemed like one of a child for a parent, while Iskander handled her with the sensitive formality of a stranger.

They made camp that evening and when Ulrika looked up at the moon and realized they had traveled yet farther east, away from her intended route, she said, "Where are you taking us?"

When he did not reply, she added, "You did not have to kidnap me. You could have asked me."

He surprised her by giving her a direct look with his black eyes, and she heard truthfulness in his voice as he said, "I am sorry for that. I was afraid Veeda was going to die. I did not want to waste a single moment getting help to her. In these mountains, we are intensely tribal. We guard our treasures and resources, we are suspicious of people from other tribes. Rivalry is our way of life. I did not know where you came from. You could very well have said no to me. And then what would I have done?"

"How long do you intend to keep me with you?"

"You can leave in the morning. I will give you food and a weapon, and directions on how to get to the City of Ghosts."

"What about you and Veeda?"

"We will go eastward."

Once again Iskander gathered twigs and leaves, and went through the motions of creating a fire, yet did not light it. He prayed over the kindling, and set the ivory horn next to it, chanting as he did so until he sat back on his heels and said, "I am searching for members of my tribe. I do not know where to go. I believe they might have fled to the east. You said you were seeking a man called the Magus, that he has answers. Do you think he might help me?"

Ulrika gave thought to her situation and circumstance and realized that, although she did not fully trust a man who had kidnapped her, she could easily get lost in these mountains and that it might be wise to keep Iskander with her.

"He lives in the City of Ghosts. Do you know where that is?"

They were dining once again on raw fish, nuts, and berries, and Iskander chewed thoughtfully before answering. "Yes, I can take us there."

Ulrika heaved a sigh of relief. Soon, now, she would be returning a favor to the prince who had helped her mother long ago. She would ask him to take her to Shalamandar where she would begin anew the intended path of her destiny, which she prayed would make her free to be with Sebastianus upon his return from China, free to love him and be with him for the rest of her life.

They heard a sound in the night. Ulrika gave a start, but Iskander laid a hand on her arm, saying, "We are safe. The traps are intact. Those men will not reach us."

She glanced over at Veeda, who slept peacefully. Her fever was gone and her wound was healing. But Iskander would not let her walk, he carried her. She was not heavy. At fourteen, Veeda had only just started filling into womanhood. Although one could see the budding breasts, her body was still slim and boyish. She wore her luxuriant black hair long and loose, but she had explained to Ulrika that when she married, she would bind her hair up under a scarf, as was her tribe's custom, and keep it hidden thereafter, only to be seen by her husband. Veeda wore a curious costume: leggings and a garment Ulrika had never seen before—tight fitting from neck to waist, with long sleeves, and secured up the front by a long row of tiny round slivers of bone slipped into slits. Veeda called the garment a "jacket" and the closure was made of "buttons." It looked like men's attire, Ulrika thought, yet it fit her very well, and seemed practical for mountain living.

Veeda expressed a lively curiosity about the world and asked Ulrika many questions. It was only when she slept, whimpering in slumber with tears streaming from her closed eyes, that Ulrika wondered what secret pain Veeda carried in her heart.

"But what if they make it past the traps?" Ulrika asked now. "What will they do?"

"They will kill all three of us. For that, for the danger I have placed you in, I am sorry. But it was necessary."

"Who are these men who pursue you?" Ulrika asked, and this time Iskander gave her a direct response.

"They are from another tribe, the enemies of my people. A feud began between our two tribes many generations ago. No one knows who or what started it, or which tribe, but revenge was exacted over an incident, and of course further retaliation was called for. Revenge is our way of life. But it is an endless cycle. When we exact revenge against that tribe, they must retaliate, creating a new reason for taking revenge upon us. And so we have fought for centuries.

"But an unforgivable act was committed five years ago. Men from my tribe, I am ashamed to say, stepped over the boundaries by raping one of their women. They declared war upon us and vowed to eradicate us from the face of the earth. They came in the night. We did not stand a chance. I was in the woods standing guard against an enemy I never saw, and returned to find my village razed to the ground, my people slaughtered. When the other tribe heard that I was still alive, they came after me. That was five years ago, and I have been running ever since."

"And Veeda?"

"I sought refuge in the village of a people whom I did not know. They were kind and took me in. I awoke to find a raid underway. My enemies had found my hiding place. They were burning the huts and slaughtering the villagers. When I saw this, I surrendered. I went outside and said, 'Here I am, take me.' They seized me. But when I saw that they were not satisfied with my capture, that they were going to continue to destroy the village as a punishment for giving me sanctuary, I broke free and I tried to fight them. But I was only one man against many. I ran to the house where I had been staying and found the family all dead. I heard a noise under the corpses and discovered Veeda. Her parents had shielded her with their own bodies to protect her. I escaped, taking Veeda with me. On a hilltop, we stopped and looked back and saw the burning huts, the dead, and we knew by the silence that the village had been wiped out."

His dark eyes seemed to look inward as he released a ragged sigh and said, "I brought those men to that innocent village. I am responsible for all those deaths."

"You were only trying to survive," Ulrika said softly, recalling a horrific battlefield in a Rhineland forest. "And you could not have known what they would do."

"Now I search for remnants of my tribe, for I believe some escaped and might have fled to the east. This is why the Magus you seek interests me. Perhaps he can tell me if any of my people are still alive. Because, you see," he said, "it is insupportable for me to believe that I, Iskander, son of Sheikh Farhad Aswari, am the last of the noble and ancient Asghar tribe."

Ulrika stared at him in disbelief. *He* was the prince she had been sent to help?

24

THEY HAD BEEN TREKKING through the mountains for days, and now they were drawing close to the City of Ghosts. It lay just on the other side of the mountain pass. Villagers and farmers along the way had confirmed that indeed the Magus dwelled in that forbidden city, and he was reported to be a very wise man.

And so forward the threesome pressed, up and up into dense forests, where the air grew thin and cold, where people friendly and hostile guarded their small territories and looked in curiosity at the unlikely threesome: the young woman with honey-colored hair and sky-blue eyes who spoke Greek but also knew some passable Farsi; the dark-eyed young man in the animal skins of a mountain tribesman, who seemed neither husband nor brother to his two female companions, a moody young man who had little to say; and the coltish girl with a ready smile, wearing the leggings and tight jacket of people in the south—a beautiful, large-eyed girl whom several men tried to buy from Iskander.

The three had foraged for food along the way, or bartered with farmers, or earned a meal with Ulrika's healing skills. They camped at night under the stars, and Ulrika heard Veeda whimpering in sad dreams, and Iskander pacing in sleeplessness. They bathed in cold mountain streams, and every morning and evening Iskander built a small fire to his god, Ahura Mazda, chanting prayers as he did so, while Veeda sang uplifting songs of praise to "the angels among us."

And now they had come to the pass in the mountains that would lead them into a world few outsiders had visited. A world where, Ulrika prayed, the Magus still lived and possessed all the answers.

She had no doubt now that Iskander was the prince she had been sent to help. But it troubled her that Iskander's people might have already been wiped out. How was she supposed to help him when she had come too late? Perhaps the Magus would tell him that survivors were waiting to be reunited with him in a new place in the east.

Iskander had not spoken much in the last few days, but Veeda was cheerful and loquacious. She walked with a limp and tired easily, and was visited by nightmares of the destruction of her village, but she was a resilient girl and when she was awake was filled with a lively curiosity, and frequently had to be cautioned to keep her voice low, and to stay close to Ulrika and Iskander. The trackers remained in pursuit—Iskander's tribal enemies whom Ulrika had yet to see but whom she had heard—in their angry growls and shouts, and heavy footfall—and who she had no doubt would slaughter her and Iskander and the girl if they caught up.

Arriving at the rough track that led between two mountain peaks, the three paused to look back. Here Ulrika finally saw them, down the slope, among the trees and boulders in the noon sun, bearded men carrying weapons, looking up at the trio at the top. The trackers stared at Iskander with fixed eyes, as the wind whistled around them and an eagle cried out from his aerie. And then, to Ulrika's surprise, the men wordlessly turned and started back down the mountain.

She looked at Iskander. "Why did they turn back?"

"This is the limit of their territory. From here, their gods are powerless. They will not follow."

"Then we are safe?" Veeda asked hopefully.

Iskander was silent for a moment as he watched the figures disappear down the slope, then he said, "They will not go far. They will camp and hope that I come down the mountain. I shall bide my time. When they have grown lazy and careless, I will go into their camp and slit their throats as they sleep. And then I will continue on to their village and burn it to the ground, leaving not a man, woman or child alive. In this way, my revenge will be complete."

Ulrika stared at him. In their days of trekking through the mountains, she had learned that Iskander suffered from insomnia. Although he would drift off after a few minutes beneath his blanket, he was soon wakened by dreams and demons, and he would pace restlessly for the rest of the night. She knew now what kept him awake. Revenge was a powerful stimulant.

"Let us go," he said and, turning, began the last steps of their journey.

Steep, rocky walls devoid of vegetation embraced the three as they followed the track in silence, their leather boots crunching stones and gravel underfoot. The wind through the pass was strong, whipping back hair and cloaks. And the sun, as if mimicking their progress, reached its zenith and then, as the silent travelers began their descent down the other side of the mountain, began its own descent toward the west.

As they crested the peaks they saw, beneath a late-summer sky that was deep blue and dotted with white clouds, a golden plain stretching before them in breathless majesty. The valley lay within a ring of lavender mountains, and the ruins of a city stood at the heart of the valley, massive walls and towering columns, charred and broken, the only testament to the savage and ruthless destruction that had taken place there three hundred years before.

Iskander, Ulrika, and Veeda were soon down the eastern side of the mountain and following the ancient royal road across an old wooden bridge over the River Pulvar. As they entered a vast stone terrace from which immense stairways rose to the open sky, they stared in humble dismay at the piles of stones and rubble and toppled pillars that had once been the palace of Darius the Great. No gardens flourished here, no trees or flowers, not even a blade of grass—just a flat, barren plain shorn to its crust. They saw charred columns and a layer of powdery dust everywhere—ash from the enormous rafters that had crashed down during the terrible inferno set by Alexander's torch, all that was left of the mighty cedars from Lebanon, and teak trees from India that were once fabulously painted columns capped with gold. Walls of dark limestone that had been laboriously engraved by skilled stonemasons depicted stiff parades of people long forgotten, now the only inhabitants of this desolate place. And as if to add final insult, proof of prior tourists visiting the ruins was found in graffiti etched into the walls: *Suspirium puellarum Alypius thraex* (Alypius the Thracian makes the girls sigh).

When they came upon a pair of stone pillars capped by a massive lintel, Ulrika stopped and stared. "I know this place," she said in a tone filled with wonder. "I have been here before."

Iskander and Veeda turned to her, their hair dancing in the cool wind.

Ulrika scanned the rows of stone columns that stood at attention on the flat plain. Pillar after pillar, perfect in their lines, hundreds of them. "I remember thinking this was a forest of stone trees."

She resumed walking. "I was told that the Magus lives north of this place. I believe my mother and I met him. We passed through these ruins when we left Persia. I can't have been more than three or four years old at the time." Ulrika took in the walls covered in bas-reliefs and cuneiform text, the stairways leading to nowhere, the sad remains of what had once been grand palaces and gardens.

She stopped suddenly, her eyes wide. "Why, there he is!" She dropped her travel packs and ran ahead, her feet echoing on the floor of the limestone terrace. Iskander and Veeda followed until they came to stand before an enormous limestone wall.

They gawked at the prince seated on a majestic throne. He was dressed in splendid robes with a tall round hat on his head, beneath which thick curls cascaded to his shoulders. His beard was thick and prodigious, covering his chest to his waist and coiled in tight ringlets. He held a staff in one hand and, curiously, a flower in the other. In front of him, a golden censer burned incense.

It was a bas-relief. Not a living man after all, but a long dead emperor, carved in stone.

"Hello?" came a voice on the wind.

They turned to see a portly man puffing up the stones steps from the grassy plain. He wore a long coat made of goat felt, a rope-belt holding it closed. His gray hair was twisted into braids, while decorative beads and bells made noise in his bushy gray beard. "Greetings, strangers! I welcome you to my home." He held out his arms. "I am Zeroun the Armenian. That is my caravanserai, down there."

They followed his pointing finger and saw the stone buildings, corrals, animals, vegetable gardens. "Come and eat, drink! Meet fellow travelers! I have comfortable rooms, and much news and gossip! You do not want to linger here for this is a haunted place, and many think it is unlucky!"

"What is this place?" Ulrika asked.

"The people who live in this valley call it the City of Ghosts. The great Alexander called it Persepolis. But long ago, another race of beings lived here, and they called their home Shalamandar."

In shock, Ulrika looked around. *This* was Shalamandar? There were no pools, crystal or otherwise. Just ruins and dust.

"Can you tell us, please," Iskander said, "where we can find the Magus?"

"Magus?" Zeroun threw back his head and laughed. "Is that old myth still breathing? There is no Magus. He was invented long ago by a charlatan who collected fees from desperate people and then vanished."

Ulrika stared at the Armenian in dismay. No crystal pools. No Magus. No man offering a key. And the prince she was supposed to save was a simple mountain tribesman who had already lost his people.

25

Ulrika's dismay soon turned to excitement because she had, after all, found Shalamandar, the place where Wulf and Selene had come together in love. The point of her own beginning, and from where she would start her new, true path.

The three made camp on the royal terrace where, centuries prior, emperors had received important dignitaries from foreign nations but where, now, only snakes and scorpions traversed the limestone floor. Iskander scavenged for dead wood and brush on the perimeter of the ruins to create a shelter for Ulrika and Veeda. Then he built the campfire, praying to Ahura Mazda, blessing the name of Zoroaster, asking the prophet to shed goodness and light into his humble servant's heart that he might find the strength to slay his enemies once and for all.

Veeda prowled the ruins until the sun reached the western horizon, creating long shadows across the golden plain, and now she moved among the toppled walls and shattered columns, tracing with her fingertips the images of long-dead people. She sang as she went, in a dialect her companions did not understand. She said she was singing to the angels who dwelt here.

"What do you do now?" Iskander asked.

Ulrika looked into black eyes that caught the fire's glow. She knew that Iskander had placed a great deal of hope in the Magus telling him if any of his people had survived. "I will meditate here," she said. "For even though we are among ruins, this is a special place and I believe answers will be revealed to me. I will begin tomorrow. I am too fatigued now to fast and cleanse my spirit. When I am refreshed and can concentrate, I will sit among these fallen pillars and crumbled walls and pray to the All Mother for revelations. Perhaps," she added with a reassuring smile, "I will learn where the rest of your tribe went."

"Can you do that?" he asked, a hopeful tone in his voice.

"I told you that I came seeking answers to a personal question. I see visions. Sometimes they are so powerful that I cannot distinguish them from memories or dreams."

Iskander nodded. "When you picked up this horn," he said, touching the talisman on his belt.

"I saw a bonfire on a mountain," Ulrika said, "and people dancing around it. Visions do not come all the time, but I am training myself in a special discipline that I hope will release my power." Drawing her cloak tighter about herself, she said, "What sort of horn is that? I do not recognize it."

She heard pride and reverence in Iskander's voice as he spoke of a creature called a unicorn. "Unicorns lived long ago but have been extinct for centuries. When the prophet Zoroaster converted my people from heathen ways, when he abolished imagery and idolatry and created the first Fire Temple, my ancestors gathered that first pure ash and distributed it among the clan. They chose precious vessels to hold that ash, and I believe mine is the only one to still exist. It is very holy, and very powerful."

He looked at her for a long moment, while Veeda danced among the dark ruins and sang her incomprehensible songs, and firelight flickered on centuries-old walls, making the graven images appear to move, and then Iskander said, "The vision that came to you when you touched this horn . . ."

His voice tightened. "What you saw was the First Fire. And although I have never doubted that this horn contained the true pure ash of that fire . . . you have given me proof that what I carry, what my father and forefathers carried, is a true relic from the days of prophet Zoroaster himself." His smile was wistful and sweet as he added, "I thank you for that, Ulrika," speaking her name for the first time.

When they saw Veeda come dancing out from behind a wall, arms over her head, pirouetting in the starlight—her leg either no longer hurting or she was oblivious to it—Ulrika said, "What is she singing about?"

"Her people worship beings called angels."

Ulrika recalled that Rachel had spoken of angels, explaining that, according to Jewish belief, they were messengers of God.

Iskander said, "They are the Bountiful Immortals. And they are everywhere among us, Veeda says, unseen, helping, protecting. The angels have special names and live according to a complex hierarchy, but that is all I know. Veeda says it is taboo to speak of her religion, forbidden to speak the names of the angels. Angels are the reason why," Iskander added in a dark tone, "Veeda's people hold such a strong tradition of hospitality. They say that when a stranger enters their home, they might be entertaining an angel unaware."

Ulrika saw eyes suddenly filled with pain and she realized: They believed Iskander was an angel but instead he brought death.

"Tell me about your people," she said, as she watched Veeda dance on the royal terrace, her slender, limber form making Ulrika think of gazelles.

"We are sheepherders. We graze thousands of them in the valleys of my land, and this makes us very prosperous." His gaze went inward and his face brightened with a pleasant memory. "Every man in my tribe must build his own house with his own hands. This is how he proves himself. It was my dream to build the largest and finest house in my village, to make my wife proud to be married to a prince, and to fill the rooms with many children."

"You can still build that house."

The brightness faded from his face. "Another destiny awaits me."

"Revenge only begets revenge," Ulrika said gently. "In Rome we say that when a man plots revenge, he should dig two graves."

Iskander shook his head, long black curls catching the firelight. "I must do this thing, for I will be held accountable."

By whom? Ulrika wondered. If he was the last of his people, and he intended to eradicate the other tribe, who would be left to judge? And how, Ulrika wondered for the hundredth time, was she to save him, as Miriam had prophesied? Unless there was *another* prince . . .

Ulrika's attention was drawn back to Veeda, spinning on her toes, her arms framing her head. Her long black hair fell like a sparkling waterfall of ink. In her leggings and tight jacket, she was a vision of slender fluidness, feather-light, agile. Her voice rose in high octaves, her eyes glowed with love and joy. Ulrika watched as the girl danced along the terrace, visiting the walls, dancing away, sprinting here and there, until she realized that Veeda was drawing closer to large, fallen blocks of which she did not seem aware.

"Veeda—" she began.

The girl was up on her toes, with her eyes closed, a beatific smile on her lips as she sang to her angels.

"Veeda," Ulrika said again, rising from the campfire. "Come away from there. You will hurt yourself."

Iskander, too, shot to his feet. "Veeda," he said.

She did not hear them. Her voice high and melodic, her eyes closed against reality as she pictured golden beings in another world, Veeda spun and twirled in the moonlight.

And when she danced dangerously close to the fallen blocks, Iskander went after her.

Veeda's shin caught the corner of one of the stones just as Iskander reached her. She cried out and tumbled. But Iskander caught her. He held her as she gazed at him with a startled expression.

From her place by the fire, Ulrika witnessed something that she sensed not even Iskander and Veeda were aware of: the way their eyes locked, the way she breathlessly held onto him, the tightness of his grip and, most of all, the long moment in which the embrace lasted—Iskander and Veeda were in love.

26

While Iskander was up in the mountain pass to begin his vigil, watching the enemy camped below and waiting for his opportunity to take revenge, and while Veeda visited Zeroun's caravanserai which lay a mile from the ruins, Ulrika was alone among the broken columns and stairs that led to nowhere.

Now she would meditate. If this place was indeed Shalamandar, then surely the answers would be revealed. Because this was where Wulf and Selene had stopped to rest. This was where her own existence began.

She chose a place on the limestone terrace and sat, crossing her legs, attaining a relaxed posture. She had not eaten breakfast, having discovered that fasting did indeed sharpen her concentration and kept her awake. And now she closed her eyes, slowed her respirations, and began her whispered chant to the All Mother.

As she prayed, she grew excited in anticipation of seeing the crystal pools. She imagined they would be beautiful—shimmering and sweet, cool, refreshing water that revived the spirit as well as the eye. How large would they be, she wondered, and how many were there? Where did the water come from? Were the pools fed by waterfalls or streams or artesian wells?

Ulrika opened her eyes. Nothing was happening.

Drawing in a deep breath, she closed her eyes and began again, sending her thoughts out into the unknown, willing her soul to explore the cosmos while she held a vision of her inner soul flame. But after a while she was aware only of the hard stone beneath her and an aching back. Her mind wandered and she wanted to eat.

She would try again tomorrow.

27

"Ulrika," Veeda said, "may I ask you a personal question?"

They were preparing breakfast while Iskander was in the brushy foothills foraging for eggs. They had been a month at the City of Ghosts, had built a comfortable camp in the ruins, and had observed the first dusting of snow on the distant mountains. Winter was coming. Soon, no caravans would be able to cross the mountain passes and the threesome would be trapped in this ancient valley.

They had fallen into a routine. Iskander went daily to his mountain pass to keep watch over his enemy, still camped on the other side. Veeda mended clothes or cooked with Ulrika, or went to the caravanserai where she was making friends among the girls who lived there.

Ulrika had kept at her daily meditations with no success. She should have received visions by now, if this was indeed the place where her life began. She should have learned the nature of the Divining and when to start on her destined path.

As she looked at the distant mountains dusted with snow, she knew she must soon make a decision: to stay and continue what was turning out to be a futile exercise in seeking answers to her gift, or buy passage on the next caravan that came through and could take her south. She had, after all, only the word of a stranger that this place was indeed Shalamandar. Zeroun had even said, "Local legend says that was the name long ago." But legends had a way of growing distorted and even completely wrong over the years. Ulrika wondered if she should return to Babylon and find another way to determine the location of the true Shalamandar.

"You may ask me anything you want," she said.

"Have you ever been in love?"

Ulrika looked at the girl's shy smile, pink blush. Setting aside her knife and the late autumn onions they had bought from Zeroun, she said, "I am in love right now, Veeda. With a wonderful man who is at this moment on his way to a far-off fabled land."

"And does he love you?"

"Yes." But, she thought, we have been apart now for a long time. Has he reached China? Does he find the women there exotic and beautiful? Perhaps irresistible . . .

She missed Sebastianus so much it was like a physical pain. Every day she read his letter, spoke out loud the words he had written, ending with "I love you." She ached for his warmth and strength, yearned to feel his powerful arms around her, needed to experience the solidness of his body and the security of his embrace.

She touched the scallop shell that lay on her breast. "Sebastianus gave this to me. It connected him to his homeland, and now it connects me to him."

"Does it connect you to his homeland as well?"

Ulrika looked at the wide, questioning eyes, dark and filled with sorrow and hope. And it occurred to her that she had more in common with this tribal girl than she had realized. They both did not know were they belonged. "I suppose it does," Ulrika said. "I had never thought of it."

Veeda looked down at her hands and said hesitantly, "How do you . . . how does a woman get a man to notice her?"

"Veeda," Ulrika said gently. "Iskander notices you."

The blush deepened. And Ulrika thought: should I tell her I suspect he feels the same way? But he is holding back. What keeps Iskander from expressing his feelings for her? The enemy on the other side of the mountain, waiting for him to come down . . .

"When he goes up there," Veeda said, pointing to the mountain that loomed over the ruins. "I feel a hole here," and she tapped her chest. "When he returns, it is filled again. But Iskander will never love me."

"Why do you say that?"

"Because of Asmahan."

"Who is Asmahan?"

"She is Iskander's wife. He thinks she is still alive."

Ulrika stared at Veeda. "I did not know he was married," she said. And then she knew the truth: Iskander was not searching for remnants of his tribe, but for one woman. And it was not out of an ancient rivalry that he sat here and plotted the deaths of the men who camped on the other side of the mountain pass, but a need to take revenge on men whom he believed had killed that woman.

Ulrika was sad for Iskander. So much senseless killing. Iskander's tribe wiped out. Veeda's clan gone. And now Iskander wanting to erase his enemy from the face of the earth. When would it end?

"Caravan!" Iskander shouted as he sprinted up the stone steps to the terrace. "A caravan is coming!"

Ulrika turned to look back over the plain and saw, beneath the morning sun, an astonishing sight: hundreds of camels, horses, and donkeys, laden with packs and riders, slowly snaking their way across the flat plain. Lifting the spit from the fire—she was roasting a skinned hare, the fat dripping into the flames and causing delicious snapping sounds—she set it aside, rose to her feet, and shielded her eyes against the sun's glare.

The familiar, and welcome, sound of jingling camels' bells rode on the breeze that wafted over the royal terrace. And Ulrika thought anxiously: will this be the last caravan? Should I go south with it?

The three hurried from their camp, excited, wondering where the traders had come from, where they were going, what exotic goods and people they brought. The prior caravan to come through the valley had turned out to be transporting the Grand Vizier's personal library, and Ulrika and her friends had learned that the Grand Vizier kept his 117,000-volume library organized while traveling with it by training his camels to walk in alphabetical order.

As she neared the noisy gathering of camels and horses and men, Ulrika heard Zeroun the Armenian's booming voice fly up to the winter clouds. "I tell you, my friend, I understand your homesickness! It is something we all feel! I myself sometimes long for my homeland! Let me tell you, holding onto something precious and dear is the way to anchor oneself in a foreign land. It is the *key.*"

She stopped and stared.

His voice rolled across the compound like thunder, rising above the noise of braying camels and shouting men. "Especially a man like yourself, sir, who goes out into the unknown, seeking for he knows not what. Oh, you can be very focused, you can be very attentive and concentrate very hard on your exploration, but if you do not hold tightly to something that has meaning for you, then you do not put your whole heart into that exploration. Something holds you back, does it not? No matter how hard you try?"

Ulrika watched him and realized that Zeroun was not looking at his guest, but over the man's shoulder, locking eyes with *her.*

And then he turned away and, putting his arm over his guest's shoulders, said, "That is the key to success in everything, my friend! I pray you have the courage to take what advice I offer here today! After all, it is free!" And his roaring laughter faded as the two stepped through the doorway of the inn.

While Ulrika remained where she was, staring after them.

And then she turned and hurried back to the ruins, leaving Iskander and Veeda to explore the caravan and the visitors.

As she ran up the steps, she thought: Zeroun is right! She had not realized it until now, but in her meditations, she always held back, afraid that her wandering soul would journey too far and become lost. Would holding something solid indeed anchor her in the real world while her spirit ventured to the other side? Was that the key, and Zeroun the man offering it, as prophesied by the Egyptian fortune-teller? And Miriam, the rabbi's wife?

She would put it to the test at once. Since they had been preparing breakfast when the caravan came, Ulrika had not eaten since the evening before—a long fast to be sure. And she knew exactly what the "anchor" would be—the scallop shell, for it was hard with sharp edges, and it was precious to her.

This time, she did not choose a random spot upon which to sit and meditate. She wanted to be as near as possible to the place where the crystal pools might have once been. But she saw nothing that looked like it could have been a reflecting pond or a bath. There were no depressions in the limestone terrace. And then she realized that walking around and using her rational mind was not going to work. She needed to tap into the Divining and perhaps a vision would come to her.

So she strolled among the columns, slowing her breathing, whispering her brief prayer to the All Mother, and clutching the scallop shell. She felt its roughness on one side, the smoothness on the other. She focused on the feel of the sharp, wavy edge as she ran her fingertips over it. The shell grew large and heavy in her hand. It weighed her down. It anchored her until she felt safe enough to send her spirit out into the unknown.

As her fear dissolved, a new understanding made itself known to Ulrika: Besides fear, other emotions made the spirit hold back. Anger, jealousy, sorrow . . . She realized that the heart must be divested of these shadows so that the spirit could walk in the light.

Ulrika felt herself grow calm and serene until, soon, her feet carried her as if with a will of their own until she came to a standstill before a massive stone archway. Two mighty columns supported a square lintel. Through the archway, on the other side, the flat terrace continued, and was littered with more debris.

She stopped and, clasping the scallop shell, closed her eyes again, controlled her breathing, and whispered, "I am here. I am anchored. I am safe. I send forth my soul into the cosmos. Holy All Mother, hear my prayer . . ."

And a reply, like a breeze, a sigh, sounded near and far at the same time.

Step through . . .

Ulrika opened her eyes and, with an invigorating intake of breath, slowly releasing it, she stepped through the archway.

Suddenly she was standing on green grass beneath a vast blue sky, the wind on her face, the sound of bleating goats as they grazed nearby. Where was the stone arch? Ulrika looked around again and, recognizing the ring of mountains that embraced the plateau, realized that she must have gone back to a time before the city had been built.

She squinted in the sunlight and saw, faintly, through the green trees and grassy plain, the dim shapes of columns and ruined walls. She was still in the City of Ghosts.

She concentrated, held onto the shell, and repeated her prayer. Now she imagined her inner soul flame, focusing on its flickering light. And the details of the landscape slowly sharpened, colors brightened until they dazzled. And the scene changed again—she stood in a sylvan paradise, surrounded by trembling poplars and whispering fountains. Here, as she watched, beautiful shimmering pools appeared, in all shades of silver and blue, and Ulrika knew she had found the Crystal Pools of Shalamandar.

A woman appeared before her, tall and beautiful, her long white robes shining in the sun.

"I remember you," Ulrika said. "You are Gaia, the ancestress of Sebastianus Gallus. Why do you visit me? Is it because of the scallop shell? Do you dwell in this shell?"

"I am your guardian spirit. You have done well, daughter, for you have learned your lessons. You are no longer arrogant but a true seeker. And so you have now come into your spiritual power. You possess the gift of the Divining, which is a conduit to the Divine. In each generation of your people, one person is born with this spiritual gift. He or she finds and identifies sacred people and places, even sacred objects, so that others might go there and draw solace and comfort from the gods."

"Yes, I see now . . ." Ulrika whispered. The shaman's cave in the Rhineland—she would have sensed it was sacred and thus was a safe place to hide. Iskander's unicorn horn filled with sacred ashes, giving Ulrika a glimpse of religious rituals long ago. And what of Jacob's grave by the Sea of Salt? Had Rachel buried her husband in hallowed ground?

"This is my purpose? To find sacred places?"

"It is your destiny, your purpose on earth, daughter, to find the Venerable Ones and tell the world about them. This is why you were brought back to the place of your beginning."

"The Venerable Ones! Who are they?"

"You will know them when you find them. Remember, daughter, the gift of the Divining is a gift from the Goddess, which marks the beginning of your new life. In this gift, you will start again on your true path, and this time you must not stray."

The pools faded away, Gaia was silenced, and Ulrika found herself standing on the stone terrace of the City of Ghosts. She took a moment to compose herself, to marvel at what she had just experienced, and as she did, realized that she felt profoundly refreshed and invigorated, as if she had slept for a long time, and drunk a cup of bracing tonic. Every muscle and sinew in her body was filled with energy. She had never known such clarity of thought. A side benefit, she realized, of focused meditation.

When she turned to walk back through the stone arch, she saw Zeroun standing there. And when she saw the smile on his face, another understanding came to her. "You are the Magus," she said.

"I am. I was a rug merchant when I first came to this valley many years ago. I was carrying carpets to the Indus Valley when my caravan stopped here to rest. But early snows trapped us in this place and we wintered here, my family and I. One cold day I was walking through these ruins when I was visited by an ancient spirit who told me I had been brought here for a special task. And so I have been giving counsel to all who seek truth."

"Why did you tell us the Magus is a myth?"

"Because I do not find lost spoons or tell fortunes. I had to be certain that you were a true spiritual seeker."

She smiled. "Why did you not simply tell me what I must do? Why did you couch your instructions in dialogue with a stranger?"

"Because the truth is within us all, and a person can only find the key within himself, it cannot be told to him. I am merely a signpost. It is up to you to find the road."

"Then dare I ask where I can find the Venerable Ones?"

"Only you can do that, Ulrika, for they are part of your personal destiny."

28

THE CARAVAN STAYED FOR only a few days, and now the merchant trader was eager to depart, for an early winter was coming. Ulrika had been able to buy passage southward. She was anxious to return to Babylon and start her search for the Venerable Ones.

And to be there when Sebastianus returned.

But when she emerged from her makeshift shelter in the ruins, wrapped in her traveling cloak, her packs on her shoulders, she looked across the plain and saw that the caravan had already departed. It could still be seen, winding its way along the southern road that would take it through treacherous mountain passes before it found the peaceful coast. Ulrika knew she had to hurry to catch up.

But when she turned to Veeda and Iskander sitting forlornly at the fire, she stopped cold.

Her friends were tragically caught in this place: Iskander a slave to ancient traditions of rivalry and revenge, Veeda a prisoner of her love. They are like me, Ulrika thought. They do not know where they belong.

She looked at the two who had been her close companions for many weeks, and she thought: they, too, need to leave this place. But she did not know how to convince them. Iskander was so obsessed with taking revenge on his tribal enemies that he could not see anything else. And Veeda, having no family, nowhere to go, was doomed to stay with him. They will sit here forever, Ulrika thought. Frozen in time like the men etched into the stone walls of this dead city.

"I must go now," she said as she picked up her medical kit. Their camp was now like a little home, with makeshift walls of timber, a floor covered in pelts and hides, and windbreaks to protect them from the elements. Ulrika had slept and eaten and laughed and cried in this strange little camp. She would never forget her short time here.

"Please do not leave us," Veeda said. She was a beauty, Ulrika thought, and soon would no longer be a coltish girl but a lovely young woman.

Ulrika glanced out at the vanishing caravan. "Come with me, both of you. We will leave this valley together and seek a new road. But we must hurry."

Veeda began to cry and Iskander stiffened with righteousness. "What you ask is impossible, Ulrika, for I have a duty to my family to carry out a final revenge upon my enemies. And I have a duty to keep Veeda safe, for it was by my actions that her tribe were annihilated."

Ulrika chewed her lip. There was still time to catch the caravan . . .

But I must set my friends free.

She sighed, knowing what she must do.

Praying that the caravan was not the last that would come through this valley, Ulrika lowered her packs to the limestone floor and murmured, "Let me help you."

They watched as she sat on a comfortable goatskin, crossed her legs, and closed her eyes. Clasping the scallop shell with both hands, she began a whispered prayer. They had seen her do this many times. She had told them the exciting news of finding the Crystal Pools through this meditation. But they were curious why she was engaged in this ritual now, when she had been so intent upon leaving with the caravan.

They waited in silence.

Anchored by the scallop shell, with the glowing soul flame filling her inner vision, Ulrika divested herself of fear, impatience, anxiety, and even the disappointment of not having left with the caravan, until her soul was set free and Gaia appeared before her. "You have done well, daughter, for you have passed the final test. There will be no caravans after this, as winter has come to the mountain passes. Your act of self-sacrifice has proven to Us that you are worthy of the gift. And now you will be rewarded, for We know the questions that fill your heart. *Behold!*"

Lights suddenly materialized around her, pink clouds of fire and heat, golden explosions dripping with sparks, soft glowings of blue luminescence. They swirled around Ulrika like giddy butterflies, engulfing her in a frenzy of hope and joy. They sparkled like drops of water sprayed from a fountain on a hot summer day. More arrived, swirling, soaring, pale phosphorous and glistening incandescence, filling the air with their melodious crooning. Beings made of cool golds and warm silvers. Rainbow colors! Shining miracles!

Ulrika cried out as she felt delicate, feathery wings embrace her and cover her and with their touch came such peace and serenity that she wept with joy.

I am hagia. I am sanctus, the feathery wings whispered. *We are eternal, we are pure. And we are with you always, watching, guarding . . .*

And then Ulrika sensed—

She held her breath.

There was Something beyond the angels and benevolent beings. Ulrika tried to reach it, to understand. But she could not. She felt tremendous love flow through her, intense waves of reassurance and compassion.

And then it all faded away and she knew she would not experience this again.

When she opened her eyes she saw two pale faces looking at her in worry and concern. It took her a moment to find her breath. She realized tears streamed down her cheeks.

"I have news for both of you," she said when she was composed again. "News that will set you free."

Veeda and Iskander exchanged a puzzled glance, then Ulrika said, "I was permitted a glimpse into a wondrous world which we can only imagine. Veeda," she said. "A being named Parvaneh spoke to me."

The girl gasped and traced a protective sign in the air. "That is an angel, a very important angel! But it is taboo to utter the names of angels!"

"The angel spoke to me and said that Teyla is gathering flowers in the marble halls of Kasha. Do you know what this means?"

Veeda's eyes grew big. She pressed her hands to her chest and looked at Ulrika in astonishment. "Teyla is my mother! How did you know this? How do you know the name of Parvaneh? And Kasha! Only my people know of Kasha!"

When Ulrika turned to Iskander, she saw bleak eyes holding a question he did not want to ask.

Ulrika smiled gently and said, "The beings that dwell in this sacred place showed me many things. I know now that we do not die, that existence is eternal, and that death is but a transformation—"

"No!" he cried, jumping to his feet. "I will not hear it! Asmahan is alive. I have searched for five years, and I will search for the rest of my life if I must."

"Iskander, listen to me—"

"No!" he screamed, turning away, putting his hands over his ears.

Ulrika rose to her feet and reached out for him, laying a hand on his arm. "I am sorry Asmahan is dead. But please believe me when I say she is in paradise."

He turned bleak eyes to her. His shoulders slumped. "I believe you, for you have seen the sacred fire altar of Zoroaster. I believe in your gift. And I suppose I have known all along that my wife is dead. I should be happy that she is in paradise," Iskander said in a tight voice, "but I am not. Asmahan and I were robbed of a life together. And those vile men who camp down the mountainside will pay. I will no longer be satisfied with merely killing them, I shall torture them for days and see that they suffer greatly."

"Iskander," Ulrika said softly, "listen to me. You are the last of your tribe. I saw that in my vision. Just as Veeda is the only survivor of her people. If you carry out this mission of revenge, you will surely get yourself killed. You have to think of your people, Iskander. Through you, they can still live. But if you die, then they will truly be dead."

He covered his face with his hands and wept bitterly. Veeda came to him and took him into her arms. He sobbed on her shoulder as she held him tightly and made soothing sounds.

Presently he collected himself and said, "You are right, Ulrika. If I slay my enemies and burn their village, someone will survive, and that man will spend the rest of his life in pursuit of me, until he kills me and my tribe is utterly erased. Yes, I have a duty to my ancestors to carry out revenge, but I have a greater duty to my *descendants,* and to Veeda, and to her people, for through us, our two bloodlines will continue."

Ulrika placed her hand on his cheek. "Iskander, make Veeda proud to be the wife of a prince. Build your house and fill the rooms with many children, for you will be the founder of a new tribe." As she said this she recalled that, before arriving at this place, Iskander had planned to go eastward, but she had persuaded him to take her to the City of Ghosts. Had he traveled eastward, she realized now, his pursuers would most likely have caught him and killed him. And so Ulrika had saved his life, fulfilling the prophecy of the prophetess Miriam—that Ulrika was to help a prince save his people.

29

When the snow came, the three abandoned their camp in the ruins and lived for a while with Zeroun and his family while Iskander built a small house, after the tradition of his tribe. They lived there through the winter, Iskander continuing to build, helping with repairs on other houses, while Veeda entertained the villagers with her singing and dancing, and Ulrika helped nurse those who came down with winter fevers. She went daily to the stone archway, where she easily summoned the vision of the Crystal Pools of Shalamandar, and there she meditated and prayed, honing her spiritual gift and its power.

At the first snowmelt, a caravan came from the north, and accepted Ulrika as a paying passenger.

Iskander and Veeda were there to say good-bye, and she embraced them in love.

When she said good-bye to Zeroun, she asked if he were the last of his kind. He said, "I am not the first Magus of Shalamandar, nor will I be the last. For as long as there are seekers of truth, there will be a Magus in this valley."

As Ulrika took her place in the caravan, she thought of her newly discovered destiny.

In Babylon, she would search for the Venerable Ones, and she would watch each day for news of a caravan making its return journey from distant China . . .

BOOK SEVEN
CHINA

30

"THEY ARE CALLED DRAGON BONES," the third interpreter said to Timonides, "they predict the future."

The Greek astrologer watched in fascination as the fortune-teller, a local man from a mountain village, smeared the ox scapula with blood, then inserted it into the hottest spot of the campfire. As everyone watched for the bone to crack and reveal a message from the ancestors, Timonides glanced over to where his son was preparing the night's dinner—a curious dish comprised of long fat threads made from rice flour, called noodles, boiled in a broth and mixed with vegetables and meat. Nestor's round face glowed in the light of his cook fire, a smile on his face as he added spices to the pot.

Timonides sent a silent prayer of thanks to the stars. His son was safe. Nestor's crime back in Antioch was behind them, and although the caravan was not far now from its destination—the Imperial Court of China—by the time they returned to Rome, Nestor and Bessas would be forgotten. The gods had clearly forgiven Timonides for falsifying horoscopes, he concluded gratefully. Perhaps they did not blame a man for wanting to protect his son.

Pulling his cloak tighter about himself against the chilly spring night, Timonides pondered the miracle of being on the other side of the world. They were camped in the mountains, a great caravan of camels, donkeys, and horses, accompanied by men, women, and children, with herds of sheep and goats to feed the great crowd. Through towns and provinces, raging rivers and grassy valleys, mountain passes, harsh deserts, and forgiving plains, the Gallus caravan was always met with great curiosity and interest. From Persia through Samarkand, over the towering Pamirs, past the shifting red-gold dunes of the Taklamakan in the arid and formidable Tarim Basin, Timonides's master had shared meals with chieftains and potentates, humble shepherds and self-important kings, conducting trade and information. He drank curdled camel's milk and feasted on lamb kebab and onions, ending with sweet rice pudding with raisins. And when his caravan departed, Sebastianus took on travelers in need of protection: a family going to a wedding in Kokonor, envoys from Sogdiana carrying trade agreements to Tashkurgan, a group of monks who called themselves Buddhist missionaries carrying the teachings of their founder from India into China. The Gallus caravan camped in sun-seared deserts and blizzard-swept mountains; sought hospitality in villages and settlements comprised of nomads' tents and mud huts; and discovered, as they moved farther east, the delight of Chinese teahouses established for travelers. Now the caravan was camped in the Tsingling Mountains near Chang'an, with their destination, fabled Luoyang, a day away.

Timonides glanced in the direction of his master, who sat at his own campfire, studying his most recently acquired map of the region. Timonides wondered briefly what was going through Sebastianus's mind—entertaining thoughts, no doubt, of Ulrika—and then Timonides returned his attention to the flames and the "dragon bone."

As Sebastianus studied his map, he was momentarily distracted by an eruption of loud, drunken laughter. He looked up to see Primo and his men, sitting at their campfire, comfortably wrapped in warm cloaks and passing around a wineskin. We have come a long way, my comrades and I, Sebastianus thought. And soon we will see the wonders of a world no Roman has ever seen, a world called the Flowery Land.

Along the route, people had told Sebastianus strange and impossible tales of the Han People, some stories too incredible to believe—"Women give birth through their mouths." "They live to be a thousand years old." Tomorrow he would see with his own eyes. If only Ulrika were here to share the triumph with him. How he missed her. He would memorize and record every detail for her, so that she could experience it with him when they were together again.

The ox scapula made a cracking sound and the fortune-teller, using bronze pincers, pulled it from the fire. Sebastianus watched as Timonides and his companions bent forward to see the dark blood-figures etched into the bone. They held their breath as they wondered what Timonides's future was. The fortune-teller frowned, shook his head, then sat back and, through the interpreter, said, "Beware the mulberry worm."

Timonides waited for the rest. When none was forthcoming, he said, "That's it? Beware of a mulberry worm? In the name of Zeus, what is that supposed to mean?" Certain that the translator had made a mistake, he had the fortune-teller repeat his pronouncement. It went through three interpreters before it was repeated exactly the same to Timonides.

As they had covered the miles, and entered regions with new dialects, Sebastianus had realized he would have to devise a system of communication, for he would never find a man who spoke both Chinese and Latin. And so they had picked up two translators along the way, happy to come along for the adventure and act as communication intermediaries: the first, speaking Latin and Persian, the second speaking only Persian and Kashmiri. A week ago, they had taken on a third man who spoke Kashmiri and Chinese. A long chain of dialogue to be sure, and one open for error, but Sebastianus knew that until he learned to speak Chinese, he would need to rely on these middlemen.

The fortune-teller lifted a deeply lined, weathered face to Timonides and said, "Your life ends with the mulberry worm."

Sebastianus saw the look of skepticism on the old astrologer's face. It made Sebastianus smile. Despite his absolute faith in the stars and their infallible predictions, Timonides was like any other man, he had a weakness for seers and their promises.

As Sebastianus returned to his map, he reached for his mug of watered wine and a strange whistle filled the night air. In the next moment, he felt a breath of wind rush past his head. He looked up in time to see the second and third arrows fly into the camp. One of Timonides's companions cried out and clutched his arm.

And then suddenly men were jumping up and shouting as a hail of arrows came down on them. As women and children dashed inside tents, men reached for swords and daggers, ducking behind boulders and shrubs, trying to see where the volley was coming from.

Inhuman shrieks pierced the night as dark shapes appeared from out of nowhere, jumping down the mountain slopes, materializing out of ravines, great formidable men wielding massive swords and axes. They bore down on the camp with a frenzy of speed and unearthly screams, swinging their weapons this way and that, bashing anything that was in their way.

Sebastianus was on his feet and racing toward them, his own sword clasped between his hands. Behind him, Primo and his trained men threw off their merchants' cloaks to charge at the invaders with clubs and spears, no longer the merry drunks they had appeared to be moments before, as no wine had passed their lips, for that was part of their ruse. Now the attackers saw the "merchants" for what they truly were, fighting men in Roman military costume, muscular, powerful, engaging the brigands with a ferocity that took them by surprise.

Almost as quickly as they had charged into the camp the brigands fell back, as so many had before them during the caravan's eastward progress, lawless mountain men seeing the fat and lazy members of a rich caravan and tasting the victory and spoils of so easy a prey. But now they were on the run, finding themselves outnumbered and outmatched by foreigners who had staged a deception. Primo and his men yelled with glee as, once again, they drove raiders from their camp.

When Sebastianus heard a strange sound fill the night, he turned and frowned. When it sounded a second time, and he recognized the unmistakable ringing of a gong, he shouted, "Wait!"

Primo and his men stopped and turned, a puzzled look on their faces. They had the brigands within reach. They could teach the outlaws a lesson, as they had previous others. But before Primo could protest, his eyes widened at an astonishing sight approaching from the mountain's eastern road.

Accompanied by swaying lanterns, an elegant carrying chair of red and gold, borne on the shoulders of twenty porters, led a procession of another twenty men, all costumed in red and gold silk with black silk caps on their heads. Two men carried an enormous brass gong between them, and bringing up the rear were pack animals laden with goods.

Sebastianus knew what this was. He had suspected that, when word of the caravan from the west reached Luoyang, the Chinese emperor might dispatch an envoy to meet the strangers. He watched as the remarkable procession came to a halt and the red and gold chair was lowered with great ceremony to the ground. As the night wind blew, causing torches to flicker and pennants to snap, the visitors from Rome watched as an extraordinary man stepped to a cushion set before him on the ground.

Tall and gaunt with a yellowish cast to his skin, he wore black silk shoes over white socks, which peeped out from beneath the hem of a lavish robe made of red silk breathtakingly embroidered with dragons and birds. The robe was wrapped around the man's slender body and secured with a wide red sash. A wispy white beard lay upon his chest, above which a long thin moustache cascaded down below the chin. His face was thin and bony with high cheekbones, his eyes almond-shaped and slanting beneath thin white eyebrows. Upon his head, a wide-brimmed hat of stiff black silk, under which long white hair had been brushed up and tucked.

He came silently forward, his hands clasped together in the voluminous sleeves of his robe. Dark, shining eyes scanned the strangers, one at a time, as if trying to determine who was the leader of the group. Finally he said, "Are you the travelers from Li-chien?" The translation was passed along from Chinese to Kashmiri to Persian to Latin.

Sebastianus knew that Li-chien was China's name for the Roman Empire, which no Chinese had ever visited but of which they had heard in mythical tales. "I am," he replied.

The man bowed. "Noble Heron, lowly and unworthy servant of His Imperial Majesty the Emperor of the Great Han Dynasty, Son of Heaven, Lord of Ten Thousand Years. I humbly invite you and your companions to visit the house of My Lord, who is interested to meet travelers from so far away."

Sebastianus had learned along the route that, two years prior, Emperor Guangwu had died and Crown Prince Zhuang had ascended the throne as Emperor Ming. "Are you here to escort us to Emperor Ming?"

Noble Heron nodded with a slight tremor of his eyebrows. "It is my humble honor to enlighten My Lord's illustrious guests on court etiquette and protocol, for how are you to know when you have never been here? It is taboo to speak the emperor's name, or the name of any royal or exalted person. You may call me Noble Heron because I am but a lowly servant at the imperial court. The emperor can be addressed in many ways, which I will teach to you."

Sebastianus saw that the man was struggling with his impulse to stare at the strangers. He wondered if what the Chinese had heard of Romans was as outlandish as what the Romans had heard of the Chinese. When Noble Heron brought out a hand to gesture in the direction of Luoyang, it was Sebastianus's turn to stare. The Chinese official's fingernails were so long they grew in curls, and each was tipped with a protective gold cap.

"My esteemed friend," Sebastianus said through the interpreters, "you would do us a great honor by sharing our camp, and while you accept our hospitality, I will explain to you as best I can our customs, which must seem strange to you."

As Noble Heron graciously accepted, and retreated while his servants prepared his tent, Primo came up to Sebastianus and said quietly, "I do not trust that man."

Sebastianus turned to him. "Go on."

"There was something strange about the attack. For weeks now we have not been troubled by local brigands, not since we entered the sphere of Chinese military influence. All the tribes and settlements we encountered were vassals of the emperor. So how is it that these brigands should attack so close to the capital city? How could they not have seen this fellow and his enormous retinue coming up the road, clearly an envoy from the imperial court?"

"It was staged," Sebastianus said. "To assess our strengths and vulnerabilities, and to learn if we come in peace or as a conquering army. We will have to be on our guard from now on. I suspect there are more tests to come."

The imperial official stayed the night at the caravan camp, eating dinner by himself and served by his personal servants. At dawn they broke camp and Sebastianus led the massive train of camels, donkeys, horses, and carts down the mountain track, with Noble Heron at his side, now riding a handsome sorrel mare.

Before starting out, Timonides read his master's horoscope while Noble Heron lit incense sticks and paid respect to the Guardians of the Four Winds: snake and tortoise in the north; red bird in the south; green dragon in the east; white tiger in the west. Along the way, as they descended to lush plains and verdant farms, Noble Heron told Sebastianus about the man whom everyone called Lord Over All Under Heaven.

Emperor Ming, aged thirty, sat on the throne with his favorite wife, Consort Ma, a beautiful woman of not yet twenty years. Ming's mother was the Dowager Empress Yin, in her fifties and known for her beauty and meekness. The emperor was famous for his generosity and affection for his family; he adhered to the moral and ethical code of the Great Sage, but he also respected the many hundreds of gods in Taoist belief, and was known to have a lively curiosity about the religions and faiths of foreigners. "The Lord of All Under Heaven," Noble Heron said, "would welcome word about the gods of Li-chien."

Luoyang was situated on a plain between the Mang Mountains and the Luo River, a rectangular-shaped city surrounded by a high stone wall and a moat with drawbridges. On the congested river, Sebastianus saw craft that he had recently learned were called junks and sampans, crowded together as floating houses. Farms covered the countryside surrounding the city, where the peasants tilled the earth, yellow from sand carried in on winds from the northeastern deserts. Farmers at their labors paused to straighten and watch the remarkable procession move by; women came out of huts to stare at the long line of animals and beasts of burden, men walking alongside wearing the various costumes of different tribes.

Crowds stood on either side of the massive stone gates, as word had reached the populace that a most remarkable caravan was coming to pay respects to the emperor. Excitement filled the air. Everyone anticipated the great festival to come, commemorating this extraordinary event.

The citizens of Luoyang were colorful in their garb, which ranged from hemp to silk, in all the hues of the rainbow, elegant men in bright robes, peasants and merchants in trousers and tunics. But Sebastianus was more interested in the guards occupying the sixteen tall towers, their armor glinting in the sun, their crossbows at the ready. Noble Heron directed the caravan to a large area on the western side of the city, where smaller caravans were already camped, and where, Sebastianus was not surprised to see, an impressive contingent of imperial soldiers waited to take their places as guards of the newly arrived goods from the west.

"You will grant us the honor," Noble Heron said, "of being our guests in the city. You might wish to retrieve personal items from your caravan."

At the city gate, carrying chairs were waiting for the visitors, small conveyances enclosed in colorful fabric and borne on the shoulders of slaves in matching costumes. Noble Heron, with his entourage, led the way, and Sebastianus, Timonides, Primo, and the three interpreters, followed. Timonides insisted upon bringing Nestor along, as he had lately developed a habit of wandering off.

When the procession emerged on the other side, the newcomers looked out the small windows of the carrying chairs and found themselves on a broad avenue lined with onlookers, behind whom multistoried pagodas rose, their red-tiled roofs shining in the sun. Tiny bells jingled on the enclosed chairs as the slaves trotted down the avenue, and when the aroma of cooking and smoke and flowering blossoms reached Sebastianus's nostrils, when he saw the upcurved eaves of the Oriental roofs, when he heard the exotic cadence of Chinese speech as citizens remarked and commented on the strange looks of the foreigners—when it truly struck Sebastianus that he was here at last, the first man from the west to enter the capital city of Imperial China, he felt his heart expand with pride and excitement. He sent a silent prayer to his ancestors—the fathers and grandfathers who had carved trade routes before him and who would be so proud of this moment: when a son of Gallus had reached the other side of the world!

He wished Ulrika were at his side. And little did he know, five years ago, when they first met outside of Rome, that he would be making such an extraordinary wish.

They were carried through another gate and into a courtyard where attendants stood waiting. Noble Heron explained that this was the special residence reserved for esteemed visitors and important dignitaries. Sebastianus and his companions would be given the opportunity to wash off the dust and grime of travel before being taken before the emperor.

They were led down a colonnaded hall lined with tall crimson columns, where servants in baggy pants and wraparound tunics stopped and stared. The quarters, though sparsely furnished with low tables and cushions, were sumptuously decorated with beautiful rugs, elegant silk hangings, painted screens, large bronze and jade urns filled with fresh flowers.

Over the miles and months of travel, Sebastianus and his companions had adapted local dress and had arrived in Luoyang wearing leather trousers and padded lamb's wool tunics. But these were discarded now, as they enjoyed steaming baths in enormous bamboo tubs filled with fragrant water. To the shock and delight of the weary men from Rome, young ladies in long blue wraparound robes scrubbed their backs and limbs, and afterward massaged their bodies with warm oil. Sebastianus, Timonides, and Primo enjoyed their first shaves and haircuts in months, and began to feel like civilized Romans again.

When Noble Heron returned to escort them into the imperial presence of the Lord of Ten Thousand Years, he stopped short and stared at his transformed guests, now formally garbed in Roman tunic and toga, Greek robes, and the tunic and leather breastplate of a legionary.

"Aya," Noble Heron whispered, his normally composed face suddenly a landscape of distress. He was silent for a long moment and appeared to be struggling with his next words. "I beg our esteemed visitor to forgive this miserable servant if any offense is caused, for I do not know your customs for mourning. If I dishonor you or your family in any way, may I suffer the death of a thousand cuts. But . . . who has died?"

Sebastianus thought the translators had made a mistake, but when the question was repeated, he said, "No one. Why?"

Noble Heron gave him an astonished look. "But you wear white and you have cut off all your hair."

"This is how we customarily dress and groom in Rome."

"Ah, I see."

But the distressed facial expression did not fade, and Sebastianus saw nervous movement beneath the silk of Noble Heron's sleeves, where his hidden hands worried clasped wrists. "Is there a problem?" Sebastianus asked.

"Smite me for my ignorance, esteemed guest, for I am truly an unworthy man without knowledge, but I do not understand your other custom . . ."

"*Other* custom?"

Noble Heron searched the bedchamber for his next words, scanning the woven mats and sprigs of bamboo as if to find them there. Then he said, "Perhaps my lofty guests would be more comfortable in Chinese robes?"

"We're comfortable the way we are," Primo growled, getting hungry and impatient. "What's wrong with the way we're dressed?"

Sebastianus recalled the people they had seen in the streets, the peasants on the farms, and the servants and attendants within these walls. Then he considered Noble Heron's appearance and it came to him: even though it was a warm spring day, only a person's hands and face were exposed. And in the case of such a high official as Noble Heron, even the hands were hidden.

The tunics worn by Sebastianus and his three friends had short sleeves, leaving arms exposed, with hems that reached only the knees, leaving much leg exposed. "We mean no offense, Noble Heron, but we are here as citizens of Rome and representatives of our own emperor. If there is to be a first meeting of our two worlds, and a cultural exchange that has never before been experienced by either of our peoples, then it would be dishonest of us to appear before your emperor as anything other than our true selves."

The white-haired official digested this piece of logical reasoning and, finding no argument, moved on to the complex issue of courtly protocol.

While the stomachs of Timonides and Primo growled and gurgled, and Nestor wondered if they would be eating noodles, Sebastianus listened politely to the many rules of etiquette and assured the man that he and his friends would follow them as best they could. But when Noble Heron arrived at the subject of a ritual called *kowtow,* Sebastianus balked.

To demonstrate, Noble Heron spoke sharply to one of the household servants who, before the astonished eyes of the foreign visitors, dropped to his knees, placed his hands on the floor, and touched his forehead to the ground. The servant jumped up and repeated the gesture eight more times in quick succession.

Noble Heron said with a smile, "That is how you and your friends will show respect to the Lord of Heaven."

"Great Zeus," Timonides murmured, and Primo shouted, "I will not scrape the floor and lift my arse for any uncivilized barbarian, king or no!"

The first translator, a citizen of Soochow who was fluent in Kashmiri, went pale and was too afraid to pass the insult to the second translator, who already gathered from the Roman's tone that his words were disrespectful and dangerous.

Sebastianus explained to Noble Heron, "We understand your desire for us to show proper respect to your emperor. And we intend to do just that. But as citizens of Rome and agents of our own emperor, it would be treasonous for us to kowtow to your king, for that would mean our emperor is a subject of your sovereign. I am certain that, were the situation reversed, Emperor Ming would not want his agents kowtowing to the monarch of another land."

"This is true," Noble Heron said, but his wispy white beard quivered. "Nonetheless, any breach of protocol means instant death and, as miserable and unworthy as my poor head is, I am not yet ready to part with it."

Sebastianus smiled. "Do not worry, my esteemed friend. We are Romans and therefore men of reason. We are amenable to compromise."

They passed through many gates and doors, around many screens and across vast courtyards before they were finally led up the hundred steps to the imperial throne room. Sebastianus and his three friends, followed by the translators, walked along a polished floor between rows of red-lacquered columns, between which silent people stood in flowing silk robes, hands hidden in sleeves, watching the procession with keen eyes. Both men and women were present, the men wearing their long hair tied up in a knot beneath black silk caps, the women bearing intricate coiffures decorated with pearls and tassels. They watched in hushed curiosity as the strangely clad visitors walked sedately behind Noble Heron.

When they neared the dais upon which the royal couple sat, young women in scarlet and blue robes held unfolded fans to their faces and whispered, their almond eyes fixed upon Sebastianus and his short, bronze-colored hair.

A gong was rung, priests in robes and elaborate headdresses appeared with censers giving off pungent smoke, and they walked in circles while the gong sounded and an unseen crier called out spells and the names of gods. While the cleansing and sanctifying ritual was conducted, Sebastianus frankly studied the man he had come thousands of miles to see.

The emperor and consort were as still as statues as they sat upon their elaborate rosewood thrones, their robes made of such a dazzling yellow silk that they looked like a twin sunrise. Ming wore a curious crown made of a stiff black board with a beaded fringe hanging on front and back, his long hair drawn up into an elaborate coiffure under the crown. Ma, young and pretty, with a heavily painted face, wore her hair in such an elaborate fashion, with jade pins and ebony sticks supporting intricate ornaments and jewelry, that her slender neck looked as if it could barely support such a weight. Like their courtiers and statesmen and attending nobles, the imperial pair exposed no part of their bodies except for their faces, from the slippered feet on golden footstools, to the voluminous silk sleeves hiding their hands, and the bright red, rolled collars beneath their jaws.

At the side of Consort Ma stood a group of graceful young ladies, elegantly coiffed and draped in flowing silk. They appeared to guard a bamboo screen, behind which Sebastianus had learned from Noble Heron that the emperor's mother, Dowager Empress Yin, would be seated, unseen yet seeing.

When Noble Heron indicated where Sebastianus and his companions were to stop, the translator from Soochow and his colleague from Kashmir immediately fell to the floor to prostrate themselves before the sovereign. The man who spoke Persian and Latin, a native of Pisa, remained standing.

Sebastianus murmured to Timonides and Primo, "Just follow my lead." Through his translators he said to Ming, "Your Noble and Exalted Majesty, we come in peace and in the name of the Nero Caesar, Emperor of Rome. According to the laws and customs of my country, all citizens of Rome are equal, with no man above another, not even our emperor, although we do address him as First Citizen. We do not kowtow to our Caesar, we do not even bow to him, but stand before him as equals. But my friends and I wish no disrespect nor offense, and so we are honored to bow to Your Majesty as we would to no other."

Sebastianus bent slightly from the waist and gave a curt nod. Timonides and Primo did likewise, while Nestor merely giggled, and when they straightened, a deathly silence hung over the court.

The Lord of Ten Thousand Years remained unmoving on his throne, his face impassive, with not a ripple in the many layers of silk and satin and embroidery that impressively covered his person. No one moved. Not a breath was heard.

Emperor Ming blinked. His voice was young and sharp and full of command when he finally spoke, "You bring trade goods to Luoyang. Are you a merchant?"

Although the question was abrupt and somewhat rude, Sebastianus had been expecting it. Noble Heron had briefed him on Chinese social hierarchy, which began with the royal family at the top, followed by the intellectual-scholars called *mandarins*, after whom came the highly respected farmer, since being a peasant working the land was considered the most honorable way to make a living. Merchants were on the lowest rung of the social ladder and greatly despised, in the Chinese thinking that it was dishonorable to make money off other people. And so it would be dishonorable for such a man to dare to approach the Lord of Ten Thousand Years.

"I am an ambassador, Your Majesty, the personal agent of my sovereign. My caravan brings gifts to the people of China. I also bring greetings from my emperor, who extends a hand of friendship to the esteemed ruler of this great land. Further, I have come on my own quest, Your Majesty, and that is to seek the wisdom of your philosophers and learned men. I offer not only an exchange of cultural goods but of ideas and knowledge."

The emperor smiled, and seemed to relax a little. "It is a welcome and honorable exchange, Sebastianus Gallus. Tell us, where are your ancestors buried?"

"Far from here, in my home country."

"Who are your gods?"

"My faith rests in the stars, Your Majesty. It is my hope that the Lord of Ten Thousand Years will grant me the right to visit with his esteemed astrologers."

"Our Great Sage, whose name it is taboo to speak, taught us that learning is the highest ideal. It will be our honor to grant you your wishes, Sebastianus Gallus. And in return, you will honor us with knowledge of your country, which you call Rome."

The audience ended and the guests were escorted to another vast chamber lined with crimson columns. Here, low tables were set with platters and goblets, and Sebastianus and his companions waited patiently as much courtly protocol was followed while the royal pair, then the dowager, and then the courtiers took their places.

While musicians hidden behind a screen played zithers and flutes, drums and bells, gongs, chimes, and wooden clappers, creating delicate exotic melodies that made the men from Rome think of mythical lands, and dancing girls performed in long graceful robes with sleeves that fluttered like birds, the emperor and his guests feasted on baked owl and bamboo shoots, lotus roots, and panther's breast. Acrobats and jugglers performed as platters were brought out, each more fanciful than the last, and the rice wine flowed.

During a demonstration of a martial art called *kung fu,* Noble Heron was summoned to Emperor Ming's table, where he kowtowed three times before receiving a message, which he quickly brought back to Sebastianus. "The Lord of Ten Thousand Years will be honored to look at maps of your empire, honorable guest, with locations of cities and military camps."

"Please inform His Majesty that I am not able to provide such information, as I am not a military man."

Noble Heron returned to his sovereign, kowtowed again, delivered the reply and received another message and returned. And thus the exchange was conducted.

"My Lord says that as a trader, Honorable Gallus, you know rivers, borders, towns. He would be delighted to see these things, and their exact placement within your empire. My Lord will provide cartographers, artists, calligraphers, and all the paper and parchment you desire. He will place as many people at your command as you need, and as many months or years as you need. Your comfort is My Lord's greatest concern, as is your spiritual need. And so he will generously allow you to build a shrine to your ancestors here in Luoyang, for a man must honor his ancestors."

The three men from Rome digested this bit of news along with sweet glazed pork and curried rice, and they understood the deeper meaning of what the emperor had just said.

Sebastianus, Primo, Timonides, and Nestor were now prisoners of the Chinese empire.

31

THEY WERE CALLED "SOCIAL FLOWERS" and their sole purpose was to give sexual pleasure to the Emperor's guests.

Little Sparrow was one such young lady in the royal court at Luoyang, a beautiful daughter of nobility schooled in the erotic arts, such as the Twenty-Nine Positions From Heaven to Earth. She specialized in "sharing the peach" and "cutting the sleeve," and had kept the Emperor's guests satisfied with these exquisite arts since she was thirteen years old.

She was twenty now and had managed these past seven years to avoid breaking the number-one rule of Social Flowers—never to fall in love. Her sisters in the dormitory had warned her against it, and she had never thought it would happen. But as Little Sparrow lay in Heroic Tiger's arms, she thought she could happily listen to him talk all night.

It didn't matter that she didn't understand a word he said. She loved the sound of his voice, the rich timbre, the exotic syllables that tumbled from his lips, the utter foreign-ness of his speech. He always talked for a while after they took pleasure, filling the perfumed evening with words brought from far away, while she lay in his strong arms, wishing the night would never end.

They lay on a mattress filled with goose down, the sheets made of silk, while a blind slave kept the air moving with the constant sway of a magnificent feather fan. The lovers were otherwise alone in the bedchamber, but they could hear the voices and music of the royal household drift over the garden wall. Heroic Tiger spoke, she imagined, of his home far away in the west. And she silently thanked the gods for this bronze-haired man to whom she had given her heart.

The role of Social Flower was a respected and dignified one, and it was a great honor to live at the royal court and serve as a pleasure-girl for important visitors. Only the daughters of the most noble families were chosen. Selection was rigid: a girl's looks, comportment, health, and ability to please a man were judged. In the case of Little Sparrow, she possessed a delicate round face, a smooth unblemished complexion, a slim, willowy body, small hands and feet. Her family had rejoiced when she was selected out of a hundred candidates. The rules were complex, and each girl was rigorously schooled in modesty and discretion, proper decorum. Her guest's pleasure was her primary aim. What she herself felt was of no importance. Once a newly recruited girl was chosen, she was moved into a special dormitory overseen by eunuchs, where she lived out her life in luxury and ease, with no other thought than how to decorate her hair or improve the painting of her eyebrows. When she was called to pay a visit to a guest, she went for the time required, did not speak unless spoken to, and returned afterward to her cot in the dormitory.

Little Sparrow was not her real name. When the Chief Eunuch had introduced her to the esteemed guest from a place called Rome, the visitor could not pronounce her name, for it was long and meant "she who awaits a little brother," as her parents had hoped for a son. And so she had told the eunuch to give the westerner her "milk" name, given to babies in their first year of life, a temporary name, as many infants did not live long. Her parents had called her Little Sparrow and only the man from the west now called her that.

By the same token, she could not pronounce the foreigner's name—

Sebastianus—and so she called him Heroic Tiger, for that was how he was in bed.

But it was not for his sexual prowess that she had fallen in love with him. Unlike former guests of the Emperor to whom she had given pleasure, Heroic Tiger treated her with kindness. He smiled at her, stroked her hair, asked her how she was feeling. To other men, esteemed ambassadors and princes who were given royal hospitality when they came to Luoyang, Little Sparrow had been a piece of furniture—something to relieve the weariness of travel and then set aside. So she had reached the age of twenty without having borne even a mild affection for any of the men she had pleasured.

And then, six months ago, she had been selected to be Heroic Tiger's bedmate, and in that time she had surrendered her heart to him. But she kept her love for this foreigner a secret. She told none of her friends, and did not bare her heart even to Heroic Tiger himself.

And as she knew he was never going to be allowed to leave Luoyang, she prayed that when she grew old and was no longer desirable in bed, he would keep her as a companion.

A distant gong sounded the midnight hour, and she knew it was time to leave. As always, Heroic Tiger kissed her tenderly on the forehead and rolled over to go to sleep. But as she dressed, she heard a knock on the outer door, and when Heroic Tiger left the bed to see who it was, Little Sparrow heard an urgent exchange of words.

When she saw the big ugly westerner named Primo stride into the chamber, followed by one of Heroic Tiger's translators, and a man who wore the robes and colors of a nobleman from a southern province, she gathered her clothes to her naked breast and slipped behind a privacy screen where she could eavesdrop.

She recognized the fourth man in the group. He was Bold Dragon, and everyone knew of his political ambitions.

His family was powerful and rich, with many friends, and, as she listened, Little Sparrow quickly grasped that he was here to offer a means of escape to the westerners. She suspected it was a way to undermine the emperor's power rather than an act of kindness. For these foreign "guests" to escape so easily from the Emperor's clutches would cause Ming to lose face.

Little Sparrow held her breath as she listened to a scheme emerge from the words the translator spoke—Bold Dragon boasting that he knew how to get Heroic Tiger out of Luoyang and back to the western borders, but that it would cost a high price. He did not need gold or riches, the young nobleman said. And as he was doing this at great personal risk, the reward would have to be something very desirable indeed.

When Heroic Tiger offered him a rare and potent aphrodisiac, Little Sparrow saw that he suddenly had Bold Dragon's attention.

She watched as a curious scene unfolded. Heroic Tiger went to a locked chest and brought out a cloth sack. He opened it and showed Bold Dragon the contents, letting him sniff them and feel some of the stuff on his fingertips. Heroic Tiger then took the teapot that was simmering with hot water, poured it into a cup, and sprinkled some of the bag's contents into the water.

While the mixture brewed, Heroic Tiger said, "I met a man in Babylon. He told me he had a farm in distant Ethiopia which lies near the source of the Nile. He noticed one day that his goats were extraordinarily frisky, and mating almost constantly. He watched them over a few days, and found that they were eating the berries off what he had thought was a useless bush. He picked some berries and tried to eat them, but they were inedible for a man. And so he roasted them in a fire, and then ground them to a gritty powder. Boiling this powder in water provided a bitter brew, but he drank it down, wondering if the berries would have the same effect on him as they had on his goats.

"His experiment worked. Within a short while, the farmer felt himself grow younger, more invigorated, and with more energy than he had felt in years. He immediately sought out his wife, and delighted her for days. The Ethiopian then took his discovery to Babylon, where I encountered him. I tasted the brew and indeed felt its stimulating affects. And now, my honored guest, you will experience this remarkable elixir for yourself."

Heroic Tiger gave it to Bold Dragon to drink , taking a sip first to prove it was not poison.

Bold Dragon sipped and pulled a face.

"Drink it all," Heroic Tiger said, while the ugly one named Primo and the translator looked on.

Bold Dragon drained the cup, smacked his lips and said, "I feel nothing."

"It takes a short spell."

The four stood in silent anticipation as Little Sparrow watched from behind the screen. Bold Dragon looked down at himself, then ran his hand over his groin. He frowned. "I have drunk only brown water."

"Patience, my friend. How do you plan to get us out of the city?"

"I can arrange for it tomorrow. You and your companion will meet me at—"

"It is not just for me and Primo. All my men are to leave."

Bold Dragon's eyebrows shot up. "*All* your men? That is over a hundred, I believe."

"I will not leave anyone behind."

Bold Dragon gave this some thought, and as he did, he raised his hand to rub his nose. But his hand shook. He held it out and the trembling increased. He whispered an oath that the interpreter did not translate. And then he said, "I am feeling something! I feel . . . invigorated!"

Sebastianus smiled. "It is a potent brew."

"Indeed! What is it called?"

"The Ethiopian said it had no name as the beans grow on a plant everyone thought useless. But he called it *qahiya,* which in his language means to have no appetite, as this brew dulls hunger."

"Perhaps it dulls the stomach's hunger, but it stimulates another type of hunger. I feel I could bed ten women tonight and not sleep! Very well, for that entire bag of *qahiya,* I will take you and your people out of Luoyang. This is my plan . . ."

Little Sparrow trembled as she listened to the details of Heroic Tiger's escape.

He was going to leave her. The only man she had ever loved.

No one could guess the dowager empress's age. Each morning, her team of personal beauticians scrubbed her face and removed every speck of hair, including her eyebrows. Then they artfully repainted her face on a background of white rice power. In order to preserve the look, the empress controlled her facial expressions and spoke with minimal movement of her lips and jaw. The effect was to give her the appearance of a ceramic doll.

"I granted this audience, Little Sparrow," she said in a voice that was as smooth and flawless as the silk robes she wore, "because I call your father my friend. But be quick, for time rushes."

Little Sparrow kowtowed nine times before the emperor's mother, and when she received permission to speak, told of the late-night meeting between the esteemed trader from Rome and a nobleman named Bold Dragon—a scheme to help the westerners escape. "Bold Dragon will bring a traveling troupe of entertainers for the Festival of the Silver Moon," Little Sparrow said as she shook with fear before the powerful woman—but she had no choice, she had to keep Heroic Tiger in Luoyang! "And while His Sublime Radiance, the Emperor, is thus distracted, one by one the entertainers will be replaced by men from the west. This will be done after each act is completed and the entertainers leave the floor. They will exchange clothes with the foreigners, who will go out into the city disguised and then through the city gates. When all the westerners have gone, then the four personal guests of the Son of Heaven will be rescued during the dead of night, and taken away to join their comrades. They plan to be far away by the time the deception is realized."

The dowager's pet cricket chirped in its bamboo cage while her ladies-in-waiting stood as still and silent as statues. The empress did not move. The gold tassels and paper birds that adorned her elaborate headdress stirred only because of a breeze that wafted through the pavilion.

Little Sparrow's heart raced as she wondered belatedly if she had committed a horrible blunder.

Finally the dowager said, "By telling me this secret, you have brought dishonor upon your family."

Little Sparrow fell to her knees and prostrated herself. "But I had thought Your Sublime Majesty would be pleased to learn of the trickery, and place guards around the foreigners!" Keeping them here. Keeping my Heroic Tiger here forever.

"Foolish child, to assume that my son would be so easily duped. Foolish child, for forgetting one of the rules of your calling, that it is forbidden to speak of matters that an honored guest discusses in the bedroom. You will go home to your family. You will tell your father that his name will no longer be spoken in the emperor's court."

"But . . . he will put me to death!"

"As is a father's right."

A quick signal from the empress, and guards stepped in to drag Little Sparrow away. She did not plead for mercy. She kept her dignity to the last, even in the final moment as she understood the cruel irony of what she had just done: by revealing Heroic Tiger's secret plan to escape so that he could not leave, she had forfeited her own life.

32

"This is dangerous business, master," Timonides said as they scanned the busy marketplace for Bold Dragon. As he spoke, Timonides kept an eye on Nestor, who still had to be reminded at age thirty-five that goods offered in merchants' stalls were not there simply for the taking. "The emperor has eyes and ears everywhere. Ming knows we want to leave and that we will be searching for any possible avenue of escape."

"And if we don't find that avenue, my friend," Sebastianus replied as he watched the Gate of Heavenly Harmony for Primo and Bold Dragon, "we will truly be here for the rest of our lives." After nine months of enjoying the emperor's hospitality, generous and lavish though it was, Sebastianus was anxious to be heading home. But Ming seemed determined to keep the westerners prisoner.

Timonides was also eager to start for home. While he found this exotic land and culture forever delightful and challenging, and he did not truly mind being a "permanent guest," he was worried about his son.

As he kept an eye on Nestor's progress among the merchant stalls, Timonides saw three women stumbling about the marketplace, their sad cries for food and mercy making his stomach churn. They were yoked together at the neck, their three heads rising from a wooden plank upon which their crimes had been listed. He could not read Chinese, but imagined they had either disobeyed their husbands or spread malicious gossip about their neighbors. Women's crimes were not as vicious as men's, but the punishments were brutal nonetheless.

He turned away and once again his eyes went to Nestor, who was watching a pair of jugglers. Timonides was worried because his son had been acting strangely of late, exhibiting an anxiety and anxiousness uncharacteristic of the otherwise placid and contented Nestor. He was acting almost as if he *knew* they were being held prisoner in this city. Timonides understood his son's simple mind, that he had no true concept of time and distance. To Nestor, the city of Antioch lay just on the other side of the Mang Mountains, and they had left only yesterday. Thus, the years and miles that would make a sound-minded man grow anxious about going home would not normally trouble Nestor.

So what was causing this strange new anxiousness?

And where was Bold Dragon, the man whom they were trusting to help them escape?

Sebastianus and his companions had not been allowed outside Luoyang since the day of their arrival. It was a show of power, of course. The emperor had proudly captured the Roman Caesar's ambassador in the same way soldiers on a battlefield capture the enemy's flags. Ming would have sent word of such, along with China's precious silk brocade, lacquerware, and porcelain, westward on trade routes, to boast that he was the benevolent host to Rome's ambassadors, in the hope that the message would ultimately reach that *other* emperor, the one called Caesar.

Of course, Timonides thought philosophically, there was a great chance the news would not reach Nero at all. And if it did, there was nothing he could do to rescue them. But it wasn't as if their captivity was unpleasant. Timonides had to concede that detainment in the capital city was surprisingly comfortable, in fact luxurious. The villa he shared with his son, Sebastianus, and Primo was spacious with many servants. Their living quarters looked out upon a garden called the Courtyard of the Pure Heart, where trickling fountains delighted the eye, lily pads floated on the pond's tranquil surface, tame egrets waded in the shallows, and songbirds in airy cages filled the air with trilling music. The visitors from the west enjoyed plentiful delicious food and delightful pastimes that included discreet young ladies, called Social Flowers, at night.

They rarely saw any other women in the imperial compound, as the sexes were separated. But they sometimes heard, during warm evenings filled with the scent of jasmine, voices on the other side of the Gate of Whispering Bamboos, feminine chatter and laughter and the clatter of *mah-jongg* tiles—the emperor's mother, sisters, nieces, aunts, and concubines, along with hundreds of female servants and eunuchs, whiling away their hours and lives in idle leisure.

A paradise on earth, Timonides thought. But it was not Rome. And as Sebastianus and Timonides and Primo had explored every inch of this city, which was two miles long and one mile wide, there was nothing left that they did not know of it—from the filthy crowding of the southern poor quarters where families were crammed in hovels and barely earned a subsistence living, to the villas of the rich in the north bordering the Imperial Palace, whose lives were filled with grace and ease.

Timonides knew that their caravan and all its goods had been confiscated by the emperor. But Sebastianus could not complain. He himself had declared them to be gifts for Ming. The slaves and servants, even Primo's fighting men, were all detained in Luoyang, in quarters suitable to their respective social status. The only ones who were thrilled with the captivity were the Buddhist missionaries who were spending many hours with the emperor, teaching him the life and philosophy of their founder, the Enlightened One.

"Master," Timonides said now for the hundredth time, "why not give the emperor what he wants? If you don't want to tell him where military garrisons are located, or vital geography, then invent them. Draw him a fanciful map of the Roman empire. He would never know!"

Whenever Sebastianus was summoned to the presence of the emperor,

Ming would request politely that his honored guest draw a map of the Roman empire, indicating military installations, troop movements, war strategies. And each time Sebastianus would aver his ignorance on the subject—which was only partially true. Timonides knew they would be kept in Luoyang until the day they died if Sebastianus did not give the sovereign what he wanted.

"Because, Timonides my old friend, as I have already explained to you, Ming is putting me to a test. He is judging my integrity and character. Whether I draw him a true military map of the empire or a false one, either way it will reveal a lack of character on my part, for the former would mean a betrayal of my sovereign, the latter would mean I am being deceitful. Ming knows it can only be one or the other. And once I lose the emperor's respect, then we are no longer his guests, I am no longer an ambassador of Rome, and we go home in disgrace, having failed utterly at our mission."

"But now we do not go home at all!"

"But if we can manage to escape and avoid recapture, then we have saved face in both the eyes of Caesar and Emperor Ming. However, we need help. Where are Primo and Bold Dragon?"

Because they knew they were being watched, Sebastianus and Timonides strolled through the marketplace, idly inspecting novelty items unknown in Rome, which needed to be demonstrated in order to understand their function: small, handheld sticks for eating; a device made of bamboo and oiled cloth, held over the head against rain and the hot sun; fans made of feathers and silk, for wafting the face in heat; a board fixed with a metal spoon that, when spun, always returned to pointing north. They saw such wonders as lanterns made of paper, glowing in the night breeze; alchemists experimenting with a black powder that exploded; bamboo frameworks covered with silk, flying in the wind at the end of a long string.

Mostly they seemed like toys and gadgets to Sebastianus, but there were truly ingenious inventions as well, such as the small hand-propelled vehicle with one wheel in the front and two handles in the rear by which a man pushed and guided it—an ingenious device that allowed a worker to transport material too heavy to carry on his own. No such tool existed in Rome.

Sebastianus wished Ulrika could see these inventions for herself. Each time Sebastianus came upon something new, he thought of her, imagining her reaction. Ulrika loved to read. What would she make of Chinese literature printed on silk scrolls or painted in books made of peach wood? How would she discuss *The Book of Changes* by Confucius; *The Art of War* by Sun Tzu; a book of divination called *I Ching* by Fei Zhi; histories, biographies, volumes of poetry, myths, and fables?

He would love to discuss China's unique philosophies and beliefs with her. What would Ulrika make of the Great Sage, whose name was taboo to utter, a philosopher who lived five centuries ago? His name, Sebastianus had finally discovered, was K'ung-fu-tzu which meant "Master Kong," and which Sebastianus and Timonides rendered as Confucius, in order to avoid breaking the law of name-taboo. The Great Sage lived long ago and introduced a code of living that stressed morality, ethics, justice, and compassion, with principles of good conduct, practical wisdom, and proper social relationships.

There was also a local folk belief called Taoism, founded two hundred years prior by a man named Lao-Tzu. *Tao* was considered to be the Cosmic Intelligence, inaccessible to human understanding, that governed the natural course of all things. The practice encompassed black magic, alchemy, elixirs of life, and hundreds of gods. Taoists revered ancestor spirits and beings they called the Immortals, and were known for their devotion to the quest for immortality, as evidenced in their search for magic herbs and minerals that would promote eternal earthly life.

So many wonders in this exotic land! Sebastianus wished he could take Ulrika to the emperor's private zoo so that she could marvel at the black-eyed pandas, pacing white tigers, and orangutans that looked like old men. He wished she could feast her eyes on other fabulous offerings in the marketplace: towering statues of pink jade, carved into the likeness of Kwan-Yin, goddess of mercy; mountains of colorful silks and satins that blinded the eye; vast amphorae filled with delectable rice wine; urns beyond counting, groaning with aromatic spices; a confection made of almonds, called marzipan, molded into the shapes of animals and flowers; and bundles of a rare medicinal plant, called rhubarb, highly prized and very costly and found only on the banks of the Chang Jiang River.

He could not wait to share with her Chinese customs and traditions: the belief in and respect for dragons; the custom of both men and women to wear their hair long in the belief that since one got one's hair from one's parents it was disrespectful to cut it; the practice of dressing little boys as girls in the hope of fooling mischievous spirit-thieves into thinking he was a mere girl and not worth stealing; the ritual of placing dried peonies beneath a bed to keep evil spirits away.

He would explain to Ulrika that preserving family honor, saving face, and paying respects to the ancestors were prized above one's life, and that a man would prefer death to failing to observe these virtues. The Chinese also had a passion for harmony, long life, and good luck, all of which were pursued through the use of incense, amulets, charms, lucky numbers, and an almost fanatical devotion to keeping evil spirits out of the house by use of deceptive screens, waterfalls, and broomsticks.

Ulrika was in Sebastianus's thoughts day and night. Every single new thing he met and marveled at made him wish to share it with her. His love for her had grown over the miles and the months. He thought of the Social Flowers who greeted him and his companions in the evenings, after a day spent with the emperor or with astrologers and philosophers and other learned men. Beautiful young women, slim and delicate, like lilies indeed, demure and compliant, sweetly scented and softly spoken. They gave pleasure, as their name promised, but Sebastianus found it to be an empty pleasure, as there was only one woman whose embrace he truly desired.

Sebastianus had achieved his goal of reaching the throne of China. He knew that honors awaited him in Rome, that his name would be spoken far and wide for his achievement. But, in the end, what he had learned from Chinese philosophers and astrologers, from the emperor and his mandarins, from people in the streets and merchants' stalls, from the Social Flowers even, was that love was more important than honors and fame and knowledge. After nearly a year of drinking in this exotic culture and soaking up China's wisdom, Sebastianus knew that it was all empty if he had no one with whom to share it.

And what of Ulrika's life? What was she doing at that moment? Where was she? Was she happy or sad? Did she find her mother in Jerusalem? Did she find an explanation for her visions? Does she now know the meaning of the Divining and the location of Shalamandar? Sebastianus did not want to miss out on the milestones of Ulrika's life. Just as he wished she could share in his adventure, he wanted to share in hers.

"Primo said they would be here by noon," Sebastianus murmured as they neared the Gate of Heavenly Harmony, which led to the crowded southern quarter of the city. He looked up at the sun. It was now midday.

Timonides sensed his master's growing anxiousness and wished there was something he could do to alleviate it. He cast Sebastianus's horoscope twice a day, but nowhere could he read when their day of departure would be, or the manner of that departure. Wondering if perhaps, because they were in China, they should employ the methods of Chinese astrology, Timonides had studied the heavens with palace astrologers, but had ultimately not been able to master the science as it was so different from that of Greece and Rome.

In Chinese astrology, there were twelve star signs, each a different animal that ruled its own year and that supposedly demonstrated the characteristics of the person born in that year. There were also animal signs assigned to each month (called inner animals) and then to hours of the day (called secret animals). And so while a person might appear to be an Ox because he was born in the year of the Ox, he might also be a Bear internally and a Dragon secretively. This made for over eight thousand combinations, each a different personality with a different horoscope.

It made Timonides's head spin. He went back to his twelve zodiacal signs, his charts, and his protractor. But no predictions were forthcoming and he was beginning to wonder if possibly the power of the gods of Greece and Rome did not reach this far.

He returned to watching Nestor, a giant among the citizens of Luoyang, as he wandered into the corner of the spice market, where food vendors were cooking over open fires. Nestor had not found eastern cooking a challenge, quickly taking to soybeans, native to China, and other such culinary oddities as cucumbers, ginger, and anise. Nestor had even learned a new way of cooking: because China did not have big forests, cooking fuel was always hard to find and so the Chinese had learned to cut up their food into tiny pieces so that it would fry quickly when stirred over a small fire.

Typical of the astrologer's simple-minded son, Nestor had already mastered such exotic dishes as rice fried with scallions; stewed crab and crispy eel; boiled turtle with ham; lotus seeds in honey. His masterpiece was deep-fried chicken feet with black bean sauce. It made Timonides salivate just to think of them.

But Timonides frowned now as he watched his son taste a pinch of pepper at a spice seller's stall. Nestor's craft had slipped of late. Too much salt, not enough oil. Delicacies such as cow's eyes and sheep's testicles over-cooked and ruined. Did the boy, in his strange way of thinking that was both simple and complex, sense that they were trying to get out of Luoyang?

Primo finally appeared in the crowd, looking cross and anxious. And he was alone. When he neared his two friends, he glanced over his shoulder before saying quietly to Sebastianus, "Bold Dragon is dead. His headless corpse was found floating in the river."

"Ming discovered our plan."

Sebastianus immediately thought of Little Sparrow, who had never come back to his bed after the night of Bold Dragon's visit. He had inquired about her, but had been met with blank responses, as if she did not exist. He was not in love with her. His feelings for her were always of the moment. While his body was with the girl from a northern province of China, his heart was always with Ulrika. But still, her absence had made him wonder.

And he wondered now if her disappearance at the same time Bold Dragon was killed was no coincidence. Sebastianus had been warned about being kind to the pleasure-girls. They could be grasping and jealous, the eunuchs had cautioned. They wove intrigue among themselves, during their long days of boredom, with each one striving to rise in rank above the others. Had Little Sparrow overheard his secret conversation with Primo and Bold Dragon, and then reported it to someone on the emperor's staff? She would have been richly rewarded, he decided, for warning the emperor of their plan to escape.

Sebastianus hoped that whatever Little Sparrow's reward for her treachery, she was enjoying it. Because now it was going to be impossible to get out of Luoyang.

"Master," Timonides wailed, "tell the emperor what he wants to know."

"You cannot do that," Primo hissed. "To divulge Rome's military extent, strengths, and weaknesses would be treason."

"And if we never leave here?" the astrologer snapped. "Caesar would understand."

"Or send us to the arena."

"Look!" Sebastianus said, pointing. They saw Noble Heron riding toward them in his familiar red and gold carrying chair.

The high official stepped to the ground. "Esteemed guest," he said to Sebastianus with an elegant bow. "It is my humble honor to inform you that the Lord of Ten Thousand Years intends to make a journey around the countryside to introduce his new empress to his vassal peoples."

A few weeks prior, Ming had been persuaded by his mother the dowager empress to elevate his consort, Ma, to the lofty position of empress. Luoyang had exploded with celebrations. Ma was popular with the courtiers, and the citizens of Luoyang loved what they had heard about her. Sebastianus himself admired the young lady, who was humble and solemn for one so elevated. The other imperial consorts and princesses were all surprised at how thrifty she was, as Ma often wore less expensive silk, and without elaborate designs. Emperor Ming consulted her often on important matters of state.

Noble Heron continued, "The Lord of Ten Thousand Years wishes to show his love and respect for his empress in front of his subjugated peoples, and to allow them the privilege and honor of paying homage to her. As part of the continued celebrations marking her crowning as empress," he said, nodding toward the many colorful paper lanterns that still decorated the market square after weeks of festivities, "the entire royal court will set out upon a journey to visit the countryside, and the Lord of Heaven wishes to invite his guests from Li-chien to join the happy journey."

Sebastianus and Primo exchanged a glance, each thinking that the festive journey most likely had more to do with parading the powerful presence of the Han Family and to gather intelligence on possible rebellions. It was well known that North Xiongnu continued to be a constant threat to both Han and her ally South Xiongnu. Although Emperor Ming engaged in a variety of military and economic tactics to try to maintain peace with North Xiongnu, the peace was shaky. A show of might was called for.

As they watched Noble Heron ride away, Sebastianus said excitedly to his two companions, "My friends, I believe this is the opportunity we have been praying for."

33

THE FIERCE HORSEMEN LINED up to face one another on the grassy plain, a hundred to each side, their husky mounts—the famous steppe horses with dense fur coats and thick skins, and known for their endurance—spirited and eager for the fray. The riders wore tall felt hats, leather trousers, and sheep's wool tunics. They called themselves Tazhkin and considered themselves to be the hardiest people alive because their ancestors came from a harsh realm at the southern edge of the Gobi Desert. It was said that, in combat, the screams of these warriors so curdled the blood of the enemy that they dropped dead before a single dagger was thrown.

And yet, somehow, Emperor Ming's father, the great Guangwu, had managed to defeat the Tazhkin with his forces and turn them into allies of the Chinese empire.

A great crowd stood along one length of the plain, men and women of the Tazhkin, but Chinese, too, from Ming's enormous retinue. The emperor himself was not in view, but rather was ensconced within his heavily guarded pavilion, as it was discovered that his wife was pregnant, and her many advisors cautioned that for her to look upon combat would instill a violent nature in her child.

But it was not truly a battle that was about to take place, it was a game. They called it "polo" and it was played by two teams of a hundred horsemen each, and consisted of swinging long sticks at a leather ball as the riders galloped at reckless speeds across the grassy plain.

Sebastianus stood with his companions in the boisterous crowd, waiting for the game to begin. He knew now why they had been invited along on this inspection tour—so that Emperor Ming could further demonstrate his power by parading his "guests" to his subjugated peoples, men from fabled Li-chien who served a powerful ruler—but not as powerful as the Lord of Ten Thousand Years.

In every province, village, and territory they visited, Sebastianus had observed the emperor with his advisors sitting beneath a magnificent red and gold canopy, surrounded by servants and guards, conferring quietly. Sebastianus listened at campfires as he made the acquaintance of strangers. He told Primo to talk with local soldiers. If an uprising were fomenting against Emperor Ming, proud warrior clans chafing under the yoke of the Celestial Ruler, Sebastianus wanted to know. An outbreak of war would be their opportunity to escape.

When Sebastianus had once considered simply asking the emperor's permission to go home, Noble Heron had warned him that such a request would be a great insult to the Heavenly Lord, as it would tell the world that the emperor's hospitality was lacking, for why else would guests wish to leave? In order to save face, the Lord of Ten Thousand Years would have to counteract by increasing his hospitality to the foreign guests by making their stay in Luoyang even more luxurious. And they would still be prisoners.

And now the tour was over, tomorrow they were to return to Luoyang. Both Sebastianus and Emperor Ming knew that the Romans' usefulness had come to an end. Both were weary of the novelty of this first meeting between east and west. Sebastianus suspected that Ming would be pleased for them to leave, to return to Caesar and inform him of the might and power of Emperor Ming. However, to allow the Romans leave would cause Ming to lose face. To allow them even an avenue of escape, no matter how cleverly staged, would be perceived as a weakness of the emperor's security guard.

And so they were at a stalemate, and Sebastianus was at a loss to find a solution.

At his side, standing in disgruntled silence, Timonides watched the polo match with a jaundiced eye. An idiotic way to pass the time, he thought as he marveled at the fever-pitch frenzy of the spectators who screamed and jumped up and down and cursed and cheered. Chariot races were so much more civilized. Timonides could not wait to get back to his own world. He was looking forward to the fame they were certain to enjoy in Rome. There would most likely be a triumphal parade in their honor, and feasting that would go on for days. Rice and noodles were all well and good, but he missed sinking his teeth into a loaf of good hot bread dipped in olive oil.

Nestor exploded with laughter and clapped his hands. It made the old Greek's heart expand with love to see his son enjoying himself so. He knew that Nestor did not grasp what he was watching, that there were points to be won and prizes to be had. The boy just liked watching the horses thundering back and forth amid the shouts of the riders. And after all it wasn't necessary for Nestor to understand the game because Timonides knew that his son's simple mind was now a repository of countless recipes for exotic dishes that were going to make him very popular in Rome.

We will open an eating house near the Forum and people will come from miles around for a taste of fabled China. Senators will sit at the tables of Timonides the Greek. Perhaps even the Emperor himself . . .

The polo game ended and the visitors from the west—who bore the extreme distinction of being guests of the Emperor of China—were invited to dine in the tent of the Tazhkin chief. Ming and his empress, and their entourage of over five hundred, dined separately in a collection of red and gold pavilions that made up a small village. Sebastianus and his friends were not part of that elite, unapproachable clique.

The banquet put on by Chief Jammu was surprisingly sumptuous, with expensive delicacies and costly wine that flowed freely. As Sebastianus and his friends sat cross-legged on elegant carpets and dined off brass plates, it was apparent that this was a wealthy tribe. Jammu's many guests, the heads of noble families, were healthy and well dressed. The men wore tall hats made of colorful felt, with sheepskin vests and woolen trousers, while the women wore pantaloons beneath long silk shifts. Maidens covered their faces with veils while the wives of prosperous men festooned their foreheads with gold coins. Many villages and settlements the emperor had visited were inhabited by farmers barely making a subsistence living, but these Tazhkin, with their platters heaped with meat, and goblets brimming with wine, were wealthy.

From what? Sebastianus wondered.

The usual dancers and musicians, jugglers and acrobats were brought out to entertain the men from the west, while Sebastianus tried to describe Rome to Chief Jammu—now with the aid of a *fourth* translator who spoke Chinese and Tazhkin, so that Sebastianus wondered how accurately his information was being conveyed, going through four men as it did.

More wine flowed and the music grew louder until Chief Jammu—a large, barrel-chested man with missing teeth and bronze skin—began to boast about something Sebastianus could not comprehend. The translators, it seemed, grew less skillful the more the wine loosened their tongues. And so when he hefted his large frame from the carpet and gestured to his guests, Sebastianus and Primo and Timonides had to rise with him and wonder where they were being taken.

Outside, they found imperial Chinese guards standing watch, as they had done since leaving Luoyang—a constant reminder to Sebastianus that he and his companions were prisoners—and they fell into step behind the small group as the chief led them through the chilly spring night.

They arrived at an enormous tent, even larger than the one in which they had dined and been entertained. It glowed from within and was guarded by Tazhkin soldiers, who snapped to attention when they saw their chief. Sebastianus could not imagine the purpose of so large a tent, or why it was guarded, and he suspected that he and Timonides and Primo were about to be shown the tribe's treasure. He imagined gold and gems as the chief bent his tall frame to step through the opening.

They followed, with Timonides making sure his son did not bang his head on the wooden door frame, for Nestor was taller even than the Tazhkin chief. As their eyes adjusted to the dim light of the interior, the visitors from the west frowned at the sight before them. "What is this?" Timonides asked, taking in the rows of tables that appeared to be covered with balls of white cotton.

They were led closer, and saw that the "cotton balls" were lined in rows and pinched between long wooden dowels, thousands of them, lying on the racks like snow. Through the translators, the visitors learned from Chief Jammu that what they were looking at were the cocoons of silk moths. The man from Pisa, who spoke Persian and Latin, explained that the special moths were husbanded like cattle or sheep, nurtured and protected until they lay their eggs on specially prepared paper. When the eggs hatched, the newborn caterpillars were fed fresh leaves, and after one month were ready. A wooden frame was placed over the tray of caterpillars and each began spinning a cocoon, attaching it to one of the long dowels in the frame. Within three days the caterpillars were completely encased in their cocoons.

The caterpillars were then killed by heat, and the cocoons were soaked in boiling water to soften the silk fibers, which were then unwound to produce continuous threads.

The guests followed Jammu as he boastfully described this process, and Sebastianus knew that he was omitting certain steps because it was illegal for anyone other than silk farmers to know the secret of making silk. So carefully guarded was the secret of manufacturing silk, in fact, that it was a death sentence to even try to smuggle a single silkworm out of China.

It took five thousand silkworms, Jammu bragged through his missing front teeth, to make one silk robe. Which was why, Sebastianus and his friends knew, silk was so costly in Rome, especially as it must pass through so many middlemen after leaving China, with each raising the price in order to make a profit. Were this secret ever to make it back to Rome, along with moths to start a small silk farm, the lucrative business here in China would dry up.

At the conclusion of the tour, the visitors were treated to a dazzling sight: rows of racks holding harvested silk that was awaiting only to be woven and dyed and made into scrolls, wall hangings, kites, clothing. The long silky filaments, bundled so thickly that they resembled a woman's tresses, glowed like white gold in the flickering torchlight. Sebastianus and his friends were speechless at the sight of the gossamer strands, worth even more than gold or the rarest of gemstones.

Thanking the chief, who was now swaying on his feet, the men from Rome retired to their tent to rest up for the journey back to Luoyang. They could not get the sight of that luxurious silk out of their minds, and as they undressed, Timonides said quietly, "Master, if we could obtain some of those worms, those cocoons, and take them back to Rome, we could be wealthy beyond measure."

Sebastianus pulled his tunic over his head and tossed it down. "The punishment for smuggling silkworms is death, my old friend. It isn't worth it."

"But still," Timonides said wistfully. "We would be the most famous men in Rome. Nestor and I could buy ourselves a villa, a comfortable retirement . . ."

"You will always have a home with me. Go to sleep, old friend. We have just one day to find a weakness in the emperor's security, and then we are prisoners in the city again."

When Sebastianus doused the lights and the tent was in darkness, and presently both he and the astrologer were snoring, Nestor lay on his pallet staring up at the ceiling.

For a long time now he had sensed that his father was unhappy, and Nestor loved his Papa very much. He had sought ways to please him, had searched for gifts in the marketplace, but nothing had shone for Nestor. A gift for his Papa had to be special.

He thought of the silken threads in that big tent. They would make Papa happy. He could buy a villa. Papa would be comfortable.

Nestor crept from his tent and loped swiftly and silently through the sleeping camp. He remembered where the shining hair was because it was in the biggest tent, which stood silhouetted against the stars. He saw the guards at the entrance and would have walked right in, but then he saw their spears and he wondered if they were hurtful men. So he went around the side, searching the perimeter of the enormous structure made of goatskins and felt, until he was on the other side, and there were no men with sticks here.

The tent was well anchored into the hard ground, but Nestor was big and strong and he was able, after much grunting and groaning, to lift the staked wall and crawl under it. By the light of the few torches that glowed inside the tent, he saw the beautiful white filaments, bundled like a lady's hair, hanging from pegs.

Nestor helped himself, curling his big thick fingers around the clump of silk strands, and then he paused to look at the white cocoons spread out on tables. He wanted one of those, too. Another gift for Papa.

Nestor was so intent upon reaching for a cocoon, trying not to break it or disturb the tiny caterpillar sleeping within, that he did not hear the guards enter the tent, was not aware of their presence until he turned around.

Nestor thought that if he smiled at the men with the clubs, they would not hurt him.

It was the final game of the week-long polo match, and tension and excitement filled the air.

Timonides searched the crowd. Where was Nestor? He would not want to miss this game.

"What is that?" Sebastianus said, pointing out onto the field where the two teams were lining up with clubs.

Timonides squinted out over the sparse grass. "It's the ball—" He gasped. "Great Zeus!" he cried.

Sebastianus and Timonides ran out onto the field, where Nestor's head rose out of the ground. They saw the packed earth around him and realized in horror that the simpleton had been buried in a deep pit up to his neck.

Before Sebastianus and Timonides could reach him, horsemen rode up and barred the way. "You must stop this!" Timonides cried. "My son has done no wrong!"

Sebastianus turned and dashed away from the field to the canopy beneath which Chief Jammu and his military aides sat on wooden chairs. When Sebastianus demanded to know what was going on, the chief said,

"The man was caught in the Silk House stealing from us. He had silk in his hands, and a cocoon. The punishment is death."

"But he didn't know! Nestor has the mind of a child!"

They heard a shout and the start of thundering hooves. Sebastianus and Timonides turned in time to see the horses racing toward Nestor. Even as the hooves came down on him, and the first great club, Nestor laughed.

As Timonides watched in frozen horror, as he saw the blood and bone and bits of brain fly up from the clubs, he remembered that silk was produced by the mulberry worm. And thus the fulfillment of an ox scapula prophecy.

SEBASTIANUS FOUND HIS FRIEND lying on a pallet, staring lifelessly at the ceiling. Timonides's eyes were red and puffy, but he no longer wept. The sun had set, the stars were out, and he had no more tears to shed.

"I requested an audience with the emperor," Sebastianus said, "and he has granted it. I am going to ask him to allow us to leave. We cannot stay here any longer. I am responsible for what happened to Nestor. I should have insisted long ago that we be permitted to leave. I only hope you can forgive me, my old friend, for allowing us to remain prisoner here so long."

Timonides did not speak, and a short time later, after following the usual, wearisome protocol, Sebastianus bowed respectfully and said to Ming: "Your Majesty, I have seen with my own eyes the wise and compassionate way the Lord of Ten Thousand Years governs his vassals, and I see that they are happy under his rule. I believe my own emperor would be interested to hear about the wise and mighty Lord of Heaven, and perhaps he can even learn from the sovereign of the Flowery Land. I humbly ask that I be allowed to return to my country and paint for my Emperor and all the high officials a portrait of the wise and compassionate rule of the Lord of Ten Thousand Years. It will be a great honor to praise Your Majesty's name from here to Rome and instill in the peoples along the way a fearsome respect for the name of the lofty one who occupies Your Majesty's throne.

"Your Majesty's generosity exceeds the number of stars in the night sky. Truly Your Majesty is the most generous man on earth. I wish to have the honor of telling the world of the greatness of the Lord of Heaven. I wish to boast of my having been your humble guest and the recipient of the Lord of Heaven's bounty and compassion. I wish to return to my country and impress my own emperor with this knowledge."

Ming said nothing. His face was without expression beneath the curious crown of beaded fringe. Ma sat silently at his side.

"In return for this generous favor, Your Majesty," Sebastianus continued, "I will tell you about the might and power of Rome. Her armies are like the seas, her soldiers are like dragons that breathe fire, her machines of war are like thunder and lightning. I tell Your Majesty these things not to betray my country, nor to boast in falsehoods—for what I say of Rome's legions is true—but to offer the Lord of Heaven the opportunity to join with a great ally that is almost as powerful as himself. Persia is Rome's enemy. And I know that the Han people would like to subjugate Persia. Together, Rome and China can surround Persia and show that lowly nation what great races we are."

Sebastianus maintained composure as the silence lengthened. He could not read Ming's face, and wondered if he had gone too far. But then the young emperor turned to Empress Ma and they exchanged a murmured dialogue.

Finally the Lord of Ten Thousand Years turned to Sebastianus and, through the interpreters, said, "Our honorable guest has anticipated a decision we had already made, many weeks ago. It is our desire to learn more about the teachings of the one called Buddha. We wish to build a shrine to him, and to share those teachings with the citizens of China. It was our plan to send some of the Buddhist missionaries, whom you brought to Luoyang a year ago, back to their home in India so that they may gather books and statues of the Enlightened One and bring them to us. We had intended to ask you, honored guest, if you would do us the great favor of escorting these missionaries back to India, and from there carry our respectful greetings to your Emperor in Li-chien.

"It is a most propitious sign that we arrived at the same thought together. It means that your journey is predestined and therefore will be a safe and lucky one. We will supply your caravan with whatever the missionaries need, as well as gifts for your Caesar and diplomatic passes that will guarantee your safe passage through territories between here and Persia. It is our wish that you depart Luoyang as soon as possible."

Sebastianus bowed and exited the pavilion. He wondered if Ming had truly meant to let them go, or if the excuse of the Buddhist missionaries were a way of saving face.

It did not matter. They were going home.

BOOK EIGHT
BABYLON

34

Ulrika stood anxiously at the prow of *The Fortunate Wind,* searching the crowded dock as she drew near.

Pray let Sebastianus still be here.

Her boat was propelled by sixty oarsmen and carried a cargo of copper ingots. The sides of the boat were colorfully decorated with figures from myth, and the sails were bright blue and red in the sunlight. Ulrika tried to mentally urge the oarsmen to row faster, faster.

The Euphrates River ran through the center of Babylon, and so the massive protective walls that encircled the city spanned the river at two ends. Watercraft sailed under stone arches and through a series of movable iron gates cleverly engineered to keep invaders out. The quayside on this sunny spring morning was crowded and bustling with industry as sailors handled oars and rigging, passengers and families cried farewells and welcomes, vendors hawked their wares, and city officials stood at their posts recording departures and arrivals, assessing incoming and outgoing cargo, levying taxes.

Ulrika was returning from a visit upriver to the town of Salama, where a shrine had been built to house clay tablets that were said to be the oldest sacred books in the world, and which held secrets that not even the priests of Marduk knew. In her quest to find the Venerable Ones, Ulrika had sailed to Salama to meet with the caretakers of the shrine. And while she was there, she had heard of a Roman party that had successfully traveled to China and was now back in Babylon, bringing a caravan filled with exotic curiosities and treasure. The governor of Babylon had thrown a feast for the Romans, who in turn allowed citizens to walk among the oddities and look for themselves at strange creatures and fabulous riches from a mythical land. The caravan was heavily guarded, the gossips said, as its goods were the property of Nero Caesar and soon bound for Rome.

Ulrika had left Salama at once, buying passage aboard *The Fortunate Wind,* and now she searched the crowd on the bustling docks for a familiar head of bronze-colored hair set upon wide shoulders. Her heart raced. *Sebastianus, are you here?*

BABYLON HAD CHANGED, SEBASTIANUS observed as he made his way through the crowd on the docks. In the seven years that had passed since he was last here, the personality of the cosmopolitan center had shifted from one of tolerance to one of prejudice. The priests of Marduk, he had learned, were growing increasingly intolerant of outside religions, demanding that the citizens of Babylon worship only at the altars of the gods who had ruled here for centuries. Intolerance against other beliefs was encouraged. Mistrust of the followers of foreign gods was fostered.

Babylon had fallen upon hard times. Men had lost their jobs, and many begged on street corners. Houses stood empty because people could not afford to pay their landlords. The sick had no money to pay physicians. Crime infested the streets. People were afraid. They blamed the gods and the government for their misfortunes. Even in Rome, Sebastianus had heard, senators had become corrupt and officials could be bribed. The Imperial Treasury was bankrupt. And Nero, in whom everyone had placed such high hopes, had disappointed his citizens. It was said that he had launched a massive work program, erecting impossibly big buildings around Rome, in the hopes of fooling the people into thinking they were enjoying a spell of prosperity.

Here, in this city between two rivers, the priests of Marduk knew that when people were discontented and believed the gods powerless, they took their lives and their destinies into their own hands. Which meant that money normally going to the priests was crossing the palms of fortune-tellers and wonder-workers. And so anyone suspected of luring citizens and their money away from the temples was arrested and interrogated. Many were executed under the laws of sacrilege and blasphemy. Even here by the water, Sebastianus detected on the shifting wind the stink of rotting flesh. Although he could not see the corpses strung up on Babylon's walls, he knew they were there.

"Pay heed! Pay heed!"

Sebastianus turned to see a city crier climb up on a stone block so that he rose above the heads of the crowd. In an impressively loud and ringing voice, he bellowed. "Make it known to all newcomers, visitors, traders, travelers, and tourists to Babylon that the following people are forbidden to move freely in the city without first registering with the Royal Guard at the Temple of Marduk: magicians, necromancers, seers, sorcerers, conjurers, wonder-workers, medicine-men, diviners, and prophets. All who ignore this edict will be subject to arrest, trial, and punishment."

Putting the world's ills from his thoughts, Sebastianus searched for a boat that looked as if it might be getting ready to depart upriver. He needed to reach the town of Salama as quickly as possible. Ulrika was there.

The moment he had brought his weary caravan to the terminus outside Babylon's walls, Sebastianus had dispatched letters to men of his acquaintance in Jerusalem and Antioch, for information on Ulrika. But because she had said she would join him in Babylon if she could, he had sent men into the city to see if she was here. In the meantime, he had had to suffer the hospitality of local government officials, to ride in a parade through the Ishtar Gate, and patiently tolerate the accolades heaped upon the first man from the west to look upon the face of China. Each night, Sebastianus would inquire of his men if there were any leads as to Ulrika's whereabouts. They had

had nothing to report until this morning. "I found her living in the Jewish Quarter, master, in the home of a widowed seamstress. But she went upriver three months ago and did not say when she would return."

As he pushed through the bustling dockside mob, searching for a departing vessel, Sebastianus wondered if Ulrika had received his letter.

"Master. Master!"

He turned and was startled to see Primo pushing through the crowd. "Master," the veteran called. "You must postpone your trip upriver. Your presence is requested at the residence of Quintus Publius."

"Again?" The ambassador from Rome to the Persian province of Babylon had already entertained Sebastianus and his companions with a victory feast at his villa west of the city. "I can't take the time. Tell him I will see him when I return from Salama."

"Master," Primo said in a grave tone. "Perhaps you should not ignore this request."

"I do not answer to an ambassador from Rome, or any other official for that fact. I answer only to Nero and he, fortunately, is many miles away. Go back and explain that I am on an urgent errand."

"But—"

Sebastianus turned and continued through the crowd, leaving his old friend and steward to scowl with worry and displeasure. Before Primo could follow his master, to persuade him to meet with the very important and powerful Publius, he saw Sebastianus head for a boat that was casting off its lines, its prow pointing upriver. And Primo realized the futility of trying to make his master see reason. To make him understand the dangerous, possibly treasonous, action he was about to take.

Primo hurried away, dreading his meeting with the powerful Quintus Publius.

❦

Clutching her packs and medicine kit, and filled with excitement and hope, Ulrika hurried down the gangplank. She had lived these past five years in Babylon searching for the whereabouts of Venerable Ones, inquiring at temples, meeting with wisemen and prophetesses, and perfecting her skills at focused meditation—always with Sebastianus in the forefront of her mind and in her heart. And now he was here in Babylon.

Was it a sign that, being reunited with the man she loved, she was going to find the Venerable Ones at last?

As she made her way through the press of humanity on the wharf, with the sounds of human cries and shouts, and animals braying and bleating, with the smells of the green river and flowering plants, the massive stone structures rising on either side of the river, monuments called ziggurats climbing to the sky in diminishing tiers, their terraces congested with plants and trees and vines—the famous Hanging Gardens of Babylon—she began to notice the conspicuous presence of temple guards on the docks, their breastplates and helmets gleaming of gold, their spears tipped with silver, as if to proclaim their wealth and therefore the power of Marduk.

Ulrika felt a frenetic atmosphere in the air that she had not felt five years ago, when she had returned from Persia. She saw now the fear on people's faces, the suspicion in their eyes. Nonetheless, she was excited to be here. The energy of the city infused her blood and bones. Babylon! With its graceful towers and spires, massive crenellated walls, enormous gates imbedded with shining tiles of blue and red and yellow, depicting mythical beasts that took one's breath away. The day was warming up. Her nostrils were assailed by the familiar stink of the city: delicious cooking aromas mingling with the acrid smell of dung fires and the stench of animal feces and human urine. Ulrika walked past obsessive gamblers playing a game of chance involving pebbles and sticks. She made her way around dancing girls twirling in colorful skirts. The streets were clogged with housewives buying olives, men haggling over wagers, snake charmers, fire-eaters, dung-sweepers, beggars, perfumed aristocrats in litters carried on the shoulders of slaves. Ulrika's ears were assaulted by an unceasing din of shouts, laughter, music, weeping. The spectrum of human emotion was compressed within a few square miles of narrow streets, dusty lanes, sunlit plazas, sagging tenements, and mansions housing unimaginable luxury and dreams.

She filled her ears with the polyglot sounds of many languages, and it felt good to hear Aramaic spoken again, and a dialect of Greek that was closer to her mother tongue than that which was heard in lands farther east.

She heard the familiar Persian, and Phoenician, Hebrew, Egyptian, Latin, and even a few tongues she did not recognize, reminding her of the legend that Babylon was the birthplace of mankind's many languages.

As Ulrika reached the base of the giant gate that led out of the city, she saw corpses hanging from the crenellated wall of the Hall of Justice. Criminals who had been slung up by their heels and left to die. This was Babylon's notorious form of execution. Here, crucifixions were never seen and Ulrika wondered if it was because of the scarcity of trees in this part of the world, making wood too precious to waste on the condemned. The dead and dying victims had all been branded, she saw, with a symbol that identified them as blasphemers and those who had committed sacrilege against the city's gods.

Whispering a prayer for their souls, she joined the busy foot traffic heading out of the city. Just ahead lay the great terminus of caravans arriving from the east.

As Sebastianus hurried toward *Ishtar's Delight,* a small boat with wine amphorae lashed to its deck, and twelve oarsmen preparing to lower their oars into the water, he saw a woman disappear through the crowd near the city gate. He stopped and squinted. Her height, her shape, her gait . . .

Was it she? Or was he so eager to find Ulrika that he was now seeing her in every woman on the street?

The crowd parted briefly. He saw her pause to look at the condemned men hanging on the crenellated wall, and as she turned, he glimpsed her face.

It was she!

"Ulrika!" he called, but she was swallowed up by the crowd.

He pushed through, shouting her name, dodging crates and dogs, trying to keep her in view. She had gone in the direction of the caravan terminus. Travel packs on her shoulders, and a medicine box slung on a strap . . . Was she planning on leaving?

He ran through the main gate, calling out. And then he saw her, just up ahead.

"Ulrika!"

She stopped and turned. He saw a look of astonishment on her face. He cried out with joy.

Ulrika ran to him, staring at Sebastianus with wide eyes as he drew near, wondering if he was real or a vision. He wore a handsome dark brown tunic, edged at the hem and short sleeves in gold embroidery and belted at the waist with a knotted cord. On his feet, sandals that were laced up to his knees, and a cream-colored cloak swung from his broad shoulders. He seemed taller than she remembered, his body more powerfully built, as if the thousands of miles had imbued him with new life and virility. She remembered that he was nearly forty years of age, yet seemed much younger.

Before she could speak, he reached out, pulled her to him, and embraced her, saying, "I found you, I found you."

Ulrika tried to catch her breath as she pressed her face against his chest and heard the reassuring thump of his heart. "It is you," she murmured. "It is truly you."

Sebastianus drew back to look down at her with damp eyes, his hands on her arms and his face so close that she saw a small scar on his chin—a new scar, so that she wondered what foreign weapon, or thorn, or cat had caused it. There were new wrinkles, too, at the corners of his eyes, as if he had laughed a lot in China, or seen too much sun. But his voice was as she remembered, deep and mellow as he said, "I knew you would be here. Somehow, I knew."

She struggled for breath. The feel of his hands on her arms, the strong grip, the heat that permeated her *palla* and ignited her skin. "I came to Babylon seven years ago. The Caravan Master said I had missed you by a month."

"Did you get my letter?"

She reached into one of her packs and produced a small scroll. It was yellowed and worn from so much handling, from being read a thousand times. "Even though I had committed it to memory," she said, "I still needed to see the words on the papyrus, written in your own hand."

"Ulrika I have so much to tell you—"

"And I, you. Sebastianus, you reached China!"

"What of you? The visions, the Divining. Did you go to Persia? Did you find the Crystal Pools?"

"Yes, yes, yes," she whispered. While citizens of Babylon streamed around them, and carts rattled by, and horses picked their way over the paving bricks of the roadway, Ulrika filled her eyes with the sight of this man. After all the sunsets and dawns, midnights and noons she had spent thinking about Sebastianus, dreaming about him, talking to him, feeling her love for him grow—here he was. Tall, solid, bronze hair shining in the sun, Galician-green eyes looking down at her with a piercing gaze.

"Come," he said, taking her travel packs and medicine kit, slinging them over his broad shoulders.

As they left the gate and the city and the crowds, as Ulrika walked at Sebastianus's side, feeling his hand on her arm as he guided her, protected her, she thought the sun had never shone so brightly, the river breezes had never been so fresh, the crops in the fields never so green.

She thought her heart would burst with joy and love.

They came to the vast staging field for caravans heading for distant places. Sebastianus led Ulrika along lines of kneeling camels, the stench of dung filling the air, with flies buzzing about, and men hurrying this way and that among what seemed like a hundred tents.

A man came around a service tent, wiping his hands on a cloth, frowning in deep thought. Ulrika recognized him as Primo, the military veteran who had been Sebastianus's chief steward. He looked a little older, a little more weathered, but she was pleased he had come through the experience unscathed, for she recalled that it was he who had been responsible for the safety of the caravan.

He glanced up and when he saw his master, grinned. But then his eyes caught Ulrika and his grin not only faded, it was replaced by a scowl.

"He's not happy about something," Ulrika murmured.

"Primo is anxious to return to Rome. He has been insisting that we leave Babylon." Sebastianus smiled. "I would agree with him, except that I knew you were here and I had to find you."

Ulrika sensed something darker behind Primo's look of displeasure. She could not pinpoint it, but she had the feeling that his anger was directed at her. Recalling her feeling, back in Antioch, that a traitor lurked among Sebastianus's men, Ulrika wondered if there was more to Primo's dark look than impatience to get to Rome.

And then she received a shock. A frail, white-haired man with gaunt cheeks and arms like sticks, his robes hanging loosely on him, came up and said, "It is good to see you again, dear child."

Ulrika stared at him. It took her a moment to realize it was Timonides. What had happened to the old astrologer? She tried to hide her dismay by smiling and saying, "It is good to see you again, Timonides."

"Here we are," Sebastianus said when they arrived at an enormous tent fashioned of thick red cloth and topped with snapping gold pennants. He took her hand and led her inside.

And Ulrika entered another world.

The heavy fabric of the walls muffled sounds from the outside, creating a cozy harbor of silence. Shiny copper lamps hung from the tent supports, emitting soft glowing light. The floor was covered with rich carpets and strewn with gaily colored pillows. Every space and corner was filled with fabulous treasure: translucent jade statues, chests filled with shimmering gold coins, fans made of iridescent peacock feathers.

Before Ulrika could speak, Sebastianus took her into his arms and kissed her hard on the lips. Her arms immediately circled his neck, to pull him against her. She kissed him back in sudden hunger.

He drew back and cupped her face in his hands. "I have so many things to tell you, and I have so many questions to ask you. But all I care about right now is this moment, being with you. I have dreamed of you . . ." He bent his head and kissed her again, tenderly this time, and slowly. Ulrika delivered herself to the love and sweet sensation, tears in her eyes.

When he drew back a second time, Sebastianus said, "In Antioch I was not a free man, Ulrika, I was not free to love you. As a member of my caravan, you were in my charge, and I have never taken advantage of that sacred trust. And also, I had to go to China. You, too, had to follow another path. Tell me, Ulrika, did you find all that you sought?"

"I did," she said, watching his lips as he spoke, wanting to kiss them, to press her mouth to his and never let go. "Was China magical, Sebastianus?"

"It was, and now I seek another kind of magic. Will you marry me, Ulrika? Will you come to Rome with me and be my wife?"

"Yes, oh yes."

Sebastianus solemnly stepped away from Ulrika and with great ceremony removed an iron ring from the little finger of his right hand. Slipping it onto the third finger of Ulrika's left hand, he softly recited the traditional Roman marriage vow: "I give you power over my hearth, power over the fire, and water in my house."

Ulrika replied: "Where you are master, I am mistress."

Sebastianus took her face in his hands again and kissed her gently. "Now you are my wife, and I am your husband. Tomorrow, we will go to the office of municipal records and register our marriage."

Ulrika closed her eyes. How she wished her mother were here to share in her joy. Ulrika knew that Selene would embrace her new son-in-law with love.

His voice then grew husky as he said, "By the stars, Ulrika, you transport me. You are magic. Are you even real, I wonder?"

"I am real, Sebastianus," she whispered, lifting her face to his.

He reached up and loosened her hair, drawing cascades of honey-colored tresses over her shoulders and breast. He bent his head and kissed her. Ulrika curled her arms around his neck. The kiss grew urgent. Their passion flared. Words tumbled out between desperate kisses, hurriedly whispered: "Love . . . need . . . desire . . . yes . . . yes . . ."

The cosmos shifted and sighed. Reality changed. The old world disappeared and a new one was created as Ulrika and Sebastianus explored each other's bodies, discovering exciting hills and valleys. Ulrika opened herself to him. He possessed her completely. The scarlet tent with the snapping gold pennants embraced the lovers as they embraced each other, and kept them safe.

SEBASTIANUS AWOKE AND LIFTED himself up on an elbow to watch Ulrika as she slept. When he touched a fingertip to her cheek, to softly trace the line of her jaw, her eyes fluttered open. She smiled.

He kissed her, sweetly and lingeringly, and then he said, "Tell me about Persia."

Ulrika recounted her experience in Shalamandar, the meditation that had revealed the crystal pools, the visit from Gaia, while Sebastianus listened in interest. "I think now that I was never meant to reach my father's people in time to warn them of Vatinius's attack, for I see now the futility of such a plan. My journey to the Rhineland was the Goddess's way of setting me free. I had felt bound by invisible ties to a land that was not part of my destiny."

She stroked his stubble-covered jaw. "Gaia also told me that it is my destiny to find the Venerable Ones. But I have been searching for five years and have yet to even know who they are."

Sebastianus laid a hand on her cheek. "I must depart as soon as possible for Rome. Can you search for them there?"

"I will search the world if I must."

He smiled. "Then I will help you, for I too am destined to travel the world."

Sebastianus cradled her in his arms then, drawing her to his warmth, while Ulrika relished the feel of his skin against hers, marveling at the power of the masculine body that held her and made her feel safe. As she listened to the reassuring beating of his heart, she listened to an amazing story of brave men crossing deserts and mountains, fighting for their lives, meeting a whole new race for the first time. He filled her mind with beautiful images as she tried to imagine Chinese women, whom she thought must be like butterflies.

"My dream to open a safe route to China route was indeed a success," he murmured as his fingers explored her curved back and delicate shoulder blades. "In Rome I will start planning the next phases of the Gallus caravan trade, sign contracts with importers and exporters, and expand the family business. I will make the name of Gallus known to the far-flung ends of the earth." He paused to kiss her hair, and inhale its fragrance. And then he said, "And you will be at my side. Together we will find Gaia's Venerable Ones."

"Will you not go home to your beloved Galicia, to your sisters and their families?"

"Perhaps, but my success in reaching China has only made me hunger for more. My heart is divided, Ulrika, except when I am with you, for never have I felt so complete as I do now."

When she trembled in his arms, from excitement, he knew, and desire, he recalled a ceramic he had found in China, manufactured only there. The clay was fired at extremely high temperatures, creating the formation of glass and other shiny minerals. Sebastianus could not pronounce the Chinese name, so he called it *porcellana,* as it resembled the translucent surface of cowrie shell. And he thought now: it is like Ulrika—strong, shining, beautiful.

She lifted her face and said softly, "And what about the astrologers in China?"

He stroked her hair, her neck, ran his hand down her bare arm, and drew her more tightly to himself. Ulrika was strong and confident, yet she seemed so vulnerable in his arms. He shook with desire. "I met with them and learned from them. Ulrika, there are many gods and spirits in China, every pond, every tree, even every kitchen has its own god. I cannot begin to name even a few. But the one thing that is the same from Rome to Luoyang is the cosmos. The same stars that shine down on the Tiber River, that shine here over the Euphrates, glitter upon the surface of the Luo. This brought me great comfort while I was in a strange land. And because they are the same everywhere, they are the one constant in the universe, I believe more than ever that the stars guide our lives. They advise us and warn us. They bring us good fortune and keep us from harm. The stars hold messages from the gods. Never have I had such faith in the heavens as I do now.

"Chinese astrologers are men of keen intelligence and insight. I spent many hours conferring with them, and I have brought back charts, instruments, devices for observation and calculation, ancient and arcane equations. I am going to take it all to the observatory in Alexandria, where the greatest astronomers in the world study the heavens, and I know they can put it all together and uncover the secrets to the meaning of life."

Night had fallen but Sebastianus did not light more lamps. There was food in the tent—dates and nuts, pomegranates and rice wine—but the lovers were not hungry. Sebastianus cradled Ulrika in his arms as they lay beneath silken sheets. If the ordinary world outside continued to exist, if Babylon was still there, they neither knew nor cared. Sebastianus placed his hand on her breast, felt her heart beating beneath the silken skin. "Ulrika, you are my horizon in the morning, my oasis at sunset. You are the moon glow that lights my way, the sweet dawn that ends my troubled sleep."

They reached for each other again, and this time the embrace went beyond physical. It was the entwining of two souls. Ulrika held tightly to Sebastianus and felt his spirit engulf her in perfection and joy. She inhaled his masculine scent, buried her face in the hard muscles of his shoulder and neck, delivered herself into his power and wanted to stay there forever. He could not have held her more tightly. She could hardly breathe except to whisper "Sebastianus," with a sigh that came from her heart.

Sebastianus nearly wept with happiness when he heard his name whispered on her warm breath. He tightened his embrace, fearful he might break her, but he felt her strong muscles and bones, as strong as her indomitable spirit. She wrapped her thighs around him as he penetrated deeper, wishing he could send his entire body into her, to be held safely and in love by this astonishing woman.

"I love you," they murmured to each other, inadequate words barely expressing the depth of their mutual devotion.

Finally they slept, intertwined in each other's arms, comforted by the warmth and feel of each other's nakedness.

"WHERE IS SEBASTIANUS GALLUS?" Quintus Publius barked when Primo came into the atrium. The hour was late. Publius had just sent off the last of his dinner guests.

Primo did not want to face this man with a thunderous expression on his face, his white toga with a purple border a reminder of his power. Publius was the Roman ambassador to the Persian province of Babylon, and a personal friend of Nero Caesar. Primo had put off reporting to Publius in the hope that Sebastianus would come to his senses and pay a visit to the ambassador at his villa west of the city.

But Sebastianus had returned to the caravan with the girl in tow, they had gone into his tent and now, hours later, had yet to emerge.

This was Primo's second summons to the ambassador's residence this week. Primo knew it was about a special dispatch Publius had received by imperial courier directly from Nero himself, demanding a report on the progress of the much-awaited caravan from China.

Primo mustered a civil attitude as he said, "My master was detained in the city on urgent business, sire, and he should be—"

"Never mind that!" Quintus Publius barked, his face red with fury. "I gave him specific orders to leave Babylon three weeks ago! Why is he still here?"

Primo thought quickly and came up with a plausible lie. "There was sickness among the women," he said, referring to a group of Chinese concubines in the caravan, a gift from Emperor Ming of Han to the emperor of Rome. They were as pretty as a garden filled with flowers, their faces white with rice powder. Primo wondered what Nero would think of them.

It was well known that Nero Caesar needed the financial capital to keep his empire going. Primo had heard tales from travelers of unrest cropping up in the many provinces. Judea, for example, where restless young Israelites were said to be fomenting revolution to gain back their autonomy. In response, Caesar was sending more legions. The Jews called it oppression, the Romans called it restoring order. But Primo had also heard that Nero's extravagant spending was not only on the army but on new buildings in the city of Rome, fabulous homes and palaces and fountains and avenues, all unnecessary and all very costly to build. Nero was bankrupting the Imperial Treasury, it was rumored, and he was desperate for sources of revenue.

What could Caesar create, Primo thought, with Sebastianus's fabulous treasure from China?

Primo knew that once Nero received Quintus Publius's report on Sebastianus Gallus's unbelievably rich caravan, the emperor would demand to see it at once, and confiscate it, as was his right as patron of the mission to China.

Primo wished the expedition had been a miserable failure. That way, his master could languish in Babylon for eternity, for all Nero would care. Because now Primo was presented with a dilemma: Obey his emperor and betray his master, or serve his master and disobey the emperor. The first would result in his master's execution, the second, his own. Primo's mouth filled with a bitter taste. He did not like this spy business. Even though he had nothing negative to report on Sebastianus, he still felt like a traitor.

"My master made many new alliances for Rome with foreign kingdoms," Primo reminded him, hoping to placate the bilious ambassador, and thinking of the report Quintus was going to dispatch to Nero by swift imperial courier. "Many of those backward tribes are so primitive, all one has to do is eat their bread, or in the farther east, share their rice, and the friendship is sealed." He did not add: the poor fools pressed their greasy thumbs to whatever document Sebastianus placed before them, and grinned with self-satisfaction to think of themselves as the equal of the greatest ruler on earth. They do not yet know of the pompous emissaries who will soon be paying visits, informing them of their duty to pay to Rome a ten percent levy on all goods that pass through their customs houses.

Primo rubbed his scarred nose. It was one of many cicatrices that decorated his soldier's body, each a memento from a long-ago battle. Primo knew he was an oddity himself, like the Chinese concubines, for it was unusual that a veteran of foreign campaigns should live to such an age. But although he was now sixty and had lost most of his hair, he still had all his teeth and was robust.

"Where did you say your master was?" Publius barked.

"On business in the city," Primo said.

Although the word treason had not been spoken, it hung in the air all the same. Everyone knew about Nero's marriage, two years prior, to a scheming spider named Poppaea Sabina, a greedy and ambitious woman with an insatiable appetite for amusements. It could be no coincidence that shortly after, Nero revived the ancient laws governing treason in order to fill the Great Circus with entertaining executions. Men were being arrested on the flimsiest of invented crimes, and thrown to lions in the arena.

Could his master's delay in Babylon be considered treasonous? After all, Sebastianus carried goods that were the personal property of Emperor Nero. He was duty-bound to get that property to Rome as quickly as possible. And yet he had tarried in Babylon. Because of a woman!

"Is there anything you wish me to report to my master?" Primo asked.

"Your master is not the only reason I sent for you," Quintus said as he reached inside the folds of his toga. He paused to study Primo's disfigured face. "Are you a loyal citizen, Primo Fidus?"

Primo was taken aback to hear his real name spoken out loud. How had Quintus found it out? And his use of it now gave Primo a strange chill. "I am a loyal citizen *and* a loyal soldier. I place my honor before my life."

Quintus produced a scroll bearing the clay seal of Caesar himself. "These are your new orders. They are secret. Keep that in mind."

Primo looked warily at the scroll. "New orders?" he said.

"This document grants you the authority, Primo Fidus, to take charge of the caravan, to arrest Sebastianus Gallus, hold him in military custody, and bring him to Rome for trial."

"Arrest him! On what charges?" Primo asked, already knowing, and dreading the answer.

"Treason," Quintus said crisply. "All goods contained in the Gallus caravan are the property of the emperor of Rome. By withholding those goods from Caesar, your master is in effect stealing, which is a crime of treason." He slapped the scroll against Primo's broad chest. "If you do not convince your master to depart Babylon at once, then pray that his execution is a swift one."

Primo looked at the scroll as if it were a scorpion.

Arrest Sebastianus! By Mithras, how was he going to do that?

Cold sweat sprouted between his shoulder blades. Since arriving in Babylon, Primo had heard strange, dark rumors about Emperor Nero, his impulsiveness, his suspected insanity. Especially his ruthlessness. *That he killed messengers bearing bad news.* But what would happen if Primo did not report his master's disloyalty and Nero found out? Primo shuddered to think. Even a hardened old soldier like himself grew faint at the thought of the grisly ways some men were put to death in the Great Circus. And what of Sebastianus? Would Primo's report result in so drastic an action as execution?

Primo decided he must prepare a response should the emperor demand to know why Gallus had tarried so long in Babylon. Primo would declare: "Oh mighty Caesar, my master was engaged in complex commerce in order to bind Babylon more closely to Rome, and to show those unworthy foreigners the advantage of being financially and economically bound to Rome—in fact, glorious Caesar, to demonstrate the lowly Babylonians' great luck to have Caesar look favorably upon them!"

It was a long speech for an old soldier, but Primo would practice it from here to the imperial audience chamber and make himself sound as convincing as possible.

He scratched his chest and felt, beneath his white tunic, the lucky arrowhead he had put on a string to wear beneath his clothes. The German arrowhead that had missed his heart by a hair. And Primo was struck by inspiration. "Perhaps the noble Publius would honor my master by receiving one of the Chinese treasures as a gift?"

The Roman wrinkled his nose. "You wouldn't be attempting to bribe me would you, Primo Fidus? I could have you skinned alive. Find your master! Tell him he is under imperial orders to get his caravan to Rome in the quickest order. I must travel to Magna today and meet with the queen. I will return in a month's time. I expect to see no sign of Sebastianus Gallus and his caravan here in Babylon!"

35

"I ONLY HAVE A FEW things to collect," Ulrika said as she led Sebastianus down a narrow, winding alley in the city, toward the house she shared with a seamstress. "I have learned to travel light."

They entered a wider street, where a marketplace stood in the shadow of the massive Hall of Justice—a towering ziggurat that rose in terraces splendidly landscaped with trees and shrubs and cascading vines. Here vendors hawked garlic and leeks, onions and beans. Sellers of bread and cheese called out their prices, while merchants shouted the merits of their various wines.

Suddenly they heard trumpets blare at the end of the street. A voice called, "Make way! Make way in the name of the great god Marduk!"

Ulrika and Sebastianus saw a contingent of priests appear around the corner, and behind them, temple guards leading five men in chains. Pedestrians immediately fell back, with donkeys and horses pulled aside. People came out of doorways to watch the curious parade.

As a crowd quickly gathered, Sebastianus drew Ulrika into the protection of a recessed doorway.

Among the white-robed priests, one stood out. The High Priest's head was shaved smooth like a polished stone. He wore no adornment over his long white robe. This singled him out of all men in Babylon, who strove to outdo each other in fringed clothes and tall cone hats, walking staffs and shoes with curled toes. When the High Priest walked down a street, people stopped and bowed and then looked away, afraid of his magnificence and power. Ulrika had heard that his authority was greater even than that of the provincial governor from Persia and the puppet prince who sat on Babylon's ancient throne.

Bringing the small procession to a halt in the square, the High Priest struck his staff on the paving stones and called out in a ringing voice: "Babylon has been infested with false prophets, wonder-workers, healers, and charlatans who seduce citizens away from the true faith. We arrested these swindlers and brought them to the Plaza of the Seven Virgins, where they stood trial for their crimes. Having been found guilty, they will be strung up by their ankles and left here to die as an example to others. In addition, their bodies will not be returned to their families for proper burial but will suffer the additional fate of being burned on a common pyre and their worthless ashes poured into the river.

"Know then their crimes," he declared as he pointed to each man with his staff. "Alexamos the Greek, guilty of selling blemished doves and lambs for sacrifice to Ishtar! Judah the Israelite, guilty of offenses against the gods of Babylon by calling them false, and making unfounded accusations against the priests of Marduk! Kosh the Egyptian, guilty of selling goat's milk and claiming it to be from the breasts of Ishtar! Myron of Crete, guilty of murdering a sacred prostitute of Ishtar! Simon of Caesarea, guilty of professing to speak to the dead."

He struck his staff again and the guards prodded the wretches forward, so that Ulrika could now see the horrible treatment they had suffered. Trial was not enough. The five had been tortured and branded.

Her heart went out to them. And then in the next instant her heart stopped in her chest. Rabbi Judah!

And then she saw, behind the guards, a group of men and women wailing and holding onto one another. Miriam and her family.

When Ulrika first returned from Persia, she had paid a visit to Miriam to thank the prophetess for setting her on the right path—Ulrika had indeed found a prince who led her to Shalamandar, as Miriam had prophesied. In the time since, Ulrika had not returned to the house of Rabbi Judah, nor had she heard him preach, but she knew of his growing reputation as a faith healer and a man who worked miracles.

"Sebastianus," Ulrika said as the five men were unchained and lined up in front of the wall. At the top, guards were lowering ropes. "We have to stop this! I know that man. He helped me once."

Sebastianus eyed the guards—the shields and spears and daggers. Then he stepped forward, saying, "Wait—"

But one of the guards was immediately blocking his path, spear lowered, lethal tip leveled at Sebastianus's chest.

Ulrika watched in horror as the condemned men's clothes were removed. She wondered if they were drugged, for they appeared dazed and not aware of what was happening to them.

But then she realized that Rabbi Judah had received no such humane treatment, for he stood tall and proud as the soldiers stripped him naked and then cut off his long curls and hacked away at his beard. Those in the crowd who had never seen a circumcised man gawked and pointed, some laughed and shouted insults.

The women in Judah's family screamed and covered their eyes. One of them fainted and fell into the arms of two male relatives. Judah remained impassive, his eyes above the crowd as the soldiers made quick work of his clothes.

When a soldier prepared to sever the leather straps from Judah's arm and forehead, the High Priest stayed him, saying, "Leave his precious religious symbols in place, so that the people will see his offense against Marduk. And also so that his god can see him and perhaps rescue him."

Ulrika went numb as she watched the guards tie ropes around the men's ankles. Without ceremony, their feet were pulled out from under them. They fell to the ground. Two hit their heads and were mercifully knocked unconscious. Another two began to shriek and beg for mercy and promised to worship Marduk for the rest of their lives.

Sebastianus put his arm around Ulrika and tried to shield her from the horrifying spectacle, but she needed to watch.

Judah remained silent as he fell to his knees, as he was then dragged like a doll to the wall, as his feet were slowly hoisted and up the wall he went, upside down, his arms dropping down. Ulrika saw his lips moving. She knew he was praying.

His family pressed forward, crying out and begging for mercy. The guards pushed them back and the High Priest, striking his staff once more, warned the onlookers that such a fate awaited anyone who did not obey the laws of Marduk and Babylon.

Then he turned and moved on, his back to five groaning men hanging from the wall, their cries ignored, their families and friends pleading for mercy. A few guards stayed, to make sure no one tried to cut them down. Ulrika knew they would stand watch until all five were dead and then bring the corpses to the garbage dump on the outskirts of the city, there to be burned along with the corpses of dogs and cats, and the filth and refuse of a city's population.

Ulrika went to the family, but Miriam said, "Ulrika, please do not look upon my husband's nakedness. Please do not witness his shame. Go home, Ulrika, and pray for him."

"But there must be something we can do! We cannot just leave him there!" She pressed her fingers to her mouth. She felt sick.

And then she felt a strong hand on her arm, and heard a deep voice say, "Come away. You should not watch this."

"Sebastianus, we must do something!"

Miriam persuaded Ulrika to leave, asking her to pray for Judah, until Sebastianus took her back to the caravan, where he held her in his arms, tenderly kissing and caressing her, brushing away her tears, holding her as she wept, until she fell asleep.

When Ulrika woke it was late afternoon, and Sebastianus was not in the tent. Her head ached and her throat was parched. Refreshing herself with water, she washed her hands and then she sat among Sebastianus's silken cushions and statues of Chinese gods, crossing her legs and clasping the scallop shell. With passion, Ulrika prayed to the Goddess to show mercy to the poor executed men.

When Sebastianus returned, night had fallen. "I tried to intercede on your friend's behalf," he said wearily. "I went to my rich and powerful friends in the city, I even went to the governor, but they all said they had no power to match that of the priests of Marduk. I then went to the temple and offered to fill their coffers if they would release the condemned men. But no amount of riches could move the High Priest. I am sorry, Ulrika."

She slipped into the comforting embrace of his strong arms and, closing her eyes, held tightly to Sebastianus as if he were an island in a stormy sea.

ULRIKA FOUND HERSELF IN A STRANGE PLACE.

She was not in Sebastianus's tent, but in wilderness. It was night, the moon nearly full, casting the desert in a silver landscape. "Sebastianus?" she called, as she turned in a slow circle. She saw that she stood in front of ruins, moonlit and ghostly, out in the middle of the dunes, with the lights of Babylon far in the distance. She recognized it as a place called Daniel's Castle, which lay some ten miles from Babylon. Legend told of a prophet named Daniel who had lived in Babylon long ago, and it was said that he was buried here. The "castle" stood against frosty stars, cold, deserted. It felt otherworldly, as if Ulrika had stepped through an invisible portal and were now in the realm of the supernatural. She turned her face to the wind and thought: This place is ancient beyond measure. Long before the prophet Daniel read mysterious words written on a wall, this ground was hallowed.

Spirits dwelled here.

It was a queer monument. Even though crumbling and falling down, its original shape and intention could still be seen: a massive square block with a smaller square block on top, with no apparent entrance or openings. And it seemed much older than a mere few centuries. There was none of the surviving detail Ulrika had seen at Persepolis. These limestone walls appeared to have been sandblasted by winds over a thousand years or more. Was the prophet Daniel buried here? Were perhaps many people buried here, laid to rest by loved ones down through the ages in the hope that proximity to a sacred site would guarantee the deceased's entry into paradise?

When a man came from around the side, Ulrika jumped. "You startled me," she said. And then she saw that it was Rabbi Judah, dressed in the familiar robes and fringed shawl of his religious calling. "You are alive!" she said, and took a step toward him.

"Do not approach me, Ulrika," he said. "You cannot come near me. I have come with a plea. Do not let them burn me."

"What do you mean?"

"My body must be preserved. Save me from the fire. Tell my family to bring me to this place and bury me here. Tell them to remember me."

The dream-vision ended and Ulrika awoke, her face damp with tears. Sebastianus was still asleep. She began to cry and he opened his eyes. "What is it, my love?" he whispered.

"Rabbi Judah is dead."

Sebastianus did not ask how she knew this. He looked at her for a long moment, in the darkness of the night, and then he sat up. "It is a blessing," he said.

Ulrika pulled away from him, hating to do so, and slipped out of bed. "I must go," she said, reaching for her clothes. "We cannot let the priests burn his body."

"Ulrika, it is too dangerous."

"I must do it," she said, slipping into her dress.

"Very well, but you stay here," Sebastianus said, reaching for his clothes. "This is dangerous business. There is a man in the governor's office who owes me a favor. And in case he has forgotten, he will certainly not have forgotten what gold coins are."

"You tried. You said not even your connections could help. But perhaps I—"

"It is one thing to save a condemned man, another to save his body. This is something I can do."

She said in a tight voice, "I cannot ask you to risk your life for a man you never knew."

"I do not do this for the rabbi, my love, I do it for you." He bent his head and kissed her, his lips lingering on hers while Ulrika wrapped her arms around his neck and pressed her body to his.

"Sebastianus," she said, "if you are successful, can you take Rabbi Judah to Daniel's Castle, which lies south of here?"

He frowned. "I am familiar with the ruins."

"I will let the family know. They will meet you there. Be careful, my love."

Ulrika stood outside the tent and watched him steal softly through the sleeping camp and vanish into the night. When she turned her face to the east and saw that dawn was not far off, she went back inside to fetch her own cloak, then she too left the camp.

THE TWO-STORY HOUSE in the Jewish Quarter had been built against the city's western wall and was embraced on either side by other houses. An outside stairway led to bedrooms above, while the business of daily life took place in the large, central room downstairs, furnished with chairs and a table, pedestals for lamps, tapestries on the windowless walls. Here the rabbi's widow sat in a high-backed chair as she received visitors who had come to pay respects.

"It was kind of you to come," Miriam said to Ulrika. The rabbi's widow was dressed all in black, with dark shadows under her eyes. Her sons, whom Ulrika recognized, stood at her side.

Ulrika glanced around at the others in the room, and those out in the garden, people from various walks of life, she saw, for not all were of the Jewish faith, nor were they all Babylonian. Apparently Rabbi Judah had reached many people with his sermons of peace and faith, and with his ability to cure illness and make the lame walk, simply by laying on his hands. Ulrika lowered her voice so that no one else could hear: "I came, honored mother, to tell you that your husband's body will not be put on the fire with the other executed men."

Miriam listened in astonishment to Ulrika's message about a Spaniard named Gallus, who had friends and connections, and the rescue of Judah's remains. Tears filled her eyes, and when Ulrika was done, Miriam broke down and wept. Immediately her sons drew close. Ulrika recognized the eldest, Samuel. He was a tall, lean young man with olive skin and jet-black hair that hung in ringlets on either side of his face. He wore a fringed prayer shawl and displayed the same leather phylacteries his devout father had worn. His dark features, Ulrika saw, were etched with pain and fury. Her heart went out to him. He had witnessed what no son should.

"I am all right," Miriam said in a tremulous voice, putting a hand on Samuel's arm. "This dear daughter has brought good news." To Ulrika she said, "God will prepare places for you and your husband in Heaven. The consuming fire would have robbed my husband of the resurrection."

"Resurrection?" Ulrika said.

"We will live again when the Master returns and the faithful are restored to their physical bodies, just as the Master was."

"Forgive my astonishment, honored mother, but this is an extraordinary coincidence, for this the second time I have heard of this rebirth among Jews. The other was in Judea when I stayed awhile with a woman named Rachel. She was guarding her husband's grave against desecration by his enemies. His name was Jacob."

Miriam gave her a startled look. "But I used to know a Rachel and Jacob in Judea! Jacob was executed in Jerusalem by Herod Agrippa. We never knew what became of his wife."

Ulrika told her of her ordeal by the Sea of Salt, how Rachel and Almah found her and her took her back to their camp.

"Wonder of wonders!" Miriam declared. "Jacob and his brother John were the sons of Zebedee. They were part of the Twelve, and we wives followed them as they traveled with the Master during his ministry of the Good News. Yeshua worked miracles and after his death, thirty-one years ago, he passed that power to his disciples. This was how my Judah was able to help people. But he will work miracles again, when Yeshua returns to this earth, as he promised, and I will be reunited with my beloved husband in the resurrection." She frowned. "But now, like Rachel, my sons and I must protect my husband's body."

"Honored mother," Ulrika said quickly, praying that Sebastianus was having success with his contact in the governor's office, "I told you once that I am blessed with visions, as I know you are. I had a dream. Judah spoke to me. He wishes to be buried at Daniel's Castle, for that is sacred ground. Sebastianus will take him there. You must send someone to meet him. But be careful. It is very dangerous."

As Miriam rose from her chair, Ulrika added, "There is one more thing. In the dream-visitation, Rabbi Judah said, 'Tell them to remember me.'"

36

Ulrika placed her travel packs in front of the tent and turned her eyes to the city's eastern wall and the Enlil Gate, through which heavy traffic endlessly flowed. Sebastianus had left that morning to inform the custom's agents of their departure, and to pay the tax. Now it was late afternoon. He should be here any moment. And tomorrow they would start for Rome!

Around her, in the spring sunshine, the caravan camp was bustling with industry as slaves prepared the many animals for the journey, and the treasure-filled tents were being taken down, folded, their precious contents secured in sealed boxes. Ulrika had not been able to eat her lunch—soft warm bread, sharp goat's cheese, and spicy olives soaked in vinegar and oil. She was too excited. And she was in love and ached to feel her husband's touch again.

She would never cease to marvel at the man she had married, his kindness to strangers at risk to himself. Sebastianus had been successful in secretly obtaining Rabbi Judah's body. He had taken it to Daniel's Castle where, out in the wilderness, far from traffic and passersby, Miriam and the family had buried him.

When she saw Timonides stumble through the camp and slip inside his tent, Ulrika's thoughts shifted to the astrologer. She had tried to talk to him, comfort him. Timonides's usual zest was absent from his speech, there was no life in his body and his eyes. She knew it was due to the manner of Nestor's death. Because his head had been trampled beneath horses' hooves, no eyes had been left upon which to lay the coins for Charon the ferryman. There was no way to pay for passage across the River Styx. Where had Nestor's soul gone? Timonides had asked. Was the poor boy destined to roam the underworld for eternity?

Ulrika wished she could use her gift to comfort him, wished Nestor's spirit would appear to her, as Rabbi Judah's had. She had meditated upon it with no success. Why did some spirits visit her and others did not?

A strangled cry suddenly tore the air.

Ulrika turned to see Timonides's small tent sway as if it had been struck. She went to the entrance and called his name. From within she heard gagging sounds. Ulrika went inside. Her eyes flew open.

Timonides was hanging from the main support, a rope around his neck, his legs kicking.

Ulrika rushed to him. Seeing the wooden boxes he had kicked away, she quickly stacked them, climbed up, and threw her arms around his legs. Lifting him up so that the strain on the noose eased, she said, "Timonides, remove the rope! I cannot hold you for long!" The boxes beneath her wobbled precariously.

"Let me die . . ."

"Help!" Ulrika shouted. "Someone help us!"

Two slaves came running in, big men with broad backs who reached up and drew the frail old man down and out of the noose. "Find your master," Ulrika said as they laid him on the floor. "Find Sebastianus!"

She knelt next to Timonides and slipped an arm under his shoulders, shocked at the feel of skin and bone beneath his clothes. His face was white, his eyes closed, lavender lids fluttering. "Why, Timonides?" she said.

He parted his gray lips and words came croaking out: "Nestor is in Hell . . . I cannot leave him there alone . . . I go to join him . . ."

"What nonsense," Ulrika said, tears rising in her eyes. "Your son was innocent and the gods know this."

But Timonides rolled his head from side to side. "Let me go to him. Nestor needs me . . ."

Ulrika rocked him gently, her tears spilling on the face that was the color of cobwebs. What had happened that would make him think Nestor was in Hell? Mother of All, please help this man.

As she listened to the camp outside, waiting for the sound of Sebastianus's arrival, she stared at Timonides's thin neck and saw his pulse flutter like a moth, weak and irregular. She feared that he might die from sheer will of not wanting to live.

"Let me go . . ." Timonides whispered.

She looked down to see him staring at her with forlorn eyes. "I spoke with philosophers in China," he said. "I met with priests and learned men. I visited temples and prayed to the most powerful gods on earth, but no one can tell me where Nestor is."

"He is with the gods," Ulrika said gently, "enjoying the next world."

"No . . . he is in Hell and he needs me."

The tent flaps flew open and Sebastianus came running in, bringing daylight and slaves with him. Dropping to his knees, he said, "What happened?"

"He tried to kill himself."

"He needs a physician."

"It is not a sickness of the flesh that afflicts him, but one of the soul."

Sebastianus thought of men he knew in the city, physicians of sterling reputation. But today marked the beginning of the spring celebrations and, for Babylon, the New Year as well. Where would he find these men?

"I have to go back into the city. Will you stay with him? I'll bring a doctor back with me."

Ulrika sat with Timonides, making him comfortable, placing poultices on his bruised neck, coaxing cool water down his throat. But when she offered food, he turned his head.

Sebastianus returned at dusk, having been unable, in the city celebrations and parades, to find a medical man who would come. "I will stay with him," Ulrika said. "His neck and throat will mend, but I fear he will make another attempt on his life."

Sebastianus stayed as well. They dined in Timonides's tent, persuading him to drink a little wine and to talk about the fears that troubled his soul. But he would not talk much. He was able to sit up after a while, and stare morosely at the carpeted floor. They heard him mutter and saw him shake his head. Devils plagued the old Greek's soul.

The next morning, Timonides told Sebastianus that he was not going to do his usual daily reading. "I will never cast another horoscope again. For the rest of my days, I will look at the stars no more."

Sebastianus became alarmed. There had been times in the past when he had had to resort to a hired astrologer—when Timonides was ill—but he had never thought Timonides would cease reading the stars altogether. Out of the old man's hearing, he said to Ulrika, "I will find a star-reader in Babylon, who will do for now, but I cannot be certain that I can find one who is willing to travel to Rome! Especially an astrologer of excellent reputation. I cannot rely on someone who is second-rate. What can we do to bring Timonides around? I dare not move this caravan without consulting the stars."

"I will talk to him."

After Sebastianus left, Ulrika said to Timonides, "Come and sit in the sunshine with me, dear friend. The daylight will make you feel better."

"Nothing will make me feel better," he said, but he joined her on a stool in front of his tent. Eyes that used to focus on the stars stared moodily at the ground. Ulrika poured him a cup of wine and placed it before him, but he did not touch it.

Timonides dwelled in thought while life and industry went on about him. The sun climbed and breezes blew from the Euphrates. Presently, he said, "Do you know . . . I am not even sure I am Greek. I was abandoned as a baby and a Greek widow took me in. She gave me my name and taught me her language and culture. She apprenticed me out to an astrologer when I was six, and when she died, I was sold into slavery. Sebastianus's father bought me and I have been serving his family ever since. Nestor was the only human being in this whole world that I was connected to by blood. He was more than my son. He was my universe. And now I am lost . . ."

He reached for the wine and when Ulrika saw how his hand trembled, she thought: He is a tangle of dark emotions. He cannot think straight.

And an idea came to her.

"Timonides, when I taught myself the skills of meditation in order to tap into my spiritual gift, I found that a side benefit was a feeling of peace and serenity afterward. Perhaps if I showed you how . . ."

He squinted at her. "Meditation?"

"It is really very simple and requires little effort, only concentration. And it is not unlike the way I have seen you prepare yourself before you read your star-charts. A clearing of the mind. A way to focus. Would you like to try it?"

"To what end?"

"To bring peace to your soul, Timonides."

"My soul does not deserve peace."

"Then do it as a favor to me. I have never taught the technique to someone else. I want to know if it is possible."

He shrugged.

"Have you an object that is precious to you? Something you can grasp in your hand and hold onto, like an anchor."

Timonides did not have to think about it. He was inside his tent and out a moment later, holding a long wooden spoon that Ulrika recognized as Nestor's favorite.

When he resumed his place on the stool, Ulrika saw, for the first time, a spark of hope in his eyes, as if just holding Nestor's spoon brought consolation. "Now hold an image in your mind," she said, "a familiar and comforting one."

A faint smile curled his lips. "A bubbling pot of stew. It is how I remember my son best."

"Create that image in your mind as you hold onto this spoon. Focus on it. Make it real in your mind. Now whisper words that hold meaning for you. Repeat them, over and over."

Timonides studied the spoon in his hands, his shoulders curved and bent. Then he nodded, as if he had come to an agreement with himself. "Stars are destiny," he murmured.

Ulrika showed him how to breathe, to sway, to focus. She spoke softly, instructing him, her simple words and subdued voice guiding him into a sensitive realm. "As you hold onto the anchor, send your spirit out . . ."

But even as she spoke, she saw his eyes moving behind his eyelids, the creases growing deep in his forehead, and she knew he was struggling.

"I cannot!" he finally cried in exasperation. "Dear child, this is not going to work!"

But she saw how lovingly he caressed the spoon, and she sensed the hope within him. Timonides did not want to kill himself, he did not want to join his son in an imagined hell. But how to save him?

Ulrika thought for a moment as she watched, in the distance, a new caravan arriving from the west, a line of weary beasts and men entering the terminus. And it came to her that her personal meditation was designed to find external places. Timonides's sickness was of the spirit. It was internal. With renewed hope, she said, "Do not try to send your spirit out, Timonides. Instead, go deep inside yourself. Find the landscape of your soul. Explore it. Do not be afraid. Tell me what you see."

He closed his eyes again, clasped the spoon, bringing it up to his chest. Breathing slowly. Swaying. Whispering, "Stars are destiny . . . stars are destiny . . ." Until he began to tremble and the chanting ceased. The breath stopped in his chest as Ulrika watched.

"Blackness," he said in a tight voice. "I see a large gaping hole. Cold winds. Isolation. My soul is lost and lonely!"

"Timonides," Ulrika said gently. "Hold a silent dialogue with your soul. Do not reveal it to me. Talk to your spiritual self. Ask questions. Ask what it wants, how it can be saved."

As she watched the old astrologer withdraw deeper into himself, his posture relaxing, the wrinkles easing on his face, Ulrika saw Sebastianus walking back through the camp, a scowl on his face. He was alone. He had not found an astrologer who would come with him.

Ulrika placed a fingertip at her lips, so that Sebastianus joined her and Timonides without making a sound.

After a few more moments of silence, Timonides finally opened his eyes and said, "I cannot do it. Ulrika, it is easy for you. You are young and agile. But my soul is old and creaks like my joints."

She leaned forward. "Many times I watched how you prepared yourself for a star-reading. I saw you close your eyes and whisper a prayer. Why did you do that?"

"To open my soul to the stars, to let their wisdom pour in."

"Then do so now."

With a doubtful look, he settled back on the stool, firmed his grip on the spoon, closed his eyes and took the first deep, cadenced breaths. "Stars are destiny," he whispered, and told himself he was preparing to do a reading. But rather than journey inward to his soul, as Ulrika suggested, Timonides knew he must send his thoughts outward and up to the sky, for that was where he belonged. As he slowed his breathing and imagined the aroma of bubbling stew and felt the precious wooden spoon in his hands, the old astrologer felt himself relax, gradually, giving up the stress and strains of his fleshly life so that his spirit could be set free and soar up to the heavens he had so loved all his life.

Soon, Timonides was flying among the forty-eight constellations, familiar friends now seen close up: boastful Orion, bested by a small scorpion and frozen forever in the heavens with his club raised, doomed never to fall. Andromeda, the chained virgin to whom Timonides now uttered the famous words of Perseus, her rescuer: "Such chains must only bind you to the hearts of lovers." And Cassiopeia, placed upon her celestial throne by spiteful Neptune, who had seated her there with her head towards the north star so that she spent half of every night upside down.

Timonides mounted winged Pegasus and rode the four winds. They neared the sun and Timonides felt the blessed radiance on his unworthy face. He saw an icy comet streak past. He tasted the moon's sweet dew.

He began to cry. So much beauty. So much divinity. And he had sullied it. For the sake of filling his miserable stomach he had soiled everything he loved and held dear. Cherished beliefs and heavenly bodies were cast aside for fear of a salivary stone.

"I am sorry!" he cried out as meteors and planets raced past him. "Forgive me!" he shouted as asteroids hurtled all around him. "Perseus, Hercules, I did not mean to disrespect you! I am but a humble man, a web of weaknesses and fears and dreads. I am nothing compared to your greatness. Give me a second chance, I beg of you!"

And then he saw the sparkling nebula, a cloud of compassion and color—the collective consciousness of the void—materialize before his eyes. It rolled toward him like a fog, obliterating stars, planets, sun, and moon until Timonides was engulfed in pure sweetness. He felt every fear and dread melt from his body as if his very flesh were dropping from his bones. He wept with joy.

He lingered there, riding the cosmic winds, while his two earthbound companions kept their eyes on him. He no longer swayed. He had ceased his chant. He appeared almost not to breathe. Time passed. Camels and men also passed. The business of the caravan terminus carried on as it had for centuries, while Ulrika and Sebastianus sat vigil with their vulnerable friend during his spirit-walk.

The sun was beginning its westward descent when Timonides finally opened his eyes and blinked at his companions in brief confusion.

"Are you all right?" Ulrika said, scanning his face, looking for signs of mental disorder. But his color was good, his skin dry, his eyes wide and unclouded. She wanted to feel his pulse but held back, fearing that touching him would break his spell.

"I am thirsty . . ." His voice as thin as smoke.

Sebastianus brought the astrologer a cup of cool water, which Timonides gulped down like a man who had just wandered in from the desert. He drew his hand across his mouth, frowning. Ulrika knew that he was readjusting to the physical world. She would not press him for word of his journey. He needed to come around in his own time.

"It was most wondrous," Timonides finally whispered, shaking his head in disbelief. "I would not have believed it possible. Ulrika, through this focused meditation, I learned things. The gods revealed secrets to me. Is this how it is, this meditation? Does it make one a conduit to the Divine? They spoke to me . . ."

He held out the cup and Sebastianus refilled it. After another long drink, Timonides said to Ulrika, "The secrets which the gods revealed to me must remain secrets, for that is part of my holy office as an astrologer. But they gave me another gift. They illuminated my inner self. And what I saw, I knew I must reveal to you, my friends."

He turned to Sebastianus. "Nestor's death was a punishment on me, master, not on him but on me. My son died in terrible agony because of my transgressions. He was innocent. Even when he beheaded Bessas in Antioch, he was innocent."

Sebastianus exchanged a startled look with Ulrika.

Timonides explained briefly what had happened in Antioch. "And then Nestor himself was killed by his having head trampled upon. I had thought it was divine retribution, a head for a head. But Nestor did not know what he was doing. I see that now. Ulrika, I explored the stars and this is what I learned: that the gods were not punishing Nestor, they were punishing me."

Sebastianus frowned. "I do not understand, old friend. What are you talking about? Why were the gods punishing you?"

"Forgive me, master, for the terrible things I am about to tell you! But I can no longer carry this burden. I must clear my conscience so that I may clear my soul. When Nestor brought me the head of Bessas the holy man, I did not tell you. I then falsified your horoscope so that you would leave Antioch at once, before the authorities came for my boy. Worse, by bringing Nestor along on the caravan I made you an accomplice to a capital crime. You were giving aid to a fugitive, which meant a death sentence for you as well, should we be caught."

Sebastianus stared at the old man for a moment, his brow knotting in surprise. "It is all right, old friend. I understand."

"There is more! I lied about your horoscopes. All of them! On that first day when Ulrika came into our caravan camp outside Rome, I lied about the message in the stars because I wanted to keep her with us, out of my own selfish interests. I thought the salivary stone might come back. And I kept lying! I kept falsifying my readings for this reason and that, always for myself. I saw a terrible calamity in your future, yet I did not warn you. But no catastrophe befell you, and so I knew it must be the gods punishing me with misreadings. I kept promising the gods that I would stop and then Nestor killed Bessas and I had to keep falsifying the readings. Oh master, in Antioch the stars said that you were to go south with Ulrika but I told you that we were to go east at once to Babylon."

Sebastianus's expression turned to stone, his silence deepened, and Ulrika saw that he barely breathed.

"I perverted astrology to suit my own selfish needs," Timonides continued, "and in this way the fates drove my son to commit a crime. It is my fault! I alone am responsible for the death of Bessas the holy man, just as I am guilty of sacrilege and offense to the gods by using the stars to my own gain! Forgive me, master." Timonides slid from his stool, fell to his knees, and grabbed Sebastianus's ankles. "Please tell me you forgive me!"

Sebastianus stared down at Timonides, while the wind picked up, bringing sounds of the city and river traffic, the smells of cook fires and beasts sweating from travel. Men's shouts, the noise of blacksmiths' hammers, the braying of mules—all flew on the air while Sebastianus Gallus stared at his old astrologer and the import of what Timonides had confessed sank in.

Finally, in a wooden voice, Sebastianus said, "I forgive you."

"Thank you, master!" Timonides cried, sobbing with relief. Lifting himself from his knees, he dashed tears from his cheeks and took a seat on his stool. "Your forgiveness is my reward. And I have been rewarded with something else, too. I know now what I should have known all along. That when Nestor's soul was brought before the gods for judgment, they would not have seen a man who had committed murder but a sweet, pure, simple soul. The gods knew that Nestor was innocent! And for this reason, he is not in Hell but in Heaven, in the bosom of divine protection."

He turned to Ulrika . "Dear child, I knew this, and yet I kept this knowledge from myself. What a wondrous thing this meditation is, for the answers to my agony were within me all along! You have given me a precious gift that I will not use frivolously."

He jumped to his feet, shouted, "I shall give you an honest reading now, master," and dashed inside the tent.

Ulrika turned to Sebastianus.

Pain shot through her heart. She tried to think of words. Tried to find a way to comfort him. But all she could do was lay her hand on his arm, to let him know she was there, that she loved him.

For on Sebastianus's face was the look of a man whose faith had been utterly shattered.

37

THEY KISSED IN THE shadow of the Ishtar Gate.

It was not a farewell kiss; they would be apart for only a short time. Sebastianus was going to meet with the supreme astrologer in Babylon, and Ulrika had an urgent errand at Daniel's Castle.

Tomorrow they were departing for Rome.

Two weeks had passed since the day of Timonides's startling confession—a day that had set Sebastianus Gallus on a quest of obsession. Needing to restore his faith in the cosmos—to undo the terrible damage wrought by an astrologer's astonishing admission, Sebastianus had embarked on a mission, meeting with every soothsayer, star-reader, and seer in the city. Ulrika had been at his side, trying to help, offering to guide him through the same meditation that had set Timonides free. But Sebastianus was not interested in answers that lay within himself. He sought answers that lay in the heavens.

"I wish you would wait, Ulrika," Sebastianus said now as they stood at the base of the massive city gate through which kings and conquerors once passed. “The priests of Marduk do not yet know of Judah’s grave, that he was not cremated with the others. But if they hear of it, they will send guards. Wait until I have seen the Chaldean.”

“I will be all right,” she said. “Primo is taking me. And I will have Timonides with me. You do not know how long you will be with the Chaldean, and I am anxious to talk to Miriam. From what I have heard, they need to be urged to leave Daniel’s Castle at once, and I think she will listen to me. This time tomorrow, my love, we will be far from this place and on our way home.”

They were in a hurry to leave Babylon. It was imperative that Sebastianus get his caravan to the Great Green before winter storms closed all sea travel. Emperor Nero would be anxious for a report on the mission, and to see the treasures Sebastianus had brought from China.

But something unexpected had happened at Daniel’s Castle. Word had gotten out that Rabbi Judah was buried there, and that he was continuing to work miracles from the grave. How this happened, Ulrika did not know, but as word spread, and more desperate people visited the ruins, the risk grew that the priests of Marduk would discover Sebastianus’s secret rescuing of Judah’s body—against priestly orders.

Ulrika looked at the shadows beneath his eyes and wished she could kiss them away—wished she could take his pain and disillusionment into herself and bring him peace. Sebastianus’s faith in the stars had been destroyed. If Timonides had lied all this time, and if a great catastrophe was supposed to have happened, but instead his journey to China was a success, then what did that say of the stars? Although Sebastianus tried to assure Ulrika he was all right, there was a haunted look in his eyes, and at night, while Ulrika held him, Sebastianus wept in his sleep. Sometimes she would wake up and find him outside, looking up at the night sky. “If there are no messages in the stars, then what are the stars for? Are men just twigs being tossed willy-nilly on a raging river with no rudder, no way to steer their courses? And what of the star-stone that fell the night Lucius died? Was it not a message from him after all, but mere coincidence? *Is everything a lie?*”

The stars had always been his comfort, his companions, his security. And now they were gone.

The blue-glazed tiles on the towering walls of the Ishtar Gate gleamed in the noontime sun, and a hundred golden dragons stood in frozen splendor. But Ulrika was aware only of a pair of green eyes filled with grief. "Dearest Sebastianus," she said, "my sojourn in Persia taught me that everything happens for a reason. I know now, as you once told me, that nothing is random, that there is indeed order in the universe. When I look back to the day when I made the decision to leave Rome and go north to warn my father's people of a military trap, I was set upon a road by unseen forces, and everything that has happened to me since was for a reason, everything that has happened to us, my dearest Sebastianus, is for a reason. Even Timonides's falsehoods. Ask the Chaldean."

"I love you, Ulrika," he said now, tenderly, laying his hand on her cheek. "I will see you before the sun sets."

"And I love you." They kissed again and then Sebastianus drew back and signaled to Primo, who stood a short distance away. "Keep her close, Primo, and be watchful for temple guards."

Ulrika was uncomfortable riding a horse, except for when Sebastianus was holding her, and as Daniel's Castle was only ten miles away, and the day was balmy and clear, they walked. Ulrika, Timonides, Primo, and six of his trained men followed the busy highway from the city until they came to a small offshoot road, and they took it out into the desert, away from villages and farms until soon they were trekking through desolation.

At Ulrika's side, Primo strode in silence, his thick soldier's body and ugly face set in grim resolve.

Quintus Publius, the ambassador from Rome, was due back soon from his visit to the queen of Magna and he had said he wanted to see no sign of the Gallus caravan. Mithras! Primo thought in frustration. If Quintus found Sebastianus still here, he would have the imperial authority, and soldiers to back it, to arrest Sebastianus and confiscate the caravan, taking them all back to Rome in chains.

They were supposedly leaving tomorrow. Sebastianus had even given orders for the slaves to pack everything up and be prepared to depart at dawn. But even though his master had promised that no matter what the Chaldean in the Babel Tower said today, tomorrow they would leave for

Rome, Primo remained cautious. He had received departure orders before, and they were still in Babylon!

"What is going on?" Ulrika said suddenly, stopping on the trail. "Look at all these people!"

The desert track, normally deserted, was busy with traffic. "It is a mob!" cried Timonides.

Ulrika stared at the donkeys and horses, wagons and carrying chairs. There was even a chariot, splendidly arrayed in shining electrum. "The rumors are true," she said. "Rabbi Judah's burial at this place is no longer a secret."

Miriam and her family had established a camp at the oasis behind the ruins—a small outcropping of palm trees, bushes, and reeds fed by an artesian pool. As soon as Ulrika turned the corner of the castle, and she saw the disorganized mob, she turned to Primo and said, "Can you and your men get these people to leave?"

He scowled. The crowd consisted of the elderly, people on crutches, impoverished women holding babies. Families had brought loved ones on litters. They carried beloved daughters and fathers, wasted by illness, and laid them beside the place where the well-known faith healer had been laid to rest. "These people are desperate," Primo said. "They have reached the end of their hope. If they believe they can find a miracle here, then all the war chariots in the empire will not budge them."

Ulrika saw Miriam, at the forefront, trying to control people who were besieging her with questions: "Can you tell me where my son is?" "Will I ever see my husband again?" "Please cure my cancer."

Primo went first, creating a path through the mob, and when Ulrika reached the distraught Miriam, she said, "How did this happen?"

Miriam came forward with outstretched arms. "It is good to see you again. I handled it poorly! You said that, in your vision, my Judah said he wanted us to remember him. I told a few of our neighbors, and people in our congregation at the synagogue. They came here to pay respects and somehow, they started saying that miracles were happening."

Ulrika's eyes widened. "Were they?"

"Oh, Ulrika, who can say? Some prayed here and went away saying they were cured. Some prayed here and went home to find something they had lost. Some prayed here and returned to the city to find a long-lost loved one waiting for them. Perhaps they were coincidences, perhaps they were the sort of miracles my Judah was empowered to perform in life. I do not know. But it has gotten out of hand and we do not know how to correct it."

Ulrika looked around in dismay. This was far worse than she had imagined. The priests of Marduk would surely hear of this—people bringing coins and offerings that otherwise would go to the temples—and then they would learn of Sebastianus's involvement. "Primo," she began—

"Help us, please. Help my little girl." A young woman carrying a small child pushed to the front of the mob, where Primo's men were using swords and shields to keep everyone back.

"Please help us," the young mother cried out. "We sold our house. I sold my jewelry. When we ran out of money for physicians, my husband sold himself into slavery and I have not seen him since. My daughter and I are homeless and penniless. I do not want to sell myself into slavery because what then will my daughter do? We have no family. Nowhere to go."

There was something in the woman's voice, in her eyes, the posture of her thin body, the tragic rags that hung on her emaciated frame, and most especially, in the way the child lay limp in her arms, that drew Ulrika to her. While others surged around, pressing against Primo's shields, the young woman held her child and pleaded with eyes that had gone deep into shadows from hunger and fear.

"What happened to her?" Ulrika said, noticing that the child seemed to be alert, as she watched Ulrika with big eyes.

Those closest by fell silent, to listen and to see if a miracle was about to happen.

"A fever swept through our neighborhood," the young mother said. "My daughter burned for days, and when she came out of it, she could not walk. It was a year ago. Physicians have said she will never walk again. Please ask Rabbi Judah to help us. I am impoverished, dear lady. I have reached the end of my road, and the last of my hope. Without my daughter I am nothing. Please restore her to life. Show me how to talk to the rabbi. What do I say? How do I address him? They say he cured people when he was alive. And some say he is doing it now."

Miriam stepped forward. “Please go back to the city. All of you! Please leave my husband in peace.”

“I will do anything,” the young mother said. “Whatever Rabbi Judah asks of me, I will do it.”

While Miriam tried to persuade her to leave, the young mother knelt beside her crippled child, bowed her head, and began to softly pray.

The Babel Tower was the tallest in Babylon, rivaling only the ziggurat of Marduk. Legend said that the tower had been built by an insolent king determined to reach heaven and meet the gods face to face. He decided to build the tallest stairway in the world, but in order to accomplish such a feat, he had needed thousands of workers, forcing him to recruit from foreign lands. As a result, with the workers all speaking different tongues and thus making errors in construction, the tower was never completed. A subsequent king converted the eyesore to a lookout tower, shaded and protected from the elements, with a complete all-around view from horizon to horizon, and the night sky with its zodiacal signs.

As Sebastianus climbed the three hundred and thirty-three stone steps that curled upward in a spiral, he struggled with his emotions. Other astrologers had not been able to restore his faith. Worse, they had come up with different horoscopes, which had shocked him. Having relied for years on Timonides for his horoscope, Sebastianus had not realized how widely varied, from astrologer to astrologer, the readings could be. They all used the same constellations and signs, the same numbers and equations, the same charts and instruments, and yet their readings were as disparate as one astrologer telling Sebastianus that his children all praised his name and would give him many grandchildren, another assuring him that his current wife would live longer than his previous two had. Was the science of astrology a sham?

But as his sandals struck each worn step, where hundreds before him had tread, Sebastianus still held hope that the famed Chaldean in this tower would restore his faith in the stars.

When he reached the top, emerging through a small wooden door, Sebastianus had to catch himself and reach for the wall. The vista! The panorama! Desert and river and hills and, most of all, the bustling metropolis that spread before him. It took his breath away.

And then he realized he had come to the end of the stairway. He was at the top of the tower with nowhere else to go. The stone wall was chest-high and the tiled roof was supported on eight columns. There was nothing else.

Where was the Chaldean?

As the wind whipped around him, threatening to strip off his cloak and carry it away, Sebastianus felt outrage rise in him. He had been duped! Was this how it happened? Gullible men like himself paid outlandish sums, only to find themselves the target of a sham? How many, through the centuries, had come up here to find themselves the butt of a joke, to go back down and tell their friends how successful the meeting with the Chaldean had been? For no man would admit to having been swindled.

I shall tell the truth! Sebastianus thought in fury. I shall shout it on the streets of Babylon that the Chaldean does not exist! That there is nothing at the top of this tower but wind and broken dreams!

A bird flew into the tower just then, startling him. It flew around in a frantic flapping of wings—a small kestrel falcon, Sebastianus saw, the color of rust and ink. He glimpsed its eyes and saw a curious film covering them. When the falcon flew into a pillar and bounced off, Sebastianus realized the bird was blind. He watched it fly in circles within the tower and then suddenly it swooped low and vanished.

Sebastianus stared at the spot. Where had the bird gone? It looked as if it had flown right into the floor.

Bending low, Sebastianus examined the marble tiles and saw, when he turned his head one way, an opening in the floor that was not otherwise observable. An enticing smell came from the opening, like sweetly perfumed incense. He heard a humming sound, as if someone were singing to himself. The Chaldean! Sebastianus circled the opening and saw a wooden step. He cautiously lowered his foot onto it, and when he felt the support, continued down.

Twelve more steps brought him to a tapestry. Pushing it aside, he saw a small cozy chamber, dimly lit by oil lamps, furnished with a table and two stools, with hangings on the walls, and shelves cluttered with astrolabes, charts, bowls, and a stuffed owl. As he entered, careful not to bang his head on the low ceiling, he surveyed the room and realized it must lie behind the spiral staircase.

The room was unoccupied, and there seemed to be no more doors or openings. "Hello?" he called out.

When he heard a sigh, Sebastianus turned and saw someone sitting at the table. He blinked. Surely that person had not been there a moment ago. It was the incense, he thought, for now it was strong and heady. Perhaps it contained a substance that caused visions.

Taking a step closer, however, he saw that it was no vision but a person sitting there, patiently waiting to speak. Sebastianus blinked again, and frowned. This must be the Chaldean, he thought, but what an extraordinary creature!

Of surprisingly humble appearance, considering his reputation, the Chaldean wore only a long white robe that had known better days. His long bony hands rested on the table, his head bowed, showing a crown of hair that was blacker than jet, parted in the middle, and streaming over the shoulders and down his back. Presently the head came up, and Sebastianus received a shock.

The Chaldean was a woman. Sebastianus was further arrested by the unusual aspect of the face, which was long and narrow, all bone and yellow skin, framed by the streaming black hair. Mournful black eyes beneath highly arched brows looked up at him. The Chaldean almost did not look human, and she was ageless. Was she twenty or eighty?

"You have a question," the Chaldean said in perfect Latin, eyes peering steadily from deep sockets.

Sebastianus took a seat opposite and it seemed that, the closer he drew to the astrologer, the more the incense invaded his head. It took on a cloying scent, with an underlying odor that was vaguely unpleasant. The room seemed to grow dimmer, the walls closing in.

"You have a question about the stars," the astonishing woman said in a voice that sounded older than the ziggurats of Babylon.

"Do they contain messages?"

"All things contain messages. They are all around us. You have but to see."

"Can the stars be relied on for messages from the gods?"

"Why do you trouble yourself about that?" the seer said with sorrow in her eyes.

Sebastianus grew impatient. The astrologer had not asked him for the day and hour of his birth, his sun and moon signs, the constellations that had hung in the night sky when he drew his first breath.

He scanned the surface of the table. It was bare. No charts, no diagrams or equations or astrolabes. "Listen here," Sebastianus began, and then he paused. The Chaldean was staring straight ahead with liquid black eyes. But there was something strange in the look . . .

Sebastianus lifted a hand and waved it in front of the astrologer's face. She did not blink.

The Chaldean was blind.

The young mother held her paralyzed daughter as she chanted her prayer: "Rabbi Judah, I beg of you to help us," she whispered with her eyes closed, as Ulrika and Miriam, Primo and his men, everyone looked on in silence. Her prayer was filled with such poignant despair, her voice touched every heart, brought tears to many eyes. "Dear Judah, I have no other recourse, nowhere else to turn. We have not eaten in days. We have no home, no family. Tomorrow I must sell myself into prostitution so that I and my daughter can live. Perhaps I should prefer death. For myself, I might, but my daughter is only four years old. I want her to live. Spirit of this place, whoever you are, if you are Judah, take *my* legs instead. Take the life that is in my muscle and bone and put it in my daughter's lifeless limbs. I beg of you, lift this curse from my baby and place it on me, and I shall revere you and speak your name for as long as I live."

Lifting her head, the young mother sent her plea to the sky. "We are a hopeless cause," she said as she began to weep. "Perhaps we are not worthy of divine notice. But I ask nothing for myself! Please *save my daughter!*"

"Mama?" came a tiny voice. "Mama?"

Feeling her daughter stir in her arms, she opened her eyes and said, "What is it, baby?"

"Who is that man?"

"What man?"

The child pointed. All heads turned. No one saw a man among the humble tents and palm trees.

"There is no one there, baby," the young mother said.

"He has honey! He has dates!" The little girl struggled in her mother's arms, pushed away, and fell to the ground.

"Baby!" the mother cried, reaching for her child.

But the girl was suddenly up on her feet and toddling away on legs that had not moved in a year.

The crowd fell silent. Ulrika turned. The child who had, moments earlier, been unable to walk, now ran. And she was running, Ulrika saw, in the direction of Judah's grave.

"Why will you not answer me directly?" Sebastianus asked in growing frustration. "You speak in riddles! Not even that, for riddles are meant to be solved. Your words make no sense!" He rose from the stool. "I have wasted enough time."

"Wait, Sebastianus Gallus . . ."

He turned. Blind eyes did not look at him as a whispered prophecy came from her ancient lips . . .

He stared at the Chaldean and when he heard her prediction, felt himself snap. "Now I know you are false!" he shouted. "For what you have just said will never come true. I promise you that!"

As he descended the three hundred and thirty-three steps, Sebastianus knew that his suspicions were sealed. What he had just heard was an impossible prophecy, and so he knew now that there were no messages in the stars. There were no gods. There was no such thing as miracles.

"Baby!" the young mother cried, running after her daughter.

Everyone watched in stunned silence, even Primo and his men, startled to see what they had thought was a paralyzed child suddenly running toward Miriam's camp.

Ulrika and Timonides watched in spellbound astonishment as the girl ran into the camp and then twirled in circles, her arms outstretched as she cried, "Honey and dates! Honey and dates!"

The mother fell to her knees before her child, her moist eyes wide as she watched the spindly legs dance on the sand. "It is a miracle!" she cried. "Thank you, Blessed Judah, for I know now that it was you who worked this miracle! I will do good deeds in your name! I will revere you all my days. I will bless your name forever, Oh Venerable Judah!"

Ulrika stared in shock. As the child twirled and her mother wept, as the mob burst into cheers and the sun moved one degree closer to the western horizon, Ulrika felt the world undergo an irreversible and profound shift.

She had found the Venerable Ones.

When Sebastianus appeared in the golden rays of sunset, galloping on horseback across the desert, Ulrika ran out breathlessly to greet him. He jumped down from his horse and drew her to him, kissing her deeply. Then he stepped back and looked around at the jubilant camp. People were lighting torches, dancing, singing, and passing around skins of wine. Many were on their knees chanting prayers. "What happened?" he said. "Who are all these people?"

"Something wonderful, my love! But tell me about the Chaldean. Did he restore your faith?"

"It is all a sham. Astrology is nothing but fakery to cheat a man out of his money. I shall never be so gullible again."

"Why do you say this?" she cried in dismay.

He described his experience, and then said, "Here is the prophecy the Chaldean uttered: 'You have a possession that you value above all others. Before one year has passed, Sebastianus Gallus, you will willingly relinquish that cherished object.' Oh Ulrika, every man has one possession he cherishes above all others! And while most men, under certain pressure and the right circumstances, will part with their most treasured possession, what the Chaldean does not know is that long ago I vowed upon the altar of my ancestors that I would never let this bracelet leave my arm as a remembrance of my brother." Sebastianus clasped his fingers around his wrist and said, "*This* is my most cherished possession, and there is no force on earth that would make me break my vow never to part with it."

Gripping her by the arms, looking into her eyes as if he and Ulrika were the only two souls in the middle of the desert, Sebastianus said with passion, "Men in their fear and foolishness try to predict their destinies, thereby hoping to control them. But the future is unpredictable, Ulrika, and destiny is as intangible as a cloud. There are no messages in the stars. I will destroy the charts, instruments, devices for observation and calculation that I brought from China. I will not visit the observatory in Alexandria where the greatest astronomers in the world study the heavens. For I know now they cannot put it all together and uncover the secrets to the meaning of life."

He looked down at her, love in his eyes. "Do not be sad for me, my dearest. Timonides's false readings and lies, and his confession revealing his misdeeds, have opened my eyes to the truth. For I am now a free man, believing in nothing, choosing my own destiny. This is why I forgive Timonides. For he is only human, and who is to say I would not have done the same under those circumstances? Perhaps he did me a favor. For now I am in control of my life. No more waiting to see what the stars portend. I will awake each morning my own master."

He gripped her shoulders and, looking deep into her eyes, said, "I climbed the three hundred and thirty-three stairs a man filled with hope, and descended them a man filled with new wisdom. From now on, dearest Ulrika, you will be my religion, my goddess, and I will worship you all the days of my life."

He kissed her then, and finally stepped back, as if bringing himself back to the physical world. He looked around. "Who are all these people? What has happened here?"

She told him about the little girl's astonishing cure.

He arched his eyebrows. "Do you believe Rabbi Judah restored her legs?"

"It does not matter what I think. When word of this reaches the city, there will be a stampede to this spot. Sebastianus, I feel responsible. I told Miriam to bring her husband here. And I told her that he wishes to be remembered. I handled it all wrong. I had not foreseen that this would happen. These people are all in danger and it is my fault. Sebastianus, my spiritual gift is to find sacred places and sacred people—I found a Venerable One!—and to lead people to them. But I must also do it responsibly, not in a way that will bring harm to others."

"Do not worry, we will find a way to fix this."

A short distance away, Primo scowled at what he had just overheard, and wondered how he was going to keep his master safe now. When word of what had happened here reached the city, there would be no containing the thousands flocking to this place. With his master insisting on fixing it!

And Quintus Publius about to depart, any day now, for his return to Babylon.

38

To my esteemed Quintus Publius. In the name of the Senate and People of Rome, I greet you. Herewith is a report on the latest activities of my master, Sebastianus Gallus, in regards to his caravan and the goods he transports for Caesar."

Primo was dictating in the privacy of his spartan military tent that had been hastily erected near Daniel's Castle. He paused to allow the secretary to write the words, dipping his pen in the ink and applying it to the papyrus. Although Primo had become proficient in several languages, he was dictating in Latin, for that was the language he shared with the ambassador from Rome.

He continued: "We are still in Babylon, honored Quintus, but there is a very good reason. Please read this report before you consider arresting my master for treason."

He had spent days worrying over what to tell Quintus Publius about Sebastianus's continued lingering in Babylon, but now he had a solution.

Primo had once been a soldier with limited imagination, who had seen the world in black and white, unskilled at fabricating lies. Yet since their return from China, Primo had found that he was more adept at lying—diplomacy, Sebastianus would call it—than he had ever thought possible. For now he must think of a clever way of covering up the fact that they were still in Babylon because his master was in love.

In his new way of thinking, going outside black and white, into areas of gray and brown and even red or green, Primo decided that the best move in this instance would be to dish the ambassador a fiction so outrageous that Publius would have no choice but to believe it!

As Primo weighed his next words, he watched the finely shaped hand move across the papyrus, jotting perfect letters. The secretary wrote almost as quickly as Primo dictated. One of the best in Babylon, Primo had been told. He wondered what the man was going to think of his next words, how he was going to react. But surely the secretary had heard hundreds of strange confessions and declarations, perhaps some even more bizarre than what Primo was about to say. If the man was truly as professional as he comported himself, and if it was true what they said about the code of ethics that governed secretaries and lawyers, the man should not react at all.

Primo knew that professional secretaries, licensed by the government and ruled by strong ethics—for otherwise they would have no clients—were paid not so much for their letter writing skills as for their silence. Whatever passed between client and secretary, whatever went into the correspondence and messages, remained there. Breaking such a confidence was punishable by death because, like lawyers, secretaries recited sworn oaths before receiving their medallions to practice—as was reflected in the title of their profession: from the Latin, *secretus,* which meant "secret."

Primo resumed dictating, "Sebastianus Gallus is under a witch's spell," and the finely shaped hand kept writing with not the slightest hesitation. Mithras, Primo thought. I might be dictating a list of vegetables for all this man reacts! He continued: "She is a sorceress who claims, among many tricks, to communicate with the dead. She holds my master in thrall by professing to communicate with supernatural beings and therefore to foretell the future. You can imagine, my esteemed Quintus, what power she has over my highly superstitious master. It is this woman, named Ulrika—and take note that she is from the same tribe that has caused the Roman Empire, and more specifically General Vatinius, much grief in recent years—who has cast the evil spell over Sebastianus Gallus, making him stay in Babylon, holding back Caesar's treasure for her own selfish interests."

Primo prayed that the story of bewitchment would divert Quintus from the charge of treason. Otherwise, the ambassador would have Sebastianus arrested, seize the caravan and, under Primo's leadership, send it off to Rome. And for a man of Sebastianus's standing in the field of merchant trading to have his caravan taken from him and his rights and privileges stripped, his family name sullied, would be the worst disgrace—not to mention what horrible fate awaited him in the arena.

Primo wondered if he could tell Sebastianus about this untenable situation. The emperor himself had sworn Primo to secrecy, and Primo had always been a man true to his oath. But, of late, he had found his loyalties shifting. He had witnessed his master's bravery in China, had observed Sebastianus's integrity and honor at work. And hadn't Sebastianus himself managed to obtain their release from the emperor's "hospitality"?

Primo scowled. He was used to wrestling *men,* not moral dilemmas.

"Send for me at your convenience, esteemed Quintus," Primo concluded, "and I shall give you a more detailed report in person, at which time I am sure you will agree that my master is more a victim than a traitor. I am confident you will encourage Caesar to be lenient with him. Your servant, Primo." He thought for a moment and then, deciding that a touch of humility would not hurt, added, "Fidus."

And the secretary smirked.

ULRIKA GLANCED IN THE direction of Primo's tent, glowing against the night with lantern light. She knew he was entertaining a visitor from the city, a man of some importance judging by the heavily fringed robes he had arrived in, the tall cone-shaped hat, and the wooden box he carried, resembling those carried by lawyers. She wondered what business Sebastianus's steward had with a civilian.

Then she looked past the tent and out into the dark desert, to see a red glow on the horizon: Babylon. A city that never slept.

Ulrika was filled with an ominous feeling. The back of her neck prickled. The sort of sensation one experienced just before a lightning storm, or a dust storm that had its unseen beginnings in faraway deserts where mythical *jinni* were said to stir up the wind to torment humankind.

Where was Sebastianus? He should have returned by now. He had left that morning for an urgent meeting with the High Priest and now he was overdue.

They had spent the past days trying to convince people to go away from this place. Instead, more had come. The crowd grew so large that Sebastianus had given Primo orders to set up a small camp and arrange for a manned guard around the perimeter.

There had been no miracles since the little girl was cured of paralysis. But that one demonstration of the magical properties of this place had been enough to generate and sustain faith. This time, there was no pushing, no protesting. Miriam and her family, Timonides, and Primo's men saw to the orderly conduct of visitors at what everyone was calling "Judah's shrine."

But they could not stay any longer. It was time for everyone to leave.

Ulrika looked out at the dark desert and felt gooseflesh rise on her arms. Something was out there, coming this way . . .

THE RIDER GALLOPED ACROSS the desert at breakneck speed, moonlight guiding his way, his cloak flying behind him as his steed kicked up clouds of sand. Sebastianus had used his powerful and influential connections, plus generous monetary donations, to keep the priests of Marduk placated. But it had come to an end. He had to warn Ulrika and the others.

They were out of time. The temple guards were coming.

As she waited anxiously for sign of Sebastianus, Ulrika looked at the quiet, faithful mob, regretful that she had given them this sacred place, only to have brought them into danger.

Was it Judah who had cured the little girl? Ulrika knew that, in the vast world, there were many different beliefs, and miracles were possible.

As the desert wind blew against her face, it reminded her of another desert, another wind—on the shore of the Sea of Salt. And suddenly she was remembering the place where Rachel and Almah had found her—on a grave. Ulrika had thought Rachel had buried her husband in sacred ground. But now, as people prayed to Venerable Judah, Ulrika wondered if it had been the other way around. Had Jacob made that ground sacred?

Remembering, too, that Jacob and Judah had been "brothers" under their master in Galilee, Ulrika wondered now if Jacob was also a Venerable One.

In Primo's tent, the secretary was packing his writing equipment and saying, "I will see that your letter is delivered safely to the house of Ambassador Publius first thing in the morning." After reading the dictation back to Primo, making corrections, and then copying it out again more neatly, the secretary had rolled it up, dripped wax onto it, and allowed Primo to seal the scroll with his ring.

"A job well done," Primo said, but as he reached into his money pouch for coins, he heard horse's hooves approaching at a gallop. Looking out, he saw Sebastianus flying into the camp.

"Wait," he said to the Babylonian. "There might be more."

Sebastianus jumped down from his horse and ran to Ulrika. "I was unable to confer with the High Priest," he said breathlessly. "He would not see me. I went to the governor, but it is beyond his control. Ulrika, not even my friend Hasheem, the powerful money-changer, could help. I have given orders to my slaves to prepare the caravan to move out. They will be ready to depart at dawn."

He looked at the frightened crowd—mothers with infants, men with useless legs, the blind and the sick—and then he lowered his voice. "The High Priest is on his way here. I was told he is bringing guards. Ulrika, I believe I can talk reasonably to the man, but we must not have a panic. If we get these people to remain peaceful and orderly, and to show no disrespect to the priests and to Marduk, I believe they will allow us to return to the city unmolested."

"Sebastianus," Ulrika said, placing a hand on his arm. "I must go to Judea."

He stared at her. "Judea! Why?"

"I believe Rachel's husband is a Venerable One and that I am meant to go there and protect him as I did Rabbi Judah. But also, Rachel saved my life, and she was one of my teachers. I owe her a great debt."

Sebastianus thought about it. "Rome has sent more legions to Judea. The unrest among the Jewish rebels grows."

"Jacob is too precious to let fall into the hands of the Romans, who were his enemies. I must go to Judea and get him and Rachel to safety."

"Where would that be?"

"I do not know, but he must be remembered as Judah is remembered. I shall do it differently. I will not be so irresponsible with Jacob. I will give it a great deal of thought."

Primo came up. "Master, is everything all right?"

Sebastianus turned to his steward. "The High Priest is coming with an armed escort. I want no provocation. We will settle this peacefully. All they want is for these people to disperse and return to the city. That is exactly what we will do. Tomorrow, I want you to see that all my goods and people get safely to Rome. I am putting you in charge of the caravan."

Primo's ugly face twisted in a scowl. "Where will you be, master?"

"I am going to Judea with Ulrika."

"Master! To *leave* the caravan?" The old soldier was nearly speechless with shock. Truly his master was under a witch's spell.

"You have your orders."

"Let me accompany you to Judea," Primo said, thinking quickly. What had he just overheard the girl say? They were going to rescue something precious? And two Jews named Rachel and Jacob? An act of treason without a doubt! Suddenly Primo was gripped with an intense desire to defend his master against Caesar's retribution. Even if it meant committing treason himself.

"You will need protection, master. Revolution is fomenting in the province of Judea, and the Roman army has increased its presence there. It will behoove you to have a veteran of the legions in your party, and I am not without connections still."

"I need a man I can trust to accompany the caravan."

Timonides stepped forward and said, "*I* will take the caravan to Rome, master. It is the least I can do for the pain and grief I have caused you."

Sebastianus thought for a moment, then said, "Very well. We must make haste now, for the High Priest will soon be here. Primo, ready your soldiers. There will be no fight, but we must be prepared. Timonides, as soon as this business is done, I want you to take my horse and ride to the caravan. See to the final preparations for departure. We have no time to lose."

Ulrika went to Miriam and said, "Men are coming from the temple of Marduk, but do not be afraid. Sebastianus will have a few words with the High Priest and then we have to send all these people home."

She paused to look into Miriam's plump face, no longer filled with despair but at peace. "I do not presume, honored mother, to tell you how to conduct your faith. But when I sent you here, I did not foresee the consequences of my actions. In the privacy of your home, spread word about Venerable Judah to friends and family, and always remember him, for that is what he asked of me."

AFTER GIVING ORDERS TO his second in command, Primo hurried back to his tent, where the secretary had been waiting impatiently. "I suggest you leave at once," Primo said. "The temple guard is coming and they might mistake you for one of those out there."

The Babylonian raised his big nose and said, "You saw the armed guards who accompany me everywhere I go. A necessary precaution in my line of work, as I carry important documents, and sometimes money. They will ride ahead of me and identify me to the priests. I am known to all of them, as I enjoy a wide reputation in the city. They will let me pass unmolested. Have you anything to add to your missive before I take my leave?"

Ignoring the man's disdain, Primo dictated an addendum to his report: "A new development, esteemed Quintus. So severely is my master held in thrall by the witch that we depart at once for Judea to rescue a treasure belonging to the enemies of Rome. This is not treason, my lord, for my master is hypnotized by the witch and knows not his own actions."

The Roman communications network was a swift and efficient system, with riders speeding along roads for which Roman engineers were so famous. The riders took fast, strong horses and galloped from outpost to outpost, in a vast relay race, bearing news, dispatches, and letters for important citizens from the emperor on down. Primo knew his report would reach Nero long before Sebastianus did. The emperor and his guards would be waiting for him and, with great luck and the power of Mithras, arrest the girl instead of his master.

As for Primo himself, he had one last important mission to carry out. In a final effort to rescue his master from committing treason, Primo would see to it that he found the insurgents Rachel and Jacob first, and kill them before Sebastianus could reach them.

"MASTER!" CAME A SHOUT IN THE NIGHT. Sebastianus and Ulrika turned to see Timonides running toward them, his white robes ghostly in the moonlight. He flung an arm behind himself. "Master! The priests and guards are coming. Oh master, there are *hundreds* of them!"

Sebastianus climbed onto the highest pile of blocks that had fallen from Daniel's Castle long ago, and from this vantage point saw an astonishing sight: a line of blazing torches winding along the highway, like a river of molten lava. Hundreds of guards indeed, Sebastianus thought in alarm. All on horseback. All carrying javelins and spears.

They come for a slaughter.

Returning to Ulrika and Timonides, he said quietly, "I underestimated the High Priest. I believe he is coming not to negotiate but to make an example of these people for the citizens of Babylon. We have to keep everyone calm. Keep them back here behind the ruins. Primo and I will stand and fight. Perhaps the High Priest will be satisfied with a few."

Ulrika took her place at Sebastianus's side as they watched the river of fire advance upon the ruins. Behind her, she heard the murmured prayers of hundreds of terrified people. Primo stood at the ready with his soldiers, weapons drawn. The wind whistled across the desert.

So many lives at stake! There had to be a way to save all these people.

Ulrika turned her face into the wind, closed her eyes, and drew in a slow breath. Reaching out, she placed her hand on the cold stone wall of the "castle" and she thought: If there is indeed a tomb under these ruins, is it large enough to hold all these people? If not all, then at least the children, the sick. And if it is a tomb, then perhaps it would be taboo for the temple guards to walk here, like the shaman's cave in the Rhineland which the German warriors avoided.

Drawing in a purifying breath, Ulrika closed her eyes and envisioned her inner soul flame. Spirit of this place, she silently prayed, I beseech thee for thy help.

She waited for a vision. When none came, she increased her concentration, focusing on the quivering soul flame, and with her free hand took hold of the scallop shell on her breast. Once again, she sent out her prayer.

But nothing happened, and panic began to steal over her. Her mouth ran dry and her palms grew moist. She had used the meditation successfully to the benefit of others—but only for individuals. Now that there were hundreds of souls in danger, would she have the power to use her gift? Or did it only work for one person at a time?

Realizing that her heart was racing—and that the temple guards were drawing closer—she redoubled her efforts. If this truly was the burial place of the Prophet Daniel, then it was sacred ground. This was her calling. This was what she was born to do. She must not panic. She must not let fear overcome her inner powers.

One by one she closed down her senses—turning deaf to the desperate prayers of hundreds of people, turning blind to the glowing torches coming up from the desert, turning numb to the feel of the wind and the cold on her skin, until all she was aware of was the rock beneath her fingers.

Again she opened herself, set her soul free, and begged the sacred being of this place to give her a sign.

Finally her spirit moved—through the solid rock and ancient dust, and across the timeless years—until she felt it touch something.

Ulrika frowned. Something was there, just in front of her and yet, unlike with previous visions, she saw only darkness. Why was her inner sight being blocked?

No, not blocked. The darkness itself is the vision.

Now she smelled a stale mustiness, felt rubble and gravel beneath her sandals, saw long corridors with dim lights at the end, heard the clanking of armor and the tramping of feet. And knowledge flooded her mind . . .

"Sebastianus!" she cried suddenly. "Before this was a tomb, it was a military outpost!"

He turned to her. "What?"

"This citadel was built hundreds of years ago as a primary defense against invaders from the south," she said, as knowledge filled her head. "The king sent his soldiers here to stage surprise attacks. Sebastianus, there are tunnels beneath us, and they lead to an oasis a mile from here, to the north! If I can just find—" Placing her other hand on the rough stones, she felt along the cold walls of the ruins. Her hand slipped inside a crevice. "Here!"

Sebastianus called for Primo and several strong men with spears. Working in torchlight, while lookouts kept an eye on the approaching guards from the city, they rammed the shafts into the crevice and, pulling back with all their might, levered one of the stone blocks so that it slipped away.

A rush of stale air blew in their faces. Taking a torch, Sebastianus slipped it in and looked around. Stone steps, dusty and littered with pebbles, descended into darkness.

"It can be done," he said, "but we must hurry. If they catch us at this, they will pursue. Primo, you will go down first and light the way."

"But you send us into a tomb, master!"

"Ulrika says the tunnel is clear."

Primo scowled. He would rather stand and fight like a man than die like a rat trapped in a sewer. But he would obey.

"The children and the elderly and the lame are to be carried," Sebastianus said. "Anyone who will hinder our escape. Primo, take several torches and place them along the way as you go, for those behind you."

Primo and a few soldiers led the way, moving obstructions, setting torches, escorting those who came behind. The rest went down in a hasty but orderly fashion, with men carrying children, strong women supporting the elders. Sebastianus sent soldiers down at intervals, with more torches. Nobody spoke. But Ulrika saw the terror on their faces as they looked into the abyss. "Do not fear," she said, "but hurry. And do not look back. Follow the person in front of you."

Down they went, one by one, the strong assisting the weak, lowering stretchers and litters into the ground, helping those on crutches and leading the blind. They carried torches and oil lamps. They found the ceiling high enough for them to stand upright and still have room above their heads—clearance enough, Ulrika thought, for the helmets of the king's soldiers long ago.

Timonides kept watch on the highway. The priests and mounted guards were coming dangerously near. "No more torches," he murmured to Sebastianus, "or they will see."

When a child began to wail, his mother covered its mouth with her hand and plunged down the stone steps.

"They are nearly upon us," Timonides said, joining Ulrika and Sebastianus at the tunnel's entrance. "We must hurry."

Two men bearing a child on a stretcher slipped and dropped the litter. Sebastianus quickly retrieved the child and handed him to one of the men, saying, "Hurry! You must run now!"

Finally, they were all down, but the palm trees glowed with light from the arriving guards. War horses nickered, armor and weaponry clanked menacingly. "Go down, old friend," Sebastianus whispered to Timonides. "Hurry! They are here!"

Timonides descended into the tunnel.

"Now you, Ulrika. Watch for those who have fallen behind. Help them move along."

She went in and then turned to find Sebastianus, not descending the steps behind her but outside, shifting the stone into place.

"Sebastianus!" she cried, reaching for him.

"There is no other way to seal this entrance. I will meet you at the caravan. Do not worry. I will be all right. I love you, Ulrika."

"Sebastianus!"

39

"I DO WISH YOU WOULD come with us, Rachel dear," the shepherd's wife said. They were the last family to leave the oasis, having decided to take their small flock of sheep to Jericho, where they believed they would be safe from impending war.

With the increasing presence of Roman military in the past weeks, there was no longer any doubt that fighting was going to break out.

"Thank you, Mina," Rachel said, "but I will stay."

As Mina picked up a stray lamb and held it to her ample bosom, she said, "We will miss you. We so enjoyed your stories. Everyone did. What a delight you were to travelers who rested here. I believe you so captivated them that they stayed longer than they normally would have."

Rachel had enjoyed telling stories to the people who lived at the oasis, as she had told them to a girl named Ulrika years ago. Rachel spun inspirational tales of faith and heroism to an attentive audience of shepherds, date farmers, wheelwrights, and travelers who rested at the oasis.

"You shouldn't be alone," Mina said, as her husband gestured impatiently to her. They needed to reach Jericho by nightfall. "Now that Almah is gone, God rest her."

"I will be all right," Rachel said. "This war will pass and people will come back to the oasis. Go in peace."

PRIMO SQUINTED UP AT the sky and saw, over the stark Judean cliffs, vultures circling.

She is hiding in there. The woman named Rachel.

He said nothing to his companions, who were surveying the deserted oasis where, just days ago, several families had lived. Primo had decided that in order to save his master from committing treason by rescuing the widow of an executed criminal, he needed to find her first. When he did, he would kill her, and tell no one. And they could continue on to Rome with Sebastianus in the clear.

"Rachel and I came here once a week to fetch water and to bathe," Ulrika said, as she looked at the pond that was fed fresh water from an artesian spring. Its surface reflected the surrounding palm and olive trees, and the clear blue sky. "We would visit with the people here, and get the latest news from travelers passing by." She traipsed over the dead grass where tents had been staked. "They don't appear to have been gone long."

"They left in a hurry," Sebastianus observed, suspecting the reason why. Roman troops had been marching through the valley for weeks, to take residence at the nearby hilltop garrison at Masada. "Do you suppose Rachel went with them?"

Keeping his eye on the vultures, and determining the landmarks over which they circled, Primo said, "My men and I will search the area. Maybe she is simply hiding."

He reined in his horse and steered it toward craggy cliffs broken into thousands of wadis, canyons, gorges, and defiles. As his eyes scanned the afternoon landscape, he thought about the strange twists and turns of fate. His master should be on a ship bound for Rome at the moment, not venturing deep into a politically volatile region on a treasonous quest! Primo knew now that they had not come to rescue a husband and wife, simply the wife.

They had left Babylon in haste, before the High Priest could change his mind and decide to make martyrs of Judah's followers. While the Gallus caravan had continued westward along the main trade route under the care of Timonides, Sebastianus and Ulrika had followed a southerly road with Primo, six soldiers, and a handful of slaves. The men rode horses while Ulrika rode a camel that had been fitted with a padded saddle for her comfort. They had traveled swiftly and constantly, stopping only to eat and rest, in a hurry to reach Judea before revolt broke out.

Looking up at the vultures, Primo noted which way their scrawny necks swiveled, the specific spot they seemed to be eyeing. He guided his mare into a rocky defile. Silence hung heavy in these narrow canyons, the only sound being the sharp clip-clop of his horse's hooves. As he inspected a series of small limestone caves, he heard a sound—pebbles avalanching down a rocky incline, as if someone had slipped. Dismounting, he continued on foot into the narrow wadi that grew so tight he had to go in sideways. Steep rocky walls blocked out the sunlight so that the way was dark with just a wedge of blue sky overhead. Primo's sturdy hobnailed sandals crunched over the small rocks littering the canyon floor. He paused to listen, his soldier's instinct telling him that something alive was hiding nearby—a large animal or a person—watching, holding its breath, ready to spring.

He stepped carefully, inspecting every crack and crevice in the canyon walls. When he took another step, he heard a gasp, and another cascade of pebbles. He looked into a crevasse and saw a dark shape huddled there.

Primo smiled. He had found Rachel.

"Will you be able to find the grave?" Sebastianus asked. "After all, it's been nine years."

Removing the blue veil from her head and settling it around her shoulders, Ulrika turned in a slow circle as she tried to recall landmarks from her brief stay here. The dun-colored landscape looked unforgiving and lifeless.

Already, the spring flowers had withered and dried up. In the distance, she saw the pale blue ribbon of water that was the sea of salt into which the River Jordan emptied. "I will find it," she said.

Sebastianus scanned the desolate landscape, the flat valley and steep cliffs dotted with caves, and then brought his eyes back to his wife. Beautiful, strong, determined. How he loved and admired her! How she had used her spiritual gift at Daniel's Castle to save all those people.

After everyone had gotten down safely in the tunnels Ulrika had discovered, Sebastianus had pushed the stone back into place and then he had gone to confront the High Priest and explain that the citizens had dispersed and wished in no way to offend Marduk. The High Priest had watched Sebastianus with a keen eye and had asked but one question, "Do you intend to stay long in Babylon?"

"I leave for Rome in the morning."

The High Priest had swept his eyes over the scene, with its unoccupied tents, scattered bits of food, sputtering oil lamps—evidence of the recent and hasty departure of a large crowd. "Marduk watches over all," he said. "He hopes his people will return to the temple and the beneficence of his supreme power. Safe traveling, Sebastianus Gallus."

To Sebastianus's amazement, the priests and temple guards had turned and headed solemnly back in the direction of Babylon. Sebastianus realized what had happened. The priests were not going to make martyrs of Judah's followers, because it would give the followers public sympathy.

Sebastianus wondered if Judah's memory would survive. Although Ulrika had urged everyone to remember him, people would always need temples and idols and priests. He thought of the ancient altar in his homeland, in a place the Romans called Finisterre—"the end of the world." An ancestress named Gaia had built the altar many centuries ago, and there had been a time, Sebastianus was told, when people had come from all over to pay homage at the altar. From as far away as Gaul and the Rhineland, it was said, pilgrims would follow ancient routes in order to pray at the scallop-shell altar. But bandits and brigands had taken to lying in wait for the defenseless wayfarers, to rob them and even kill them, so that pilgrimages to the scallop-shell altar eventually stopped and Gaia's altar was forgotten.

Would the same happen in Babylon? Would the priests, like those long-ago bandits, succeed in frightening worshippers into abandoning Rabbi Judah?

PRIMO DREW HIS SWORD and raised it to deliver a swift death blow. But the woman rose to her feet, drew the veil back from her gray hair, and said softly, “I pray, noble sir, go in peace. I am not an enemy of Rome.”

Suddenly, the Judean wilderness vanished and the years rolled back. Primo was in that small village in Galilee once again, surrounded by angry men determined to tear him apart. It was not her face he recognized, but her voice, the accent of her dialect, the very words she used.

He gasped. It was not *she*—not that young mother of the village long ago. But so very like her . . .

Primo froze, suddenly held by two beseeching eyes, dark and liquid. A strand of hair escaped her veil and fluttered across her cheek. A memory from long ago fluttered across his mind, like that strand of hair: his mother, drawing a comb through her rich tresses, while her son Fidus watched. She was crying. Her shoulders were freshly bruised. The comb was made of wood, some of the teeth were missing. Fidus wished he could buy her an ivory comb. He wished he could kill the men who used her.

His body shook—not then, when he was nine years old, but now, in the Judean wilderness—as a truth came to him. His mother had done what she needed to survive, as this woman named Rachel was doing. His mother, uneducated, without family, giving her little boy a dog’s name, not knowing, in her naïveté, the life of cruelty it would bring to him.

She had loved him in her way, and he had worshipped her in return.

Primo nearly cried out as he felt the years roll away, the aches and pains leaving his joints, making him feel robust and virile again. He left the rat-infested room he had shared with his mother and came forward to the springtime of his life, when a young woman had interceded on a stranger’s behalf. And now the memory of that kind gesture—combined with a fresh new tenderness for his mother—began to melt the stone wall that guarded his heart. Because of his ugliness and how women reacted to it, Primo had always thought he could never be loved. But the sight of this soft-spoken woman, and how she reminded him of a mother's love long ago, made him realize he had been wrong.

In an instant, his whole life came into question. His military career. Perhaps it is easier to blindly follow orders than to question them. It was easier to betray a master than a Caesar. Easier to hate women than to yearn for their love.

He lowered his sword.

"We are here to rescue you, if you are Rachel, the widow of Jacob."

"Rescue!"

"A woman named Ulrika, and her husband, myself, and a few soldiers."

Rachel frowned. "Ulrika? That name is familiar. Yes, I remember. Years ago, a young woman stayed with me for a while. Her name was Ulrika."

Primo nodded. "That is the one."

Her eyes widened. "She is *here?*"

"We have come to take you to a safe place."

"A safe place . . ."

"You have nothing to fear from me," Primo said, sheathing his sword in its scabbard, feeling his throat constrict with emotion. He held out his hand. "I swear by the sacred blood of Mithras, dear lady, that I will let no harm come to you."

They found Ulrika and Sebastianus in a nearby canyon, and the two women embraced in a tearful reunion. They took Rachel to the campfire Sebastianus's slaves had built, and gave her some water, bread, and dates, which she ate delicately despite the fact that it was obvious she was very hungry. Questions flew: "Did you reach Babylon?"

"Why did you not go with the families when they left the oasis?"

"How can you stay here now, all alone, with Almah gone?"

Finally, as shadows crept across the valley and all questions were answered, Ulrika told Rachel about her focused meditation, the answers that came to her in Shalamandar, her search for the Venerable Ones. She told her about Miriam and Judah, and the miracle at Daniel's Castle. "I believe your husband Jacob is a Venerable One, and his remains must be protected."

"How?"

"I suggest," Sebastianus interjected, "that you come to Rome with us."

"I cannot go to Rome. We must be here when the master returns. And it will be soon, for Yeshua promised he would come back in our lifetime. This is why I did not leave with the others."

Ulrika said, "Many of your faith are now in Rome. Miriam told me of a man named Simon Peter, whom she knew in Galilee, and she said he is there, as head of the congregation in Rome. We will take you to him."

Rachel's eyes grew big. "Simon is in Rome? I will think about this and pray for guidance."

PRIMO COULD NOT SLEEP.

Rolling onto his back, he looked up at the stars and saw by the position of the moon that dawn was near. He threw off his blanket and rose to his feet. The others slept on in silence—Sebastianus and Ulrika in their tent, Rachel in a tent she shared with no one, the slaves and soldiers under the stars.

Primo looked out at the cold and barren desert, and realized he had changed. He was no longer the man he had been hours earlier.

Rachel. So like that village mother of long ago . . .

The oasis had several ponds. At sunset, Rachel and Ulrika had bathed in one behind protective screening. As Primo had stood guard with his back to the women, he had heard the soft whispering of water, delicate splashes, gentle trickles, and he had imagined the feminine skin and curves down which the water cascaded. In that moment Primo had understood why Sebastianus had acted the way he had all these months. He was simply a man in love.

Primo strode across the cold sand to the place where Rachel had said her husband was buried. The grave was unmarked. Ulrika had convinced Rachel that her husband's remains were no longer safe here but would be protected by the congregation in Rome.

As a chill breeze blew through his thinning hair, Primo thought about his report to Quintus Publius, which the imperial courier would deliver to Emperor Nero long before they themselves reached Rome. Nero would want to know about the witch who had cast evil spells on Sebastianus. He would be particularly interested in the treasure Primo had mentioned. Nero would most likely be anticipating the legendary secret hoard of gold supposedly spirited away from the Temple in Jerusalem before it was destroyed by Babylonians.

Caesar had become obsessed with money. When their small party had stopped at oases and caravanserais, they had heard stories of the emperor's increasing instability and irrational behavior. He trumped up charges of treason against men of wealth, had them executed so he could seize their estates.

When he reads my report, Primo thought, he will think that I am bringing fabulous treasure to him. Instead, they are the bones of an executed criminal. He will have the bones destroyed. I cannot allow that to happen. Rachel gave up her life to protect them.

Primo drew in a deep, sharp breath and felt his heart come to life. It expanded in his chest like a bird expanding its wings until his heart was normal-sized again, beating with passion, full of life and feeling. Suddenly Primo no longer saw the world in black and white but in shades and hues of all the colors of the rainbow. Because Primo, who had lived his life by a code of honor and duty, now knew that there was a higher duty than that to master and emperor—a duty to love.

ULRIKA WOKE SUDDENLY WITH a vision: a papyrus document rolled up and sealed with red wax. Primo affixing his ring to the wax.

He is the one I sensed as the betrayer in Sebastianus's midst.

Slipping into her cloak, she went into the cold pre-dawn in search of him, and found Primo sitting at the campfire, staring into black coals.

"I had a vision of you back in Antioch," she said. "I saw you betraying Sebastianus. And yet you did not."

He looked at her with the eyes of a man who had not slept. In a voice curiously soft for so rugged a man, he told Ulrika an amazing tale of oaths and emperors, spies and secret reports—and when he was done she thought for a long moment, taking in the deformed nose and scarred face, and said, "You are a man of honor, Primo, and also one of great strength. You have been burdened with a moral dilemma since the day we left Rome, and you kept it to yourself. I believe now that what I saw in that vision back in Antioch was not a traitor but a man who feared he would betray his own loyalties. I misjudged you."

"And I, you," he said softly. "From the moment I first met you, I thought you were going to bring harm to my master. But I know now that you have in fact been good for him, that you helped him to tap his own strength. We should have been friends, all this time. I am sorry now that we were not."

"I, too," she said with a smile. "And now we must tell Sebastianus the truth about Nero."

Ulrika roused the slaves, ordering them to build a fire. Then she woke Sebastianus, who immediately threw on his cloak and stepped out into the biting air. Wakened by voices, Rachel looked out and, seeing her companions gathering at the fire, wrapped herself in her cloak and joined them.

"Noble Gallus," Primo began, startling Sebastianus with such formality, making him wonder what extraordinary confession they were about to hear. "I have always been loyal to you, but as a soldier I thought my first loyalty was to my emperor. I became caught between these two loyalties, and in my desperate attempt to serve both masters—that is, to satisfy Caesar and yet save you from charges of treason—I laid the blame on Ulrika and sent it in a report. I told Caesar that you are under a witch's spell."

"A witch's spell!" Sebastianus said.

"I accused Ulrika of being a witch."

She stared at him in shock. And then her blood ran cold.

In Rome, it was legal for a husband to force his wife to undergo abortion if he suspected the child was not his, or even if he did not want the child. But it was illegal for a woman to procure an abortion for any reason. And so such women sought the help of those who knew the secrets of ending conception. Midwives, wise women, female physicians, and herbalists were all suspected of being abortionists. When their deeds were found out, they were called witches and the punishment was death by stoning.

Primo looked at Ulrika and said, "I am so sorry."

"You had your reasons," she heard herself say, but she had suddenly gone numb with fear. Was that how her life was going to end? Before she was even thirty years old, tied to a post in the Great Circus, while gladiators hurled rocks at her until she was dead?

"Master, we must take a ship to Alexandria," Primo said quickly, "and find a place that is beyond the emperor's reach. I will protect all of you, upon my oath as a soldier."

But Sebastianus shook his head. "I must go to Rome to clear my name, my family's name. But you will take the women to Alexandria."

Ulrika placed her hand on Sebastianus's and said, "I will not let you face Nero alone, my love. Besides, I must clear my name as well. It is not just for my sake, but for my mother's. Wherever she is in this world, she is an honorable healer whose reputation is unblemished. If her daughter is condemned for witchcraft, and executed, it could have disastrous consequences for her."

Rachel then spoke up, saying, "And I have been in hiding long enough. It is time I joined my own kind. I will join the congregation under Simon Peter."

Finally Sebastianus said to Primo, "Then save yourself, old friend, for now you are party to treason and you have broken your oath to Caesar." But even as he said it, Sebastianus knew Primo would return to Rome with them.

As the first golden rays of dawn broke over the distant cliffs in the east, and the four at the campfire felt the promise of the day's warmth, each pondered the fate that awaited them in Rome.

BOOK NINE

ROME, 64 C.E.

40

"There it is," Sebastianus said quietly as he scanned the vast caravan terminus. He counted twenty legionaries standing watch around his caravan—an elite cohort in shining breastplates and red brushes on their helmets—not only guarding his tents and camels and goods from China, but on the lookout for the caravan's leader, he was certain, with orders to slap him in chains and drag him before the emperor.

Stepping back behind the protection of the blacksmith's tent, from which sounds of clanging metal rose in the morning air, he said to Ulrika, "It appears the emperor has seized the caravan as well."

As soon as they had arrived in Rome, they had gone to Sebastianus's villa and found guards surrounding it, with a sign on the main gate declaring it to be the property of the Senate and People of Rome. "We will have to assume that my friends are also being watched, in case I go to them for assistance."

Ulrika felt a wave of emotions wash over her. It had been ten years since she was last in Rome, and the sight of the city brought back a rush of girlhood memories. She thought of old friends who would be married now, with children—Julia, Lucia, Servia.

Behind those towering walls, in the warren of streets and lanes that covered Rome's hills, Ulrika had lived in a villa with her mother. There, she had learned about the Rhineland, had yearned to meet her father's people. But in that same villa, Ulrika had spoken harsh words to her mother and apologized in a letter that her mother had never read.

Did my mother return to Rome? Is she here now?

"What should we do?" she asked, scanning the crowd for a familiar face. They had yet to find Timonides.

The caravanserai south of Rome was vast and noisy, with camels bellowing and donkeys braying, dogs running about on ground covered in sludgy manure and chopped straw. The air was choked with pungent smoke from cook fires, and from the stench of animals recently sodden with sweat. The whole encampment was a hubbub of industry and care, and surrounding it were Roman soldiers in brass and scarlet, standing watch to make sure no one touched the emperor's treasure.

And then Ulrika *did* see a familiar face. "Timonides!" she cried.

He had been coming from the direction of the southern gate, wringing his hands, his face filled with worry. Ulrika called out, glancing at the soldiers to make sure they had not heard. The old astrologer stopped and turned. His face broadened with joy as he came toward them at a trot.

They embraced in the shadow of the blacksmith's tent, Timonides's cheeks wet with tears. "I never thought I would see you again, master," he sobbed on Sebastianus's chest. "It is so good to see you both."

"You are well, old friend?" Sebastianus said, wiping his own tears away.

"I am well, master, but I have been in hiding, waiting for your arrival. Nero is out of his mind with fury!"

"But the caravan arrived intact, did it not?"

"Yes, but too late for his taste. And he came in person to pick through everything here. Nothing pleased him."

"But there are treasures in there!"

"Not the sort Nero wants. They say he has a new passion—for gemstones! He carries an emerald and peers at the world through it. He needs money. You have heard of the terrible fire that destroyed much of the city. Rumors are that Nero himself set it so that he could clear room for new buildings. Master! You cannot go home. Soldiers are there to arrest you. I have come to the caravan terminus every day, hoping to find you before the soldiers did."

"I know, old friend."

Timonides's white eyebrows flew up. "You know about the charges of treason and witchcraft?"

Sebastianus laid a hand on the old astrologer's shoulder. "It is a long story."

Timonides turned to Ulrika. "While I have been awaiting your arrival, I have not been idle. I asked around and learned that a well-known healer-woman named Selene now lives in Ephesus, where she practices her arts."

"You found my mother?" But Ulrika was not surprised. Selene had enjoyed a sterling reputation here in Rome. Word of her whereabouts would have made its way back to where she had been so loved.

"You can write to her. I know where to send a letter."

"Oh Timonides, this is wonderful news!"

"But what of your journey to Judea?"

Sebastianus told him of finding Rachel at the oasis near the sea of salt, where he and Primo had reverently moved Jacob's remains to the small cedar chest in which Rachel had kept her clothes. From there they had made their way to the coast to take a merchant ship across the Great Green, arriving at Brundisium a week ago, the first day of October. There they had purchased horses and carts and fresh supplies, and had struck out along the Via Appia, the highway that connected the main cities of Italia. Fifty miles south of Rome they parted ways with Primo and Rachel, believing that the two would be safer on their own, and Primo knew an old friend, a retired centurion he had served under, who would offer them safe haven at his hillside vineyard.

"Where are you going to take the relics?" Timonides asked.

"We had thought to a man named Simon Peter, a friend of Rachel's."

Timonides shook his head. "Your friend Rachel is not safe here. I have heard of this Simon fellow. He leads a group of Jews who are waiting for the Messiah to come. As they are a closed and fanatical group, Nero has decided to blame them for the fire that destroyed much of the city. They have all been arrested and await execution in the arena."

"How bad was the fire?" Ulrika asked.

"Terrible! It happened three months ago, on the night of July the eighteenth, starting at the southeastern end of the Circus Maximus in shops selling flammable goods. The fire spread quickly and burned for over five days. Hundreds of houses and shops were reduced to cinders. Nero began rebuilding at once, but they are extravagant projects. He is building a splendid new residence for himself called the Golden House—a project certain to bankrupt the Treasury, as you might imagine by its name. Did you know that Nero has proclaimed himself a god? He is insisting that he be worshipped alongside Jupiter and Apollo. Come with me, master. I will take you and Ulrika to a safe place."

Sebastianus turned to Ulrika, "Go with Timonides. Send word to Primo and Rachel. Italia is no longer safe for them."

"What about you?"

"I have an appointment with our emperor. Ulrika, you go with Timonides—"

Ulrika shook her head. "I am going with you."

Timonides spoke up: "Master, I will also go with you. You were led astray by my false horoscopes. If there are any charges of treason, they should be upon me. This is something I must do."

"Very well, but we must find a way to get into the palace."

"It is a madhouse, master. This is Nero's jubilee year. Emissaries have come from all over the empire to bring him gifts. You cannot even get near the Imperial Palace. Best to let one of *those* take you," Timonides said, flinging an arm in the direction of the Roman guard.

But Sebastianus said, "I will not stand before Caesar in chains. And I especially will not have my wife paraded in chains. We are free citizens of Rome and deserve to be heard before we are found guilty." He rubbed the bronze stubble on his jaw. "The problem is how to get into the palace without risking arrest? For if we are arrested, we could languish in prison for days or even weeks before we are brought before Caesar and our case is heard. We need only get in the door. But how?"

"Sebastianus," Ulrika said. "Primo told us that he said in his report to Nero you went to Judea to find hidden treasure. You need only appear at the entrance and give them your name. If Nero is truly desperate for money, he will have you brought into his presence at once."

"But you have nothing to give him," Timonides protested. "I have seen the visitors arriving at the palace. They bring fantastic gifts for Caesar. You will not be allowed to enter empty-handed."

Sebastianus smiled. "But I do have a gift for Caesar. A very rare and unique gift that only I can give."

Timonides wrinkled his nose. "What might that be?"

"You yourself gave me the idea, old friend, in something you just now said. But we must hurry."

They went first to an inn, where they bathed and changed into clothes Timonides purchased for them in the marketplace—Sebastianus would not have Ulrika and himself arrive before the emperor in anything less than the finest garments. Ulrika wore a dress of several layers, all the shades of a sunrise, with a daffodil-colored veil that went from the crown of her head to her feet, and draped artfully over her right arm. Sebastianus donned a black knee-length tunic edged with gold embroidery, and a matching black toga draped over his broad shoulders and arms. Adding new sandals that laced up the calves, and expensive belts made from the softest kid leather, Sebastianus was satisfied that he and Ulrika made an elegant couple, aristocratic enough to pass the scrutiny of any palace steward or chamberlain. And now that Timonides had regained all health lost in China, and wore clean white robes that set off his handsome flowing white hair, he made for a fine servant to the patrician couple.

Before they left the inn, Sebastianus took Ulrika's face in his hands and kissed her on the lips. "Whatever happens today, my love, remember that I will always love you. Wherever destiny takes us from this day forward, I will carry you forever in my heart. Now listen to me. Let me do the talking. Say nothing to Caesar. Do not try to defend yourself. I will find a way to exonerate you of the charge of witchcraft. Above all, do not divulge to Nero your gift, for he will want to keep you for himself. They say he has become obsessed with the gods and knowing the future. Ulrika, if he learns of your spiritual gift, you will be kept a prisoner in the palace, and Nero will torment you with his insanity. Promise me you will say nothing."

"Sebastianus, what is your gift for Caesar? He has taken everything. We are left with nothing except the clothes we wear."

"Do not fear, my love. From what I have learned of our emperor, it is something he will not be able to resist."

It was a short walk to the Forum and the base of the Palatine Hill, but the way was crowded with onlookers lining the wide avenue to gawk at the visitors who continually arrived in the hopes of an audience with the emperor. But Sebastianus managed to get himself and his two companions through the maze of stewards and chamberlains, and finally into the palace itself.

The waiting hall outside the imperial audience chamber was so crammed with people and animals it was nearly impossible to make one's way through. Visitors hoping to impress Nero had brought extravagant and fabulous gifts, filling the colonnaded hall with a colorful spectacle of comically dressed midgets on golden leashes; dance troupes with drums and torches; trained dogs dressed as lions and tigers; enormous chests brimming with rare bird plumage and animal pelts; statues carved in the likeness of the emperor. A staff of imperious chamberlains, dressed in impressive long blue tunics embroidered with silver threads, saw to the sorting of the guests. The hall was filled with the dull roar of many voices mingling with the peculiar barks and howls and squawks of the exotic animals that were waiting to be presented to the emperor. The chamberlains checked rosters of names—those invited and those to be banned. Sebastianus Gallus and Ulrika were on neither list.

The fat steward who had the final say-so at the enormous double doors looked them up and down. He held a tall ebony walking staff tipped with gold, intended to be rapped on the floor for attention. "You say you have a gift for Caesar? You do not appear to be carrying anything."

"It is for Caesar's eyes only," Sebastianus said.

The man waited, sucked a tooth, shifted his heavy staff to the other hand.

"I will not bribe you," Sebastianus said. "I will simply send word to Caesar that, due to the negligence and greed of a certain steward identified by a raspberry mark on his neck, one of Caesar's oldest and dearest friends was kept from presenting him with a prize above all others."

The chamberlain met Sebastianus's eye with the air of one who had faced many an arrogant, and threatening, visitor to the palace.

"And you are to personally escort us," Sebastianus added.

The chamberlain's brow arched in frank surprise. He sucked his teeth again, taking the measure of the unusual trio, then he said, "I think I shall call a guard instead. I see no gift for Caesar. Especially none more valuable than any of *these,*" and he gestured toward thirty African slaves bearing massive elephant tusks on their shoulders.

"Apparently," Sebastianus said calmly, "you enjoy a special intimacy with our emperor to know what he would prize above all else."

Sebastianus kept his eyes on the chamberlain, who met his gaze for a moment, and then he faltered, looking away, clearing his throat until he said, "Come this way."

Going through a smaller door, they followed the chamberlain into the audience hall, remembered from ten years prior, and joined a cacophonous press of colorful humanity. Nero's guests were mostly from the Roman patrician class, judging by their elegant gowns and togas, and the ladies' hairdos, which seemed to compete for height and number of curls. They stood about murmuring amongst themselves, turned every now and then when a foreign guest was admitted, and ogled the gifts laid at Nero's feet. Young slaves in pale-blue and silver tunics moved among the guests with platters bearing cups of wine, or tasty treats such as roasted sparrows and figs dipped in honey.

Ulrika was flung back to the last time she had stood in this hall, ten years prior. She recalled seeing the same apparition that had appeared to her in the countryside when she was twelve—a woman running with her mouth wide in a silent scream, her arms and hands covered in blood. Ulrika had not known why the vision had appeared to her in this audience chamber, and she still did not know. But should it happen again, this time she would have control of the vision and learn its meaning.

The crowd was dense, so Sebastianus allowed Timonides and Ulrika to go first as they followed the chamberlain, with Sebastianus behind them, shielding them from elbows and feet. Ulrika tried to glimpse the emperor at the other end of the domed chamber, but she could not see him over the heads of so many.

One personage, however, caught her eye.

The Vestal Virgins were priestesses of Vesta, goddess of the hearth, and Rome's patron goddess and protector. The Vestals were freed of the usual social obligations to marry and rear children, and took a vow of chastity in order to devote themselves to the guardianship of the sacred flames of Vesta, seeing that they never burned out. The Chief Vestal, who had caught Ulrika's eye, sat on a high throne surrounded by handmaidens and wore a stunning gown of many layers in colors of blue, aquamarine, and peridot green. She was the most powerful priestess in Rome and was always seen at important events, at chariot races, or being carried through Rome in her private chair on important business.

Beneath her impressive crown, rising tall and heavy on her head and covered with a long, pale-green veil that cascaded over her shoulders, a passive face watched the spectacle, and she paid no attention to two chamberlains who had begun to argue over protocol.

Ulrika deduced from the gestures of the more important of the two stewards—tall and thin and wearing a curious robe that had sleeves and a pleated skirt—that the three newcomers must wait their turn. "Master," Timonides murmured, "if we are forced to wait, it could take *days.*"

But now they were near the emperor, and could see the golden throne he occupied, the dais that lifted him above the crowd, the men surrounding him wearing white tunics and togas edged in purple. Empress Poppaea Sabina, Ulrika noticed, was not present, and she wondered why.

Nero was fretful. "I do not need midgets and dancers!" he snapped. "Can no one understand my plight? Rome must be made beautiful again. Do I pay for such a feat with beads and feathers?

During their walk from the inn, Ulrika had seen the charred ruins left by the great fire. Rubble was being hurriedly cleared by gangs of slaves, and alongside the skeletons of burned-out buildings new edifices were hastily going up, with scaffolding that seemed to Ulrika of dubious strength, supporting stonemasons, brick layers, carpenters, painters. Even the Imperial

Palace was undergoing massive renovation, also at a frenetic pace, as if Emperor Nero were racing to stay ahead of a pursuing calamity. The audience chamber in which Ulrika now stood had been transformed—she could not believe that such a grand room could be made even grander. She looked up at the ceiling that, ten years prior, had been a dome of geometric squares, but was now a blazing panorama of the night sky, with a throned Nero at the center of a circle of zodiacal signs. The mosaic of Nero was executed in a rainbow of colors, while the constellations were composed of gold and silver tiles. Ulrika wondered how long it had taken the masterpiece to be rendered, for she could not imagine Nero exhibiting much patience with its progress.

The atmosphere, too, was different from ten years ago. Ulrika felt the tension in the air. There was none of the optimism that a young new emperor had generated. People's eyes shifted about with mistrust and anxiety while Nero sat on a new throne fashioned in solid gold beneath a purple canopy festooned with gold fringe and tassels. He was still handsome, Ulrika thought, with an imposing nose, thick curly hair, and a stylish beard that decorated his neck but left his jaw clean-shaven. He wore robes and a toga of purple silk, with a gold laurel wreath on his head. He was the most powerful man on earth, and he was twenty-six years old.

Sebastianus and his companions watched the two chamberlains argue, until Sebastianus suddenly strode forward, past the guards and the chamberlains, and, stopping squarely before Nero, declared, "Greetings, noble Caesar, from Sebastianus Gallus!"

"Wait!" cried the mortified chamberlains, and members of Caesar's elite Praetorian Guard jumped forward.

"Gallus!" Nero held up a hand to stay the others, and studied the impudent visitor through his notorious emerald monocle. "Sebastianus Gallus is a traitor to the people of Rome. Why is this man not in chains?"

The fat chamberlain with the raspberry mark vanished, while those nearby fell silent. The Chief Vestal slowly swiveled her head, as if her massive crown were the weight of Rome itself, and she watched with half-closed eyes as Sebastianus said in a commanding voice, "I have come of my own volition, great Caesar, and I stand before you not only as a friend but as your personally chosen ambassador to the faraway land of China. My mission was a success, Caesar, and I return with a gift."

Nero signaled for the Praetorians to hold their position. "What is this gift, Sebastianus Gallus?"

"My gift is this: Personal greetings to Most Honored Caesar from His Celestial Magnificence, the Emperor of China."

Nero stared at him. "That is it? That is all you bring me? A *greeting?*"

"Emperor Ming of Han invites Caesar to send Rome's gods to China. Shrines will be set up to house them. This would include your own divine self, Caesar, to be worshipped by many Chinese."

Nero grunted. "They are a backward people. I want nothing to do with China."

"I thought Caesar would be pleased that he would be worshipped by another race."

"You thought wrong, Gallus. I repeat: What else have you brought me?"

"You have been through the goods in my caravan, Caesar. You have seen and heard all that I brought back from China."

"What of precious gems?" Nero said, bringing the emerald monocle to his eye.

"Jade—"

"Worthless!" Nero leaned forward, placing an elbow on the arm of his golden throne. "Sebastianus Gallus, we have been told that you tarried in Babylon for no known reason while you kept your emperor waiting. Your emperor, who was in *need.* How do you account for yourself, and why should we not consider this a treasonous act?"

"My master is innocent, great Caesar!"

Attention shifted to Gallus's white-bearded companion. "Who are you?" barked the emperor.

"I am Timonides, my master's astrologer. For personal and greedy reasons I falsified my master's horoscopes, leading him in the wrong direction, forcing him to divert his path from Rome. Sebastianus Gallus is not guilty of treason, only of trusting an old servant."

"What of Judea, old man? Did you tell your master to go there?"

When Timonides faltered, having not expected the question, Sebastianus spoke up: "I went on my own, great Caesar, on a personal errand."

"It is well known that I am not honored in Judea, and that Rome is despised there. Why, I wonder, would someone loyal to his emperor visit a place that was disloyal to that same emperor? Unless of course it was to rescue treasure for your emperor, in which case it would not be an act of treason."

"There was no treasure, Caesar. I went to Judea in aid of a friend."

"I think you are lying. Everyone knows that the temple in Jerusalem was filled with gold and gemstones, and that the Jews took it all to safety when the Babylonians invaded. You found it and you have hidden it somewhere."

"There was no treasure, Caesar."

The chief chamberlain stepped up to the dais and murmured something to one of Nero's aides, who in turn whispered in the emperor's ear. Nero nodded, and a moment later a side door opened. To Ulrika's shock, Primo and Rachel were brought in, ropes binding their wrists. Behind them, a soldier carried the small cedar chest that had once held Rachel's garments.

Nero said to Sebastianus, "My agents sighted you at Brundisium and followed you to Rome. Did you really think you could sneak back without your emperor knowing, or that you could hide your partners in treason?"

"They are merely friends, Caesar," Sebastianus said. "There are no traitors here."

Nero pointed to the cedar chest. "And what is in that?"

"The box contains the bones of a man who wishes to be buried with his kin."

Nero ordered it opened while everyone watched in eager anticipation. The legendary Jewish treasure was said to be so great that even slaves' chains were wrought of gold.

As the Praetorian lifted the lid, Nero rose to his feet, his eyes fixed greedily on the chest. "What is it?" he said sharply. "What do you see?"

"It is as Gallus said, Caesar. Just bones."

The emperor made a show of disgust and sat back down. "You shall pay for your deception, Sebastianus Gallus, and for thinking you could make your emperor appear the fool."

"If I may speak, Caesar," Primo said, stepping forward. "I am Primo Fidus and I served in Rome's legions for many years before I retired and went in service to Sebastianus Gallus. It was my report, written by me and dispatched to Ambassador Quintus Publius in Babylon, that led you to believe my master went to Judea in search of treasure. I was mistaken. I had been misinformed."

Nero said, "I read that report. Were you mistaken about the witch as well?"

Primo's eyes flickered toward Ulrika. "I was, Caesar."

"So many mistakes from a man who survived a multitude of foreign campaigns. It is a wonder you are still alive." A rumble of laughter went through the crowd. "Where is this woman you *mistakenly* called a witch? Is she in Rome?"

When Primo did not respond, Nero gestured with his right hand, and a Praetorian stepped forward to deliver a swift blow with the butt of his spear against Primo's head. Primo dropped to his knees, and at once blood appeared on his scalp. "Where is the witch?" Nero repeated and the Praetorian stood ready.

"I am the one, Caesar," Ulrika said, stepping forward to stand with Sebastianus and Timonides before the emperor. "But I am not a witch. It was gossip and rumors spoken in Babylon. This man is not to blame." She looked at Sebastianus and murmured, "Forgive me, for now I must speak."

Ulrika saw the way the emperor narrowed his eyes at her head. "You are fair-haired like a Barbarian," he said. "Are you unaware that we are at war with Barbarian insurgents?"

"My father's people live in the Rhineland," she said, her heart racing. If he inquired about her mother, what would she say? The truth, that her mother had been a close friend of Claudius Caesar, Nero's predecessor whom he had assassinated?

She braced herself for the question, but instead Nero said dismissively, "I know you are a Cherusci. It said so in that oaf's report. Unless of course he was mistaken in that, too!"

More soft laughter.

"Do not deny that you made outrageous claims in Babylon," Nero said, pointing a finger at Ulrika, "that you are able to see the dead. I know this because that blockhead wasn't the only man reporting to me. I received a more detailed report of your dramatics in Babylon from my ambassador there who wrote to me of miracles and cures. Show me how you speak to the dead. I wish a demonstration."

"It is not that simple, Caesar," Ulrika said, recalling how Sebastianus had cautioned her against demonstrating her talents to Nero, who would make her a prisoner for his own amusements. "But I am not a witch. I do not cast evil spells or—"

He waved an impatient hand. "I care nothing about that. Can you speak to the dead or not? Answer me."

A young slave arrived at Nero's side, bearing a platter of garlic-fried mushrooms. He stood patiently for the food to be noticed. Nero looked the offering over, casually, then he reached for the serving fork, which was two-tined and made of silver, and in a lightning-quick gesture, thrust it into the boy's abdomen.

A collective gasp rose from the onlookers, but no one made another sound as Nero leaned forward in his throne to watch the youth die.

Then he straightened and said to Ulrika, "He is dead. Speak to him. Ask him something."

She was too shocked to speak.

"Perhaps it is *you* who speaks from the grave?" he said, holding up the bloody fork. "If I were to kill you right now, would you speak to *me?* I am, after all, a god."

Ulrika tried to think of a response that would satisfy Nero when suddenly, at her side, Sebastianus said in a loud voice, "Great Caesar did not give me a chance to finish my report, for I bring another gift besides the greeting from China. You asked about gemstones. I have a stone that is even more priceless than the emerald you hold to your eye."

Nero gave him a suspicious look. "Why did you not say this before?"

"You inquired after gems, great Caesar. What I offer you is not a gem."

"Yet it is more valuable? How can that be?"

"Sebastianus, no—" Ulrika began.

Sebastianus took a step forward, holding out his arm. "You see this gold bracelet? It is decorated with a simple stone, somewhat ordinary in appearance. But it is in fact a piece of a star."

Nero sat up, his face alive with interest. "How is that so?"

"Years ago there was a star-shower over my homeland of Galicia, and when I went into the field where stars fell, I found this fragment, still hot from its flight."

Nero looked at his advisors, from one to the other, who averred that it was possible.

"If the stone is indeed what you say it is, then I accept your gift."

"I wish to strike a bargain with you, Caesar. I will exchange this bracelet with you for something in return."

"And what would that be?"

"This woman's freedom."

A mixture of laughter, gasps of surprise, and murmurs erupted from the onlookers.

"This star that fell from the heavens is yours, Caesar, if you let my wife go free."

"What is to prevent me from just taking it?"

"Because, Caesar, this stone was a gift from the gods. Unless I give it freely, the man who steals it causes great offense to the gods. It would bring him many years of bad luck."

Nero thought about this, then said, "We will have it authenticated. If your bracelet carries a star fragment, and you give it freely to me, this woman is yours and you may both leave."

"Caesar, these people have done you no harm," Sebastianus added, pointing to Rachel and Primo. "As you can see, they are members of the general populace who are so fond of you. By releasing them, and the remains of the widow's husband, you confirm what all of Rome already knows: that you are the protector and benefactor of the masses."

Nero waved a hand. "You can all go. What is it to me? But first my astronomer must examine the stone."

The chief astronomer, his three assistants, and three respected astrologers were brought before Nero. They took the bracelet and withdrew behind a plain door, to emerge now and then with questions: Where precisely did the star fall to earth? What was the exact date and hour? From which direction did the star-shower come, and what was its duration?

Sebastianus was filled with confidence as he awaited the verdict, knowing that Nero would accept the bracelet, for it was just as the Chaldean in Babylon had foretold, that Sebastianus would be parting with his most cherished possession.

The astronomers finally returned to confirm the stone's authenticity, as records showed that precisely such a shower of stars occurred in that exact location and at that exact moment. The astronomers were also familiar with the feel, weight, and appearance of fallen stars.

Nero said, "I wish to have this stone as it must contain great power that makes it, as you say, more priceless than any gemstone in my possession."

"Then I give it to you freely," Sebastianus said.

As Nero slipped the bracelet onto his wrist, pausing to admire it, he said, "Sebastianus Gallus, I find you guilty of treason and I order your execution in the arena."

"But . . . we have an agreement!"

"You yourself said that this stone came from the gods, Gallus, and as I am now a god, I take it back on behalf of my fellow deities. And I will think of an amusing entertainment for the masses, among whom you say I am so beloved. Yes, the common people love me. I lowered taxes, I lowered the price of food, I give them free bread and free games in the arena. And the people love nothing more than to see the mighty brought down. A man of your fame and wealth and stature will bring record crowds to the Great Circus. Half the population of Rome will cram itself within its stands in order to watch your execution."

Before Sebastianus could protest further, Ulrika spoke up, saying, "Mighty Caesar, you asked for a demonstration of my powers. I will give you one. But only if you set this man free."

"What is this?" Nero quipped. "Market day? Suddenly I am being bargained with as if I were a seller of wine."

His aides laughed.

But Ulrika remained unfazed. "I can communicate with the dead, as you were told, Caesar. But it comes with a price. If you are satisfied with my demonstration and believe that my gifts are genuine, then I will stay here and be your channel to the realm of the dead. But only if you let Sebastianus Gallus go free."

Nero said archly, "You will give me a dead man for a living man?" and one of his advisors, a portly senator wearing a purple-edged toga, said, "The dead man is invisible, Caesar. How do you know you are getting a fair exchange?"

His comrades laughed. Another quipped, "Perhaps what the girl 'sees' is with her mind's eye!"

"Well said, Marcus."

Ulrika turned to the one called Marcus and stared at him for a long moment, slowing her breath, clasping her scallop shell and imagining her inner soul flame. After intense concentration, she said, "Then how do you explain the boy I see at your side, perhaps ten or eleven years old? He is speaking to me. He says his name is Faustio."

The aide named Marcus blinked and his smile fell.

"Shall I go on?" she said.

Nero waved a hand. "You are inventing a fiction! There is no way to prove what you claim."

But Ulrika noticed that Marcus no longer smirked.

"Can you read objects?" Nero asked. "Among my seers is a man who can see the future when he handles a personal object."

"I have experience, Caesar."

"You will do a reading for me, and I have the perfect object," the emperor said, delighted with himself and this new amusement.

He handed his emerald monocle to an aide, who gave it to Ulrika.

"Can you see the future?" Nero said impatiently.

Ulrika cradled the sparkling green crystal in her hands. The gem had been set in a frame of delicate gold filigree, with a long handle fashioned from ivory. All eyes turned to her as she looked down at the gemstone. The chamber grew quiet.

She studied the surface of the emerald, rough in places and smooth in others. It was irregularly shaped, with cloudy spots inside. But it was a stunning green such as she had never seen before, and the small spaces that were clear all the way through shot back captivating highlights.

Spirit of the emerald, she silently prayed, please send me a message. Give me a sign, or words that I can pass on to this man who holds my beloved husband's life in his hands.

The imperial audience chamber grew silent, it faded from her peripheral vision, and another vision entered Ulrika's line of sight. *Soft fabric . . . panels of diaphanous material . . . Hangings over a doorway. Ulrika is on the other side, looking into a sumptuous bedroom. A woman is there, at her vanity table, removing cosmetics from her face. Agrippina, widow of Claudius and mother of Nero. She is suddenly startled. Interrupted. Someone enters. A man. He carries a dagger. She jumps to her feet. Not frightened, defiant. She knows he has come to assassinate her. She turns to him and says contemptuously, "If you must do this deed, then smite me in the womb and destroy that part of my body that gave birth to so abominable a son."*

The vision disappeared and Ulrika swayed briefly. Sebastianus caught her. Pressing her hand to her forehead, Ulrika drew in a breath and steadied herself.

Nero leaned forward on his throne. "Well?" he said. "What did you see?"

She trembled. She knew she had just witnessed Empress Agrippina's murder, and that her son had been watching from behind bedroom drapes. Ulrika recalled the rumor that Nero had hired an assassin to kill his mother and then had himself killed the assassin to keep the man from speaking.

No one knows what Agrippina said in her last moments. But Nero knows. And now I do, too . . .

Ulrika glanced at Sebastianus, at Timonides and Primo and Rachel. She felt hundreds of eyes upon her, and those of the emperor, as they narrowed in suspicion. She did not know what to say. Nero wanted her to tell him something that only he could possibly know and that would therefore prove that she did indeed have a gift. But what the emerald had told her was something that put herself in danger—any hint that she knew it was he who had had Agrippina murdered jeopardized her own life.

"Speak up!" Nero barked. "What does the emerald tell you?"

But proof of my powers will set Sebastianus free because Nero will not be able to deny that I have indeed communicated with the spirit world.

"Great Caesar," Ulrika began. "I see a woman—"

Suddenly, the massive double doors that were the main entrance to the audience chamber crashed open, and all heads turned.

When legionaries tramped in, their hobnailed sandals striking the marble floor, Nero shot to his feet and shouted, "Who dares to barge in unannounced and without my permission?"

Ulrika turned and her eyes widened when an impressive man appeared behind the unit of soldiers, massive red plumes rising from his shining helmet. He wore a white leather breastplate with a golden lion emblazoned on the front, a white tunic underneath, edged in gold. The greaves on his shins, and cuffs protecting his forearms, were also made of gold, making him a blinding sight as he marched forward with long strides, stiff and confident, right hand clasping the hilt of his sword.

"Sebastianus," Ulrika whispered as the man drew near. "It is General Vatinius!"

Nero's look turned to one of puzzlement. "Vatinius? What is this all about? You come without invitation, without announcement. Explain yourself!"

"I bring a special gift for Caesar," the general declared in a voice that rose to the domed ceiling. Vatinius turned and outstretched his arm, and another unit of soldiers entered the audience chamber, with a manacled prisoner at their center.

"Great Caesar," Vatinius cried, "in honor of your Jubilee Year, I give you the insurgent Barbarian who has led campaigns against Rome for thirty years. Wulf, who claims to be the son of Arminius!"

Ulrika reached for Sebastianus as the man in chains was led through the crowd. She filled her eyes with the sight of him—he was tall and broad, his long blond hair in tangles and braids and streaked with gray, his beard long and gray. He wore a dark brown tunic of rough homespun cloth, leather leggings, and fur boots that reached his knees. A man in his late fifties, he walked with an erect posture, and a proud bearing of his head. He looked neither right nor left, but directly at Caesar.

Ulrika struggled for breath. There stood the man she had dreamed of since she was a child, had fantasized about, had yearned to meet. He had filled her girlhood thoughts and blazed across her imagination in heroic proportions. She had searched for him. She had been told he was dead.

She saw a look of keen pleasure on Nero's face and she was suddenly sick to her stomach. She knew what that wicked smile meant.

All of Rome gossiped about Nero's failure to secure victories in his name. The war with Parthia had ended the year before with Rome agreeing to a truce, and while Nero had been successful in quelling the revolt in

Britain led by Queen Boudica, he had been robbed of a victory celebration when Boudica had committed suicide. Everyone in the audience chamber understood the significance of Vatinius's surprise gift for his emperor.

Nero made a show of rising from his throne and approaching the general. "How is it I was not informed of this?"

Vatinius smiled. "The capture is recent, Caesar, and the few men who knew of it were sworn to secrecy. I wished to make it a surprise."

"Well done, noble Vatinius!" Nero said as he circled the prisoner, looking him up and down in satisfaction. "I will hold games in your honor, General. You are a hero of the empire."

The onlookers erupted in cheers and Ulrika felt herself go cold with fear.

"For you, Barbarian," Nero said with glee, "we will have a special punishment in the arena. Perhaps I will pit Sebastianus Gallus against you. Barbarian against Roman patrician. And see who wins!"

Ulrika's heart went out to her father. She wanted to run to him, embrace him, and protect him.

Thirty-three years ago my father was taken prisoner during a battle in Germania and sold on the slave market. Three years later, he left my mother in Persia, at her urging, to return to the Rhineland and fight General Vatinius. And then, a mere ten years ago, General Vatinius dined in Aunt Paulina's house and bragged about his military strategy against my father, vowing to end the German insurgency once and for all. And now here we are.

It must not end this way.

Finding her voice, Ulrika said, "Great Caesar, the emerald has spoken to me. There is a woman here who wishes to be heard. A very powerful woman with a message for you. But I must now demand a higher price in exchange."

Vatinius turned and gave Ulrika a perplexed look.

The Barbarian also turned. He stared for a long moment at her face, a look of puzzlement in his blue eyes. And then Ulrika saw his lips move, and she read the one silent word he mouthed: "Selene . . . ?"

Nero frowned, displeased at the interruption, but intrigued also. "I do not bargain. And if I am satisfied that you possess the powers you claim to, I will keep you here in the palace, as my conduit to the spirit world."

Ulrika shook her head. "No, Caesar, you cannot steal me as you did

Sebastianus Gallus's star-stone. I cannot be forced to use my gift against my will. I have a message for you from the spirit world. If you wish to hear it, I insist upon the freedom of Sebastianus Gallus. And then, Caesar, if you are convinced that I possess the power to speak to the dead, to be a messenger between this world and the next, I will stay willingly in this palace and serve you for the rest of my days. But as I said, my price is now higher. Not only do I ask that you set Sebastianus Gallus free, great Caesar, but the Barbarian as well. In return I will speak to the dead for you, I will receive their messages and deliver them to you. I will show you the future. I will tell you whom you can trust and whom not."

When General Vatinius began to protest, Nero silenced him. "Show me what you can do. If I am pleased, then I will grant your wish and let these men go. Who is this powerful woman who sends me a message?"

Forgive me, Sebastianus, she thought. Perhaps this is why the Goddess brought me to this place at this time—to set you and my father free.

"Great Caesar," Ulrika said, as everyone watched, anxiously anticipating her message from the spirit world. As she braced herself for the emperor's reaction to his mother's final words—"Smite my womb"—she was distracted by movement at the corner of her eye. Had someone stepped forward? She turned.

The wolf was there, sitting beside her father. Golden eyes fixed on her.

Ulrika stared. Was it indeed her wolf-spirit?

"Get on with it!" Nero snapped.

Yes, it *was* the spirit, because no one else saw the creature.

He is here for a reason . . .

She looked at her father and thought: His name is Wulf. And twenty-nine years ago, at the hour of my birth, I was given the name Ulrika, which means "wolf power." There was a reason for it, and now I know what that reason is.

All things are connected. *We* are connected.

And in that moment, Ulrika remembered another wolf, and she knew that the gods had come to her aid.

She grew calm. This was the moment for which she had been born. From the hour of her birth in faraway Persia, through all the miles and years she had traveled, all the people she had encountered, both helpful and hindering, all the learnings, the awakenings, and the love of the finest man on earth—her road had brought her to this crucial hour.

And suddenly it was not Agrippina with whom she was in contact.

"Well?" Nero said impatiently.

"Great Caesar," she said, "we stand on a holy place. Your palace was built on Rome's most sacrosanct spot. Romulus and Remus were suckled on this hill by a she-wolf."

"Every child knows that," Nero snapped, referring to the legend of twin brothers Romulus and Remus, said to be the sons of the god Mars and a Vestal Virgin. Because their mother had broken her vow of chastity, the infants were placed in a wooden trough and set upon the waters of the River Tiber. The tide carried the trough ashore, where the babies were found by a she-wolf. Instead of killing them, the wolf took care of them and suckled them with her milk. They grew to manhood and to become the founders of the city of Rome.

"The woman who is here," Ulrika said, "wanting to be heard . . . her name is unfamiliar to me. She speaks an archaic form of Latin."

"What is this specter's name?" Doubt and suspicion in his tone.

"She is called Rhea Silvia. She brings a message."

"Stop!"

All turned to the Chief Vestal,who gestured to Ulrika. "Come forward." When Ulrika stood before her, the priestess said, "You dare to claim to be in contact with Rome's first Chief Vestal?"

"She is in contact with *me,* honored lady. And she has a message."

"Tell it to me," the priestess said. "Whisper it so that no one else can hear."

She leaned forward and, drawing back her veil to expose her ear, listened as Ulrika whispered the message. The Chief Vestal went pale.

Sitting back on her throne, the priestess folded her hands in her lap and said softly, "What you have just told me is known only to the Vestals. It is recorded in our sacred chronicle, the Book of Prophecies, handed down to us through the ages. We Vestals are the chosen keepers of Rome's secrets. Do you understand?"

“I do.”

“And you do know that what you have just learned, if you were to broadcast it, calamity would come to Rome. The city would plunge into chaos. Do you understand this?”

Ulrika nodded solemnly.

“Then you must swear to me now, upon that which is most sacred to you, that you will never utter a word of this to another soul.”

“But, honored lady, I must prove my powers to the emperor so that he will set my husband free.”

“I will see to your husband’s freedom, and that of your friends and the Barbarian.”

Ulrika knew that the Chief Vestal possessed such power. Ulrika looked at Sebastianus and, swearing upon her love for him, said, “You have my promise. Rome’s secret is safe.”

The Vestal turned to Nero. “Caesar, you must release these people and let them go in peace.” She then turned to Ulrika and added quietly, “Once you leave this palace, you will no longer be safe. My protection goes only so far. You must leave Rome and never return.”

“Yes—” Ulrika began.

But Nero, rising from his throne, said, “I will not release these people. They are guilty of treason. And this Barbarian,” he said, pointing to Wulf, “is a known enemy of the empire.”

“You cannot defy the wishes of Vesta,” the priestess said, a mortified look on her face. “If you do, Caesar, you risk bringing calamity upon your people. Vesta will withdraw her protection if you offend her.”

“I am more powerful than Vesta,” Nero declared, and a collective gasp rose from the crowd. Those at the rear and nearest the doors began to back away and seek hasty exit. “Take the prisoners away!” he said to the chief of his Praetorian Guard, sweeping his arm over Ulrika and Sebastianus and Timonides, Rachel and the kneeling Primo, and Wulf. “I have tried them and found them guilty. They will be executed in the Great Circus!”

The crowd shifted and murmured, exchanged glances. There was no mistaking the horrified look on the Chief Vestal’s face. Bad luck was going to strike Rome.

And then suddenly—a distant rumble, as if thunder had clapped over Rome's seven hills. The floor of the audience chamber began to shake, and then the walls, and the air was filled with the sound of a dull roar. Statues swayed and toppled, crashing down. People screamed. Nero sprang from his throne and flung himself behind a giant marble statue of Minerva, wedging himself between the heavy, immovable effigy and the walls, throwing his arms protectively over his head. When an onyx bust wobbled in an overhead niche, threatening to topple, General Vatinius ran to protect his emperor, pulling Nero out of the way as the bust crashed to the floor.

Rachel fell to her knees to wrap her arms around the cedar chest. Primo dropped beside her and covered her with his thick torso, shielding her from falling debris.

As people ran to and fro, looking for exits, escaping from being crushed by falling statues, as they pushed and shoved and trampled those who fell, Wulf dashed away from his guards and fled to the outer balcony, where potted trees swayed and water splashed out of the fountain. His wrists still shackled, he climbed upon the balustrade, he poised to jump, but then stopped and looked back. His eyes went to Ulrika. He hesitated. Then he jumped back down onto the balcony. As he ran inside the chamber, he held onto the walls but the floor shook. He was thrown off balance and had to cling to a pillar for support.

And then the silver and gold mosaic tiles began to drop from the domed ceiling.

Looking up, Sebastianus saw sparkling bits come drifting down, like silver rain. He pulled Ulrika to him, draping his toga over her to protect her. She held tightly to him and pressed her face into his chest as she imagined the massive palace crashing down about them. Sebastianus stared up at the domed ceiling, unable to take his eyes away. The constellations were breaking up. He watched in amazement as, fragment by fragment, the gold and silver mosaic pieces came loose from the dome and drifted down. More and more fell, exposing gray plaster behind, the zodiacal signs disintegrating as the throned Nero in the center began to break up and drop away in small shining bits of tile.

"Ulrika!" Sebastianus said. "Look!"

She brought her head out from the protection of his cloak and lifted her face. "Why . . . it is a star-shower!"

"Just like the one the night Lucius died," Sebastianus said as he watched the stars rain down from the domed ceiling.

Nero Caesar began screaming: "Get out! You are free! All of you! And take the wretched Barbarian with you."

"Caesar!" General Vatinius shouted. "You cannot do this!"

"Vesta preserve us!" Nero screamed, and grabbed for the General, clinging to him like a man drowning.

"This way!" the Chief Vestal called out. She stood against a wall, holding aside a heavy hanging to reveal a door.

The earthquake subsided and finally stopped, but tiles and dust continued to rain down on the few who remained in the massive hall. Sebastianus raced over and freed Wulf's hands while Primo scooped up the cedar chest. The six ran to the door where the Chief Vestal said, "This will take you to the Holy of Holies in the temple of Vesta. Go quickly."

They were covered in sparkling little tiles, their hair and clothes glittering as they hurried through. As they ran along the corridor, where torches flickered in sconces, and busts and statues stood in marble niches, Ulrika saw that the earthquake had not struck here. And when they reached the end, where the corridor opened into a quiet sanctuary, they saw ahead, through an open colonnade, that the city had not been affected by the earthquake at all. Rome was quiet and all was as usual.

"This way!" Sebastianus said.

They ran through the colonnaded temple, where priestesses looked at them in surprise, and down the steps to mingle with the crowds in the Forum. At the far end, where steps led up the Palatine Hill to the Imperial Palace, Sebastianus saw Praetorian Guards coming down. "Vatinius has sent them after us," he said.

"Follow me," Primo said, and the five hurried after the military veteran, who loped through the marketplace with the cedar chest in his arms. Sebastianus saw to it that Rachel kept up, while Wulf watched after Ulrika and the elderly Timonides.

Located in the center of Rome, between the Palatine and Capitoline

Hills, the Roman Forum was a rectangle surrounded by temples and government buildings. The site of triumphal processions and government elections, venue for public speeches and nucleus of commercial affairs, the Forum was the beating heart of the empire. Here statues and monuments commemorated the city's great men, gods, and goddesses. It was also a marketplace, where stalls were crammed between marble buildings, and everything from books to carpets was sold.

Primo led his companions along the busy Sacred Way, past the Curia, Rome's Senate House, and around the side of the Temple of Castor and Pollux, where they found a small grotto carved into the hillside, with a trickling fountain and vines cascading down. A marble altar had been built into the rock long ago, and a terracotta plaque above the altar showed a young man riding a bull, and underneath was written: *Sol Invictus Mithras.* It was a shrine to Mithras, and from here they could remain hidden while watching the progress of the Praetorians.

"Selene," came a deep voice. Ulrika turned to look up into blue eyes filled with questions. "And yet not . . . You resemble her."

It had been a long time since she had spoken German, but it came back easily to her lips. "Selene is my mother, and you are my father." He was so handsome, so strong and heroic looking, as if he normally lived with Thor and Odin. She could see why her mother had fallen in love with him.

Frank surprise stood on his face. "I am your father?" His eyes roamed her hair, her features. He smiled. "You are Selene's daughter, yes, but now I see my mother in your eyes, your chin. I did not know . . ."

He drew her into his arms and clasped her in a strong embrace. He held her for a long moment, while Ulrika heard the steady thumping of his warrior's heart. Then he drew back and said, "Your mother is well? Our time together was short, but it was memorable."

"Mother is in Ephesus. And I believe she is well. How did Vatinius catch you?"

He smiled. "I am not as swift as I once was."

"This is Sebastianus," she said. "My husband." Ulrika then introduced her father to Timonides, Primo, and Rachel, and as she explained how they had all come to be standing before Emperor Nero, she thought: What an odd mix we are—a wealthy Spanish trader; a veteran of the Roman army; a Greek astrologer; a Jewish widow; a hero of the German revolt; and myself, a girl once lost but who has found her way.

"Where do you go from here?" Wulf asked in halting Latin, and Sebastianus said, "We go to Galicia."

Primo muttered, "We won't be going anywhere if we don't find a better hiding place. The Praetorians are getting close."

Wulf's look darkened. "It is me they want, not you and your friends. Vatinius will not rest until I am recaptured. If I go, they will come after me, and you will be free to go your way."

"No!"

"Ulrika, I must return to the Rhineland, and you must go with this man who is your husband."

"Wulf, my friend," Sebastianus said, "travel with us to the port of Ostia, for there I can see that you are disguised and well provisioned, and placed with a safe and trusted caravan leader. They are all known to me, and many owe me a favor."

Wulf nodded in agreement, and then he went to stand guard with Primo, who was keeping an eye on the throngs filling the Forum, and the Praetorian guards searching among them.

Ulrika first made sure that Rachel was all right, and found that she was already being taken care of by Timonides, who had cleared the marble bench of autumn leaves to make Jacob's widow comfortable. The cedar chest with its precious contents was tucked securely against the altar of Mithras.

Ulrika then turned to Sebastianus, who was also keenly watching the crowds among the temples and government buildings. "Why do we go to Galicia?" she asked.

In the intimacy of the small and ancient grotto, Sebastianus took Ulrika by the shoulders and looked long and deep into her eyes before saying, "Ulrika, someone might say it was the coincidence of an earthquake and shoddy craftsmanship that brought those mosaic tiles down. But I call it a miracle, for the tiles came down in a shower of stars that looked just like the star-shower over my homeland the night Lucius died. It not only saved all our lives, Ulrika, but pointed the way as well. I believe it was a sign that I am meant to return home after years of roaming. It is also the answer to where we are to take Jacob's relics. To Gaia's altar, which is a sacred place."

Ulrika turned to Rachel and said, "You will not be safe in Rome."

Rachel nodded. "We will take Jacob to that sacred place."

"Master," Primo said, "we must be going. We cannot stay here any longer. The Praetorians are searching around the Treasury building. This is a good time to make a quick escape."

"But where do we go?" Timonides asked, rising from the marble bench. "Nero confiscated your estate and caravan. He left you penniless."

"Do not fear, I have many friends who will help."

"I, too," Primo said.

"And there are members of my faith," Rachel added, "who will help."

Ulrika opened her hand and discovered, to her amazement, that she was still clutching the emerald. Timonides whistled. "That will be worth a good price!"

"But not with Nero searching for us," Primo said darkly. "He will eventually regret letting us and the Barbarian go. He will send legions after us."

But Ulrika, gazing into the green heart of the gemstone, shook her head and said, "Nero will not search for us. After today, his popularity will rapidly decline. When word spreads of how he treated General Vatinius, robbing him of a victory parade with his prisoner in chains, the army will turn against the emperor. In four years he will become so unpopular that the Senate declares him a public enemy and orders his execution. Nero will die by his own hand, with a dagger in his throat."

"It is time to go," Sebastianus said, gesturing to his small party. "The Praetorians will not see us. There is a man who lives north of the city. He will take us in for a while. I did him a favor once . . ."

41

"We have arrived!" Sebastianus cried as he urged his horse into a quick gallop, while Ulrika rode in his arms.

They had sailed from Ostia and crossed the Great Green to land at the Roman colony of Barcino, on the northeast coast of Hispania. From there the caravan of horses, mules, wagons, and people had struck westward, to follow newly laid Roman roads and ancient trails carved long ago by forgotten ancestors. They trekked past tiny hamlets and scattered farms, isolated Roman villas, and the occasional military outpost. The terrain was variously flat, mountainous, green, and rocky, with a deep blue sky traversed by enormous billowing clouds. The capricious winds blew at their backs and in their faces, while nights sparkled frostily and days glowed with warmth. In the far distance to the north they saw the towering mountain range named after the mythological princess, Pyrene, beyond which lay the land of the Gauls.

After weeks of travel, the weary caravan had finally crested the last hill of their journey, and they now saw below a verdant countryside of such deep and wondrous green that Ulrika thought it could not be real. Set amid steep, wooded hillsides were whitewashed buildings surrounded by pastures and orchards. The villas stood far apart, with footpaths connecting them, and beyond, a bustling marketplace with a blacksmith shop, small ateliers for metal and stone workers, and a wooden fortress housing Roman soldiers. A settlement on its way to becoming a town. More rolling green hills undulated to the horizon, dotted with dwellings, pastures, vegetable gardens.

Sebastianus's eyes filled with tears as he sat atop his horse, and he could not for the moment speak. Ulrika sat in silence as he steadied her in a tight hold.

"That is my family home," he finally said, pointing to a sprawling villa with several buildings and gardens and penned animals. And that way," he said, pointing westward, "is the end of the world, which Romans call Finisterre. It is a day's journey by foot. You can stand on the rocky promontory and look out over an ocean that goes on forever. There is no more land after that."

Ulrika gave him a radiant smile. "From Luoyang to Finisterre, you have spanned the world."

Before Sebastianus could give the signal for the caravan to move on, the afternoon air was pierced by a high, keening sound. "Look, master!" Timonides said, pointing. He sat astride a donkey, while behind him Rachel rode in a cart drawn by oxen. "Someone is coming!"

"My little sister," Sebastianus said, dismounting, and then helping Ulrika down. "I see she has been making tarts. I hope you like cherries, Ulrika," he added with a grin. "My brother-in-law is rather proud of his orchards."

Ulrika stared in astonishment, for rushing up the hill toward them, holding her skirts as she sprinted over the grass, was the plump young woman of her vision long ago. Ulrika saw now that she was not running *from anything* but *toward* something, and the open mouth was screaming with joy, not fear. The "blood" on her hands was the juice of red fruit.

Ulrika watched as brother and sister met in an emotional embrace, laughing and crying at the same time.

"We received your message days ago and have been preparing for your return ever since!" Lucia declared breathlessly.

When they landed at Barcino, Sebastianus had sent a swift rider accompanied by an armed guard with greetings to his family, announcing his homecoming. Ulrika knew the names and histories of all the family members, who were numerous, as his three sisters lived in that sprawling villa with husbands, children, and a variety of in-laws.

Lucia looked prosperous, Ulrika thought, and she saw the resemblance to her brother, saw the copper highlights in her long hair. She turned to Ulrika with shining eyes. Her Latin was thickly accented, and so Ulrika knew she must learn the dialect of this region. The sisters-in-law embraced as more people came running from the villa, men in short tunics, women in long dresses, children and dogs, all calling out to their returned brother and uncle.

The caravan continued on and arrived at the villa in a noisy affair of welcomes and introductions, and everyone talking at once. A lively feast followed, lasting late into the night—a celebration with music and dancing, much wine, and generous offerings of steamed clams, boiled octopus, fried squid, and an endless array of cherry tarts.

Afterwards, as Ulrika lay in Sebastianus's arms, in the room he had shared with his brother Lucius years ago, she thought of the letter she had sent to her mother from Ostia, placing it in the care of a sea captain bound for Ephesus who promised to deliver it personally. Ulrika had filled the missive with all the remarkable news of her life, and ended it with an invitation, praying that Selene would come to this northwest corner of Hispania for a long visit.

And now Ulrika's family was complete. She had traveled from Rome to Ostia with her father, during which time they had spoken of their lives, and Ulrika had gotten to know the great Wulf at last.

A tour of the villa was mandatory the next morning, with the children skipping and running in excitement, and then the noon meal, after which Sebastianus announced it was time to visit the ancient altar.

They went alone to the hill that rose in a gentle wooded crest, following an ancient path together, through poplar trees, oaks, and firs—a sylvan paradise that reminded Ulrika of the place where she had seen the Crystal

Pools of Shalamandar. One would not have known that the jumble of stones and seashells at the end of the path was Gaia's altar, for it looked haphazard and untended. But Ulrika closed her eyes and sent her spirit out into this protected glade, and she knew they stood on sacred ground.

"We will lay Venerable Jacob to rest here," she said. "We will rebuild the altar, and then a shrine so that people can come and seek the help and solace of the Goddess and pay respects to the holy man who sleeps here."

As she placed her hand upon the altar, Ulrika closed her eyes, calmed her breathing, whispered her mantra, and received a vision. "Years from now," she said, "a magnificent house of worship will be erected upon this spot, and millions of pilgrims will come from the far ends of the earth to pay homage to the remains of Venerable Jacob, whom they will know as Sant Yago. And this place will be remembered for the stars that fell in the nearby fields, the campus stellae."

Sebastianus said, "I will make the route of the pilgrimage safe once again. I will put up signposts and establish resting places. I will place guards along the route who will patrol the roads, for I know now that this is what I have been called to do, to be a protector of pilgrims. This is the real reason I was sent to China, so that I might perfect my skills in escorting caravans, and in learning how to keep travelers safe."

Thinking of China and his visit there, which now seemed almost like a dream, Sebastianus knew that, because of Nero's madness there would be no more expeditions to China. Perhaps not for years, or even centuries. Sebastianus would always cherish his time there. He had walked upon the yellow soil of Luoyang, had exchanged ideas with a wise emperor, had known such friends as Noble Heron and Little Sparrow. But now Sebastianus must turn his eyes to the future.

"Ulrika, I have for so long thought I was fated to yearn to explore new lands while longing for my home. But I am home now, with my true work about to begin. I realize, too," he added, "that there is both order and predictability in the world, and randomness. Life is neither one nor the other. Just as there are fixed stars and falling stars, in our own hearts we are certain of some things, and uncertain of others. We may never understand why, all we know is that while we walk this earth, we do our best, and live in love and peace."

Ulrika removed the scallop shell from around her neck and placed it on the altar. "This is the end of my road, for I will be the guardian of the shrine. When people come for solace and answers, I will teach them my meditation. Perhaps all people have the gift of the Divining. It simply has to be found and tapped into. Or perhaps, in the end, the Divining is not about finding sacred places, but finding the sacred within ourselves. And I will teach others how to identify the Venerable Ones, for surely St. Jude and St. James," she added, using their Romanized names, "are not the only ones."

A familiar voice now whispered in her mind: "You have done well, daughter. I will not be visiting you again, for you no longer need my guidance."

"One question, Honored Lady," Ulrika said silently, with her thoughts. "Why did you come to me? Why not go to Sebastianus, for you are his ancestor and this is also his destiny?"

"Because I am not his ancestress, I am yours. The Gallus family came late to Galicia, and although you were born of a Roman mother and a German father, your bloodline reaches far back into the mists of time, on the rocky coast of Galicia where I built an altar of scallop shells. You are my descendant, Ulrika of Galicia. And while you will not see me again, be assured that I am with you always. Farewell, daughter, and remember to guard the secret from the Book of Prophecies."

The cryptic secret that Rhea Silva had told her, and that Ulrika in turn had whispered to the Chief Vestal: that the reign of the gods of Rome was coming to an end. Ulrika wondered if laying Jacob to rest in this ancient altar were part of that change, for he had been the follower of a new faith, he had believed in one God, and now he was buried in ground sacred to the Goddess. Perhaps not a change, she thought, nor an ending, but a joining . . .

Ulrika took Sebastianus's hand and said, "Long ago I asked a question of a fortune-teller. Where do I belong? Does where I belong define me? She did not give me an answer, but I know now that who you are doesn't depend on where you are. Who you are is something you take with you wherever you go."

Sebastianus smiled. "And now we are here. Home . . ."

BARBARA WOOD
is the international bestselling author of
twenty-five acclaimed novels, including the *New York Times*
bestseller *Domina*. Her work has been translated into over 30
languages. Barbara lives in California.